A Winter's DATE

J. Epps and S. Brümmer

A Winter's Date
Published by Jessica Epps and Sasha-Lee Brümmer
Copyright © 2015 Jessica Epps and Sasha-Lee Brümmer
2015 Edition
ISBN: 978-0-9863049-2-7

Editor:
Lisa Aurello

Cover Designer:
Judi Perkins

Interior Design and Formatting:
Christine Borgford, Perfectly Publishable

The following story contains mature themes, strong language, and sexual situations. It is intended for adult readers.

This book is dedicated to *our readers*—to all of those who share a love for Heather and Noah's story.

Soundtrack

Bright—Echosmith

Cookie—R. Kelly

Desire—Meg Myers

Elastic Heart—Sia, ft. The Weeknd and Diplo

Falling—Florence and the Machine

Fine by Me—Andy Grammer

Going Down for Real—Flo Rida

Happy—Pharrell Williams

Hey Mama—David Guetta, ft. Nicki Minaj, Bebe Rexha & Afrojack

High for This—The Weeknd

Lay Me Down—Sam Smith, ft. John Legend

Moondance—Michael Bublé

Moving Pictures Silent Films—Great Lake Swimmers

Once Upon a Dream—Lana Del Rey

Skinny Love—Birdy

Summertime Sadness—Lana Del Rey

The Sea and the Rhythm—Iron & Wine

The Trapeze Swinger—Iron & Wine

#1 Crush—Garbage

Chapter One

KEEN SENSATIONS

NOAH

An ominous storm delivers its wrath over the heart of London, opening the sky. Through the darkening night, thunderous cracks and bolts of lightning strike in concert. Rain beating against the window in Heather's room on the thirty-fifth floor is the only audible sound in the apartment, distracting me from my studies when it pulls my gaze out of the window and into the capturing beauty of the turbulent storm.

The love of a woman can make a man do dubious things, and the way Heather loves me has made me do some ridiculous shit. For instance, dropping everything and flying across an ocean to track her down and claim her as my own again. I've been in London for two weeks now; I couldn't care less about my surroundings, just as long as she's there. I haven't broached the subject on how long she plans on staying, though, and, quite frankly, I'm not okay with a long-distance relationship. I did not like the distance when she left Arizona, but London? Yeah, not happening. I can be dominant when I want to be, but the problem is . . . Heather doesn't respond well to dominance unless it involves us being naked and my dick between her legs. I haven't—and I won't—push her to go home with me, although that's ultimately what I want.

I've been studying day and night for the bar exam while Heather has been dancing her little ass off; she's exceedingly dedicated to her ballet career, now more than before. The only recurring problem seems to be Alexis Keeley. Every time I swing by the studio to have lunch with Heather or pick her up, Alexis is waiting. She's like a vulture waiting on my relationship to perish, so she can swoop in and pick up the pieces. I refuse to let that happen.

I'm lost in my thoughts when I feel her lips graze the skin on my neck. I didn't even feel her walk up to me, let alone hear her pad into the room. I can feel her smile against my skin, and she's bubbling with energy. Turning around quickly, I knock her off her feet, and then catch her before she is able to fall. She moves her gorgeous self onto my lap while giggling sweetly.

"Good evening, little ballerina. How was practice?"

"Hi, baby. It was good, but I couldn't get my mind off of you."

Damn, she smells like heaven. "Oh yeah? Why was that?" I taunt.

She nuzzles herself into my neck and nips at me. "Because I've wanted you since you got up at five in the morning to study. I didn't want to interrupt, though; you were so invested in your books. And twelve hours later, you're still studying."

I close my book, remembering the page number before sliding it to the other end of the desk.

"Is that better? You now have my undivided attention."

She sighs dramatically. "Finally."

The smile that forms on my face is the one that's been there since I made love to her during an intense storm while in the London Eye. Her hands move down to grasp my cock through my sweatpants, surprising me with her urgency. Blood rushes through my veins all the way down to my dick, forming an unmistakable tent in my sweats when she moves her hand away. Her body is so attuned to mine that she starts grinding those hips on me before I can even get my hands on her pale skin. I know she's wet and ready for me, and I'm going to satisfy this budding need in her until she can't stand my touch without exploding in a rush of orgasm.

Before I can finish that thought, there's a knock on the door, interrupting the flash of heat between us. Shit, more like a fucking pounding.

"Heather? Noah? You two better be clothed because I'm busting in."

The door swings open before I have a second to adjust my painfully aching cock. As much as I enjoy Heather hanging out with her best friend, Dillen, living with her is something else. She's a ball of energy waiting to blow—blow my friend she met in New York, that is. I've lost track of how many times she's asked me when Coen is coming to visit her in London. Hell, I know I won't be getting any sleep when that dipshit arrives. Heather and I might have to retreat to a hotel during his stay, or at the very least purchase some earplugs.

"Dillen," Heather mockingly scolds.

"What? Oh, were you two about to do it?" she asks sarcastically. She knows Heather can't stay off of my dick for more than twelve hours. She's like one hell of an athlete, thriving on sex to calm her and rein in her body before performing.

Heather looks down at my still-hard cock. Her little hand is wrapped around my shaft through my sweats, and I'm sure Dillen is staring by now.

"Holy shit, Heather."

Heather's eyes shoot up swiftly, "Go get your own," she says, attempting to hide my straining erection in the fabric of my sweats, but there's not a hope in hell. My gift to women, to Heather, is no longer a curse.

Dillen hauls ass out of the room, slamming the door shut behind her.

"We need to get a deadbolt on this door if I'm ever going to be able to ravage you like I did in that capsule."

Dillen's voice comes screeching through the walls of her apartment, "Is there even a condom that fits you, Noah? Damn."

"Uhh . . . ballerina? Do you want to answer that?"

"I'm on the pill, you butthead. He doesn't need to wear a condom," Heather blurts out as she deftly works to get my sweats off.

I hear Dillen snort, then sarcastically reply, "Yeah, because that's one hundred percent effective."

Dammit, Dillen, way to kill the mood.

Heather's head quickly snaps up, and she looks into my eyes for the briefest moment. There's nothing like throwing in the risk of pregnancy to get someone's juices flowing. And before I can say a word, Heather looks as if she's drawn some sort of conclusion and shrugs. The growl that escapes me is louder than I expected, as she dives back in and wraps her hand around my bare length.

Dillen must have heard my growl, because the next thing I hear is her yelling, "You lucky little shit. I'm so envious of you right now."

Her words are soon lost to the both of us as we become entirely consumed in each other.

"Please? Do what you did to me last night?" she begs, and I'm going to give it to her all night until she is too sore to take me anymore.

"You better be ready for me, ballerina. I'm not wasting any time tonight. That little pussy belongs to me." I can feel my pulse thrumming in my dick as she takes it into her mouth, sucking me off like I'm her favorite flavor of the month. I hear Dillen yell something, but I couldn't give a shit. I know Coen just showed up on her doorstep and she's about to damn well lose it with excitement.

Hell, I should probably send out a note of apology to all of our surrounding neighbors tomorrow because of the onslaught of screams that will be coming from this apartment tonight.

The flicks of Heather's tongue bring me back as I unconsciously run my hands into her dark-chocolate hair. I meticulously pull her farther down my shaft and watch gratifyingly as her lips meet the base of my cock.

Countless hours pass before Heather and I emerge from her bedroom, only to find clothes strewn all over the living room and kitchen floor. I believe the pictures on the wall are crooked; either that, or I'm still trying to recover from my last orgasm.

"Was that Coen at the door?" She sounds genuinely surprised.

"Yeah, and I'm guessing his dick is currently wet. I'm sorry I didn't tell you he was coming, but the two of you girls share everything and he really wanted it to be a surprise for Dillen."

She jumps up and circles her arms around my neck, holding me fast as she presses those soft, rosy lips to mine. "You are the most amazing man. I'm so in love with you, Noah Ryan."

"Mmm," I hum against her lips before taking her bottom lip into my mouth and sucking. "I love you too. I'll never get tired of hearing that."

She beams and stares me down with those gorgeous jade green eyes. Her little frame shivers in my arms, and I hold her closer. "Am I giving you goose bumps and orgasms now?"

"You know exactly what you do to me, Noah." Her teeth graze the skin of my throat as she growls cutely.

"Are you complaining?"

"No," she snaps out, "not one bit. Plus, if they weren't in there . . ." She nods toward Dillen's bedroom just as a violent, ear-piercing scream fills the apartment. We both freeze and stare at the door before she finishes her sentence. " . . . I would be the one having a few more orgasms."

"Holy fuck, that's what she sounds like? I would be deaf after one round with her. I hope Coen is wearing earplugs."

She smacks my chest and playfully scolds me, "Baby, you aren't having a round with anybody except me."

She gets a chuckle out of me, and I squeeze her firm ass. "Come on, let's get some food in you before you wither away," she says, playfully biting my jaw, and I fucking love it.

"I am not withering away. Can we order in tonight, please?"

"I'm fine with that."

I carry her over to the couch and sit down with her on my lap. As I turn my head to look for the remote, my nose comes within mere inches of a bright green bra hanging from the sofa back. "Fuck, Dillen . . ." I jerk away as Heather's laugh fills the room.

"Why in God's name is her shit everywhere?"

She shrugs cutely. "When the moment hits, we're not worried where our clothes go."

I laugh at her response, and she reaches for her tablet. We spend the next few minutes playfully arguing about what to order before we finally decide to order enough Chinese food to feed us for days.

"Damn, someone worked up an appetite."

She nods excitedly. "I'm sure Dillen and Coen have too."

"Yeah, from the sound of it."

With the remote in hand, I flick Dillen's bra off the back of the couch so I can relax. A smile is already playing at my lips because I can feel Heather moving around on the couch. She's trying to get comfortable, and I know it won't be long now, so I sit and wait patiently. Within minutes she gives in and curls back up on my lap, sensually wiggling her ass as she rests her head against my chest. Her ice-cold fingers stray underneath my shirt before she starts pulling at my V-neck to get it off.

"Are you cold?" I ask in a low voice.

"I'm always cold."

I pull my shirt off and she rests her head back down against my bare skin, running her fingers up and down my torso. I think she enjoys our skin-to-skin contact. My fingers trail along her arm as we watch one of the latest movie releases.

A half-hour passes before Coen and Dillen walk out of her bedroom. They both look battered up and fatigued.

Heather lifts her head from my chest and looks up at her friend. "Dillen, you are so stinking loud."

"Heather, you be quiet . . . Coen is a maniac between the sheets."

Coen laughs and slaps my shoulder as he walks past the couch and to the front door.

"Did you wash your goddamn hands before touching me, you ass-fuck? Welcome to London, by the way. How was your flight?"

"Yeah, thanks for making me get a cab, dipshit," he says as he swings the door open to accept our food delivery.

"The cash is on the table to your right, and you're welcome."

Heather moves off of my lap to help Dillen spread out the food on the dining room table; the two of them are whispering, and I would love to know exactly what they are talking about. This woman has my attention at all times, and I don't think she even realizes it. I get up and pull my shirt back on before joining the three of them at the table.

"Eat up, you sex fiends," Heather chimes in, and I have to clear my throat because she is definitely not one to talk.

The evening passes quickly, with excited chatter filling the confines of Dillen's apartment. A few hours later I'm back to the grind. I have my notes splayed out in front of me and a few textbooks taking up every inch of available space on the desk in Heather's room. The thudding of

Dillen's headboard on our wall has stopped, and I'm grateful for the silence; I can finally concentrate.

My brain aches from staring at all of the cramped words on the page. Laws are laws, but they vary greatly from state to state. I try to not let my stress show because I don't want Heather to see me that way, and I don't want a single thing to keep her from her lifelong dream. She's got her first performance with this company in less than a week, and I'll be damned if she doesn't have the lead role already. Of course she does: she's remarkable.

I never gave much thought to the dedication of a dancer before. When I attended the ballet with Mae, it was just a show, just a few hours out of my night. But fuck, Heather is such a dedicated performer; I'm constantly in awe of her. Dillen is pretty noteworthy as well, but she still has nothing on my girl. There's something behind her smile when she dances, and I love watching her. She's happiest onstage, and I know when I see that smile, she's where she's meant to be.

I know how disheartened she would have been if she stayed in the States. I must admit, I'm pretty damn pleased that she's away from that prick in tights. I was damn close to knocking out his over-bleached teeth at the bar that night, and I'd do it again, but the lying pussy never came to London. But now we have to deal with Alexis, trading one problem for another.

She's relentless, that girl. Heather hasn't asked me any more questions about Alexis, and thank fuck. She's trouble with a capital T. One thing I figured out while dating in college was how to identify the crazies. Alexis is a textbook narcissist with psychopathic tendencies. Keeping my distance from her is my main objective. I just wish Heather didn't have her head filled with nonsense on a daily basis by the crazy bitch. I can tell every day when she comes home that Alexis has messed with her in some way. She won't admit it to me, but I can see it. I've watched my girl, and I know when she's hiding something.

I cannot concentrate tonight.

My thoughts drift from my studies to a few nights ago. I was beyond exhausted from reading the same book repeatedly. The words were on replay in my head. I got up to stretch and grab some ice water when I noticed that Heather wasn't in her bed.

When did she leave the room? I walked down the hall and into the kitchen when I noticed the TV flashing in the dark. Quietly, I made my way over to where Heather was curled up on the couch, half asleep, watching the . . . *Smithsonian Channel?* The volume was almost inaudible. As I rounded the couch, she looked up at me with tired eyes.

"Baby? What are you doing out here?" I asked as I crouched down beside her head, kissing her forehead gently. She looked so damn adorable when she replied, her eyes fighting to stay open.

"I couldn't sleep; I was too cold."

Smirking, I picked her up and carried her back to bed. She nuzzled against my chest and before I had her under the covers, she was out like a light. I guess I never gave any thought to how her sleep might be screwed up from my studying. She's slept on my chest every night that we've been together—a habit that we've formed since the beginning.

I'm pulled from my thoughts when I hear her rustling in the sheets behind me. I turn in my chair to look, and Heather is tossing in her sleep; she seems restless and I can't stand it. I check the clock, and it reads almost two in the morning. *Damn.* I get up and strip down, turning the lamp off before climbing into bed. Almost instantly she stops moving when I curl my body around hers. I must radiate a shit-ton of heat because her body feels like an ice cube next to mine. Within a minute she's breathing, deep and slow, and I feel her body finally relax.

Damn, I need to start going to bed sooner.

Chapter Two

FILTHY MOUTH

HEATHER

Coen has been in London for a few days now and I can tell Dillen is having a hard time walking, let alone dancing. I'm sitting on Noah's lap, impatiently waiting for her to get her shoes on. "Dillen, we are going to be late, and this is our last practice before the show."

I can hear Noah chuckle, and I snap my head at him and glare. His hand squeezes my ass as we both watch her scramble to put her shoes on.

"Shit, maybe Coen needs to lay off for the next twenty-four hours. He's still passed the hell out, isn't he? You've fucked him into a coma," Noah says, trying not to laugh.

I nudge him with my shoulder and nuzzle his neck, whispering, "I'm going to miss you tonight. Don't study too hard because when I come home you're going to cuddle with me and much, much more."

"In that case, you better make sure you are warm and sweaty when you get back from practice." Dillen groans at Noah's words.

I smack his chest lightly before biting at his neck. "Behave," I say, reluctantly getting off of his lap to grab my duffel bag, sighing loudly.

"Wish me luck, baby." I lean over and kiss Noah quickly before walking over and yanking Dillen up off the floor. "Come on, lazy butt."

"Good luck, beautiful. You too, Dillen," Noah calls out before the door shuts, and Dillen starts whimpering in pain.

I all but drag her down the hallway to the elevators. "Honestly, Dill . . . you two should cool it."

"But it feels so good during," she whines as we get into her car and head out into the London traffic to get to the ballet studio.

I don't have the heart to scold her anymore because I know exactly how she feels. I'm completely addicted to Noah, and I would never want her to tell me to stop. I don't think I would be able to regardless: this addiction is here to stay. As we pull up to the studio and park, I find myself getting excited about the upcoming show. I close my eyes briefly and picture myself on stage as a clear white spotlight focuses on me, bringing my choreography to life.

There's a lot of chatter and excitement when we make it into the studio, and I can hear Alexis' voice ring clearly over the others.

"Little shit, I'm so glad you beat that whore and stole the solo from underneath her big feet," Dillen says, giggling, as she plops down to put her pointe shoes on.

I grin devilishly and sit down to put mine on as well. "It did feel pretty good," I whisper so only she can hear.

"I knew it," she says too loudly, and before I know it, our conversation gets sideswiped by the crazy troll herself.

"Dillen, Heather . . . It's nice to see you both. Oh Heather, if something happens to you from now until the show, Mistress Nadine is going to put me in, in place of you. I know all of the choreography . . . probably better than you do." She smiles malevolently. "Please do tell Noah it was really sweet of him to take me out for coffee a few days ago while he waited for you to drag your non-existent ass out of the practice studio."

My heart jumps into my throat, and I almost choke on it. I'm staring up at her, trying to keep my cool as I slip my pointe shoe on. "Excuse me?" I say, unable to believe what I'm hearing. My Noah? Took her out for coffee? No. Why? Jealousy surges through me, and my good mood evaporates instantly.

She rolls her eyes and peers down at me, speaking as if she holds some sort of authority over me. "I said, tell Noah thank you for taking me out for coffee. He was so, so sweet."

"Back the hell off, you crazy bitch," Dillen yells up at her. "Noah is obviously with Heather, so why don't you take the fucking hint, and stop trying to stir up shit?"

My body shakes with this startling revelation: I'm so fucking angry.

I feel betrayed.

What in the hell was he thinking?

I stand up and grab Dillen's arm. "Come on, Dill. Practice is starting."

She pulls back and scolds me with her eyes. "You seriously believe her right now? When the fuck would Noah have time to see her skank-ass? Huh? *Never*. He's so busy studying and the rest of his available time he spends working out or with you. Alexis—"

"What? I'm not intimidated by you," Alexis spits out as she steps closer to Dillen.

I don't even want to tell Dillen that he had plenty of time to go get coffee with her the other day while I was in the private studio with Mistress Cora. My practice session with her took up more time than I wanted, and I felt bad that he waited on me. Now I don't know what I feel. I'm hurt. No, I'm way beyond hurt. I tug on her hand and start to walk away.

"She's not worth it, Dill. Come on."

Dillen reluctantly steps back with me but throws both of her hands up in the air, flipping Alexis off, and taunting her. "Fuck her," she yells, and we move to the other side of the studio to continue to stretch.

"Heather, there's no way in hell he took her out. He's literally chased you around the world; why the hell would he just throw that away?"

I shrug as I stretch in silence. I'm blocking every emotion out right now.

"Fine. I'll call him." She flippantly reaches into her duffel and grabs her phone, quickly dialing.

I hear him answer, "Hey Dillen, is everything okay?"

I can't hear his voice right now or I'll break. I get up and walk over to the barre. I can hear Dillen as clear as day, though, as I'm sure every-one in the studio can.

"No. Listen, Alexis is causing shit again, and I've about had it with her exaggerated, confronting bitch-face. Heather's upset, and you need to come and right this problem, like, now." She goes quiet as she listens to him respond before replying to him.

"Crazy-feet told Heather that you took her out to get coffee this week, while Heather was in her private session."

She goes quiet again, and I hate it.

"I can try; hold on."

I'm watching her in the mirror as she gets up and marches over to me, shoving her phone in my face. "Talk to him," she demands.

I stare her down before taking the phone.

Damn her.

My voice is quiet when I speak. "Hello?"

"Hey baby."

My entire body relaxes at the sound of his smoky, confident voice. Ugh, I hate that he has that effect on me when I'm trying to be mad at him.

"I love you. You do know that, right?"

I sigh and bite the inside of my cheek. "Yes."

"Do you believe me when I say that I didn't see her when I was wait-ing for you, let alone take her out? I would never hurt my beautiful girl like that."

God, he makes it impossible to stay mad at him.

"Noah, I . . ."

" . . . you love me, and you trust me. I didn't take her out. Do you want me to come down there?" I can hear him moving around, and then I hear a set of keys jingling and Coen asking where he's going, in the background.

"No. I'm okay now, Noah. Please stay at home. I believe you. Just finish studying, and be done by the time I get home. You promised you'd cuddle with me."

"I know I did, but you mean the world to me. I can't lose you over something some ex-girlfriend of mine said; you're too damn important."

"I'm not leaving you. Now go study."

He sighs, and I hear him put the keys down on the countertop. "All right. I'll be ready for you when you get home. Have a good practice."

"Thank you, I will."

"Goodbye, baby," he says before we hang up.

Dillen is still standing behind me with her hands on her hips. "I told you he loves you, little shit. Now get a grip and don't let that skank fuck with your relationship."

I nod and hand her the cell phone back—I hate it when she's right. "Okay, okay."

"That's what I thought." She reaches over and puts the phone back into her duffel, and we finish warming up as Mistress Nadine walks into the studio, clapping her hands loudly to get everyone's attention as practice begins.

When I get back to the apartment with Dillen, he's waiting for me just as he promised. I haven't showered and I'm sure I look like a hot, sweaty mess. He's on his feet as soon as he sees me walk through the front door, when he smacks my ass playfully before picking me up and tossing me over his shoulder.

"Noah!"

"Fuck, I missed you. You better be warmed up for me because the only thing I'm studying tonight is this beautiful naked body of yours," he says confidently as he whisks me into my bedroom, shutting the door quickly behind us. I take this golden opportunity to stare at his gorgeous butt and whack it a few times.

He gently tosses me onto the bed then runs his hands up my thighs as he hisses through his teeth, causing me to giggle.

"Damn, I love the sound of that," he says before his teeth find the inside of my thigh. He bites down and breathes in my scent through my tights; I'm needy and all too hot already. The sexual attraction between us is astounding—I can't get enough of him.

I gaze up at him, my cheeks already burning red from my unasked question. "I want you inside of me, but not in here. Will you fuck me in another room tonight?"

"There's that filthy mouth that I love," he says, cocking his eyebrow up at me, "and that's five dollars in the swear jar, little miss. I wouldn't mind taking you in another room, but what about Dillen and Coen?"

I moan with the sudden rip of my tights; he's pulling on the fragile material until he has exposed enough of my lower body to satisfy him.

"I think they are going out."

I can't breathe as his hands wildly strip me until I'm lying naked in front of him, my breasts painfully heavy. I bite the inside of my cheek when he pulls his shirt off—it's apparent he's been running recently by the sheen of perspiration that jackets his divine body. I lean forward and scoot up the bed as he takes off his sweat pants and boxer briefs. What springs free is monstrous and stiff and in need of me, in need of my body.

He follows me up the bed, looking like a predator stalking his prey. *Mmm*, I think, he can eat me whenever he wants me.

"If they are leaving tonight, I'm fucking you on every surface of this apartment. Then when we're done, I want you naked in my arms, trying desperately to catch your breath."

"That sounds so good . . ." I respond breathlessly.

"Tell me what you thought when you first felt my cock in your hands, Heather."

His full lips graze my earlobe, and I can feel his storm brewing, and before I am able to speak, he's moving lower, teasing my neck with his tongue. Tasting me.

"Your mouth watered when you felt how big my dick was . . . didn't it?" he asks, and I gasp when I feel his teeth sink into my neck. He's biting at my collarbone, and I can now feel my arousal drip from between my legs, trickling further down to my ass. I'm squirming beneath him, willing him silently to say more. His deep, sexy voice speaking these erotic words will be my undoing. He grinds his hips seductively against my body, and I can feel every hard inch of him. *Oh my God . . . he isn't even inside me, and I'm about to come.*

"Tell me, Heather." His tongue flicks against my peaked nipple, and then he nips along the taut skin over my ribs, causing my hips to jerk. "I want to hear that dirty little mouth of yours say it. Tell me how fucking full you feel when I bury my dick inside that hot little pussy of yours."

I swear to God, I'm dripping like a faucet now. I can't even speak.

My clit is throbbing beneath its hood, and I will shatter if he touches me there.

I'm aching, and I need to feel him—I can't take this internal throbbing any longer. "Noah, please . . ."

"Begging now, huh?"

He rolls me onto my stomach, and I push up on my hands, so he has the perfect view of my butt. His hands move all over my backside as he kneels up on the bed, positioning himself to drive into me.

When it comes to this man, I can't manage my feelings—I lose every ounce of control I have over myself.

"Tell me how bad you want me, Heather."

Oh God, he sounds so sexy when he's taunting me. "I want to feel you . . . please don't make me wait any longer."

I'm watching him as his chest heaves, and he sinks the head of his throbbing cock into me, "Noah. .!"

"I'm going to give it to you just like you wanted it. You'll be able to feel every fucking inch of me." He's slowly pushing into me, one inconceivable inch at a time. I need him harder and faster than what he's giving me, though.

"Baby . . . please, I need it harder."

"You do, huh?"

With that, he thrusts his full length into me without holding back. I can hear him breathing through his teeth as he starts a slow, painstaking process of pulling out of me and then slamming his immense cock into me repeatedly, until my tight grip on him gives a little. I don't think he can concentrate if he hasn't stretched me first—I'm too tight. I love it, though, and tomorrow, after the show, I'm going to be the one on top, deciding the depth and pace of the moment while my body stiffens and he drives me to the edge of eruption.

I'm brought back into the moment as his long, swift thrusts become deeper, heavier, and full of lust. He's almost frantic as my walls tighten around him when he rotates his hips.

The bastard.

"Do you like that, Heather? Can you feel how fucking deep I am?"

"Oh yes . . . just like that." I push back on him as he pushes forward, sending him so unbelievably deep. A twinge of pain peels through my body, but I decide to ignore it and relish this body-shattering delight that is my boyfriend.

My limbs are already shaking as I lower my chest to the bed. He's taking me from behind, exactly how he wants it. He rarely loses himself, and it excites me when he does.

"Mmm, yes, baby, please don't stop."

My voice is erotic yet needy when I speak with my cheek pressed against the mattress. He feels so good inside me that I grip the sheets and moan loudly.

He's panting through his teeth with each intake of breath and each hard, painful yet pleasing thrust he sinks into me with his ample cock. He takes up every bit of space I have to offer him, filling me with his sizeable girth.

I love the way his rock-hard thighs stay pressed against me, the way his fingers grip my hips, and the way his balls feel as they slap against me with every powerful lunge.

"Heather, you're so fucking tight."

My body coils, and I know he knows that I'm about to come, but he suddenly stops moving. He pulls on my hair while he wraps his arm around my waist, pulling me upright. His chest is pressed against my back while he's seated fully inside of me. I'm panting heavily, trying to move, but he has complete control of my body. I'm losing myself to this Greek god and to get one more stroke against my spot would do me in, but he doesn't budge. His hand moves from my waist to slide up my body, and kneads my breast while he's biting my ear.

His deep, husky voice, full of lust, reverberates through my body when he speaks. "You're so close . . . aren't you, ballerina?" His tongue flicks my earlobe and down the column of my neck. "Your pussy is quivering against my cock . . ."

I whimper, and his hand tightens in my hair, yanking my head back harder.

"Tell me . . ."

He's biting down my neck and kneading my other breast, pinching my nipple hard. The jolt that rolls through me is almost enough to make me come. "Tell me how bad you want my come, Heather."

I can't respond; the pleasure is too immense as I try and focus on our wet, hard, and pulsing connection. I can't take it anymore. I rotate my hips a few times before his hands move down to my hips, forcing me to stop, but it's too late. My body jolts as waves of vibrant energy slam into me and a rush of pure euphoria racks my body. My walls hug him securely, and I can feel him start to pulse as he emits copious amounts of pleasure into me.

His fingers clench in my hair, and all I can do is moan. His low growl fills the room as he loses himself inside of me. "Ahh fuck," he groans through clenched teeth against my neck. My pulse point is racing, and I have no doubt that he can feel how he electrifies my body.

We're utterly still for moments until he loosens his grip on my hair and gently lowers us onto our sides. His movements are slow and deliberate when he pulls out of me and turns me to face him as he slides his hand down my rib cage and to the curve of my butt. He reaches his destination when he pushes his finger deep inside of my wet sex. When he removes it I feel empty, but he soothes me by placing the same finger against my lips. He no longer has to ask me to suck, but I wait for his command anyway.

"Suck, Heather."

I do. I take the length of his finger into my mouth to taste our mingled orgasms until all I can taste is him. Slowly, he removes his finger from my mouth and places his lips on mine as a thank-you.

I'm spent.

Completely done for.

I'm so weak that I can't even nuzzle his warm, damp chest. My eyes are heavy, and I allow myself to close them for a moment. His fingers lazily trail up and down my naked back, and I'm about to pass out in his arms when I hear him speak.

His voice is almost a whisper. "Don't you know that I would never hurt you, Heather?"

"Mmm . . . I know," I manage to say.

His heart is beating rapidly, and his arms tighten around me almost painfully. "Stop letting her get in your head. I don't fucking want her. Do you hear me?"

I stiffen and open my eyes to gaze up at his strong jaw. "You mean Alexis?"

"I don't want her. Do you understand?"

I nod because I realize this must have been weighing on him. I know he loves me, and yes, I'm petrified that she's going to steal him from me, but I also know that he won't leave me. Yet I let her get to me daily. I think he's noticed more than once now.

I maneuver my arm so I can lace my fingers with his. I feel his body relax ever so slightly when he tightens his fingers around mine. I tilt my head up to place soft kisses along his jawline, whispering, "Tell me you love me, Noah."

His available hand moves to grip my ass and squeeze again when a low, assertive rumble emerges from his handsome lips. "I fucking love you, Heather, more than words could express."

I can't describe the feeling I get when he says that to me. I've never had a man draw these kinds of emotions out of me before, and I love him for it. Every single bit of him. I can't believe I left this man, and more importantly, I can't believe he wanted me back after I crushed his already-wounded heart.

"Get some sleep; you have your performance in the morning."

He pulls me on top of his chest, holding me where I always want to be—the spot where I feel completely safe.

"Mmm, you're right. Goodnight, Noah."

He hums his approval of my response before he inhales deeply. His chest expands before he exhales slowly, contently.

"Goodnight, Heather."

Chapter Three

BEAUTIFUL RUIN

NOAH

I'm backstage in Heather's dressing room while she gets ready to go on stage for the first time in London with the Royal Ballet. She's sitting in front of her mirror, and I can tell she's nervous as hell. Coen is out in the audience guarding our seats, so I can wish my ballerina good luck before the show begins.

"Noah?" She shakes her head and looks at me in the mirror as I sit behind her. Her eyes are wide and haunted with fear and doubt. "I can't do this."

"Of course you can, baby. You were born to do this. I can't wait to see my girl show London what she's made of."

I spin her chair around and stand, before lifting her effortlessly into my arms, pulling her glittered up body against my black tux.

"I'm not ready. I know I'm not; it's just too soon." Her petite body trembles in my arms and for the first time, I'm not sure if my touch can calm her down.

"You are going to kill it. I'll be backstage the second you get off, and we can go home, or get drunk, or do anything you want to do." I lift her chin up and press my lips to hers in another attempt to help settle her frayed nerves.

She finally sags in my arms and holds onto me for dear life as our tongues graze each other's passionately. There's a hard knock on the door and a stagehand calls out, "Heather Lane? Five minutes."

"Go kick some ballet ass, baby."

Her smile is reassuring and jacks up my testosterone. I place my lips on hers once more before letting go of her and setting her down on her feet. Her pointe shoes make a slight thud when they hit the ground, and I know she's ready now.

"Promise me that you'll meet me back here after the show?" she asks as she backs toward the door, trying to keep me in her line of sight for as long as she can.

"You have my word. Now go and show em' what you've got."

I wink at her, and she blows me a kiss before stepping out of the room and following the stagehand out into the hallway.

I walk out after her and close the door. I watch the two of them walk down the hallway as she shakes out her hands as if she's trying to get rid of every ounce of nervous energy. I turn and pace down the hall in the opposite direction, to head back to my seat next to Coen. I don't want to miss a second of her glowing on stage. The hallway is dimly lit, and I'm surprised I haven't run into a wall yet. I'm about to reach the end of the hall when I stop abruptly as I'm about to collide with a blonde-bunned dancer.

"Whoa, shit, I'm sorry about that."

"Oh, it's okay . . ." she turns around and gasps loudly, "Noah."

Ah fuck me. Alexis.

"Excuse me," I say politely and try to squeeze past her. She darts in front of me before I can avoid this encounter.

"What's the rush, handsome?" She purses her lips in a suggestive manner as her eyes roam down the center of my body and stop right below my belt buckle.

For fuck's sake.

"I'm going to my seat, Alexis. Now if you'll excuse me . . ." I try again to shove my way past her, but she doesn't budge, and I'm not interested in toppling over a female, regardless of our past. Her avaricious hands move to the lapels of my tux, and I raise my eyebrows in dissatisfaction.

"I want you to fuck me."

"*Excuse* me?"

"I want to feel how deep and hard you can go. God, I cannot begin to tell you how often I dream about your tongue on my body. I don't think I can take seeing you without touching you anymore; you turn me on more than anyone else has before. How do you want me, Noah?"

I laugh once in amusement and grab her wrists, removing her hands from my tux. "You couldn't pay me enough to fuck that used-up body of yours. I have a hard enough time stomaching the sound of your voice to begin with. Now get out of my way, Alexis."

I try using a stern voice on her, but she seems undeterred and practically exhilarated. She's fucking delusional. She fists her hand on my lapel again while her other hand slides down to the waistband of my slacks. I glance down, and before I figure out what her intentions are, she grabs my cock through my slacks and tries to plaster her withered-up lips on mine.

I grab her shoulders and shove her away as quickly as I can. "Fucking hell, Alexis. Take a damn hint; I didn't want you for long in college, and I sure as hell don't want you now, and I never will."

"You can't resist me for too much longer, Noah. You loved playing with my rack, and Heather basically has nothing for you to play with. Quit fucking with that bulimic piece of trash and come back to me, where you belong . . . I have no idea what you see in her."

I don't even try to hide my scowl because now she's pushed me too far. "You're a real piece of work, Alexis. I don't want you; my cock doesn't want you. Get out of my way. *Now.*"

"You can't be serious about her—she's an atrocious dancer, and I'm sure she makes you do all of the work in bed. You're too good for her, Noah. I'll be right here when you need a new pussy to play with . . . one that plays back."

I'm fed up with hearing her shit; this crazy-ass bitch doesn't understand a fucking thing I'm saying. I'm still trying to register the first thing that came out of her mouth mere moments ago. I've never had a woman be so blunt with me before.

"You have legitimately lost all sense of morality, Alexis. There is no point in insulting you because, unlike most people, it does not appear to deter you in the least, nor would a battle of wits go over well since you seem to have lost yours. Your endless attempts of trying to capture my attention have continuously gone to waste. As I've demonstrated, I will not, and refuse to show you the slightest bit of affection or waste a second longer of my time on you. Your constant conniving and endless torment of my girlfriend stops right now, and if you refuse to cease all harassment of her . . . I sure as fuck will be dealing with you firsthand.

"Oh, and don't get your head wrapped around that and try to exploit it in a pathetic attempt to win me over because I can tell you right now, without a single doubt in my mind, that there will never come a time when you will outwit, outsmart, or outlast my relationship with Heather. The faster you're able to process and accept what I've said, the faster you'll be able to overcome your psychopathic tendencies. As far as I'm concerned, you are a part of my distant past, a dark part that I will never revisit. Now move before I make it impossible for you to stand."

As soon as those words leave my mouth, my head is forced to the right. I bring my hand up and rub my cheek, massaging the sting from where she just smacked me. "Nice one," I respond calmly.

She stands there unmoving, unrelenting, and overly confident as I shove past her sluggish frame. I can tell I've struck a chord within her, and I know that will not be the last confrontation I have with her, but it will have to do for now. I stride through the set of double doors and into the emptying lobby, where I am finally free of crazy-feet, as Dillen so aptly named her.

I hear her whine in protest as the doors swing shut behind me, and if I remember correctly, she's about to throw one of her idiosyncratic tantrums.

I make my way to my seat as the lights are going down on the audience, hiding us from the dancers' view. My cheek stings, but I try not to pay attention as I finally reach Coen and take my seat. Our seats are only four rows from the orchestra pit, so I can watch Heather perform her impeccably choreographed solo meticulously.

I'm watching the dark, veiled wings on the side of the stage where I know she'll be. I'm anxious as all hell to see her again, especially after my recent encounter with the bitch. Then the curtains are drawn open across the dim stage, and she stands in position as the spotlight hits her. When the music starts to play, her gorgeous, angelic body starts to move and rotate in faultless turns in front of everyone. The white spotlight holds tight on her glittered body, which holds her audience captive.

Her choreography is slow and precise, and she's executing it flawlessly.

She has everyone enthralled.

I'm so proud of this woman that I can't begin to explain it. She's such a gifted performer; there's no wonder why she's incredibly sought after. Minutes go by when her solo scene comes to an end and she disappears behind the curtain, and a throng of ballerinas floods the stage. I'm trying my hardest to stay seated; I want to go back there and find her and tell her how magnificent she was. I look over to my right and see Coen searching the stage for Dillen. He seems confused as he leans over.

"Dude, they all fucking look alike. I can't find her," he murmurs.

The dipshit has never been so into a girl before that I'm almost proud of him. Dillen moves up front, and I nudge him. "She's the one in the middle—focus, man."

He leans forward, smiling like a drunken idiot when he spots her. "Damn . . ."

I chuckle silently, and I'm about to fuck with his head when Heather moves back onto the stage, and I'm sideswiped by her beauty. She stands in the center of the stage and starts to rotate, her gorgeous body in sync with the music. I'd lose my breakfast if I had to spin like that. I have no idea how she does it.

We all get addicted to something that relieves the pain, and she's my opiate. She's perpetually graceful: it's engrained into who she is, and she does something to me every time I see her. I know I'm grinning from ear to ear as I watch her show London what she can do. There are so many ballerinas on stage that it's almost hard to decipher who's who; I understand Coen's confusion. But I know where my baby is, front and center. Everyone is in formation, where they're supposed to be, but something catches my eye. I'm not sure how I noticed it, but someone seems to step out of place. I sit up straight as Heather moves closer toward the crowd. Something in my gut is telling me this is wrong. The other ballerinas are dancing all around her in perfect chaos, and then it happens again: that same ballerina steps out of place, moving eerily close to Heather.

I watch intently as Heather slows her turns, and she's about to come to a stop when life switches into a blurry slow-motion picture. The ballerina that kept moving out of place hip-checks Heather, and although anger floods me, I expect Heather to catch herself, but the amount of energy, momentum, and force in the impact must have been too much because she's propelled forward at such a speed that she's unable to find her balance.

Even though it looked like the other ballerina regained her balance, she falls backwards before crashing onto the solid black stage. I cannot move my eyes away from Heather as her body swings in the balance between life and death. Gravity takes control of her agile body and pulls her efficaciously over the edge of the stage. Her fate is no longer in her hands nor is it in mine as the incident happens too rapidly for me to wholly comprehend what has happened. In the intense silence I hear a distressed scream fill the theater, and it tears through me like a shard of glass. The scream that made my blood run cold comes to an abrupt stop when her body falls out of view and then there is a boisterous sound and her body crashes into instruments, which brings the music to an unexpected halt.

Holy shit.

My body goes rigid and sets itself into motion at the same time. That scream ignites something within me, making adrenaline surge through my veins at vicious speeds. My eyes look back to the stage as my body automatically gets me onto my feet. Coen curses in the silence of the theatre, saying the words that I am unable to form. My fists clench with blanched knuckles when I see that Alexis is the fallen ballerina, a vindictive leer plastered on her face. I feel Coen move next to me, but I'm faster than he is. I leap between the seats in front of me as people stand up and gasp at the dramatic scene unraveling in front of them. The room is noiseless except for the sounds of hysteria and disbelief coming from the audience members' mouths.

I can't get to her fast enough.

"Move!" I yell out to an asshole that won't let me by. I shove him aside, not giving a damn who he is, or if I've hurt him in the process. I struggle desperately to maneuver through the people and jump over the next two rows, before I haul myself over the wall separating the orchestra pit from the gaping crowd.

As soon as I see her, my body stills; the air around me is unstirred and my own breathing seems to die as my heart slams against my ribs. My stomach lurches as I let the scene in front of me sink into my line of vision as a faint metallic scent fills the air. My beautiful girl is lying unconscious on the cold concrete floor. I find my feet again and rush to her side, where I drop down to my knees next to her broken frame as the musicians try desperately to pick up their instruments. My voice reverberates in my own ears as I yell out for someone to help . . . to do anything. I take in her features, trying to assess her limp body. Her face is soft, yet her complexion is off by the amount of makeup covering her face, making it impossible for me to truly see her. My eyes move over her again, noticing her arms, which are strewn aside carelessly, seemingly irreparable.

The grip of silent panic consumes me and my vision blurs as I looking around helplessly for someone—anyone—to help her. I can hear my heart pounding wildly in my ears as the tangible knot in the pit of my stomach grows.

Her color is unlike her own as she lies in a rapidly expanding pool of blood. I cannot tell where the blood is originating from, nor can I apply pressure to a wound that I cannot find. She has a few gashes along her arms, but not enough to make up for the vast amount spilling onto the concrete. I glance down her body and to her mangled legs where the deep red gore advances further.

"Baby?" My voice is hoarse, and I don't recognize it. "Heather, can you hear me?"

She doesn't respond in the slightest as I move closer to her. Her eyes that were dancing with joy moments ago are now closed, and her body lies in front of me as if it's vacant of a soul.

A few men in dark designer suits rush over, one of them already on the phone with whom I can only assume are the medics. "Sir, I need you to step back from her please. We can't move her before we fully understand how the fall has affected her."

"Fuck off, man. I'm not leaving her."

I hear Dillen yell out from the stage, "Mr. Norwich, he's the only family she has here."

He looks down at me and nods before looking back at Heather.

"Heather? You're going to be okay," I say, moving my hand to her throat, feeling a faint, but steady pulse under my fingers.

Please be okay.

There's an obscene amount of blood; it's pooling around her head and underneath her pallid body. I'm terrified to move her, but I'm about to scoop her into my arms and carry her to the hospital because the damn medics are taking too long. Rage, adrenaline, and panic join forces to flow through me as I shout at nobody in particular, "Where in the fuck are they?"

"They will be here shortly. I'm going to need you to stay calm for her sake," Mr. Norwich says, before turning and speaking to someone behind us, "Clear the stage, and call for a cleanup crew for this mess. The show must go on once we've gotten her out of here safely. We dance when we're broken, so somebody please inform the understudy to be waiting in the wings."

Are you fucking kidding me?

I look upward toward the stage where Dillen stands, her hands cupping her mouth and black tears raining down from her wide eyes.

A few feet over, a distorted view of Alexis comes into my vision, and she doesn't look remorseful in the slightest. She has a smug, triumphant grin on her face, and right then, I know that this stunt was intentional. She hurt my girl because of me, because I refused to give her what she wanted.

I want nothing more than to pull my body up onto the stage and confront her. I don't even want Dillen that close to this selfish bitch.

"Dillen, go find Coen."

She hesitates and stares down at her best friend, my girl. "Go!" I command her and this time she listens just as the medics run in with their equipment and stretcher.

I watch, horrified, as the medics assess her and gently move her from the solid concrete onto the board; thankfully they're quick, because within a minute they have Heather strapped down securely before they attempt to move her onto the stretcher. The pool of blood that was underneath her is massive. The amount of blood loss she's suffered seems to frighten the medics: I am able see it on their faces when they look at each other. They know something but aren't telling me shit. They maneuver the stretcher carefully through the crowded orchestra pit when I get up and follow them as they move through the dark hallways backstage. One of the medics calls out over his shoulder, "I need a list of medications she is on, as well as any allergies she might have."

The question catches me off guard. "I don't know and I'm the only one she has here," I spit out quickly, keeping up with them as we move through the hallways and out into the mild April air.

He doesn't say anything to me, but they quickly get her into the ambulance. When they are good to go, they instruct me to get in and seated. Once inside, the medic who is seated in the back with me reaches over and slams the door shut as the ambulance sirens start blaring and we take off into the streets of London. My eyes are on her, silently pleading for this to be an atrocious but mere projection of an unimaginable nightmare.

Chapter Four

LONELY DEVASTATION

NOAH

The ER is chaotic.

The air feels stuffy with an undertone of sanitizer wafting through the dustless corridors, as the nurses try to appear unhurried and serene—they are anything but. There are doctors and nurses everywhere, poking and prodding her, and inserting an IV into her delicate skin. The nurses are supposed to be calming, right? Well, they fucking aren't. Everyone's causing a commotion and yelling out words I've only heard on television while my girl is lying motionless on this table, causing me to feel dead inside.

I can't function; I cannot even manage to replay the scene that unfolded in front of my eyes moments ago. Beside me, there's a woman firing off questions: "What is her full name? What is her date of birth? Is she allergic to anything? Is she taking any medications?"

Fuck! Would she just shut up?

My fucking life is lying lifeless in front of me. The love of my life, my ballerina, is inert and unresponsive, and she's worried about that shit? I can no longer feel the spark that hummed gloriously between us.

She's bleeding.

Unconscious.

Ruined.

My chest is aching; I can't believe this is happening. I want to bellow and tell everyone to get the hell off of her but at the same time, I want to yell and tell them they aren't doing enough to help her. I finally hear the woman beside me again, as she ardently shoves herself into my unwilling thoughts.

"Sir? Sir? Does she have insurance? What is her United States Social Security number? What's your relationship to her?"

I'm shaking my head to clear it, rubbing my hands over my face to try to be as much help as I possibly can, but her clipped tone is not aiding me.

"I'm sorry, what?" I reply as calmly as I can.

Abruptly I'm being forced from the room as they pull the curtain closed and close the door, shutting me out of the operating room they wheeled my broken ballerina into. "Hey! What's happening?" I demand.

The nurse with the infuriating questions and clipboard grabs my bicep as I walk toward the door. "Sir, you can't go in there right now."

I whip around and stare down at her cruelly. "Why can't I be in there? She needs me." My voice is laced with annoyance and fear; my veins swell as they wait for me to explode in a rush of ferocity. I need to help her in any way I can.

"Sir, please calm down. They are doing all they can. Please have a seat and fill out her paperwork. Someone will be with you when they have answers."

She leads me to a waiting room not far from where Heather is being worked on, and hands me the clipboard with papers attached to it. I take a seat in the sterile room and watch as the nurse promptly leaves me alone with my troubled thoughts.

Will she wake up?

Why wouldn't she open her eyes for me?

What's been broken?

Why was there so much blood?

I glance down at the papers and read over a few questions, and I don't have a single answer to any of them. I know a lot about Heather, but nothing that will help me with these vital questions. Fuck, how do I not know her birthday? Or her middle name? Christ. I need to call Dani. She needs to be here, but what do I say? How do I tell her that her sister is unconscious because of me; I never meant to trigger Alexis like that.

I drop the clipboard into the adjoined seat and lean forward, resting my elbows on my knees with my fingers laced together, begging nobody in particular for strength, for both myself and Heather.

Unable to bear the fluorescent lights for another minute, I drop my face into my hands. This has to be a nightmare, filled with paralyzingly raw emotions. One in which I feel undeniably helpless. I haven't been able to form a single response in my head to the simple questions I should be able to answer. All I keep thinking is how I couldn't protect her today; I just sat and watched her fall from afar. A cold sweat bathes my body in this uncomfortable armchair as I visualize her fall once more; my beautiful angel lost her wings and fell.

Minutes later . . . an hour passes? Fuck, I don't know, but a doctor in light green scrubs walks into my line of sight as I'm looking at my feet.

"Sir? Are you Miss Lane's contact?"

My head flies up, and I'm on my feet before I can acknowledge the movement. "Yes. Is she awake? When can I see her?"

I'm just now recognizing the somber look on his fatigued face. My eyes move to his name tag, but I don't even care to read it.

He shakes his head. "Sir, she's suffered quite a few injuries from the fall, some of which are non-life-threatening, and others that are. She has yet to respond to us verbally. She has cranial swelling, and we have her in a medically induced coma to treat it."

My world is crashing around me as he speaks.

"We have her scheduled for surgery while she's sedated to rejoin the bone fragments into a normal position. She broke the bones in her midfoot, which is what we call a Lisfranc injury, but it's a rather simple surgery to take on. We're more concerned about her cranial swelling and any damage it may cause."

I take a deep breath and exhale, running my hand down my face again. "Will you wake her up after that?"

Again he shakes his head, and my heart sinks further into the pit of my stomach.

"Once we determine that the swelling has gone down, we'll decide whether or not it's safe to wake her up from her comatose state."

I nod and am about to ask if I can see her when he speaks again, placing his hand on my shoulder. "I trust that you are Miss Lane's significant other, in which case I am tremendously sorry to have to be the one to tell you this, but she lost the child in the fall."

What? No.

My eyes find his solemn expression, and I try to explain. "No, Heather wasn't pregnant. I think you've confused her with another patient," I reply adamantly.

His face is grim when he replies, "I'm sorry, but it looks as if she was five to six weeks pregnant. I've been the one helping her through this accident, and I will be the one to perform her surgery. You have my apologies." He squeezes my shoulder while I stare at him in shock. "We'll let you see her once she's out of surgery and in the recovery room."

I'm at a loss for words.

He turns and leaves the waiting room, and I'm left standing there alone again in an attempt to process the worst news of my life.

Heather was pregnant? *Was.*

I can't describe the body-crushing weight that sits on my chest as I replay his words in my head, trying to make them sink in as far as they will go. I'm anxious and need an outlet but my body is too weak to pace the room at the moment.

Did she know?

Why wouldn't she have told me?

I was going to be a father. She was going to be my baby's mother.

A thousand questions flood my mind while pictures of a pregnant Heather will their way into my head. No, she couldn't have known. She's been drinking. She wouldn't have drunk, would she? She wouldn't have hurt our unborn child or herself; she would not have put herself at risk. I need her like I need air, and she knows that.

Fuck Alexis.

She took this from me. My girl and now my child, one of them is gone forever while the other needs aid in breathing. Rage flows through my veins, and I stand up to leave this oppressive room to find my Heather when a nurse comes in.

"Sir? Were you able to fill out her paperwork?" She tries to soothe me with her flat, gentle voice.

"I'm going to need more time."

She nods in understanding and leaves the room to me, and my irrational thoughts. I stare blankly at the clipboard lying on the seat, and before I know it, a couple of hours have passed. Soft footsteps on the cold tile bring me back from a muted, dull place. My eyes meet a nurse's and I stand up to greet her.

"Sir, Miss Lane is out of surgery and in her recovery room. You are welcome to go and see her now."

She signals for me to follow her, and I can't move my feet fast enough, but she isn't moving quickly enough to suit me. Doesn't she realize I need to be with her? I'm seconds away from bypassing her and searching rooms on my own when she walks into a room at the end of the hall.

My feet keep stop cold when I see my beautiful girl, lying in this bed all alone, tubes connecting her to machines that surround her.

"It's okay, you can come in and talk to her. It's better for them to hear voices than just the constant beeping of the machines," the nurse softly says while checking an IV bag that hangs above Heather's still body.

I will my feet to move and walk over to the side of her bed. I've never felt so helpless before in all of my life. She's motionless and my heart is aching in my chest because I can't help her while she suffers . . . but it's much more than suffering. She's in a fixed, comatose state that is keeping her universe at bay, keeping all of the painful and heavy sorrow out of her life.

The nurse leaves the room and shuts the door behind her, leaving me alone with Heather. The only sounds that fill the confined space are the maddening beeps, hisses, and clicks from the machines that surround her, moving air into her lungs and monitoring her vitals. I sit in the chair next to her bed and reach for her hand. It's always cold, but this is colder than usual, lifeless. I want to cover her body with mine and keep her warm, but I'm afraid I'll break her.

"Baby? Can you hear me?" My voice is weak and quiet as I look up at her emotionless face. Her beautiful eyes are closed as if she is resting peacefully, but I know she's fighting underneath the stillness of her body. I can't stand the tube that rests between her roseate lips; it shouldn't be there . . . none of this should be there. My lips belong there.

I want her to breathe on her own. I look down and bring her hand to my lips, placing soft kisses on it, whispering things to her, keeping her hand warm.

"God, baby, please wake up for me. Please?"

I gaze down her body and slowly place my hand on top of her flat stomach as the loss that I was just told about sinks in further. My child used to be here; I rub my thumb gently against her as I feel her stomach rise and fall with every aided breath. I never gave any thought to being a father, but would I have been one? Eventually one day, I think I might have. I sit still in the cool room before throwing my head back and staring up at the acoustic ceiling tiles separated by white grids.

If she didn't know, will she be mad? I don't even know this simple thing about her, among many others. Did she ever want to have a baby and would she have had mine? How is she going to react when I tell her? Tell her that she's no longer pregnant with my child. I feel wet, salty fear run down my face. Fuck, this beautiful woman has brought so many emotions out of me; she has no idea how much I love her.

"Come on, baby, open those beautiful eyes," I whisper as I kiss each one of her fingers. Even though I know they have her heavily sedated, I still try to wake her up because this is too much to wrap my head around. "Do you know how much I love you? I love watching you . . . I always have. I watch you dream, I watch you dance . . . I could watch you for the rest of my life, Heather, but I don't like watching you in here. I need you to wake up. Open your eyes and look at me." My voice is stern yet pleading, but she doesn't respond.

I've been sitting in this chair for hours while my head rests near Heather's arm, holding her hand in mine. The door swings open, and I look up with tired eyes into Dillen's.

"Oh holy shit . . ." Her hands fly to her mouth as she walks forward. "Noah . . . is she. .?"

I sit up straight for the first time since I've been in her room. "No, she just cannot wake up because they have her sedated," I answer her quietly, as if she's just sleeping.

She walks over to me in a rush and throws herself against me, hugging me from the side with her arms wrapped around my shoulders. Her cheek is at my back and I can feel her tears fall onto my white shirt.

I pat her arm, in an attempt soothe her, but I'm currently unable to soothe myself, let alone someone who has known Heather for most of her life. Normally, crying women make me uncomfortable, but this is different. She feels the exact same way I do, but she has a better way of showing it. I'm sure it's better than boxing up all of these emotions into compartments that will dig at my soul. I'd rather be the one in her place.

Her sobs fill the room. "Noah, it happened so fast," she says, sniffling, and lets go of me. "Have you talked to the doctors? What did they say?"

I won't tell her about the miscarriage because Heather needs to be the first to know; she'll need to deal with it in her own way rather than having the world rain down on her.

My voice is tight when I respond. "The doctor said she broke a few bones in her midfoot in the fall. They did surgery, but it will be a while before she heals and is able to dance again."

Dillen whimpers and cries harder, knowing that Heather will have to work harder than ever to regain her career.

"She's got something called cranial swelling." I clear my throat to continue. "Her brain is swelling, and that is why they won't wake her up."

"She's going to be devastated when she wakes up, Noah. I'm so glad you're here for her because she's going to need you so, so much."

I squeeze my eyes shut. "She wouldn't be lying here if I hadn't come to London. I ran into . . ." I pause before I say too much. "Alexis has this stupid fucking vendetta against me, and she has taken it all out on Heather."

Her eyes find mine, sympathy flooding her red, flushed face. "No, Noah. This isn't your fault. Alexis is psycho!"

I nod because I agree with her about Alexis, but this is my fault. I'm the reason she's here, and I'm the only one to blame for her losing what

I didn't know we had.

"Do you have her purse? The nurses are asking me all these questions and I don't have answers to them." I try to sway the conversation because I'm still coming to grips with being at fault.

"Yes, I'll text Coen to bring her stuff in." She pulls out her phone and hurriedly moves her fingers across the screen, then hits send. It makes a noise before she looks at me again. "Okay, he's on his way up now."

"Dillen? Would you do something for me? I don't think I could call her sister right now. Could you call Danielle? She needs to know what happened."

"Oh . . . I mean, I suppose I could. Are you sure you want me to be the one to do it?" I don't think she wants to do it either by the conflict in her voice.

"Yeah, I'm sure. Please, Dill?" She looks at me nervously. "Dillen, I don't want to leave her side, and I doubt I could get all of the appropriate words out over the phone."

"Okay, I'll make the call from the hallway. Please let me know if there are any changes while I'm out there."

I think she's about to start sobbing again when I turn my attention back to Heather and kiss her temple. "I love you, little ballerina."

Dillen walks out of the room and into the hallway. A few seconds pass until I can hear her voice; I cannot make out the words she's saying, though, but the hum of her voice pacifies me slightly.

I look back down at my sleeping beauty and squeeze her hand. "Please be okay, Heather. I need you back here with me. I'll do anything you ask. Just please, come back to me." I kiss the tip of her cold nose and sit back down, resting my hand on her stomach, rubbing gently with my thumb in an effort to appease her loss.

Dillen walks back into the room and takes a seat on the other chair as Coen follows her in. He looks from me to Heather, obviously surprised at how ghastly she looks, but I still think she's the most beautiful thing I've laid my eyes on. Bruises cover her pale skin; they've slowly been darkening over these few hours. The only color that belongs on her pale complexion is pink—her pink and nothing else.

"Damn . . ." is all Coen can manage to say as he walks over to Dillen to wrap his arms around her shivering body as she quakes with uncontrollable sobs.

"Noah? Dani said that she'd be on the first plane out of LA," she says through sniffles and tries to breathe through her mouth. "I don't know if Brannon is coming with her because he has a huge project he's working on and can't just leave his team in the middle of it."

"That's fine. Thank you for doing that, Dillen." I take a deep breath and exhale slowly as I search Heather's face for any changes in the seconds my eyes strayed from her.

Coen walks over and places his hand on my shoulder. "Can I get you some coffee, man?"

"That'd be great, thanks."

"No problem. You like it black, right?" he asks, and Dillen stands up to join him.

"Yeah," is all I can say; I don't have any more words for him as they both walk to the door.

"We'll be back, Noah. Please call me if she wakes up," Dillen asks softly before they leave the private hospital room.

I take Heather's too-cold hand again, willing her to open those stunning jade green eyes for me, but she doesn't.

I'm unsure of how much time passes before the two of them come back. I'm missing my girl although she's right in front of me, and I'm mourning our unborn child. I feel like someone has reached a bare hand into my chest, grasping my heart and squeezing it with all possible might, as it's twisted and turned and dragged painfully out of my body. I feel myself sinking into an abyss, one I didn't know even existed. How am I going to tell her? She must have just gotten pregnant before she left for London. She's had a piece of my heart the entire time she was away from me, thrumming wildly inside of her being.

Dillen interrupts my thoughts. "Noah? We got you coffee and a sandwich."

I feel like all of my energy has been drained. It takes too much effort to look up toward the two of them. "Thank you, both of you."

I can hear Dillen tear up again and to avoid the overwhelming emotions, I look back down at Heather. My world has collapsed. I push the sandwich aside and take a sip of the steaming black liquid.

"Man, do you need anything else? We can stay or go, just let us know what you'd like us to do."

"Shit, I don't know. Could you bring a change of clothes? Or even my toothbrush?"

"I can get that for you. I can run out right now," Dillen says kindly, but I shake my head.

"No, it's okay. You two go and get some sleep. I'm going to stay here tonight."

"All right, man. We'll just be a phone call away," Coen says when he gets up and rubs his hand down Dillen's back. I'm happy for the two of them; I don't know if they are exclusive or not, but it's more than Coen has had before.

"Thanks, have a good night."

"Bye, Noah," he says as they walk out.

I get up and close the door quietly in order to shut out some of the overbearing noise leaking through the hospital hallway.

Chapter Five

INTIMATE RELATIONS

NOAH

I've had maybe two hours of sleep in the last twenty-four hours. I feel like death, but it's not because I'm worn out. Heather won't budge, not even an inch; her fingers won't move, her eyelids won't flutter, and I'm begging her to do anything for me. I stretch and look behind me, spotting her duffel bag. I get up and grab it, before sitting back down in my chair next to her bed. Unzipping the duffel, I look inside and see all her possessions. I've never searched through a woman's belongings before because it's simply not my place, but right now, I need to know more about her. I need to be able to answer these questions in order to do my part. I grab her oversized purse out of the duffel before setting it down at my feet.

Opening her purse, I peer down into it and smile immediately. The first thing I see is a small bag of Swedish Fish. Dammit Heather, my little candy fiend. Of course she would have candy in her purse; it really should not surprise me. I move the bag of candy onto my thigh and look farther in, where I see things that I would suspect most women carry around in their purses: lipstick, those little hair things they wear on their wrists, and a small bottle of perfume. All of these things are normally meaningless, but they mean a fuck-ton to me right now. Grabbing her wallet, I open it up and find her license.

She's smiling in her picture, my beautiful baby. I read over the small print on the plastic card: her full name is Heather Adalyn Lane, and she was born on October twenty-second, 1990. How the fuck did I not know her birthday?

I commit her birthday to memory, making damn sure I won't forget it.

Damn, I didn't even know she was five years younger than I am. I was expecting a year or two, but shit, I was way off. I glance up at her still-too pallid body. "You're still flawless, baby."

I'm about to put her license back in its place when I see a small photo tucked away. I pull on the corner of it, revealing an infant lying in its mother's arms. I run my thumb over the image, assuming it's a photo of Heather with her mother on the day she was born.

I put her license back along with the photo and search for her insurance card, and for whatever reason it's not in her wallet. Fuck, I feel like I'm an intruder, searching through her things like this. I unzip a side pocket of her purse and reach in, pulling out her insurance card and a piece of . . . card stock? What in the hell is this? I turn it over in my hands and catch a familiar scent. It's my cologne, with the name of it written in her elegant handwriting along the white strip.

She's got my cologne sprayed on this small strip of paper. Fuck, I love this woman. I put her bag down and move closer to her, leaning onto her bed to whisper in her ear.

"I love you, baby. Please wake up for me?" I kiss her ear and nuzzle her, hoping like hell it'll wake her. "I'm not leaving you for a second, Heather Adalyn Lane." I exhale and run my fingers through her hair, dwelling on her current situation. "You've got a beautiful name, and it fits you perfectly."

The door opens behind me and my conversation with Heather is cut short. I turn around to look and see another nurse come in. She moves to the bedside and starts checking Heather's fluids and vitals.

"She's looking much better today," the woman says to me, but I know she's lying through her teeth.

She doesn't look any better; in fact, she looks worse. Her leg is swollen and bruised from what I can see under her bandage, and her head is wrapped tightly. There's a bruise on the side of her face and staples in the back of her head. Lord only knows what she feels like internally. I remain quiet instead of offering her my hoarse voice. I watch her closely as she writes down a few things before departing from the room, leaving me alone with Heather once again.

I lean back down and drape my arm across her stomach gently. I need to wrap her in my arms, but I can't. I'll break this fragile girl lying before me if I do. I start whispering things to her, but once again I'm interrupted by the door opening behind me. For fuck's sake, lady, you were just in here. I scowl and turn to look when my eyes land on hers.

Alexis.

She stands in the doorway and raises her eyebrows. "I didn't think you'd be in here, Noah. How's your face?"

I abruptly stand up, deepening my scowl. "Get the fuck out."

"Oh, don't be an asshole. I came to give my condolences."

I stare at this insane woman for a long minute before I can actually say anything. "She's not dead, Alexis. Now get the fuck out of here before I call for security."

"Oh, I like you bossy and emotional. Maybe I should have shoved the little bitch off of the stage ages ago."

I storm across the small room in mere seconds and stare her down, towering over her as my body vibrates with fury. "What the fuck is wrong with you? You're psychotic, Alexis. You could have killed her."

"I couldn't care less. You're lucky she's still breathing. I basically threw myself at you and you denied me each time. Payback's a bitch, just like her spoiled ass. It's a good thing you were here . . . I could have done much worse."

I can't fucking believe how crazy this girl is. I'm stunned. My voice is menacing when I finally speak. "You think I would ever touch you after what you did to her? You are unquestionably nothing compared to Heather. You're going to pay for this, Alexis."

"Oh please," she scoffs and rolls her eyes. "I already got in trouble with Mr. Norwich."

My blood boils when she air quotes the word trouble.

"I told him it was merely an accident, shed a few crocodile tears, and bam, I'm back on top."

"Get your crazy ass out of this room."

I reach for the phone on the wall to call security when I feel her lips on my cheek. It takes all of my self-will not to shove her out into the hallway. I move back and call out, "I need security in here."

"Ugh, you're so dramatic, Noah. Fine, I'm leaving."

"Fuck you, Alexis."

She steps back through the doorframe, and I slam the door shut in her face. I stand there, breathing harshly.

I haven't showered or shaved in a couple of days. I look like shit, but I'm not moving from this spot. Coen and Dillen keep trying to force me to leave for a little while, or at least shower, but what if she wakes up? No fucking way in hell am I leaving.

Something must be wrong. She hasn't responded to anything. Not one damn thing. There are a couple of doctors who keep coming in and checking on her. They talk in hushed voices and write shit down. They keep telling me to wait patiently, but I've got zero patience left.

I want answers.

I have nothing left inside of me. I get up and check her body over: I know every bruise, every cut, and every stitch on her body. The bruises are fading to a greenish-yellow color now. The nurse says it's a good sign because her body is healing.

I'm sitting here holding her hand, inspecting her nails. Shit, she's going to be mad when she sees how her polish has grown out. I chuckle to myself knowingly when suddenly her finger twitches. I can only stare. I think I'm seeing things, but then her finger moves again. My head snaps up to look at her.

"Baby?"

She doesn't respond, but I get up and lean in close. "Come on, beautiful, I'm here. Come back to me, Heather. Open those eyes."

I watch her hand closely for any sign of movement before I look back up at her face. Her lashes flutter ever so slightly, and my heart leaps. Today of all fucking days! "That's it, baby, come on, you can do it."

I reach for the call button and press it continuously, coaxing her while I wait. "Heather . . . open your eyes, baby. You can do it. I'm here, and I'm waiting for you."

The door swings open, and a nurse walks in. I can't contain my eagerness. "She moved; she moved her finger just a second ago."

The nurse frowns and walks over. "Sir, that's just not possible. We have her sedated."

"No. It happened, or I wouldn't have called you in here." I move my hand and stroke her hair gently. "She wants up, and she's obviously fighting the drugs. Can you not take her off that yet?" I ask hopefully.

"The doctor needs to okay that decision."

"Well, get him in here," I reply with a bit too much irritation.

She leaves the room, and I turn back to Heather, smiling at her. "Keep fighting it; listen to my voice. Follow my voice, Heather. I'll do anything you want. I'll eat crinkle fries . . . you can have all of my bacon for the rest of my life. Just wake up for me."

I watch her closely, but there's no movement. I'm begging, willing her to move. "Come on, beautiful, tell me you love me. I need to hear it." A few minutes later the door opens, and the doctor walks in, looking concerned.

"Well, let's see what she's doing here," he says with authority as he walks over to Heather. He takes a small light and lifts her eyelids. Looking for what, I don't know, but he grins.

"It seems as if Miss Lane doesn't want to be asleep anymore."

He turns to the nurse, and gives her instructions regarding her IV and then turns to me. "For whatever reason, her body is fighting off this medication. She's trying to wake on her own."

I can't help my smile, and my chest fucking swells. Damn right she wants up.

The nurse nods as she reaches up to the IV bag, turning a switch to stop the drip. She quickly replaces the current bag with another. I'm guessing it contains fluids to keep Heather hydrated, but I can't be certain.

"Is she going to wake up soon?" I ask the doctor as he's writing more shit down.

"I'd give her a few hours. The sedative usually has to wear off first. I'd like to do a CAT scan on her when she's awake and functioning. Would you prefer to give her the news about her miscarriage, or would you like for me to do it?"

I look over at Heather, frowning. "No . . . I'll do it."

He nods and walks toward the door. "I'll make my rounds and be back shortly to check up on her."

He leaves the room and I grab my phone. I send both Dillen and Coen a text, as well as Dani, giving them an update on her progress:

> *Hey. Heather's been fighting the sedative and they just took her off of it. The doctor said it'll take her a few hours to come around, but hopefully she'll be awake once you guys are back from the airport.*

I get a text back almost immediately after I've sent it, as if Dillen is waiting for updates with her phone in hand.

> *My little shit! She's going to be okay, right? Oh please tell her I love her if she wakes up shortly. Dani is due to land in forty minutes, and I think we'll be back at the hospital in an hour or two.*

I quickly type out a reply:

> *Okay. I'll keep you posted.*

It's been over a fucking hour. My forehead is resting on the edge of her bed while I stare down at my feet. Damn, I thought she was coming around sooner. I sigh and rub my thumb over the top of her hand. The constant beeping in the background is getting annoying, and I count them sometimes: it's usually around eighty-eight beats per minute. Without warning, in the middle of my counting, the beeping in the background accelerates.

I lift my head and look at the machine with tired eyes. *What in the hell?* It's beeping frantically. I sit up straight and look over at Heather. My heart slams against my chest when I see her eyes are open. I leap out of my chair, sending it toppling over.

"Heather? Baby?"

I push the call button again and cup her face. Her eyes are darting from side to side in a frantic attempt to see around the room. "Baby, calm down for me. You're safe."

She's flexing her fingers then brings them up to the tube in her mouth in an attempt to pull at it. "Hey, I'm here. Calm down."

I take her hand gently and kiss it as her eyes well up. She's panicking. I can see her chest heave as her heart slams again and again.

Her gorgeous eyes find mine, and I smile down at her. "I'm here. I love you so fucking much." I move my hand to cup the side of her bruised cheek and kiss her temple as tears stream down her face.

"Don't cry, baby, it's okay."

I reach for her hands and hold them in mine so she doesn't try to pull on the tube. Her rapid beats are coming quicker, and at the rate she's going, she'll pass out. "Heather, please calm down."

I try using a commanding voice. "Squeeze my hand if you can hear me."

She does, and her eyes don't leave mine. The doctor and nurse finally walk in. *About fucking time.*

I don't let go of her hand, but I move out of the doctor's way. They instruct her to try and cough as they take the tube out of her throat. She coughs, and it looks painful as hell to watch. Fuck, she's been through so much.

I just want to hold her, and make her feel safe again. Shit, does she even know what happened? The nurse brings over a cup of chipped ice, and then slowly moves the bed upright.

The doctor starts talking to Heather, discussing her injuries. He stops and stares at me when he's about to mention the miscarriage

"Why don't I give you two a few minutes before I take her back for the CAT scan . . ." He trails off as he excuses himself and the nurse.

Heather's eyes shoot up to mine. My eyes are stinging with an unnamed emotion as I look down at my broken ballerina.

I smile softly at her and pull my chair close to the bed. I cup her face as I kiss her lips. "Hello, my sleeping beauty. Did you have a good nap?" I take an ice chip and bring it to her lips.

She takes a deep breath in and opens her mouth, trying to talk, but her throat is too dry, "Shh, baby, listen to me . . ." She takes the ice chip into her mouth and sucks on it. "I'm going to ask you some questions of my own, okay? Don't talk, though. Just nod or shake your head."

She nods her head, but there's confusion in her eyes.

I lean forward and kiss her lips softly. "Do you remember what happened?"

She nods her head slowly and opens her mouth to speak, but I stop her. "Shh . . ."

"Okay," she replies, and it kills me. Her voice is odd and raspy, unlike her own.

"Baby, please don't speak. As much as I want to hear your voice, I don't want you to strain your body. About the fall . . . do you know why you fell?" I ask as I lace our fingers together.

She shakes her head, and her eyes pool with tears again.

I sigh and move my hand to her flat stomach. "It was Alexis."

She breaks my heart when the tears steadily fall down her cheeks. I wipe them away with my thumb, grazing her soft skin.

"I'm so sorry. You looked so beautiful on stage. Fuck, I haven't been able to breathe without you. The doctor wants to take you for a CAT scan soon. Dani, Dillen, Coen, and possibly Brannon are on their way as we speak."

She nods and tries to speak through her tears. "What happened?"

"The medics brought you back here. You broke . . . fuck, what was it called? You broke the bones in the middle of your foot. I think he called it a Lisfranc injury. They performed surgery on you, and you're going to be okay, but it's going to be a while before you can dance again. We'll need to ask the doctor for specifics on that injury. You had brain swelling and . . . and . . . you've been sedated for two days now."

Why the hell can I not say it? I need to tell her.

Her eyes overflow with tears as her chest heaves. Fuck, this is going to kill me. I want to take away all of her pain and grief, but right now . . . I'm about to make it worse.

"I know, and I'm so sorry. I'm here, though."

Her trembling hands squeeze mine weakly, and I look down, dreading what I have to do next. "I need you to stay calm, okay?"

She nods and closes her eyes. I hand her the cup of ice chips and kiss her wet cheeks when the door opens, and everyone who loves my girl quickly fills the room.

"Oh Heather!" Dani rushes briskly to her sister's side.

Fuck. I guess I'll have to wait to tell her. I know this is going to bite me in the ass somehow.

I let go of Heather's hand and move away from the bed, giving everyone a chance to get close to her. I'm in protector mode when I speak, addressing everyone.

"Guys, they just took her breathing tube out about a half-hour ago. She's having a hard time speaking, so let's give her voice a little break."

I feel their eyes all shoot up at me at once; I know they are all extremely protective of her too. I couldn't give a fuck if they're pissed at me right now. All I'm concerned about is her. I look over at Coen, and he is wearing a smirk . . . he knows exactly what mode I'm currently in.

The doctors come in and announce that they need to get Heather rolled downstairs for her scan and that only her next of kin may accompany her. I step forward at the same time Dani does.

Fuck.

I ask the doctor if I can speak to him privately. Everyone in the room stares us down as we walk out of the room and shut the door. I lower my voice. "I haven't had a chance to tell her about the miscarriage yet. They came right as I was about to tell her."

He assures me that he won't mention anything while she is having her scan done, but it's imperative that I tell her as soon as possible. We both re-enter the room, and I step back to lean against the wall. I cross my arms over my chest as I watch them unlock the wheels on her bed. She hasn't been out of my sight in days, and this makes me anxious. I've even been taking a piss with the door open, so I can see her. She would have been mad as hell if she had woken up during those times.

I watch as they wheel her out, and Dani hurriedly follows them out of the room. Coen is at my side before I can move. "Hey man, how are you holding up?"

"I'm better now that she's awake."

"No shit, man, I bet." His hand meets my shoulder. "She sure as shit won't be able to beat this year's gift, will she? Happy birthday, man. Now go shave because you look like shit."

I bark out a lighthearted laugh before smirking at the thought. "Thanks. No, she won't."

I'm grateful for Coen's sense of humor, which he brings with him into trying situations. He knows when to pull out his smartass remarks when I could use them the most.

Dillen helps me gather my shit together before I say goodbye to them and make my way back to the apartment to shower and change.

On my way back to the hospital after the quickest shower of my life, I stop at a Starbucks to pick up a cool drink for Heather, which I know will feel good on her raw throat. I ask the barista for a Strawberries and Crème frappuccino, knowing the pink hue will lift Heather's spirits. It took about an hour and a half from the time I left the hospital to when I walk back into Heather's room.

Heather sits up straight and calls out, "Noah . . ." Her voice is strong, not as strong as it should be, but I can recognize my girl. I feel like a thousand pounds have been lifted when I see her. I choke back tears when I can feel the electricity buzzing between us again; our love has developed from lust and want, to passion and an intense desire to be together. I stride to her bedside and reach for her hand.

"Hi, beautiful." I press my lips to hers without hesitation.

"I missed you," she says against my lips.

I chuckle lightly. "Now you know how I've felt."

"Oh, I know how you feel . . ." Her eyes sparkle with mischief and I know she's talking about my dick.

"Oh yeah?" I place my lips against her neck and speak softly, ensuring only she can hear me. "Damn, two days of sleep and you're ready to go?"

"Little shit?" Dillen interrupts. "That's the first time he's left your side since you fell. I've been bringing him meals and clean clothes to change into."

"I'm sorry it took me so long to get back here. I made a pit stop on the way."

"It's okay. Can I please be alone with Noah?" she asks in a hushed tone.

She eyes the pink drink in my hand and smiles softly. "Is that for me?"

I know she's talking about the Starbucks drink in my hand, so I wink at her and joke, "Nope. It's for me."

I hand her the cool pink drink and take a seat beside her bed.

"Thank you."

God, she's still so incredibly enthusiastic.

"I guess we'll see you guys later," I say in an attempt to dismiss them.

Dani frowns and gets up. "You want me to leave my sister when I just flew around the world to be by her side?"

Brannon stands up next to her and squeezes her shoulder. "Let them be, babe. She needs him just like you need me."

"Brannon! Don't take his side. I'm her sister, and he's . . . I'm the one that's supposed to be staying with her."

Shit, I didn't know she had beef with me, especially since she helped me get Heather back.

"Dani, please? I love you, and I'm so happy you're here, but I need him right now."

"Whatever, Heather." Dani grabs her shit and stomps out of the room.

"Damn, I'm sorry, you guys. I'll try to talk to her," Brannon interjects before walking out to go after her.

I turn to Heather and look down at her. "I'm sorry; I didn't mean to piss her off."

She gives me an apologetic smile. "Don't be. I want you here."

"We're going to head out too; we'll be back in the morning," Coen says as he and Dillen move toward the door.

Turning to glance at them, I say, "Thanks guys," before looking back down at Heather as she says goodbye to them.

Her bruised little face lights up when it's just us again. "I love you," she says before tugging on my t-shirt, successfully pulling me down to kiss her.

I smile against her lips and pull back. "I love you too," I say, looking her over. "Are you hurting? What did they do to you while I was gone?" I ask as I put another thin blanket over her legs carefully.

"I had that scan done and then . . ." She trails off, and I look up, noticing her little nose is scrunched. I can tell she doesn't want to tell me.

"What?" I prod.

"They took my catheter out," she quickly replies and turns her head. I can't help but chuckle. She's so fucking adorable.

"But I'm still bleeding. I don't know why. I guess that's what happens."

My eyes flicker down to her stomach, and my smile suddenly falls.

Shit. Here we go.

I've had plenty of time to look up what happens after a miscarriage while I waited for her to wake up. Her bleeding isn't from the catheter removal. Well, not all of it anyway. I clear my throat and sit on the edge of the bed. Taking in a deep breath and exhaling, I look behind me at the door and pray that nobody interrupts this because I'm going to go apeshit if they do. I look back at her, keeping my emotions masked.

"Heather, there's something you need to know."

I bring her hand to my mouth and start kissing her fingertips. She's watching me with those eyes of hers, and they're free of tears for once.

Ah hell.

"Heather, I don't know any other way to tell you this . . ." A little wrinkle forms between her eyebrows, and I exhale audibly. "You were pregnant . . . but you've had a miscarriage." I kiss the palm of her hand while I wait for her to process what I'm saying. I know that this probably won't go over well, but I'm not letting go of her.

"I'm sorry." I whisper into her palm and kiss it again.

"I . . . you got me pregnant?"

I look up at her, and it's as if my worst fears are realized. She's angry. I nod because I'm struggling to find the right words. "Yes, I did. I'm sorry, Heather."

"It's gone? I'm not pregnant?" The look of shock on her face is scaring me—I'm unsure how to decipher her emotions.

It? I frown at her wording. We had a baby growing inside of her, and her reaction is not what I was prepared for.

"No . . . not anymore."

She doesn't speak for the longest time. Her eyes glass over, and she's staring at me, but looking straight through me.

"Hey . . . talk to me."

I try ducking my head to get into her line of vision.

"This can't be happening . . ." she says in a silent whisper.

I don't even know how to console her. She's so silent. Is she wondering what we could have had? What if?

I'm numb.

Chapter Six

EMPTY

HEATHER

Pregnant?

I cannot put into words the depth of sorrow I feel right now.

Blankness.

Numbness.

Nothing.

How do I forgive my broken body?

How do I tell that baby goodbye, when I didn't get a chance to say hello, or that I loved it? Not only did I not know I was pregnant, but I lost my baby. Our baby. A baby I held for every second of its life and now? Nothing.

My mind is running over everything I could have done differently if I had known. I wouldn't have been drinking and . . . oh God. This is my fault, and I have no explanation for it.

My emotions are in turmoil as the world around me moves on as if my heart has not been shattered into hundreds of unfixable pieces, and a million words or emotions could not bring our baby back. I glance back up at Noah, and he's holding my hand, but I feel isolated and alone. I feel utterly empty.

How is this affecting him? Is he devastated? Relieved?

"Noah?" He kisses my palm again and looks down into my eyes. "I didn't know . . ."

"I'm sorry, Heather."

"No . . . I'm sorry."

He lowers his head to my stomach and kisses it gently, melting my heart. He's quiet for a long, agonizing minute, but then he speaks and I almost can't hear him. "Are you mad at me?"

"Why would I be mad at you? I'm so happy that you're here," I say, attempting to smile for him, but I'm almost sure he can see through my broken heart and empty, aching arms. Every part of me hurts: my mind, my soul, and every inch of my disgustingly bruised, broken body is mourning and pleading that this is not true.

He moves and tilts my chin up. "Tell me what you need."

I'm confused by what he says because what I need has been taken from me—from us. I shake my head and stare out of the window to a clear blue sky. "I don't know what I need."

He laces his fingers with mine. "Why don't you try and get some sleep then?"

I reposition myself on the bed, not wanting to look out onto a clear, gorgeous day while I'm in my own personal hell.

My body cries out in loss as I lie still, unmoving, as I try and fight through this news. I know that there will be months and years of mourning that I need to get through. It's hard to imagine anything more heartbreaking than this loss. How can I love something so much that I didn't fully have, that I didn't know even existed? The only way I can work through this grief is to let it hit me with its full force of intensity and take it. I know I have to grieve because it's the emotional and physical price I need to pay, but I feel blindsided.

I unconsciously move my arms down to my midsection, holding my empty tummy.

This grief will not expire, and I will not be intoxicated by memories and feelings of this loved angel, an angel whose heart stopped beating before mine could beat for it. I will never know what it would've been like to carry this child; I will not have memories of being pregnant or being excited to hold my newborn or watching it sleep in my arms while Noah sat by my side. I have nothing.

Desolation.

When I wake up, Noah is fast asleep, half of his body draped onto the bed with his head resting on my stomach. Did he even sleep while I was sedated? It doesn't seem like he did. I try stretching out my legs, but they are stiff and sore. I wince and look up when I realize we're not alone. "Dani?"

"He shouldn't be crowding you like that. He's probably hurting you."

"It's nice to see you too, sister."

"Heather . . . I'm going to call the doctor. He shouldn't be using you as a pillow," she all but yells, which causes Noah to stir.

"Please stop . . . I can tell he hasn't slept. If this was Brannon, I would never ask him to leave."

"Well, he's not Brannon. You've been with this man for all of five minutes."

I scowl at her. "What the heck is your problem, Danielle?" I try to sit up more without waking him.

I think he feels me move, and it's hurting me more than anything, I look down at my man as he forces his bloodshot eyes open. "Mmm, do you need me to take you to the bathroom?"

Dani clears her throat and glares at me expectantly.

I shake my head and whisper, "No, not yet. Go back to sleep," and glare at Dani when his eyes close.

"That's it. I'm calling the doctor." She gets up and strides over to the call button, hitting it twice. Two nurses come into the room a moment later.

"Miss Lane? Is everything okay?" one of them asks.

"Yes, I'm fine . . . it was pressed by mistake. I'm sorry," I say as she eyes my handsome sleeping Greek god.

"Actually," Dani pipes in, but I stare her down. "Never mind. Thank you."

The nurses leave, and I'm not even sure what to say to my sister in this moment.

"I'm sorry, Heather . . . it's just . . . I just went into mom mode."

I sigh quietly. "Dani, Noah loves me. Why are you so mad at him?"

"Because I want to be the one taking care of my sister; it's my job to do it. It always has been. He comes into the picture and takes you away from me . . ." She sniffles, and I know she's being selfish, but I understand now. It's always been just the two of us.

I look down at Noah. He's proved to me over and over again how much he loves me. "Dani, it's not just you and I anymore, and he's been taking care of me."

"I know he has. I'm just . . . ugh! I'm just jealous," she sobs and wipes at the tears that have fallen down her cheek.

"Jealous? Dani, you're being ridiculous. I'm lucky he even wants me."

"I'm sorry," she says softly and gets up, walking over to me and hugging me gently. "I love you."

"I love you too." I know she wants to feel needed, so I quickly think of something for her to do. "Umm, do you know when I get to leave?"

She eyes my bruises before she smiles again. "I can go find out. I'll be right back."

She quickly leaves the room, and I sag back against the pillow just as Noah opens his eyes slowly, greeting me with a sleepy, lazy smile.

"Bathroom?" he asks groggily.

I hold in a giggle and nod. "Please?"

I've got both Noah and Dani wanting me to need them.

"Mmm, I need a kiss first, ballerina," he says as he sits up.

I lean into him and tilt my head up, pressing my lips to his.

He growls aggressively against my lips and smiles. "You have no idea how happy I am about you being awake and okay," he says as he stands up and removes the thin blanket from my legs. I reach out and grab hold of the IV stand before he carefully lifts me into his arms.

I'm sore all over, but I try not to let it show. He carries me gently and sets me down on the toilet. I don't even have to say anything because he already knows what I'm thinking. He's looking down at me, his face as serious as ever.

"Get over it, ballerina; I'm not leaving you in here alone."

"Noah, please?"

"No way in hell am I leaving this room."

He turns around and faces the wall, giving me as much privacy as I'm going to get. I huff angrily and as loud as I can, so he knows how mad I am.

"Don't even try that with me. You know I love it when you're pissy."

This is so not right. I sit there quietly and cross my arms in a full-on pout. I am not peeing in front of him.

He turns around and raises his eyebrow at me. "Heather . . ."

I glare at him. "Yes, Ryan?"

"You are so fucking stubborn. You know that?" he says as he steps just outside of the door, leaving the door wide open. I growl in frustration and try to reach for the faucet unsuccessfully.

"Noah?"

"Yes, baby?" he calls from around the corner.

"Can you at least turn on the water, so you can't hear me going?"

He chuckles before walking back in and turning on the water, then walks out again, waiting for me.

The rush of running water eases my discomfort, and I start to go. As soon as I do, I regret it. It's so painful to go that I squeak out and quickly hold onto my abdomen.

"Are you okay?"

I can hear that Dani is back in the room.

"Can you go check on her please?" he asks my sister.

"Why couldn't you wait until I was back, Noah?" she bites out. She's seriously killing me.

I hear him reply, and I can tell he has a tenuous grasp on biting his tongue. "I didn't know you were here, Dani. She told me she needed to go."

She walks in, and I frown at her. "I'm fine," I say to her sternly.

She shuts the door, completely excluding Noah.

"Dani, please stop it."

I'm emotional and in physical pain, and she's being such a butthead.

"He won't even let you use the bathroom alone. He's obsessed with you, and it's not healthy."

"I asked him to take me," I snap back and wince when another sharp pain hits me. "Get the nurse."

"Oh shit . . ." She pushes the button and the nurse comes in minutes later.

Noah's standing in the doorway with a look of concern on his face.

"If you don't mind, I need both of you to give me and Miss Lane a few moments alone, please," the nurse says sweetly, and Noah nods, but I swear Dani is about to jump down her throat. I watch as my Greek god walks away from the bathroom and I think he goes to stand outside in the hallway.

The nurse shuts the door behind her, and I ask her if it's normal to have this type of pain and cramping. She nods and explains that it's normal to have both after a miscarriage, and that my bleeding should stop within a couple of weeks.

I'm deflated with this news, and it sets off something inside me. I don't know what it is, and I can't begin to explain it, but I'm unhappy. She helps me get cleaned up and back into bed. She says I'll be able to go home tonight, but I have to wait for the doctor to sign a release form. After she leaves the room, I'm once again surrounded by the tension that engulfs Noah and Dani. I can feel myself slipping further into this veil of darkness.

Chapter Seven

APOLOGY ACCEPTED

NOAH

I'm waiting for the nurse to emerge from Heather's room when Dani turns on me. "Listen, I know Heather means a lot to you, but you need to let her breathe. You are completely suffocating her from all directions, and I'm not going to stand by and watch you do it."

What the hell just happened?

"Excuse me?"

"Noah, don't be childish. She needs her space from you. I don't know what you did last night, but I can tell she is incredibly upset today. You were the only one who could have done or said anything to her."

I laugh because this is just fucking ridiculous. "What the hell makes you think I did something?"

"You were the only person around her last night. I don't know what you did to her, but you completely mess with her emotions. She's not herself."

I can't stand being accused of upsetting Heather. "You have no fucking idea what is going on, Dani. What the hell is your problem?"

"*You* are. You should leave . . ."

"Are you fucking kidding me? You have no clue what we're going through."

"Oh? And what would that be? That you can't have my sister underneath you?" she spits out angrily as she steps closer to me in the fluorescently lit hallway.

"How about the fact that she had a miscarriage? That she lost our unborn baby . . . Or is that my fucking fault too, because I fucked her, and that was the reason she was pregnant?" I run my hands through my hair when the nurse walks out and says we can both go back in.

Dani is speechless.

She just stares at me as if I have two heads. "Noah . . ."

"Just drop it. Contrary to what you believe, I would never hurt her. She's the one good thing in my life, and I would never compromise that."

I reach for the door, and she reaches for my elbow. I automatically pull away from her—I don't need her or anyone else's pity.

"Don't . . ."

I walk into the room with my heart in my throat. I feel like I can't breathe.

"I'm sorry," I hear her say as I walk into the room and sit down next to my girl.

"Are you okay?" I ask Heather anxiously.

"I'm fine, handsome. What's wrong?"

"I let it slip to Dani about the miscarriage. I'm sorry, Heather. She just had me by the throat." I take her hand and look down toward her flat stomach as I tremble with anger.

"Oh . . ."

She doesn't say anything else. I look up at her, and she won't even make eye contact with me.

"I fucked up. I'm sorry."

I get up and start pacing the room. I'm petrified of losing her. I can't and won't lose one more single person in my life. I'm beyond pissed right now, and thirty seconds later Dani walks into the room. She gazes at her sister and then at me, before walking over to Heather. I can tell Heather is uncomfortable, and I want to protect her, but every time Dani is involved, I have to bite my tongue. I can't be in the same room as her right now, so I walk out.

My face is masked of all emotion when I walk up to the nurse's station, mustering the lowest, most controlled voice I can. "When will Heather Lane be able to leave the hospital?"

"Oh yes, give me a second." She lowers her glasses to look at the screen. "The doctor will be by to do his rounds shortly. He is the only one who is able to sign the release form for her. She's going to need crutches, which her insurance will cover. Her doctor will be the one to bring them in when he signs her release form.

"Okay, great. Is there anything I will need to pick up for her?"

"We'll be sending her home with a list of things she can and cannot do. The doctor will go over the list with her to ensure that she understands all of it."

"Good. Thank you for your help." I head back to Heather's room and walk in. I'm unsure of what I've missed, but Heather is in tears.

I look directly at Dani. "What in the hell did you say to her?" My fury is barely contained.

"Noah," Heather croaks out and reaches for me, "it's okay. She just apologized."

My shoulders sag in relief.

I move close to her and kiss her tears, whispering, "You and I are going to be okay."

She nods, but I know she doesn't believe me. "I love you, Noah."

"I love you too, beautiful."

"Heather? Noah? I'm so sorry for how I've been acting. There's no excuse for it."

Heather looks up at me, judging whether or not I'm in the right frame of mind to forgive her sister. I reassure her by squeezing her hand and accepting Dani's apology.

Chapter Eight

LOVE REASSURED

NOAH

I'm fucking petrified.

I don't know what to do. I've never dealt with anything like this before. Heather has been lying in bed for three days now. She won't come out of her room, she barely eats, and I can't get her to stop crying. I've had to deal with Dani jumping on my ass—she's pissed at me for God knows what, and I have to say that I couldn't care less. My only worry is Heather: she's not herself.

At first I thought she was upset about her foot, and dancing. Then I thought she might have been in pain from the stitches in her head. But now I know . . . it's the miscarriage. I've tried everything I can think of. I've even joined an online forum for people who have suffered through this loss before. I'm heartbroken for her and for us. I just need time to figure out what she needs.

HEATHER

How can I miss something I barely had?

Something I didn't know I had the pleasure of having?

There's too much that time cannot wipe away.

I feel like I've lost my way.

Nothing in this world can describe how devoid of life I feel. A life I didn't know I had inside of me was ripped out of my body, out of my womb. I never thought I'd want a child, but knowing that the child was Noah's baby . . . it pains me like nothing I've ever felt before. I think I want that from him now. I think I want something that belongs to the both of us.

I feel like I can't move, and I don't want the sunshine spilling into my room, even if the weather is gorgeous outside. Noah's tried to open the curtains a few times, but I just can't bear it. I'm wallowing in the darkness and in his arms. A rose that was once held up with such elegance and grandeur is now wilted, bent over and crying dark blood-colored petals.

I can't tell when Noah's down, upset, or when he cries . . . if he even cries. He's been putting me first since he told me about our loss. He hasn't turned away from me once, and I know he won't. I know he's going through as many complicated emotions as I am, but he still manages to be my pillar, the strong stalk of my wilted rose. He stands tall and holds me up; I would crumble without him. I think he's awake as he holds me. *What do I say?*

"Noah?"

"Mmm? I'm here, baby," he replies softly as he kisses my neck.

"Are we going to be okay?"

He turns me over and presses his lips to mine. "We're more than okay. You're the sweetest thing in my life."

I grin because I know he's talking about my sweet tooth, "Can we go get some ice cream? Or see a movie? I think I'd like to be outside today. Well, I'd like to try."

His smile is all the light I need. His tanned arms tighten around my fragile frame. "We can do anything you want to do. I'll do anything to wash all of this pain away."

I feel like the pull between us has intensified since we first met.

"I know you will. Would you mind if Dill and Coen came too?"

He hums against my skin. "How about we go with Dani and Brannon to the airport, and then we'll go out with Dillen and Coen?"

"My sister leaves today? How has it been that long already? Oh, I'm such a horrible person. I have hardly spent any time with her, and she flew all the way out here to be by my side."

"You are the furthest thing from a horrible person."

His love for me is undeniable.

He's been the world's best companion, lover, and friend; I couldn't ask for more of him. I sigh heavily and will myself to move to the end of the bed and reach for my crutches. Noah sits up quickly and stands in front of me with his arms stretched out toward me. He's ready to support me in any way I need him. "Do you need help getting up?"

"No, I'm okay. I need to do this on my own." I try to convince myself too, because I'd much rather have help, but I need to force myself; I need to survive this. I struggle to get up, but eventually I do, and I am able to maneuver myself with the crutches to the bathroom, where I start running the bath. I swear I can hear him smiling from in here.

It takes me longer than usual to get ready with this damned boot on my foot, but when I emerge from the bathroom the curtains are open, and the spring sun lights up my room in all its glory. I can't help but smile and remind myself that our baby is in a better place that is filled with undying love and warmth.

My bedroom door is open, and for the first time since waking up in the hospital, I don't mind it. I walk out with the help of my crutches to my awaiting family.

"There she is," Noah announces, and they all turn around with smiles on their faces.

Dillen bolts toward me and throws her arms around me. "Little shit! I've missed your ass." She swats at my butt, and I yelp.

"Hi, Dill, I'm sorry for being such a downer."

"Shush!"

I hear Dani sniffle, and before I know it she's hugging both of us. "I love you, sister."

I start to tear up, and I hug them back. "I love you too. I'm so sorry I haven't come out of my room."

"We understand, Heather. It's okay," Dani croons as her squeeze tightens. "Brannon just ordered breakfast, and it should be here soon."

I nod and look over at Brannon, Noah, and Coen. I'm suddenly embarrassed and want to go back into my room. Everyone here knows I lost our baby. They know I wasn't strong enough to keep it safe.

I think Noah senses that I'm about to fall apart, because he walks toward me and drapes his arms around my body, so I can lean against him. I take in a deep breath and will myself to relax.

He whispers in my ear, "Are you okay?"

I wipe at my newly shed tears and nod, tasting the salt on my cheeks. I'm unable to make eye contact with anybody. "I'm okay."

"I'm here for you, ballerina. We all are." He kisses my neck, and I can feel everyone's eyes on us. There's a knock at the door, and Brannon says he'll get it.

"Oh, that must be the breakfast. Dani? Will you help me set up the table?" Dillen asks politely.

I hear them talking happily as they set the table together. They're going on like everything is fine. How can everything be fine? I look up at Noah. "They blame me, don't they?"

He reaches for my hand and laces his fingers through mine. "Blame you? Heather, they don't blame you for anything. Your fall and our loss is not and never will be your fault."

Do I believe him? I don't know.

My head is telling me to, but my heart refuses to agree.

"Okay . . ." is all I can manage.

Breakfast passes quickly, as we all eat and everyone tries to make small talk with me. I'm trying, but all I want is to be alone. After breakfast, Dill and Coen bid their goodbyes to my sister and Brannon, before the four of us head to the airport. I'm slowly getting used to these crutches as we make our way to the security checkpoint.

"Thank you both for coming."

Dani grips me in a tight hug. "We love you, Heather, so much. Please come visit us. We miss you." She's sniffling in my ear, and it makes me emotional again. My puffy red eyes can't take any more tears.

"I will, I promise," I say softly when she lets go of me.

Noah's at my side a second later and snakes his arm around my waist, so I can lean on him, rather than my having to hold myself up on the crutches.

"Thank you for your hospitality, Noah . . . Heather," Brannon says as he pulls out their passports. Dani steps forward and hugs Noah too.

"Thank you for taking care of my sister. I'm glad she's got someone like you."

He shows slight emotion when he replies, "You're welcome, Dani. Don't worry, I won't leave her alone."

"I know. Thank you."

We hug each other again before they walk through security and out of sight.

"Noah?"

"Yes, ballerina?"

"Can we have a date in our room tonight?"

His face lights up, and it makes me smile. I can't do much to make him happy, but I'm trying.

"You never have to ask me for that. The answer is always going to be yes." He tilts my chin up to get a better view of me. "Are you okay?"

I take in a deep breath and let it out slowly before nodding. "I will be."

His lips meet mine, teasing the seam of my lips with his tongue. "Come on, I've got a date with a beautiful girl tonight, and I need to get home," he says playfully before letting me go.

We walk out to Dill's Fiat and drive home. "Are you sure this won't be a waste of a date? We can't even have sex . . ."

I look over and see him scowl before he hides it from me.

"Heather, that doesn't matter to me. And how is it a wasted date when I have my girlfriend lying against me all night?"

I giggle as he drives back. "You just want me naked and in your arms . . ."

"Damn right I do."

I look down at my foot in my boot and frown. He reacts by reaching for my hand and squeezing it gently.

"Hey. Don't you worry about that. You'll be dancing again in no time at all. Just think of this as a well-deserved vacation for your feet."

He winks and brings my fingers to his lips and kisses them as he drives us back to the apartment.

"And I'll make you a deal: if you keep that beautiful smile on your face, I'll help you paint your toe nails when you need me to. I'll try at least." He laughs at himself, and I join in.

"Awww, baby, I promise. I can't wait for that."

"I think I'll suck on them tonight and make you squirm," he jokes as we pull into the garage of the apartment building.

"Ah!" I smack his arm. "Noah!"

"What? What happened? I blacked out," he asks innocently while using my own line against me. He gets out and walks around to help me out of the car and to the elevator to get up to our floor.

When we get into the apartment, he scoops me up into his arms, causing me to drop my crutches as he takes me to our room. Ours. It's not mine anymore; it's ours.

I haven't smiled this much in I don't know how long. He's jovial today and it makes me happy. He's so gentle with me when he picks me up and lays me down.

"I've missed you."

"I've been right here, baby. Can I get you your pajamas?" he asks as he starts pulling at my yoga pants.

I bite my lip and nod. This man is gorgeous.

He moves quickly as he carefully removes my boot, followed by my yoga pants and shirt, so I'm lying there in my bra and panties. "Don't you move, I'll be right back."

"Hurry up."

He walks out of the room and closes the door behind him. I feel good—for once, I feel happy. His good mood is radiating in waves, and I love seeing him like this. I pull the covers up over my chest and lie there.

Moments later he's back with my favorite pair of pink loose-fitting satin pajama pants, my pink camisole, which I know he enjoys due to the amount of cleavage it shows off, a bag of Reese's Pieces, and a roll of Starburst.

"Are you cold?" He pauses to look at me—it didn't take him long to notice that I'm completely covered up.

I laugh at him and watch him undress.

"I am. Can you come and warm me up?"

"Damn right I can."

He tosses his boxer briefs across the room and pulls the blankets off of me. His eyes devour me, every inch of my semi-naked body. I bite my lip as his cock grows in front of me, and I want nothing more than to take him into my mouth and suck him dry.

"Fuck, you have the most amazing body."

I'm feeling energized from his good mood, so I crook my finger, beckoning him. "Come here, handsome."

His growl fills the room as he lies down on top of me, kissing my neck down to my collarbone. I can't help but moan because his lips feel so, so good on my cold skin. I'm so worked up already. I move my fingers up into his hair and pull, encouraging him to keep going.

He kisses down my chest where he teases his tongue along the lace edging of my bra. My body comes alive, and I sigh in approval. "Baby, I want to . . . but I can't."

"Shh . . ." he says against my breast. "Just let me have my lips on you; I want to watch you enjoy it. Do you like the way it feels?"

His breath is coming fast against my skin as I mumble out what words I can, "I . . . yes . . ."

I don't want him to stop because it feels unbelievable. I'm squirming, just like he said he'd make me do. I blink my eyes open when I feel him lift his body off of mine. He's braced above me, searching my face. I know he's checking to see if I'm okay. He must be satisfied with what he sees because moments later, he runs his thumb along my lower lip. He softly caresses it and teases the seam of my lips, pressing in with the slightest amount of pressure. His eyes darken when I swirl my tongue around his thumb. He groans, and I can feel him growing, pushing his girth into my delicate panties; it's monstrous.

"Those lips should be wrapped around something else."

I bite down and moan. "Put your cock in my mouth, Noah," I say in the most erotic voice I can manage. I know he loves it when I talk dirty to him.

"Fuck, baby. I want you. I'll . . ." He pauses when we both hear Dillen's dramatic shrill cry rip through the walls separating our bedrooms.

My mouth drops open, and his eyes go wide.

"Jesus," he says as he looks at the wall above our headboard. "Is she okay?"

"I think so. She's always been loud, but this is a new octave level, even for her."

He groans loudly and rolls over onto his back, pulling a pillow over his head and muttering a curse.

I look over at him and giggle. "Way to kill the mood, huh?" I reach over and grab my book and sit up against the headboard, pulling the sheets up with me. "I'm sorry, baby," I say before laying my hand on his naked chest.

He stuffs the pillow under his head and reaches for a beer and his tablet.

"Don't apologize, ballerina."

He grabs his glasses that he only wears when he's reading the news-paper on his tablet or studying. He's so unbelievably sexy in them—I almost wish he'd wear them more often. I look at the two of us, and almost snort. We look like an old couple in bed, without a sex life.

A minute later there's a banging against our wall, and we both look at each other. Poor Noah is so sexually frustrated and now we've basically got a porno beating against the wall behind us. I giggle when he groans and slides down the bed, flinging his arm over his eyes.

"Dammit. I cannot stay in here. Get dressed. We're going out." He gets up and walks toward the closet while I take in his naked tush.

God, this sucks. I'm broken and can't even make love to my boy-friend. As Noah gets dressed, I try to wiggle out of bed without hitting my foot.

He's in the closet pulling his shirt over his head when the noises in the other room reach an all-time high. *Holy F!*

Noah groans in a protest.

"Oh, come the fuck on."

When he emerges from the closet, he already has clothes for me in his hands. "Here. It may not match but I have to get out of this sex den."

He helps me get my pants on, and then does my boot while I work on getting my top on. Of course he doesn't get me any panties to wear. Classic Noah. Soon after we leave we're at a local cafe, picking out gelato flavors for each other to try and help get our minds off our frustrated libidos.

Chapter Nine

UNPREDICTABLE REALITY

NOAH

Almost two weeks have passed since we lost something precious. Dani and Brannon have been gone for a week now, and the apartment has been quiet. I believe Coen leaves tomorrow, so we've decided to give Dillen and Coen some alone time. Heather and I are sitting in Costa, working on our second lattes.

I'm playing with her fingers—just touching her comforts me. "Heather? I need to talk to you about something."

She's looking at her phone and not paying much attention to anything else. "Okay, what about?"

"It's about my parents." I watch her carefully. "I want to meet them, and I want you to be there with me."

She shifts uncomfortably in her seat and squeezes my hand as she sets her phone down. "I would love to, but I also need to talk to you about them. I uhmm . . . ."

"Would either of you like a refill?"

We're interrupted by our waitress, and I notice Heather's shoulders slump. I answer her while Heather searches for something in her purse, pulling out a bottle of her medication.

"Yes, please."

I watch her carefully as the waitress places our mugs on her tray. I look up at the waitress. "I'd like a warm buttered croissant too, please." I know that Heather can't take those pills without eating because they make her sick.

"Of course, I'll be right back with your drinks," she answers politely and walks away. I rub the tension out of my jaw and take her hand again.

"Baby? Are you in pain? Do you want to leave?"

"No, I'll be fine. Okay, so . . . your parents?" She urges me to continue.

"I'll need to tell Joel I'm ready to meet them. I don't even know how in the hell this is going to go."

"It's going to be emotional for everyone involved. Are you going to call them or will Joel?"

"I don't know. Maybe this is a bad idea." I start questioning everything I've been thinking about. "Shit, maybe I should just wait."

As she's about to reply, I interrupt her to say, "Hell, they've been waiting for thirty years. I can't make them wait any longer."

"Wait . . . I thought you were twenty nine? Ugh, I'm such an awful girlfriend."

I laugh and shake my head. "I may be your Greek god, but I still age, baby."

"Noah Ryan," she sits up straight with a frown marring her face. "Why did you tell me you were twenty-nine then?"

"I was twenty-nine when we met. I turned thirty on April third."

"But . . ." Her mouth drops open, and surprise fills her eyes. "That was almost two weeks ago!" she shouts in realization.

"I know, and you gave me the best gift by waking up for me." I lean over and kiss her when the waitress gets back, attempting to calm her.

"Noah . . . I'm so sorry," she says, frowning, and throws her arms around my neck. "Why didn't you tell me?"

I laugh at her scolding me. "It just wasn't important. Your waking up and being okay was." I breathe her in and smile. "You gave me exactly what I wanted."

She narrows her eyes at me. "I'm still mad about this, Ryan."

"You can make it up to me. How does that sound?"

She easily grins and kisses my jaw. Her little storm has passed. "Okay, fine, I will."

"What does your sexy little ass have in mind?"

"No, it's a surprise."

"I like surprises, Miss Lane, especially if they involve your naked body."

She nips at my lip, and I growl, "Now swear to me that you'll be there to meet my parents with me . . ."

She stares at me for a few minutes, and I'm worried she'll say no, but then she smiles softly. "I swear I'll be by your side, Noah."

"Thank you, ballerina. Now eat your croissant."

She kisses me quickly, and then starts to eat. I'm feeling much better about the situation, and I'm relaxed for the first time in a while. I lean back in my chair and put my arm around the back of hers.

"Mmm, this is good. Do you want a bite?" she asks as she holds up the croissant to my lips. I take her fingers into my mouth and suck on them, before biting off a piece of the croissant. She whimpers, and I wink.

"Don't tease me."

"Ballerina, you love being teased. Now get that little ass on my lap."

I watch her squirm in her seat, before she gets up and sits down on my lap. I'm the luckiest son of a bitch to have this gorgeous woman. She keeps me stable and strong. I'd crack without her in my life. Hell, I did crack.

She lays her head on my shoulder and whispers, "This is hardly the place for me to be sitting on your lap."

"I couldn't give a fuck. I want you here, and this is where you want to be." I tap her ass playfully so she knows not to argue with me. "I . . . uh, I wanted to tell you that I got an email this morning from the character and fitness examiners of New York State . . ." I trail off, thinking about what the email said.

"What did it say?" She's staring up at me with those beautiful jade green eyes.

"It said that I passed."

Her smile is beaming, and I swear it lights up the entire coffeehouse. "Baby, that's wonderful."

"Yeah, I'm excited for this nightmare to come to an end."

"You're going to do great. When is it?"

"It's at the end of July, but I'm going to sign up for a six-week course before I take it. I need the refresher." Shit, I'm basically telling her that I'm leaving.

She stares up at me, and I wait for the tears. "I . . . can I come home with you?"

I think my heart just stopped. *Wait what?* "You want to go home?"

She nods. "I want to go home."

I sigh deeply and rub my face in disbelief. "Wait a minute, let's think about this. Of course I want you to come home with me, but you followed your dream all the way here. Are you sure you want to just up and leave?"

"I got my chance, and they are not going to wait on me. They've already replaced me, Noah. Mr. Norwich sent me an email telling me that they are going to go ahead with Alexis because of my carelessness."

"None of that was your fault, Heather."

"I know, but I want to leave."

I hurt for her in this decision she has to make, because there is no going back once she decides to leave. "I'll take you home; you just let me know when." I'm trying damn hard to hide how fucking ecstatic I am about this. I want her in my bed, in her bed.

"Now tell me, how are you feeling? And no, I don't want a one-word answer this time."

"I'm fine," she replies, and I raise my eyebrow. "What? That was two words. I'm serious, I'm okay, really."

I move my hand off of her little ass and bring it back with a vengeance. She yelps, and we get a few glances from the other patrons nearby. "Heather Lane . . . you'll tell me the second you aren't, correct?"

She's been texting all day, and I'm anxious to know who she's texting. "Do you mind putting down your phone for a few minutes and talking to me?"

"I'm sorry," she says as she puts her phone down again. "Yes, I'll talk to you."

I sigh and take her lips, kissing her intimately in front of all of these people.

"Now . . . I want *you* to tell me. How do you feel? I want the truth," she asks as she stares me down.

"Me? You don't give the truth, but you want it? We're playing that game, huh?"

I take a few seconds to breathe and rein in my emotions before continuing. "Okay. I'm pissed. I'm anxious, and I don't fucking understand why everything good in my life turns to shit and makes my life a living hell."

She scowls and gets off my lap, sitting down in her chair. "All right . . . but what do you mean I'm not giving you the truth?"

I move closer to her and pick her stubborn little ass off of the chair and move her back onto my lap. "I know you're hurting. We haven't discussed this, but we're going through it together, ballerina. I'm here."

Her body is tense and unmoving. She stares forward, and I regret my comment. I don't want her irritated with me. She's silent. *Fuck.* I exhale and rest my forehead on her shoulder. My voice low so only she can hear, I tell her the truth, "I'm devastated, Heather. I'm hurting, and I want you to open up to me."

She moves in my arms and curls up, nuzzling into my chest. "Me too. I'm sorry I couldn't keep your baby."

"You have nothing to apologize for. You were incredibly strong and you fought through the pain. I fucking love you—do you hear me?"

"Yes, I hear you."

HEATHER

I can't wait anymore for him to wake up. It's just after six in the morning, and I'm wide awake. I think I've finally snapped out of it. Last night after we got back from the coffee shop, Noah and I had a long, emotional conversation about our baby. The baby we lost. We came to the conclusion that we'll have each other, and we need to lean on each other as well. No more hiding things.

Of course I agreed, but I just can't tell him everything, at least not yet. I'm not sure how he'll handle it. I still haven't dealt with it myself. Keeping this a secret will come back to haunt me, I'm sure, but there is no way I'm telling him how I know his parents. Dani keeps pressuring me daily and has threatened to let him in on my secret herself. I keep telling her that I'll tell him, but I just need more time, time that I seem to be running short of. He's just as emotionally unstable as I am right now, and I'll know when the time is right.

I can't lie here any longer, so I get out of bed as quietly as I can and grab my crutches. I make my way into the bathroom to use it while he's asleep and try to shower. I'm almost in shock when I realize I'm no longer bleeding. I haven't had any pain in over a week and now this. I'm so excited I could scream. I'm so beyond overjoyed that Noah could walk in here right now and catch me peeing, and I wouldn't even care. Gah . . . If only I could dance right now, I'd be ecstatic. I feel like a heavy weight has been lifted off of me. I'll finally be able to please my man with more than my mouth. I shower as quickly as I can without falling and get dressed, sneaking my way past Noah and into the closet.

Last night Noah told me he was going home soon to start studying for the bar exam. I can't stand the thought of being without him now, so I told him I wanted to go home with him. I made that instantaneous decision without regret; I won't leave my Greek god ever again. I start taking all of my clothes off of the hangers and begin packing them into my suitcases. An hour later, my hair has air dried, falling in loose, messy waves down my back, and I've packed almost everything of ours.

Noah must have been exhausted, because I moved from the closet to the bedroom to pack, and he never woke up. There are clothes scattered all over the bed that I've yet to pack, but I need a break. My foot is in a lot of pain, and I think I've overdone it. I'm about to get back into bed when he stirs and reaches for me. He lifts his head when he can't find me.

"Baby? What's wrong? Why are you up?"

I can't help but smile. He's so perfect, and he's always concerned about me.

"I couldn't sleep. Go back to sleep, I'm fine," I lie through my teeth because my foot really hurts, but he doesn't need to know that.

He sits up and rubs his eyes before forcing them open. Blinking, he takes in the mess that is now our bedroom. He peers down at the folded clothes on the floor and the outfits I have strewn on the bed. "What are you doing? Can you not figure out what to wear?"

"I'm packing," I say as I sit on the bed.

"Packing?" He swings his legs off of the bed, and I watch his muscles shift with each progression of his limbs. He walks into the closet and turns to face me when he notices that nothing is in the closet anymore. "You packed my shit too?" he asks with a cocky smile playing on his lips. He's got a five o'clock shadow, and it looks unbelievably titillating.

"Yes," is all my worked-up body can squeak out.

I think he notices my eyes roaming his toned, gorgeous body because the air shifts between us. His body moves toward me, and I'm about to drool, but I'm out of breath and panting. What is he doing to me?

"Is this you telling me you want to go home sooner than later?"

He's so close—I can feel the heat radiating off of him. My body defies me by getting up and moving even closer. I blink up at him seductively. My body has a mind of its own as I trace the outline of his nipple before trailing my finger down the middle of his torso to the deep end of his carved-out V, right where his boxer briefs begin.

"I want you to take me . . ." I pause and watch his eyes darken. " . . . home."

"Take you?" He repeats as I slide my finger under the hem of his boxer briefs. I think he's lost his mind too. His cock is straining and stretching the material of his boxer briefs to its limit. I glance down to take in the monstrous view.

My pulse is already racing because I know he can touch me. He just doesn't know it yet. I sit down on the edge of the bed and pull his briefs down a little until I'm eye level with his monstrous erection. I slowly lick the head of his cock, and he groans loudly.

The aching in my sex is almost painful as I bare my teeth and slightly bite down just below the head of his cock.

"Holy shit!"

I insert the tip of my tongue into his slit and get a taste of his sea-salty pre-come. I whimper in delight as I take what I can of his heavy, palpitating cock between my lips. He reaches back against the dresser to steady himself as I start pumping him with my fist. My hands look minis-cule compared to his length. He's so thick and now wet from my mouth that I want him in more than one place.

"Do you like that, Noah?" I ask him as I lean back and pull my tank off and toss it. I look back up at him, and his chest is heaving with deep breaths.

"Shit, baby, you're a fucking expert at pleasing me. I . . ." He hiss-es through his teeth when I scrape my teeth up his shaft ever so gently. " . . . motherfucker!"

I love the feeling I get when I hear him lose his cool. I feel exception-ally powerful. He genuinely enjoys every touch, bite, and lick I give him. I cup his heavy balls and feel them tighten with the need for release.

"Fucking shit . . . I'm going to bust in that dirty mouth of yours."

His fingers move into my hair, and he grips momentarily, but lets go almost instantly as if he remembers himself. He brings his hand down underneath my chin, cupping my face gently, reverently.

"I want it," I breathe out, taking him in my mouth once again. "Come in my mouth, Noah," I say when I pull him from my mouth to take a much-needed breath.

His cock jerks violently when I wrap my lips around his shaft again. I keep a fast and steady rhythm with my mouth and hand as I pump him. That's when he erupts. His hot, silky come spurts into my mouth and coats my throat as he struggles to stand upright. His sultry storm is back with a vengeance as I taste his liquid candy.

I hum my appreciation and swallow everything I can, but there's still so much that spills from my lips. I look up at him through my lashes as I continue to swallow him. He's wearing a look of pure euphoria. He tangles his hand in my hair, removing his cock from my mouth. I feel his eyes move down my throat to my breasts, following a trail of his salty pleasure.

"Holy fuck . . . good morning to you too, you sexy piece of ass."

Before I'm able to say a word, he's got me on my back on top of the clothes scattered on the bed. I can't help but giggle and kiss his bare chest. "Good morning."

"How are you feeling? Are you okay this morning?"

Feeling? The only thing I can feel is the painful ache between my thighs and his hard, pulsing cock pushing against my skin. I pull him down to kiss me hard. My body is coiled and needy. I shake my head no when I release his lips. "Not good." I whisper out breathlessly. "I'm aching."

A wrinkle forms between his eyebrows when he frowns. "Your head?" He exhales in a frustrated rush. "I'm so sorry, Heather. I remembered as soon as I pulled. I . . ."

I shake my head to stop him. "No, I'm aching here . . ." I lower my hand down and touch myself when I see recognition flash into his eyes.

His eyes follow my hand, watching me slowly caress my oversensitive skin. "Will I hurt you?" His lips drift across my skin, biting me in every spot he wants and needs.

"No." I'm clawing at his skin anxiously. "Please, I'm not bleeding anymore, and I haven't been hurting." I'm arching my body into his, trying to entice him. God, if he turns me down, I'm going to cry. I want him that badly. His hot hands move down my body and rip my lacy thong off of me.

"Yes . . ." I wail in ecstasy as his finger runs down through my folds.

He's grinning when he pushes one finger inside; my tight walls lock around his finger as he moves it in and out swiftly. "It's been a while, ballerina; I think this is going to wear you out. Maybe I should just make you come on my fingers."

My eyes roll back, and all I can do is gasp. He's right. There's no way he's getting in. I'm too tight.

"We're not leaving this bedroom until I've satisfied your every need," he insists, and I whimper, reaching for his face and bringing those charming lips to mine.

"Mmm, I love you," I say quietly as I wrap my arms around his neck, holding him to me.

He licks my teeth and then my bottom lip as we kiss, replying under his breath, "I love you, Heather Lane."

He pushes his finger up to my sweet spot before adding a second. My body jolts, and I moan against his lips. He's pushing me to the brink—and fast; I'm so, so close. It feels like it's been forever since we've been intimate.

"Oh . . . yes, right there."

He's using his thumb to help me chase my orgasm as he coaxes my little bundle of nerves from beneath its hood.

"Let me feel that pussy come."

Right then he nips at my neck, and I crack under the pressure of his fingers.

"Ah . . . Noah!"

I convulse uncontrollably as thunderous quakes rack my body. I scream out as the paralyzing bliss overwhelms every cell inside of me. I can feel his low rumbling growl against my neck as he moves and bites another spot.

My fingers dig into his arm, and I start begging, "Please, please don't make me wait. I need you now. I don't care if it hurts."

"You're going to wait whether you like it or not. I will not damage or hurt you. No exception," he states as he kisses my breasts and down my stiff, needy body to the inside of my quivering thighs. I'm panting, and I can't wait. I want him so badly that I'm about to take it from him. I move my body down, and he stops moving. I reach for his shaft and try to maneuver myself to get what I want. I've never felt this way before. My hormones are raging.

He grabs my hips and halts my movements. "Heather, no." I can feel the tension in his grip as he moves me up the bed.

"No!" I argue back and try to squirm back down. I've never really been mad at him, but dammit, I'm so close.

His fingers lock around me and pin me to the bed. He's stern and serious when he says, "Listen to me."

I stop squirming and look up at him. "What?"

"You're not rushing this. You're going to let me do what I want to this gorgeous body of yours. You're going to let me make you come as many times as I see fit. I am going to make you mine, solely mine, and your libido is not going to get in the way of my taking my time with you."

Ugh! I cannot believe this.

"But . . ."

"But nothing. Now stop fighting me and let our bodies get reacquainted."

His lips are on me again as he pushes my legs apart. He bites and licks the inside of my thighs, teasing me. *How can I say anything to that?* I exhale in a rush when his tongue moves slowly against my skin.

"Baby, please? I can't wait."

"Be patient, little miss."

I can feel his warm breath hit my sex in a caress. His mouth is on me the second he stops speaking, and then I know. I know that he's struggling to keep his cool. I know he wants to slam his heavy veined cock into me with all of his might, but he won't, because he cares more about me and my well-being than he does his own.

His tongue is moving faster, and I need to watch him. I lift my head and watch this gorgeous man eat me out. It's the sexiest thing to see, and I can't believe I've never watched before. His eyes are closed, and he's ravenous. Suddenly his teeth nip at my folds, and I come undone.

My body shudders as he continues his determined assault on my sex. He pushes his middle and index finger into me while I'm lost in my orgasm to stretch me out. He's enjoying this too much.

His eyes meet mine when I can no longer move. "Fuck it," he yells out and pulls my body to the edge of the bed, before stroking his cock with one hand.

By the look in his eyes, his self-restraint is shredded; he's just as wanton as I am. I don't know how he's lasted this long. I'm feeling triumphant: my begging must have finally gotten to him. His expression is controlled when he leans down and braces himself over me. "You make me lose control, Heather. Now I'm taking control over your body."

Holy F!

I'd let him control any aspect of my life. I love his cockiness. His dominance. My lustful thoughts are interrupted by confusion as I watch him slide a latex barrier over the thick head of his cock, before he places himself at my entrance.

"Wait, what is that?" I ask and close my legs even though I know the answer.

"Exactly what it looks like. Now open your damn legs, so I can watch myself sink into that pussy. We're playing by my rules now."

My thighs have a mind of their own, and they open willingly, allowing him the space he needs to push the head of his cock between my folds and into my awaiting walls.

"Oh shit!" I blurt out before I can stop myself. My eyes lock with his as he stops moving. His palms are resting on my knees. He doesn't say anything for the longest moment, but then he continues to move achingly slow, stopping just inside my folds. He squeezes my knees and growls low and deep, my heat engulfing just the head of his cock.

"Fuck, you are beyond tight," his voice breaks the sound of our rapid breaths. "Do you want more?" His question drives me insane because he already knows I want so, so much more.

"Yes!" I pant and watch his expression as he slides farther into my channel.

He feels unimaginable, and the feeling that ruptures through my body is one of a kind. I arch my back as pleasure takes over. I'm so high off of him and he's once again so contained, so reserved. I hate that he won't let himself enjoy this. He's so tense in his effort not to hurt me.

I need a way to calm him so I reach up and press my palm to his abs, halting him. His face is pained when he looks at me.

"Kiss me," I say in the softest voice I can manage.

I can feel the restraint he's using in his core when I sit up and kiss him slowly. I want him to revel in this. He needs to know he's not hurting or damaging me.

I slip my arms around his neck and run my fingers up into his hair while I kiss him slowly, passionately. Whispering against his lips, "I'm okay, baby . . . I'm reeling. I'm not in any pain. Please, please make love to me."

His grunt reverberates through me as his hands stop holding me down and start roaming my body. My eyes flutter closed at his soft, warm touches. He pulls my back up and off of the bed so that I'm sitting up at an angle on the edge of the bed. Both of his large tanned hands move down my spine to my butt, as he pushes the rest of his length into me.

I whimper into his mouth and suck on his lower lip. "Yes . . . just like that, baby."

We both relax, allowing him to slide in easily. I'm holding onto his muscled shoulders, as we rock on the edge of the bed: my butt is half on and half off of the mattress. His sizable cock is pressing up into me, grazing my spot repeatedly.

"Ballerina, you are so damn gorgeous," he trails off as his cock convulses inside of me.

I'm kissing every part of him that I can reach: his lips, jaw, and down his neck.

"You're going to make me come," he whispers in a strained voice.

My hands move from his broad shoulders, down his spine, where I drag my nails across his taut skin.

I think he likes it, so I apply more pressure. I know I'm leaving my marks on him, but I love it. His heavy balls are slapping against the curve of my butt as he pounds into me swiftly.

I whimper out in delirium as it all overtakes me when he digs his fingers into my butt cheeks. "Baby!"

His growl is so sexy when he hears my cries. He thrusts up into me over and over again. Noah's so long and insanely thick that I can barely keep my thoughts straight. My heart is pounding out of my chest. He slows his movements and pulls back to look at me, running his hand up my neck and slipping his thumb into my mouth. At that same moment, he circles his hips and pushes into me with more force.

I come with a body-shaking, heart-racing, toe-curling orgasm that takes control of me.

His groan reverberates through my body, and he buries himself deep inside of me.

Every single movement between us stops as his sexy, raspy grunt fills the room, and I feel how hot he is for me. He's spewing every last drop deep into the damned barrier between us as I contract around his shaft.

I collapse onto the bed, completely exhausted. I know I didn't do much work, but my body hasn't been through that type of exertion in quite some time. His breathing is hot and heavy as he leans his forehead between my breasts. We're both damp with perspiration from our lovemaking.

I'm so in love with this man. I cannot believe I got so lucky. I move my fingers into his damp hair and gently massage his scalp. He groans and kisses between my breasts, and it makes me smile. He's so affectionate, so unlike the others I've been with.

He hums his appreciation before pulling his length out of me and removing the now slick condom off of himself. He moves us both farther up the bed, tossing a hanger from the bed onto the floor so we can get comfortable. He rests his head between my breasts again and murmurs, "I love you, little ballerina."

Chapter Ten

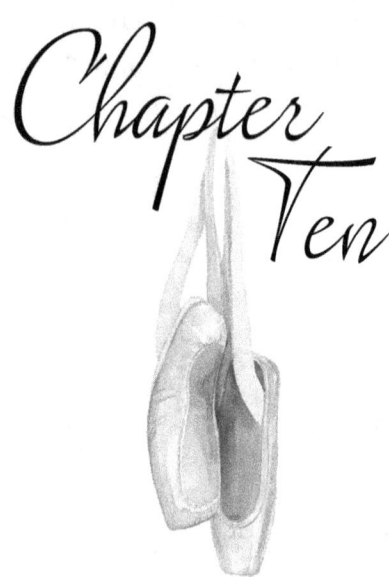

DEFENSIVE RESPECT

NOAH

My ballerina is fast asleep as I purchase our plane tickets to get us back to New York City. I figured she'd want more time in London to spend with Dillen, so we leave in a month from today. Coen left this morning, and I can hear Dillen sputtering about it in her room. I understand how much distance can hurt a person. Whenever I'm too far from my girl, I feel homesick. I can't imagine going through that again, and I'm fucking delighted that she asked to come back home with me.

It's late and I should get to bed soon, but I have one more thing I need to do before I can shut down my laptop. I have to email my parents. Joel got in contact with them this past week, and he's explained my situation to them. He hasn't given them any of my information, and I'm grateful for that. I don't think I could cope with an onslaught of questions or an outpouring of love I think I'll get from them. I'm not even certain if that's what I'd get. I have their information, and this entire situation is lying in the palm of my hands.

Perhaps they have an entire family without me; I wouldn't be surprised. It's been thirty years since they saw me last. They have missed every second of my life. Every accomplishment, every fucked-up thing I've done, and every lie I've told. But they won't miss the first girl I bring home. I can't imagine how they must be struggling with this information. Hell, they probably assumed I was dead.

I decided to look up the articles that were supposed to be in Mae's white binder, the binder that tore me apart limb by limb in the cruelest and most merciless way. I find an article that is dated April 5th, 1985, two days after my birth.

Investigation to Find Missing Newborn Continues

NEW YORK—An investigation to find the kidnapped two-day old infant, Jorden Somer, is well underway. The infant was stolen mere hours after his birth. Search crews have swept the hospital, as well as hospital grounds with no success.

Yesterday's search didn't turn up anything substantive, but investigators say they will continue to follow up on leads today.

"We're not leaving a single stone unturned when it comes to this newborn baby boy," said Officer Nathan Hunt, of the NYPD. "Yesterday we were checking trashcans in the immediate neighborhood, searching any area where this infant might possibly be located. Today we are focusing on a centralized area, then working outward. This target area has been a prime spot for a certain serial kidnapper to discard any child he or she does not approve of. However, there are no signs of Jorden Somer yet."

Police have searched every street, alley, dumpster, and crevice and are once again questioning witnesses about Jorden Somer's disappearance. His parents, Henry and Ellery Somer, have decided to remain silent in this difficult and unfortunate time in their lives. Both parents were questioned soon after they reported their baby missing.

If you have any information, you're asked to contact your local police department.

I manage to breathe and exit out of the scanned-in article. I will myself to open up my email and type out a brief message to the two of them before I get some shut-eye.

To: Henry Somer, Ellery Somer
From: Noah Ryan
Subject: Jorden Somer

Henry and Ellery,
   It has taken me weeks to compose this email, and I'm still unsure of what to say. I'd like to meet both of you soon, though. I'm sure Joel Aldrich has caught you both up on my situation, and I'm also sure you have just as many questions as I do. I believe it will be easier to speak about this in person. I'll be back in New York in a month if you'd like to arrange a date to meet. I'd be happy to rearrange my schedule for you.

Your son,
Noah Ryan/Jorden Somer

I reluctantly hit send before closing my laptop, and I get into bed, moving Heather on top of my chest. She's been sleeping soundly lately. I think the grieving process of our unborn child has developed into a journey that we both need to take. Everything about that situation was over my head. I still have no idea how to handle any of it, but I'm not giving up on my girl. Not now, not ever.

I don't know where Heather is. I can hear her music playing in the background somewhere. I look around at an unfamiliar place, and I'm confused. *Where in the hell am I?* I turn and look behind me, through a set of glass doors that peer out onto a beach. I'm in someone's living room. The items in the room look familiar; they look like my things . . . and hers. I like this place, and it feels like home. It feels right. I call out for her, "Heather?"
   I don't hear anything except her music playing. Suddenly, something tugs at my jeans. I look down when I feel something sit on my bare foot; smiling up at me is a little girl—a beautiful, little brunette girl, sitting on my foot with her little legs and arms wrapped tightly around my leg. She tugs at my pant leg again. "Dance with me, Daddy."
   My heart slams against my chest, and I'm jolted awake, sitting

straight up out of bed, gasping for air. I look down beside me and see my girl sleeping peacefully on my pillow.

I rub a hand over my eyes and down my face. Holy fuck, what the hell was that all about? My eyes are mostly adjusted to the dark, and I look back down at Heather. She's sound asleep. Quietly, I get out of bed and walk into the bathroom, closing the door almost fully before turning on the lights. My eyes protest when the bright lights bathe the room.

Damn, that dream.

Why?

I brace my arms on the counter while I look at my tired reflection. It's the studying. Yeah, that's it. I need to cut back on the studying. My brain needs a fucking break. I sigh and turn on the faucet, leaning down and splashing cold water on my face, before looking back up at myself. Fuck Ryan, get your shit together. It was just a dream.

"Baby?" Heather calls out before pushing the bathroom door open. She's still half asleep, with her hair half in and half out of her ponytail.

"Hey beautiful, let's go back to bed."

"Are you okay?" she asks, before inspecting me. Fuck, she's the cutest sleepy little mess.

"I'm good."

I walk over to her and sweep her off of her feet, carrying her back to bed, being sure to turn off the lights before I lay her down.

She curls up on top of my chest, and I wrap my arms around her little frame, keeping her secure on top of me.

"I love you, Noah."

I kiss the top of her head and grin. "I love you too."

When I open my eyes again, the sunlight is pouring into the room, and Heather is sitting at the end of the bed with her legs crossed. Surrounding her are golden foil packets, and I smell the unmistakable scent of latex. I sit up, confused, and try to focus. When I see what she's done, my eyes go wide.

"Heather, what in the fuck are you doing?" I scold her.

She looks at me and replies with a flippant shrug. "Taking care of business."

I frown when she takes the scissors to another condom, cutting it in half while making a show of it. She looks downright unrepentant.

"Why?" I almost shout in disbelief.

She glares at me. "Because I hate that you wore these with me. I don't want it happening again, so I'm doing what I had to do."

This stubborn woman. Fuck.

"You won't let me win this one, will you?"

She stares at me as if the question I just asked is redundant, so I try to change the topic instead, to avoid an argument. "I bought our plane tickets last night. We leave in just under a month."

Her eyes are unhappy, and I can't stand it. "Oh . . . okay."

"Is that okay?"

She tosses all of the cut-up bits of condoms into the trash, before sitting down on one of the bags she's stuffed full. I'm not going to lie: she looks cute as fuck with the little boot on her foot.

"Sure. I assumed we would be leaving sooner rather than later."

"We can. I don't have a problem changing the tickets, but I thought that Dillen might need you here, seeing as Coen left yesterday."

"But . . . I . . ."

"You what?" I move to the end of the bed and take her hand as she sits there pouting.

"I want to go home. I want to be as far away from this ballet company and Alexis as possible."

I frown because I want the same thing. I think it's fucked up that the company hasn't done shit to penalize Alexis Keeley. Dillen said they actually went on with the show the night my ballerina fell. Apparently Alexis took Heather's spot and stole the show. I can't fucking bear the sadness in Heather's eyes. I know she's upset about their lack of actions too.

"Come here." I offer her my hand, and she takes it, moving onto my lap and curling up. "We can leave at the end of the week. Would that be better?"

She nods and lays her head in the crook of my neck. "I should have never come here," she says quietly.

"Don't say that. You were chasing your life's dream. I'll have you home soon, baby, I swear." I move my hands underneath the thin material of her shirt to glide my fingertips over her skin when my phone beeps loudly.

Her body relaxes under my touch, and she makes the sexiest sound, but my eyes move to my phone. I see the name Henry Somer on my screen before it turns black again. *Fuck.* She moves her hands over my chest and down my abs. For the first time ever, my mind is preoccupied when her hands are on me.

"Ballerina? I need to check something really fast." I'm anxious, and I can feel my heart racing in my fingers.

She stops touching me instantly and drops her hands. "Oh, okay, I'm sorry." Before I can do anything, she's off my lap and hobbling to the door. "I'll be back; I just need my medicine." Her voice sounds dejected and it kills me.

"Heather . . ." *Fuck. What do I say to her?*

She turns around to look at me.

"I emailed them last night, and he just responded."

Her lips part in a gasp. "Why didn't you wake me last night?"

"You were sleeping so soundly. I didn't have the heart to wake you. Come here, I want you to read it first."

I don't know what's wrong with her, but she looks like a deer in headlights. "I . . . n-no, you need to read it first," she stutters.

"Okay. Will you at least come here?" I grab my phone off of the nightstand and look at her dazed expression. She moves slower than normal as she walks over to me; her foot must be hurting. She joins me on the bed, sitting close beside me, so I place my lips on her softly before I swipe my finger across my phone's screen and click on the email notification.

To: Noah Ryan
From: Henry Somer
IN RE: Jorden Somer

Noah,

It's an honor to finally talk to you. Ellery is too shaken up by your email to respond, but we both like the idea of sitting down together and having a chat. We could meet you in the city, or you're more than welcome to come to our home in Southampton. The choice is yours.

Your parents,
Henry and Ellery Somer

I look up and hand her my phone, imploring her to read the email from Henry. I don't think I could call him Dad, or Father. Henry will have to do.

"Go ahead and read it."

She takes the phone from me and I watch as her jade green eyes move back and forth over the screen until she's done reading it.

"Noah, they are so excited to meet you. Are you going to go to them when we get home?"

"I'd like to, but only if you come with me. You're going to be the first and only girl I bring home."

She's chewing on her lip nervously. "Noah . . . there's something I need to . . ."

There's a knock on the bedroom door, and she stops talking. The door starts to swing open, and I hurriedly throw the comforter over my waist. Seconds later Dillen walks in with a tear-stained face.

"Little shit?" She sniffles and walks over and lies on our bed, curling up into a ball and starts to cry.

Ah fuck. Tears. I gotta bail.

"Dillen," Heather croons as I wrap the blanket around my waist and grab some sweats out of a bag Heather packed.

"I'll let you two have some time alone," I say before kissing the back of Heather's head and walking out of the bedroom to the kitchen to get my ballerina's medication ready.

HEATHER

Dillen is a complete mess. I would say her emotions have been wrung dry, but her tears are still falling. I've never seen her so emotional before, especially over a man. I'm trying to console her, but it doesn't seem to be working in the slightest. "Dill, you're going to see him again. No man flies across an ocean just to screw my best friend. Did you tell him you would visit?" I ask and stroke her hair softly.

"Yes, but I don't know if I can. Flying back and forth takes up so much time, and I don't think I can take that much time off from the studio." She sniffles then loudly bursts into tears again without warning.

I sigh and move her head onto my lap. I know exactly how she's feeling because I was devastated when I left Noah.

"I-I don't even know if he wants to see me again," she all but squawks out at me.

"Oh Dill, of course he does. It's obvious that you two cannot get enough of each other."

She snaps her head around so that she's staring up at me. "Do you think he left to get away from me?"

"No, sweetie. He has to go back to work, or else I'm sure he'd love to stay."

She dashes her tears away and hugs me. "I'm sorry. I'm such an idiotic fool. I shouldn't be so stinking upset over a man like this."

I laugh and pat her back sympathetically. "Oh hush. You listened to me cry for weeks when I moved here, and now it's my turn. Plus, you're my best friend, Dill." I pull back and hold her at arm's length. "Now let's pig out on ice cream and candy to get your mind off of things."

She nods approvingly and throws her arms around my neck, squeezing the life out of me. "Can you get Noah to make his grilled cheese sandwiches for us? They're my favorite."

I smile and hug her back before I pull her off of my bed. "Let's go give him the puppy-dog eyes." She wipes her raccoon eyes, and we walk out of the bedroom, crooning his name at the same time, "Noahhh?"

He lifts his eyes off of his textbooks and gives me the most dazzling, panty-wetting smirk. Oh dang . . . he's wearing his glasses again. I could jump him right this freaking second.

"What can I do for you, ladies?" he asks in that cool, smoky voice.

We're both stunned into silence. I can't even make a sound, and it seems like Dill can't either. Holy crap, I'm going to combust from within.

"Well?"

He's waiting patiently for an answer while we stare at his perfectly sculpted body. I think Dill has completely forgotten about her cheesy carb request.

"I . . . we . . ."

I've forgotten everything. He's staring at us with his eyebrow raised now, imploring me to say something with his silent gesture.

"We wanted something, but I forgot what it was." I glance at Dill in a daze. "What did we want, Dill?"

Her facial expression reminds me of the many times she's just been caught walking into the dance studio late, trying to get around the extra workout session that comes along with it.

"Uhh . . ."

I shove her with my hip trying to get her to say something, anything.

She must be so embarrassed because her cheeks have taken on a radiant crimson color—Dillen never blushes. She sighs dreamily and swats my arm good-humoredly. "You lucky little shit. Noah, can you make us grilled-cheese sandwiches, please?"

I laugh and rub my arm to soothe the sting out of it. "Hey . . ." We both pout at him, and I swiftly forget the red handprint that has made a quick appearance on my bicep. "Please?"

He chuckles and puts his book down, then reaches up to take off his reading glasses. My eyes roam down his bare torso and to the flaccid yet obvious gift in his sweat pants, "Baby? Will you leave your glasses on today? Please?"

"Leave them on? Why?" he asks suspiciously as he gets up and brings over a glass of water and my medication.

I reach out and take my pills from him while I rack my brain for a true and simple explanation. "Because you look like a sexy professor in them . . ." I watch him closely as I take the glass and sip the water before swallowing my medicine. " . . . and I'm a naughty girl who needs detention."

Dillen busts out laughing beside me and walks into the kitchen muttering, "I'd gladly take a detention."

"Well, shit, I'll need to put you on academic probation if that's the case." He grabs me and smacks my butt hard in front of Dillen, leaving a stinging sensation in its wake.

I squeak loudly and grin as his behavior sends a welcome thrill through me. "Are there spankings involved with academic probation?"

"I wouldn't think so, but I can make an exception." He swoops me up and carries me to the kitchen counter to where Dill is about to ice down her libido. She's gotten everything out for Noah to make his delicious sandwiches.

I sit on the counter and watch him move adeptly around the kitchen.

"Thank you, baby," I say sweetly.

"Yes, thank you, baby," Dillen mocks in a voice that is too high-pitched to resemble mine.

Noah chuckles as he starts assembling the sandwiches, and Dill joins me on the counter. We're now both watching Noah's muscles move underneath his taut golden skin as he does the simplest of tasks.

"You two are a couple of hornballs."

"So?" Dillen protests, shifting uncomfortably on the counter and nudging me with her elbow as she tries to fight her libido.

I laugh and almost melt when Noah tilts his head up at me, and winks—what a panty dropper. A few minutes later he's perfected our sandwiches and slides each one onto a white ceramic plate before handing one to each of us. He slowly tilts my chin upward to meet his lips; my body sags as the sexual tension between us takes over, and I almost drop my plate. He bares his teeth and tugs on my bottom lip before breaking our kiss and walking back to the living room, leaving me winded.

"Enjoy, ladies."

"Thank you, Noah," she says as we both stare after him and his mighty fine, taut rear end.

Dill and I are still eating on the counter when she looks at me. "Okay, for real . . . we've been friends for, like, ever, but I would absolutely have a three-way with you if it meant I got to taste-test that." She points her thumb toward Noah, and I almost choke on my food with laughter.

"Dillen!" I shriek.

"What?" She giggles deviously and jumps off the counter. "I may not be into girls, but at the very least, I'd make an attempt. Now, I need a girl's night in, please?"

"Deal. Movies, candy, drinks, and more drinks. Maybe we can get Noah to play a game with us?"

"What kind of game, little shit?" She eyes my man and bites her lower lip.

I snap my fingers to get her attention. I don't know why, but jealousy courses its way through my veins as I think of her picturing my man naked and positioned over her.

"Hey lady, he's mine. Not the kind of game you're thinking of."

"Okay, fine . . . for now, but I want alcohol to start this evening off right."

"Well, duh. Now go shower, and I'll do the same, and then we'll make Noah make us some drinks tonight."

"Ugh! As much as I adore Coen, I'm still envious of that Greek god."

"He is pretty amazing, huh? Okay go." I push Dill toward her bedroom. "I need to go kiss my man."

Noah gets up and walks up to me when Dill stumbles into her room—drunk on the sight of my man. Noah pushes my legs apart with his hips and wraps his arms around my waist. "Then kiss me, ballerina."

I look up into his eyes. "How did you . . . ?"

"I pay attention to what my girl needs," he says softly, before pressing his lips to mine passionately.

I sigh against his lips and wrap my arms around his neck. He's always so warm, and he knows exactly what I need. *Him.*

"I'm going to study tonight; you two have a good time, okay?"

He helps me down off of the counter, and I pout. "You're not going to hang out with us?"

"In a week's time you'll be all mine, and I won't have to share you with anyone. Go have some fun with Dillen."

I scowl and cross my arms, officially throwing a fit. "I don't want to wait."

"Wait for what?"

"I don't want to wait a whole week. Please come have a good time with us?"

"How about we have our own fun afterward? I'll get you naked and bite you all over your gorgeous body."

I run my hands down his chest, over the grooves of his abdomen. He closes his eyes briefly, and I think I've got him right where I want him.

"Ballerina?" His hands move down to my butt, squeezing.

I grin devilishly but hide it before looking up at him, playing coy. "Yes?"

"I'll be in our room when you need me. Enjoy yourself."

My mouth drops open, and I stare at him in disbelief. Before I know it, he's already grabbed his books and shut our bedroom door, completely dismissing me.

I'm standing there staring at the door when Dillen's voice startles me.

"Hey little shit? Did you shower yet?" I turn around and see her already showered and in her lounge clothes, combing her wet hair.

"Oh . . . uh, crap. No, I got sidetracked, sorry. I'll be right back."

"Why does that not surprise me? I'll start making margaritas. Would you like traditional or strawberry?"

"Strawberry, please," I call out before opening my bedroom door and stepping inside. I look over and see Noah is at the desk. He is focused solely on his thick textbook. I walk by him, and he doesn't even notice me. Glancing back over my shoulder, I sigh. He's been so wrapped up in studying that he barely notices anything anymore.

"Heather?"

I'm startled, and I reach for the bathroom light as I open the door. "Sorry, I didn't mean to bother you. I was just about to shower."

The next thing I know he has me up against the cool glass of the shower door, and his lips are moving down my neck to my collarbone. I can only gasp as I weaken under his touch.

"You never bother me. You are my girl and the most important person to me. Do you understand?"

"Yes," I breathe out.

He reaches past me and turns the shower on. "Let's get this boot off of you, and then I'm going to wash this gorgeous body of yours."

"Baby, go study. Dillen is making us drinks and is waiting for me."

"Fine. On the condition that you'll enjoy yourself tonight and come tuck your sexy little ass in bed with me after you've had too many margaritas."

I manage a small smile and kiss him briefly. "I promise."

"You're such a distraction," he says in a deep, raspy voice. He pulls back and smacks my butt before going back into the room to bury himself in books and laws.

I quickly get undressed and step into the warm steam shower, where my mind wanders as I wash myself. I feel so bad for Noah. He works so hard but never lets himself have a good time.

I think it might be a way for him to escape his own thoughts. I know he still has problems with everything that has happened, and I am able to tell on which days it gets to him most. I can tell when he's lost all of his self-will; I can even tell when he's thinking about Mae, and on those days he's somber and reserved.

I quickly finish up my shower and get dressed. Then I sit down to put my boot back on, brush out my hair, and spray a spritz of Noah's cologne on his sweatshirt that I pull over my head. I love how he smells: it comforts me in ways I've never been comforted before, outside of his actual embrace.

As I walk to the door, he turns around and smiles before I leave the room. "You look beautiful, Heather."

I feel my cheeks heat at his comment. He devours my body with his eyes as I leave the room. "Thank you, professor."

I blow him a kiss before walking out to Dillen who is sitting on the couch, holding up a margarita and candy. "Let's go, little shit. I need my best friend's help getting ruthlessly drunk."

"If I could run, I would so jump on you right now."

She sticks out her tongue at me. "Try your best, butthead."

I laugh and shake my head as I walk over with my noticeably bulky, highly un-sexy boot.

"You know, they could make these things look better if they wanted to," I gripe as I sit down at the other end of the couch and reach for my glass. I hum my appreciation when my lips taste the sugar on the rim of the glass. "Mmm, I love these."

She scoots over and lays her head on my shoulder. "We are getting drunk, Heather, whether you're on your damn medication or not."

She seems so sad, so unlike herself. "Deal." I nudge her with my shoulder. "We better get the bottle of tequila then because these just aren't going to be enough." I take another sip of my margarita and almost spill it when she sits up quickly.

"I'll get it," she shrieks happily and just like that, her good mood is back. She skips to the kitchen on her toes and pulls the freezer door open overdramatically. "Do we have limes or are we sending Noah out to get some?" She grabs two shot glasses before pulling the tequila out of the freezer.

I set my drink down and turn to rest my chin on the back of the couch. "No, we should have some. Plus, we can't bother the professor; he's in hardcore study mode." I pout cutely as I watch Dill cut the limes.

"We could always trade," she offers up nonchalantly.

"Trade? Trade what?" I turn back and reach for my drink. I bring it to my lips when I see her devilish grin.

She walks over and places our shots on the coffee table. "We could trade dicks."

I choke on my drink, and strawberry margarita spills from my lips and down my chin. I'm sputtering, and I can't believe what I'm hearing. I feel her pat me on the back and laugh.

"WH-WHAT?" I cough out my words.

She's in a riff of laughter, trying to not spill her shot of tequila that is filled to the brim. "Oh little shit, won't you please let me go for a ride? Just once? How big *is* he? Does he know how to use it?"

I can't even stop my gasp before it leaves my lips. "Go for a ride?" I shriek. I'm not mad—just completely shocked. "Are you completely insane? Hell no, you can't ride him!" I bust out laughing and shove her.

She spills her overfilled shot onto her tank and I reach for mine. Our laughter fills the room, and we sober long enough to hold our shot glasses to each other's.

"To girl's night," she shouts, and we down our shots after clinking the small glasses together.

I grimace because I hate the smell of tequila, but I shoot it regardless. The burn seems to fill my lungs and I exhale deeply. "Whew, dammit, that burns." I reach over and grab her knee, locking eyes with her. "Oh, and Dill . . ." I pause to look over my shoulder at the closed bedroom door, and then back at her. "He's enormous."

She's sucking on her lime when she freezes and takes it from her mouth. "Oh professor . . ." she calls out sensually and arches her back against the couch. Her head falls back as an erotic sound comes from her lips.

I can't stop laughing as I fill our shot glasses again. Unable to resist teasing her more, I keep talking. "And oh my God, Dill, he so knows how to use it."

"Oh yes!" she screams, and Noah cracks open the bedroom door.

"Is everything okay out here?"

My eyes go wide, and my back stiffens. "Oops," I giggle and turn my head to look at him.

"Sorry, professor, we'll keep it down." I try and cover Dill's laughter with the blue beaded throw pillow, and she fights me with more laughs.

His cool, smoky laugh fills the room before he shuts the door, and I'm unsure if it's the alcohol or my libido, but his voice just soaked my panties.

I sag against the armrest of the couch and sigh dramatically.

"Holy fucking shit, Heather. I'm going to jump your boyfriend," she proclaims, before forcing me to take another shot.

"I think I'll jump him instead, and I'll make sure he keeps those glasses on tonight." I down the shot and scrunch my face as it burns all the way down the back of my throat.

She pouts and buries her face in a pillow. "Ahhh, I'm so jealous."

I laugh and am about to play with her hair when her head shoots up, and her hair is wild around her face.

"I'm serious, you have to tell me. I want every detail. Let's swap stories." She reaches for her margarita, and I take mine. "So . . . tell me, does he talk in bed?"

I lick my teeth and decide to give her a little insight into my sex life. "He does when he takes me. It's more hair pulling, biting, and oh . . ." I hesitate before I give away the sexiest thing he does. " . . . when we are done and I can't muster one more solitary orgasm, he takes my finger and . . ." I stop speaking while my mind goes to his thick girth moving our orgasms in and out of us.

"And?" she prods with her drink almost to her lips. Her eyes are wide in her eagerness to know more about my sex life.

"He runs my finger through our . . . uhm . . . our orgasms and makes me taste us together." I sigh and bite the inside of my cheek. Feeling the warmth flood my cheeks, I risk a glance at her.

She's staring at me with her mouth completely agape. "I'm sorry, do you mind repeating that so I can enjoy it again?"

I take another much-needed shot, and I can feel my head swim. "I know, right?" A goofy grin forms on my face, and I lean back against the armrest.

"I officially hate you. Coen didn't do anything like that. He's a big fan of anal, though."

I sit up and gasp, grabbing her arm, causing her to spill her drink on her leg. "Oh my God, Dill. Does it hurt?" I can feel the alcohol running through my veins, and I can tell my filter has gone out of the window.

She licks her hand and giggles. "Does anal hurt? Uhm, holy shit, yes. But it gets better—so much better—and Coen sure as hell knew how to do it too."

I cover my eyes just thinking about it and start laughing. "Why am I not surprised?" I reach for a lime and bite into it. The muscles in my cheeks protest, clenching when the sourness invades my taste buds. Quickly, I take a shot. Absentmindedly thinking . . .

Did I do that backwards?

I don't really mind the burn anymore; maybe I've killed all feeling in my esophagus? I look up at her and point. "And I don't believe you about it feeling good. There's no way we are even going there. Besides, I don't think he's into that.

She gets up and turns on the music on her smart TV. "It feels incredible, and you are completely missing out. And I guarantee you that he's into it."

My face is burning . . . from what? The alcohol or this conversation? I try to stand but my boot feels like it weighs a thousand pounds. "Take this off of me." I pout and look at my foot.

She jerks her head to the side to drunkenly inspect my boot. "Why isn't it pink?" she asks, then twirls around the living room before she crashes into the couch and falls backward onto it, snickering like a schoolgirl. I reach my arm out to her to make sure she's okay when my bedroom door swings open again.

We're both laughing now and I completely forget about my boot and any pain I should be feeling. I don't know why, but I find it hilarious that she fell and I hold my stomach with all the laughter. "Oh my God, don't! I'm going to pee."

She turns onto her stomach and crawls over to me then reaches for the tequila bottle. "Take a shot from the bottle," she insists, but before I can respond a warm, inviting shiver runs through my body and I look up into his eyes. My occasional professor and always Greek god is standing in the doorway in his boxer briefs. His hair is disheveled, and I realize that he must have been asleep.

I have the bottle in my hand, and I just stare. My lips are numb and I can barely feel them when I put my lips together to shush her. I press my finger to her lips in a drunken mistake. "Shh . . . we woke the professor." I giggle and throw my head back when she peers up at him through her long eyelashes.

"Whoa momma," she murmurs all too loudly.

He runs his hand down his face and walks into the living room. When Dill sits up she's practically panting. Noah sits down on the single seat as if he's fully dressed, and Dill and I are now two horny, incredibly drunk women.

I'm actually so drunk that I don't even care that he's almost naked in front of her. "Did we wake you?" I take a drink from the bottle before Dillen practically rips it out of my hand and drinks from it, her eyes devouring him the entire time.

He rubs his eyes again, and I'm incredibly drawn to him. I get up and hobble over. His warm arms are around me in a second, and he pulls me onto his lap. Noah is always warm, but now his skin feels like he's on fire. Even with the tequila messing with my head, I know that this is the place that I will always want to be.

I hear Dillen giggle behind me, and I look over. I try not to laugh but things are just so funny to me right now.

"Hi, Noah . . ." she basically moans his name and eyes his gorgeously sculpted chest.

He smiles his panty-dropping smile and replies, "Hi, Dillen. It seems like you two have gotten into the hard stuff, huh?"

I laugh and bite his chest playfully.

She huffs and pouts at the two of us. "I think you two should have anal."

I gasp so loud and lean over to try and cover her mouth. "Dillen . . ." I shriek as she howls in a fit of laughter.

Noah's hand moves down to my ass and he squeezes with too much confidence. "Would I fit?" he whispers in my ear.

I feel my face get red-hot again, and I forget we're not alone. "No. No way. I already told Dill you were ginormous."

I look over and see Dillen nod adamantly and fan her face. "It's true. She did."

He presses his lips to my neck and I can feel him smile sleepily against my skin. "Exactly how much have you had to drink, Miss Lane?"

I look down at my hand and count on my fingers before looking at the bottle. "Uhhh, one time?"

Dillen busts out laughing and gets up to get more alcohol.

"One time, huh?"

His chest reverberates with his deep, smoky laughter before he kisses the back of my head. I nod and lean into him, smelling his cologne that I love so much. My inhibitions squashed by tequila, I whisper in his ear while Dill is in the kitchen, "Do you want that?"

I can feel his eyes roaming my body and then his cock jerking against my butt. "I'd like to try it at some point."

My body thrums with excitement and I bite at his earlobe. "Do you think I would like it?"

"Possibly. Coen said Dillen loved it when he fucked her ass."

I gasp and pull back to look at him. I grab his face with both of my hands and stare at him. "HE TOLD YOU THAT?"

He moves my body so I straddle him and holds onto my butt, "Yeah, he did, and he asked if you enjoyed it too, but I didn't give him an answer."

I look down at him in my drunken state and a small giggle escapes me. "Does he know that your . . ." I cup my mouth and whisper the word cock, " . . . is huge?"

He tilts my chin up and kisses my numb, drunken lips, instead of answering my question. "Let's get you some water, ballerina."

I pout against his lips. *Why won't he answer me?* "I don't want any."

His lips move to my ear, and he chuckles. "You're so fucking stubborn, Heather."

I smile and bury my face in his neck and bite. Probably harder than I meant to, but I can't feel my teeth now either. He sucks in a sharp breath of air and pinches my rear end. "Where the fuck did Dillen go?"

I look up and over at the couch and then into the kitchen. "Dill . . ." I scream out and wiggle off of Noah's lap.

He straightens up his boxer briefs before he stands, and I get a "Shh . . ." from Dillen.

I start to laugh when I hear her and I stumble over to the sound of her voice. "Come out, come out, wherever you are."

I step into the kitchen and look down at my boot, but instead my eyes focus on Dillen lying on the tiled floor in just her bra and panties.

I gasp at the sight and cover my mouth before the giggles hit me. "Dillen Alice Ascher, where are your clothes?" I kneel down and karate-chop her flat stomach before leaning against the cabinet.

She makes an "oof" noise and sticks her tongue out at me. "I'm so hot, even my boobs are sweating."

My smile feels unlike my own, but it's plastered on my face. "At least you have boobs." I nudge her leg with my boot when I remember it's still on me. "Get up, and take this off of me. And I'm still thirsty."

Noah walks into the kitchen, and he laughs at the sight of us on the floor, "Hell, put your damn clothes back on."

"You're one to talk," she shoots back at him quickly.

I look up and realize that she's right. "Hey! Yeah, put your clothes on, professor." I smack the cold, hard tile with my hand and laugh at my own lame joke. "And will someone get this boot off of me? Frick."

"That boot is staying on, ballerina. All right, girls, I'm heading back to bed. Yell really loud if you need anything, and for the love of God, don't play with the knives." He winks and moves the knife that Dill was using earlier into the sink before walking back into our bedroom.

I almost melt when he winks at me, and I swear he flexed his butt muscles when he walked away. I look over at Dill, and she's watching me with dreamy eyes. "What?" I smile and lean my head back against the wood.

"If you two ever break up, I get first crack."

My mouth drops open and I reach over and grab the oven mitt that hangs nearby. Throwing it at her, I yell, "Hey butthead, if we break up, you better be on my side. Now take this boot off of me."

She pulls herself across the floor to me. "Fine, but you can't tell anyone that I helped."

I cross my heart and hold my fingers up. "I swear."

I barely watch her do it because I don't even want to see what it looks like off. I hear and feel Velcro being pulled and then instant relief. I sigh because it feels so good as the rush of cool air washes over my foot. "Is it gross?" I ask through my drunken, numb lips.

"You have a sock on, little shit. I can't tell, and no, I am not removing that."

"DO IT!" I yell.

"No, no way in hell am I removing that stinky sock."

"It doesn't stink, you jerk."

She pulls on the thin material covering my big toe and pulls just a little more before stopping. "Oh my . . . nope. That's gross. I can't do it."

I growl in frustration and reach up into the junk drawer. "Fine. I'll do it." My hand finds the pair of scissors, and I bring them out of the drawer and show her.

Her eyes go wide, and she stares at me. "No!"

"Yes, this is happening."

I reach down and slide the blade underneath the edge of my sock, and I snip it. Dillen gasps loudly and covers her mouth dramatically, "Oh shit, don't do it. You are going be in so much trouble, Heather. I'm not going down with you for this."

I laugh and continue to cut along the top of my foot. My eyes go wide when I see the discoloration in my skin. My stomach turns, and I get a twinge in my belly. *Oh sick. Now I know why he never wants me to look at it.* I finally get it cut all the way to my toes, and I peel away my sock.

"Ewww!" Dillen shrieks out, and I laugh hysterically. My fuzzy brain doesn't even register how I'm going to get this back on. I'm just happy to have the dang thing off.

I'm trying to get up off the floor unsuccessfully when I hear Noah's voice above me.

"What in the ever loving fuck are you doing?"

I can't hold in my laughter when Dillen points at me like a little tattletale. "I told her not to do it."

I look up at him and see the frown he's wearing. "That's it, play time is over," he says as he bends down and grabs the scissors from my hand. "You're drunk and playing with scissors? Shit, Heather, so much for me hiding the damn knives," he scolds and picks me up, walking us toward the bedroom. "It's time for bed, Miss Lane."

My head starts to swim with the movement, and for the first time all night, I start to feel sick. My stomach has an odd, hot bubbling sensation.

"'Night, Dill," I mumble as he walks.

"Dillen, don't move," he says in a highly dominant, sexy command before we reach the bedroom.

I feel like I'm drifting to sleep when I feel cool sheets beneath me. My eyes blink open in the dim light and I watch him walk out of the room with my throw blanket.

Where's he going with my blanket?

Moments later I feel the room spin and I look up. He's back and undressing me. "Are you mad?"

He's quiet before he speaks. "Yes, Heather, I am. Go to sleep."

I smile a drunken grin. "Spank me then."

He smirks as he takes off my pants and gently eases my foot from them. "I just might. I'm on the verge, and your little ass is just begging for it. Go to sleep, Heather."

I willingly close my eyes and feel the bed dip behind me. "Mmm . . ." I purr when I feel his warmth engulf me. He wraps his arm around my waist and pulls me closer to him. "Where's my blanket?" I ask sleepily.

I feel him exhale into my hair. "I wrapped Dillen in your blanket before I picked her up and put her to bed."

My God, could he be any more perfect?

I'm not sure when . . . minutes . . . maybe seconds, but soon after he kisses the back of my head, I pass out and remember nothing else.

Chapter Eleven

BODIES OF TRUTH

NOAH

The living room looks like we hosted a rave in it last night. My girl sure as hell went to town. I'm glad Dillen was able to get her mind off of things, and I'm equally as glad that Heather got her to stop crying. However, I am fucking pissed beyond belief that she took her boot off of her foot.

What in the hell were they thinking? How was she planning on walking without it? Her doctor specifically gave her instructions . . . I could wring both their necks for last night's stunt.

I hear Dillen's bedroom door open slowly, and she peeks out at me. "Good morning, Noah."

Her voice sounds timid as she steps out of her room. Her hair looks like it was caught in a windstorm, and she's squinting her eyes in the bright morning light. I haven't decided if I'm going to go easy on her or not.

"Yeah, morning. Now tell me, what in the ever loving fuck were you thinking when you let her take her damn boot off?"

I watch her eyes go from slits to wide as saucers as she shamefully stares at Heather's boot on the floor next to me. I wait as she tries to explain. "Noah, I swear I told her not to, but she kept begging me to take it off."

"And you let her? I know you weren't in your right mind, but hell, Dillen. She could have seriously injured herself."

I can tell that she's genuinely sorry as I watch her bring her fingers to her lips and chew nervously on her nails. "Is her foot okay?"

I sigh heavily. "Yeah, she's fine. I got to her before she stood up and I put a new sock on her, but not the boot. I need her to be awake when I put it back on so I know it's not hurting her."

She nods in agreement and sits down at the island across from me. From the looks of it, she's nursing a hangover, as I'm sure my ballerina will be. I turn my back to pour her a glass of orange juice and grab the Advil when I hear her say, "I'm sorry, Noah."

I walk over to her and hand her the tall, cool glass. "It's okay. She's just been through a lot, and I want her to have every chance possible to be able to dance again."

I start to clean up the mess in the kitchen from last night when I hear her sigh. "Seriously, Noah, you are like the sweetest guy I know. I'm so jealous." I pause briefly at her admission as I toss the shriveled-up limes into the trash.

"Coen's a lucky guy to have you, Dill. He should have landed by now, right?"

I don't hear a reply, so I turn and look. She's picking at her nails, and I know from living with this girl for a few weeks now that she's got something on her mind.

Finally, she shrugs. "Probably."

"Probably? What's going on?"

She leans back and puts her hair up in a messy bun on top of her head, before she takes the Advil and sets the glass down.

"I don't really think he's wanting anything out of our relationship," she replies and puts her forehead in her palm.

Ah fuck, please don't cry.

"I'll be honest with you, Dillen. I've known Coen for roughly eight years now, and I've never seen him so enamored with anyone before. He's a 'fuck and dump' kind of asshole who gets all the pussy he wants. That was until he met you, and he hasn't bragged about a woman to me since."

She cradles her chin in her hand. "Really?"

I shrug and nod. "Yeah, but you seem rather uninterested."

"No, I'm interested. I just . . ."

I have to chuckle.

"What?" she prods.

I shake my head and grin. "You females overanalyze everything." That gets a smile out of her, and she throws the bottle of Advil at my chest.

"Oh shut up."

"It's the damn truth, and you know it."

"No, it's not."

I laugh when she refuses to admit the truth. "Okay . . . whatever you say." I shake my head and pour some juice for Heather.

"I think I'm going to tell him we're over."

I'm thrown for a loop by her words. The juice almost overflows in the glass but I stop pouring as soon as I notice. "Excuse me? What the hell did you say? You know that I can't un-hear that, right?"

I look up, and she just stares at me while chewing on her lip.

Well fuck me.

"I'm sure he'll be fine. He never alluded to the fact that he wanted exclusivity," she replies and fidgets with her glass.

I put the carton of orange juice away and turn back around, racking my brain for the right thing to say. "I'm sure he'll miss you."

She winces and is about to speak when we both turn at the sound of Heather's voice.

"What are you guys doing up?" she asks, and I take in her appearance.

Fuck, she looks cute as hell hung over. Her hair is just as wild as Dillen's was, and her eyes are just as tired. She makes her way over to the island with the help of her crutches, and I remember how angry I was with their little stunt.

"Good morning, trouble." I walk over and kiss the top of her head before setting the glass and Advil down in front of her.

I swear she's about to complain when I raise my eyebrow, challenging her. Her shoulders slump and she lays her head on the cool countertop. "Heather, let me get the boot on your foot."

"Okay . . ." she replies begrudgingly and sits up. I walk over with the boot and kneel down in front of her, carefully putting it back on.

I make sure it's on correctly, just as the doctor showed me, and I stand back up. "Does that feel all right?"

She looks down at it, and I see a hint of disgust on her face. "Yes, it's fine."

I watch as she glances over at Dillen when she asks Heather, "Do you remember last night? We got in a LOT of trouble." Dillen snickers before she drinks her juice.

Heather shrugs her shoulders, and I know today isn't going to be a good day. I pull her into my arms and kiss the top of her head.

Dillen laughs, and her eyes are bright with mischief. "Do you want to do it again tonight?" she asks Heather excitedly "Oh, and I'm breaking up with Coen," she adds, like it's the best thing she's decided on in a decade.

"What?" Heather shrieks and looks from me to her friend.

I shrug and shake my head. "Don't look at me, ballerina. I want nothing to do with this."

"I don't think that we'd get anywhere fast, little shit. Plus, I'd rather go out and have some fun."

I can see the confusion in Heather's eyes as she looks at Dillen. "Oh . . . I . . . really? Are you sure, Dill? I mean, he really, really likes you."

"I'm sure," Dillen says without hesitation.

Heather looks over at me with a worried expression on her face, and I shrug.

"I'm going to shower and then head to practice, so I'll see the two of you later?" Dillen asks as she walks toward her room.

"Okay, Dill," Heather replies in her soft voice, and I take the seat next to her, angling myself to face her.

I reach over and move her hair behind her ear. "Ballerina?"

"Yeah?"

"Last night before I went to bed, I got a phone call from Ellery Somer. I didn't answer because I wasn't sure of what to say. It went to voicemail, and I haven't listened to the message she left me either. I was hoping you'd listen to it first?"

I watch as her eyes widen with surprise. "Oh. I . . . of course, but . . . are you sure? I mean, don't you want to hear her before I do?"

I get off of the barstool and offer her my hand. "No, I need you to do this for me, please."

"Okay . . ." She seems to be as nervous as I am.

We walk into her bedroom and shut the door behind us. I unplug my phone from where it's charging and hand it to her. I watch her look at my phone, and then she does something I've never seen her do. She turns her back on me.

HEATHER

Oh crap, oh crap, oh crap.

Okay, don't panic.

You knew this was coming.

I chant to myself internally as I bring his phone to my ear.

I have to turn my back because I know my face will give me away as soon as I hear her.

"Hi, Noah, this is Ellery Somer, your . . ." She clears her throat. "Uhm, I just wanted to call and let you know that Henry and I are notably looking forward to speaking with you." She pauses and takes in a shaky breath. I can hear a man whisper for her to go on in the background.

"We-we would love for you to come and visit with us, darling. Please feel free to call at any time of the day. We cannot wait see you again." Her voice is so genuine and just like I remembered. I find myself smiling and tearing up just hearing that voice again.

"I cannot tell you what it means to me to just hear your voice." She pauses again, and I hear a rustling before his voice comes on the line.

"Noah, it's Henry." He sighs but also chuckles, and it broadens my smile. "You'll have to excuse Ellery, as she is a bit emotional. Give us a call whenever you'd like. Have a good evening."

The message ends, and I pull the phone away from my ear as I turn back around to face him. I look up into Noah's expectant eyes as he searches my face for answers.

I smile and hand him his phone. "Noah, they're wonderful."

"Yeah? What did they say?" he asks as he stares down at the phone in his large tanned hand.

"They can't wait to talk to you." I wipe my cheek with the back of my hand. I'm so happy for him; he has no idea just how amazing they are.

His almost-smile turns into a frown as he watches me wipe my tears away. "Heather, what is it?"

I shake my head and beam up at him. "Nothing. I'm just really happy for you. You're finally going to get to meet your parents, Noah." I walk up to him and wrap my arms around his waist, and dwell in his warmth.

"You're still coming with me, right?" His arms move around me, and I breathe in his clean scent.

I nod against his chest and grip at the back of his shirt. The turmoil I feel inside is excruciating. "Noah?" My heart is racing, and if I don't tell him now, it'll only be worse later on.

"What is it, beautiful?"

It's now that I remember the picture I have in my purse. The one I've carried around for as long as I can remember. I look up at him and let go before looking around the room for my purse.

I hear Dillen yell out, "Bye guys, be home tonight." And then the front door slams shut.

"Bye," Noah says, but by the sound of his voice he's more interested in what I'm doing.

I leave the confines of our bedroom and search for my purse in the kitchen. I have nothing else on my mind but finding that picture, and I barely register him calling my name. I finally find my purse and look up at him, his broad shoulders framed by the white doorframe.

"I need to show you something . . ."

I'm shuddering. I don't know him well enough to know how he'll react. He may leave me, and I wouldn't blame him—this isn't the kind of secret I should have kept. But what are the odds? Out of all the people in the world . . . ?

He walks up behind me, snaking his arm around my waist.

"Heather? What's wrong?"

I fumble in my bag and start tossing things, searching for my wallet. My hands shake when I find it, and I can't even open it. It feels like a thousand pounds in my hands. I can feel my heart beating against my rib cage, and I'm having a hard time calming down.

"Baby? Talk to me, please?" He presses his lips to my shoulder, silently telling me that he loves me.

I turn, and he lets go of me. Before I chicken out, I take his hand and lead him to the couch. I can't even look at him as I sit on the edge. I force my body to turn and face him, my hands clenching my wallet as I take a huge breath.

"Okay, so I have this picture . . ." I trail off and open my wallet and find it hidden behind my driver's license. I pull it out and look at the infant in the picture. Before I can say another word, his finger is under my chin, tilting it up and forcing me to look at him. His smile is heartbreaking because I know it won't be there for long.

"I know, Heather, I've seen it. I had to look for your license when you were in the hospital, and I saw it."

I swallow hard and shake my head.

He pulls me onto his lap and nuzzles my neck. "Is that your mother? I know you miss her, baby."

My voice is only a whisper when I reply. "No . . . it's not me."

I feel his body stiffen, and he pulls away from my neck. The tears that threaten are stinging my eyes, and I can feel his storm brewing.

His voice is tight when he replies, "That's your baby?"

He moves me off his lap. *God, why is this so hard to tell him.* I can't even look him in the eye.

"Why didn't you tell me you had had a child, Heather?" He sits there and rubs his hand through his hair and over his ridged jaw.

"Dammit, Heather . . . how could you keep that from me?"

I refuse to look up and meet his eyes. I can hear his breathing quicken, and I know for a fact that he's upset. A tear trails down my cheek, and I shake my head. How could he think it's mine? Finally, I look up. His face is masked of all emotion as he stares across the room and focuses on anything but me.

"Noah, it's not my child."

No, he's wrong. It's not mine, but I don't have the words. I can't find a single one, so I simply shake my head as I turn the photograph over in my hand and stare at the beautiful handwriting that gives the picture its age, *April 3, 1985.*

"It's not yours?" he asks, yet his voice sounds accusatory.

"No." I hand him the photo and wait. I watch him take it, and his eyes roam over the picture.

"Okay, Heather, then tell me who . . ." He stops speaking as soon as he sees the date written in Ellery's handwriting. He's silent for the longest time, and I'm praying he doesn't get up and leave. Surely he's figured it out now, and maybe I won't have to say the words.

"How did you get this photograph, Heather?"

I look down at the floor and focus my eyes on my boot, trying to avoid looking up at him while I tell him my secret. "I took it when I was twelve. I was with them for three months before Dani turned eighteen and she was legally able to be my guardian. My parents had just died and they—the Somers—had lost a child years before, a boy, born on April third, 1985. I-I know who your parents are, Noah."

Guilt floods my blood, and I think I'm going to pass out. I should have told him weeks ago. My heart is pumping the spoken secret through my veins faster than I thought I could ever feel. I can't breathe, but somehow I manage to look up at him. I think he's stopped breathing entirely as he tries to absorb everything.

"Your parents were my foster parents, Noah."

His face is blank and completely devoid of emotion. He sits back against the couch cushions and stares at the wall at the far end of the room. "You know them?"

"I used to. I . . ." His eyes narrow slightly and I can honestly say I have no idea what he's thinking. "When I left . . . I never went back. I haven't seen them since Dani got custody of me."

"Since you were twelve?" I think he's trying to make sense of all of this information, information that I should have shared with him as soon as I saw that picture of Henry. His smoky voice interrupts my thoughts. "And they know you're with me?"

I shake my head adamantly. "No. No, I lost touch with them. I haven't spoken to them since . . ." I trail off, feeling ashamed at how long it's been.

"Why didn't you say anything? I've been second-guessing myself for weeks, and you just . . . fuck."

He shifts and gets up from the couch. He runs his fingers through his hair, and I watch as his muscles move under his lightweight V-neck. When his fingers reach the back of his neck, he grabs a fistful of the material and pulls it up and over his head.

"I need to shower," he says quickly and balls the shirt up in his hands as he retreats to the bathroom connected to our bedroom.

I feel like I can't move. I just watched him walk away from me, and I can't even summon the courage to go after him. I knew this would happen; Dani even knew it would. She warned me that he would be pissed. I guess that's why I kept it a secret for so long. I don't even know if I'll ever be able to make him understand.

I hear the water turn on, and I will myself to stand up. I hobble into the room and shut the door behind me, making sure to lock it because the last thing I want is Dillen barging in here. I slowly take my boot off and then my clothes. I stand and make my way over to the open bathroom door and walk in. I'm exposed, completely.

He needs to know that I didn't mean for this to hurt him. I just . . . I was in shock, and by the time I got past the shock, I realized I wanted him to have a family, the one he never got to have. I had my parents for twelve years, but he barely had his for a day. Salty tears mar my face as I stand in front of the shower door. I'm trying to avoid applying any weight to my fragile foot when I step inside, holding onto anything I can. His back is turned toward me, and I watch as his muscles stiffen when he realizes I'm close. I swallow my guilt and wrap my arms around his torso.

I wait for him to say something, but he doesn't. He doesn't move nor does he touch me. I can't let go of him because I need him. I need him to know that.

"Noah, please? I'm so sorry," I say over the spray of the water as I lay my forehead against his back. I feel his arms move and his hands grasp my wrists. Relief floods me for the briefest moment until he pulls free from my grip.

When he turns to face me, my eyes meet his; his face is flushed like he's been physically ill for days. He speaks before I have time to take in the rest of his mood. "I flew across the world for you, Heather. I've given up my life to come after you, not once, but twice. Goddammit, Heather. I fucking love you with every damn fiber of my being, but I have never felt . . . Hell. You are the one person I have trusted with every aspect of my life, and you know everything I've been through. Why did you feel the need to hide this from me?"

"I . . ." I try to reply but he holds his hand up.

"No, never mind. I don't want to hear any bullshit. Why you insist on keeping shit from me is beyond my comprehension."

I blurt out the words, so he doesn't have time to cut me off this time. "I didn't know how. How do I tell the man I love that his parents cared for me in the way that they never got to with him?"

I watch as he stares down at me like I just smacked him. I never thought he would take it this way. I search for any sign, any signal, that he would welcome my touch. My touch always calms him . . . but I find nothing. His stance screams anger and frustration toward me.

I feel his heated and heavy gaze move down my body, and he stops when he sees my foot. "What the hell are you thinking, huh? Are you trying to further damage yourself?" He easily removes me from the shower without any injury to my leg.

I don't move because I'm scared he won't want to touch me after this. My body weakens when the thought of this possibly being the last time he touches me creeps into my mind like an incoming storm, waiting to inflict its worst and rain down on me. To sting my skin, to hurt me, and tear everything I love away from me because I kept a secret.

Noah sets me down on the bed without drying me off first. I watch his retreating back as he walks out into the living room, naked with cool water droplets covering his gorgeous body. When he comes back he's got the bottle of Woodford Bourbon to his lips, and his throat is working overtime to down the liquid burn.

I'm nervous. Not for myself, but for him. I remember the last time he drank when he was angry. It didn't escalate to what could have been, but now . . . it just might. In the back of my mind, I notice that he doesn't even have an erection. He's never been in proximity of my naked body and not been affected. The fleeting moment passes when he kicks my boot toward the bed.

"Put it back on," he says in an icy-cold voice.

He pulls out two towels from the closet and tosses one at me. I can't tell if he's mad at me for knowing them or mad at me for keeping this secret from him. My mind is running, trying to place his mood.

"Noah . . . please."

He pauses as he dries off and picks up the bottle again to drink from it. I know I just bought that bottle and from the two large drinks he's taken from it, he's put a substantial dent in it. My eyes sting with tears, knowing what state he's trying to force himself into. He'd rather be pissed at me than acknowledge how hurt he is. I love this man unconditionally, but I keep hurting him like he's never been hurt before. It's not on purpose, I promise myself. I pull the towel around my body as my hands tremble.

I'm still for at least thirty minutes, lying on the bed and staring at the ceiling while I can feel his eyes on me. I eventually find the energy and willpower to move up the bed and watch him, as he does the same from a slumped-over position in the seat on the opposite side of the room. The bottle of bourbon sits on the floor next to his feet; it usually takes a mountain to knock my man over, but today, all it took was me.

I move to get up, and his head lifts, but his eyes stay almost closed. I'm cold, not only from lying here in just a towel, but from the dark heaviness that blankets this room. I never put my boot on like I was told, so when I take my first step without it, an excruciating pain travels up my leg. I bite the inside of my cheek to keep from crying out—I don't want him to know. As I reach for my robe, I look over at him.

"Are you going to speak to me at all?" I ask quietly.

"I told you to put your damn boot on." He completely ignores my question and straightens up in the chair.

My stubborn side rears back and spills from my lips before I have time to filter. "I heard you the first time."

"Oh yeah? It sure as hell doesn't look like it. It's a funny thing, isn't it? You have a knack for doing the opposite from what is best for you."

I don't pretend that what he said doesn't sting, but I'm not used to him being like this. "I've tried hard to protect myself from feelings, Noah. You have to understand that I just wanted my parents, not anyone else, so I blocked out that part of my life."

"Apparently you blocked out everything from me too. I've fought to get your walls down—since New Year's Eve—and you refuse to let me in. If you don't fucking want me in, then stop letting me warm you up and just fucking let go. Break me again. You've gotten pretty damn good at it."

I suck in a sharp breath. I can't believe what I'm hearing. "I do want you, Noah . . ."

He snorts and throws his head back in a laugh that isn't his. "You sure have one fucked-up way of showing it."

I know he's drunk, and I know I've hurt him, so I can't blame him for what he says, but I'm completely devastated. I refuse to let any more tears fall in front of him, so I take the painful steps toward the door as I tie my robe around my waist.

"You don't mean that, Noah."

"Just like you didn't mean it when you said you love me, huh?"

I turn, causing another shooting pain to go up my leg, but I ignore it. "I have never lied to you about how much I love you. Not once, and I wouldn't ever."

"Yeah? I sure as fuck don't understand why you're insistent on keeping all these damn secrets from me."

Guilt and anger surge through me simultaneously. "Stop it, Noah."

I look into his eyes and flinch when his drunken smirk hardens his face.

"Stop what? Stop calling you out on shit? I'm sorry you don't like hearing it. What else do you have hidden from me?"

"Why would I hide anything from you that I thought you could handle?"

"Apparently I can't handle anything, Heather."

"Noah, stop it. This is not fair. You don't understand."

"You wouldn't give me a fucking chance to understand, Heather. You just keep shit from me like I'm a goddamn child."

"I'm not hiding anything from you. I'm sorry, Noah. I should have told you as soon as I saw his picture."

I watch as he stares at me. He doesn't believe me, and I don't know what to do to fix this. He takes a long swig from the bottle before setting it down and picking up his phone to listen to Ellery's message. He turns away from me again.

I stand and watch his muscular back tense up. I want to go to him, but he doesn't want my touch. I'm on the verge of a breakdown, and if I don't get out now, he'll use it against me, I'm sure. He puts down the phone and picks up the bottle of liquor again. I know this isn't going to end well.

I walk out of the room and shut the door because I don't think my heart can take it anymore. We've been arguing for what seems like hours now. I lie down on the couch and shut my eyes, trying to warm myself up.

I'm startled awake by the apartment door closing, and I sit up quickly, thinking that it's Noah leaving. Thankfully, Dillen flitters into the room with a day-conquering smile on her face.

"Hi, little shit. Guess what I did today? I broke up with Coen," she answers herself before I can get a word in. She tilts her head to the side when she notices my mood.

"Uh-oh, is everything okay?"

I look back over my shoulder at the closed bedroom door and then at the clock. It's after eight and it's dark outside. My eyes burn from crying, and I shake my head. "No, we're not okay."

"Oh Heather." She walks over to me quickly and pulls me into her arms, hugging me tightly before letting go and holding me at an arm's length away to inspect me.

"Where is your boot?" she sighs and smacks the side of my butt playfully in an attempt to cheer me up, but she gets nothing besides my blank, somber stare.

"Okay. Go in there and get your boot, and I'll help you put it back on."

It's probably a good idea to put it back on since it's been hours. I hobble over to the door and crack it open just enough to step inside before shutting it again.

Noah is sitting at the desk with his broad, muscular back to me. There are a few textbooks open and scattered around him, and papers are strewn all over the place, along with a few bottles of beer that I didn't hear him come out for. He's resting his elbow on the chair's arm and staring intently at the desk.

"Noah?"

His head slowly rolls to the other side of his shoulders before I hear his rough voice. "You know, I have a secret of my own."

I reach down and pick up my boot and start to walk over to him; no matter how angry, or upset I am, I can still feel the pull that buzzes between us. The electrifying love I feel for this Greek god is fierce and unmistakable.

He turns before I can reach him, and when he turns around in the chair, his eyes meet mine briefly before going back to the desk. I suppose he's waiting for me to respond, but I stubbornly stay quiet. He moves his alcohol-impaired body from the seat and stands up shakily. Swiping his hand across the desk, he grabs a small black box. He's staring at it with red-rimmed eyes when he pops the top open, revealing a stunning solitaire round-cut diamond ring.

"You want to know what my fucking secret was?"

I can only stare. I don't even know what to say. I never in a million years expected this. I didn't even expect him to be awake.

"Nothing, huh? I figured, fuck, if she's going to keep shit from me, then I'll be the one with the balls and tell her everything."

He tosses the open ring box too hard onto the desk, causing the ring to fall out of the box and onto the floor. "Fuck it, right? Why the hell would I want this when you can't be honest with me for two damn minutes?"

"Noah, you don't want to marry me."

"You're right, I don't," he says as he stares at me with cold, emotionless eyes.

His words gut me, and I haven't even managed to say a word as he stumbles across the room to the bed, where he lies down and reaches to turn off the light, completely blocking me out. My eyes well up with tears as I look at him and then back to the diamond ring on the hardwood floor.

It feels like a deep, dark haze has overtaken me as I reach out for the wall to steady myself. I can't catch my breath; I can't think straight.

"Noah . . . please," I choke out and look over at his shirtless torso on the bed. He's lying on his stomach, and he's completely still.

I think the alcohol finally won.

Chapter Twelve

NECESSARY APOLOGIES

NOAH

It's been two days since I found out that Heather knows my parents. Two days since I gave away my secret. I'm lying in bed staring at the ceiling as she lies on her side, facing the bedroom door. She's hardly said two words to me since she hurt me . . . since I broke her. Since I tore the air from her lungs, leaving her with nothing to breathe, and no matter how deep a breath she takes, she comes up short. I caused this. I caused her to feel like she's alone when we're with each other; I caused her to feel paralyzed, unable to move on with what we are. I think sleep is the only way she's been able to escape the pain.

I feel like a prisoner of my own actions.

I need to fix this.

Our plane leaves for New York tonight, and I can't say whether Heather will be getting on that plane with me or not. There's a heavy weight in the room and I cannot stand it. What I did to her, in spite of her deciding that keeping that information from me was best, was the vilest and rashest thing I have ever done.

She moves minutely, and I turn my head to look at her. I don't know if she's asleep or not, but her tiny frame shivers. I reach for her throw blanket that separates us and drape it over her, careful not to touch her. Hell knows she doesn't want me touching her.

I no longer have the confidence that she's mine, or that she'll ever forgive me. I've lost who I am, and as a result, I've lost my ballerina to an intensely dark place where she feels so low. All of her energy and desires are gone as she lies still.

"Heather?"

I watch as her shoulders move with each breath. She doesn't respond for the longest time, and I come to the conclusion that she is in fact asleep when her quiet, emotionless voice breaks the silence.

"Yeah?"

Her voice is like ecstasy.

Our pull is still there—you could cut it in the air with a knife. Hell, I love this woman more than anything, and I fucked it all up. I chance it and roll onto my side and spoon her from behind. I slowly slide my hand around her small waist and wait for her to react. I know that this will be the best way for us to talk about what we did to each other. She doesn't have to look at me and be disgusted, but I can feel her. I can feel her body react to my words, and it'll tell me the truth. She's bruised and tender from the fight, and I'm going to make these bruises fade. I don't want a stalemate in our relationship, so I'm going to let go of my anger and stop defending myself because I was in the wrong.

"You didn't deserve what I did." I swallow the lump that's forming in the back of my throat. "I ruined something for you that was supposed to make you the happiest woman alive. I took that out of foolishness and anger. I don't know how to fix it, but the numbness, shame, and fear I feel when I think about not having you is all consuming. It's torture. I don't know how to adequately apologize, but I'm going to start with saying I'm sorry."

I close my eyes as I speak those last two words and wait. I wait . . . and wait . . . and wait. The entire time I'm waiting, I'm thinking of my next step, my next plan of action. What do I do or say to make her believe how disgusted I am with myself? She has every right to pull away, to remove my hands from her body the way I did to her. Her body lies tense in my arms, and I hate it. I fucking hate the way that makes me feel. I don't want to feel the rejection from her, so I remove my arm from her waist and instantly feel cold. I'm cold . . . for once. I feel the icy sting of her silence as it creeps up my spine. I decide to try and bank on the one thing I have in my corner. I have no shame in what I'm about to say. I exhale all my tension and move my hand up into her long, dark hair. Gathering it gently and pulling it away from the back of her neck, I lean in close and whisper my only shot in hell as I kiss the back of her neck.

"You said you'd never leave me again."

The waiting continues for seconds or minutes, I'm not sure, but I finally get the glimpse I've been waiting for. Her tense body relaxes ever so slightly and she moves back toward me. The move is so slight that I doubt she even knows it, but I do. I've used the guilt card, and I don't regret it for a second. Her voice rings clear when she speaks my name; even if it were only a whisper, I'd hear it anywhere.

"Noah . . ."

I try my hardest not to squeeze the living shit out of her. My body is telling me to take her, but my mind is telling me to shut my fucking mouth.

You've said enough, Ryan.

"I'm here, Heather . . . right here."

My lips move of their own accord and drift across the back of her neck as she speaks. The fact that she hasn't pushed me away yet is giving me all the hope I've silently begged for in these last two days.

"I never meant to hurt you, Noah. I just didn't know how to tell you . . . I didn't want to spoil this big event in your life."

"I get that. I also understand if you'd rather not fly back to the States with me today. I'll do what it takes to make this right; just please give me that chance. Being without you would be like living in a world without color . . . a fog of nothingness . . . one that would pass me by without a second glimpse . . . and every day would be a struggle. It would be the cruelest of punishments, but if it's what I need to go through to have a chance at you giving me one last glimpse . . . I'll do it. Just please . . . don't leave me."

I exhale deeply and kiss her skin again, tasting her for possibly the last time when she abruptly turns to face me. I'm caught by surprise but try to hide it. Her beautiful jade green eyes look tired and swollen; I add it to the list of things I already hate myself for. I bring my hand up and cup her cheek, my thumb gently rubbing her eyelid.

"Don't leave me. Please?"

She leans into my touch and briefly closes her eyes before looking right at me. "I'm not leaving you, Noah."

With that, I know she loves me to no end. She doesn't have to say those three words right now, but after everything I put her through two days ago, and after losing our child, she still hasn't run away. No matter how hard our situation has gotten, she hasn't left my side, as I haven't left hers.

Shutting my eyes, I press my cold lips to her temple and take in a deep breath when her hand moves up my chest. "I will never deserve your love, ballerina."

Her breathing sounds shaky as she looks up at me, and I think I'm hearing things when the words leave her lips. "Will you kiss me, please?"

My eyes meet hers when she angles her face toward mine, pleading with me for physical contact. I run my hand through the waves of her dark-chocolate hair and hold her as I bring my lips down to meet hers for the first time in what feels like an eternity of waiting and wanting. Our lips skim the surface of each other's nervously. She draws back ever so slightly and I take in every signal she is giving off, assessing if it's okay to kiss her again.

Our lips meet again, and they stay closed as we continue to place slow, gentle, and lingering kisses on each other. She presses against me, and I move my other hand to the small of her back, as her hands move up to my shoulders and slowly wrap around my neck.

I need her as close to me as possible, so I shift my weight until her body is pressed tightly to mine. Her lips become a little more eager, and it's hard for me to be a gentleman at this moment when all I want is to slip my tongue between her lips and taste my girl again.

She pulls back and hides her face in my chest, nuzzling me.

"You're not getting on that plane without me, Noah."

Jesus, thank you, I silently reply to myself as I kiss the top of her head and hold her close.

She sighs quietly and all of the tension in her body melts away. I watch her shut her eyes and take in a long, deep breath before sleep overtakes her.

I won't let her go as she lies in my arms. I'll wake her when we need to leave, but she needs this right now. I can tell she hasn't been sleeping, and I won't wake her. I press my lips to the top of her head, and my muscles unclench as I breathe her in.

The desire to incessantly apologize to each other was finally put to rest earlier today. Heather hasn't let go of me for more than the two minutes it took for her to get dressed before we left for the airport. When we said goodbye to Dillen before going through airport security, she wouldn't let go of my hand while she hugged her friend goodbye. Dillen was in tears again, and I feel guilty because I'm the reason Heather is leaving London. Yet I feel elated to be going home.

We're standing in line at the gate to board our flight once they call first class. Her small hand grips mine, and our fingers are laced together. I squeeze her hand and she looks up at me with an overwhelming amount of love. The emotional pain we've been through in the past two days has had no effect on her love for me. Our love can bring the strongest person to their knees; I know, because I've experienced it. I was vulnerable.

"Ballerina, are you okay? I know you're not looking forward to this flight."

Her fingers tense around mine and she shakes her head. I had a feeling this might happen, and there's really nothing I can do to help. I pull her into my chest and kiss the top of her head, trying to give her as much as I can.

"You're going to be just fine. I won't let anything happen to you."

"I know," she says softly when the line starts moving. We get our tickets scanned, and then walk down the jetway and onto the plane to find our seats.

"Which seat would you like, baby?"

She's still holding onto me; fuck, I wish I could take this fear away from her.

It looks as if she's pausing to think. I've never seen someone so terrified of flying before. Her body language gives everything away as she slips into the row and sits near the window. I put her carry-on bag above us and look back down at her; she's trembling. I can't imagine what this flight was like for her when she flew alone.

I take my seat and lift the armrest between us, thankful that I can at least hold her. I look down and take her shaking fingers, bringing them to my lips.

Fuck me, this is going to be a long flight.

"Did you take those sleeping pills yet?" I ask as I try to calm her with my touch.

"No, not yet."

"Are they in your purse?"

"Yeah."

I ask the flight attendant for a mimosa and water, and I lean down to get Heather's purse. When I look back up she's fidgeting nervously. *Christ, I can't stand seeing her like this.*

"Hey . . ." I reach for her chin and make her look at me. "Calm down. You're going to be fine. I promise."

She takes in a deep breath and clutches at my shirt. "I can't do this."

"I won't ever ask you to get on another flight, baby. We'll drive everywhere. You have my word."

I watch her to make sure she takes her sleeping pill, and then I pull her into my arms and hold her as her body quivers wildly.

She looks up at me with frightened eyes as I rub her shoulder. "Do you think we're going to crash?"

I chuckle and shake my head. "No, we're not going to crash," I manage to say without laughing. But damn, she's fucking adorable.

After the flight attendants have been through their final checks, they sit back down, and Heather digs her fingers into my forearm. After we taxi out, the plane lurches and starts jetting down the runway at full speed. Her fingers are clenched around my arm to the point of her knuckles turning white. I try to make her laugh to keep her mind preoccupied.

"Damn girl, you're going to bruise me."

She smiles the slightest bit, but she refuses to let go of me, and I'm okay with it. I love that she needs me too. Once the plane reaches its altitude, she finally relaxes—either because of me, or her medication is finally kicking in.

"Go to sleep, baby."

"Mmm," she manages, and I get up to grab her pink blanket from her carry-on. I lay it over her before I take my laptop out and sit down to study while she sleeps.

I look over as I wait for my laptop to power up, and she's already passed out. Thank God.

The flight attendant walks by, and I ask her for a glass of orange juice for when Heather wakes up. She's been asleep for just over four hours now, and I've gotten a lot of studying done. We hit a rough patch of turbulence, and I keep my eye on Heather, hoping that she doesn't wake up right now. A few minutes pass, and she seems to be okay until we hit another rough patch.

Moments later she stirs and must feel the plane jolt because she sits straight up in a panic and grabs the armrest to her left. She gasps as her eyes go wide.

"Are we crashing?" Her voice trembles noticeably.

I reach out to her and cup her face, making her look at me. "We're not crashing. Relax for me, ballerina. We're fine, and I'm here."

I can feel her heartbeat fluttering against my fingertips when I graze her neck.

Her eyes are locked onto mine, and I move in closer to kiss her slowly. I shut my laptop and make her lie back down, reclining my seat too. I'm thankful that this armrest moves, enabling me to lie down next to her. I pull her body into mine and move my hands under her shirt. She sighs heavily and puts her blanket over the two of us.

"I'm not going to let you go. You have my word."

"Please don't."

The turbulence intensifies, and her breathing follows suit.

"Shh . . . just relax." My fingers graze her flat stomach.

She's radiating nervous energy so I kiss her, wanting her to know that we're going to be okay. I need to get her to calm down. "Heather . . . be quiet, okay?" I move my hand lower and under the light lace material of her panties.

She quickly grabs my wrist and halts my movements. "Noah, you . . . what are you doing?"

"Do you trust me?"

She nods but doesn't let go of my wrist.

I move my hand down farther regardless and run the pad of my index finger around her clit.

She jolts under my touch. "Noah, no."

"Don't say that word to me, Heather." I kiss her collarbone before nipping at her. She's already forgotten about the flight, and she's completely ensconced in my touch.

I know that she's not opposed to sexual acts in public; in fact, I know she enjoys them just as much as I do. I'm not sure if she can keep her moans and gyrations to a minimum, but I'm going to try. Discreetly, I slide my middle finger inside of her warm pussy. She doesn't fight my daring movement, but instead seems to delight in it.

"Oh God . . ." she whispers and grips my wrist tighter.

"That's not my name, but you can call me whatever the fuck you want, beautiful. Just make sure you let that pussy come all over my hand."

She bites on her cheek to stop herself from moaning out loud as I add another finger into her soaked channel. I start applying more pressure and moving my fingers faster, pushing up on her most sensitive spot.

"Noah, I can't."

"Shh . . ."

I remove my fingers from her pussy and pull my hand out of her panties. She's still holding onto my wrist when I put my two fingers into my mouth and taste her sweetness.

"I love the way this pussy tastes."

Her eyes widen and just as I'm about to dive back in, I'm interrupted. "Sir, miss? Would either of you like a drink?"

I look at the glass full of orange juice and shake my head. "We're all set, thank you."

She moves on, and I turn back to Heather. To my surprise, she's sitting a little straighter and her blanket is nearly at her waist.

I raise my eyebrow in a challenge. "Going somewhere? I'm not finished."

"I have to pee," she lies, and I shake my head.

"No, you have to come."

I move toward her and slip my hand below the blanket. "I haven't had your pussy in days, Heather. I know you're aching for my cock." My lips graze her earlobe as I speak.

She lies back down and watches me intently as I lower my hand, and holy shit, my feisty girl has pushed her panties and leggings down to her knees. The grin that spreads across my face is hard to hide. "Mmm, there she is."

I slide a finger into her again when she moves her hand on top of mine.

She turns her face toward mine and sucks in a breath. I focus my eyes on her lips while my finger focuses on her warm, wet pussy. "You miss my cock, don't you?"

She rotates her hips as if she's begging for me. "Noah . . ."

"Yeah? I fucking love when you beg me." She licks her plump lips and presses down on my hand.

"Give me more."

I meet her needs and slide in a second finger, pushing up at her spot at a faster pace as her walls grip my fingers. My cock is hard as hell, and I'm thinking of all the ways I could get her off. My fingers are drenched, and her juices are dripping into my palm and down my wrist.

I can't help but groan into her ear. "I'm going to come the moment I get inside this pussy, Heather."

She whimpers, and I swear to God she starts leaking like a faucet. "I need your cock, Noah."

I slowly remove my fingers from her and undo my jeans with my other hand, just far enough to get my cock out. "Turn around and give me your ass."

"I-Noah, we'll get caught," she whispers as she watches me.

I reach up and turn our reading lights off before I flip her over and pull her ass to me. "Everyone is asleep, and the lights are out in the cabin."

She looks back at me with a worried expression on her face. I lean in close, groaning when I grip my cock and drag it through her soaked folds.

"This is your one and only chance at joining the mile-high club." Sucking on her earlobe, I add, "Slide that pretty pussy down my cock, Heather. You're soaking wet—I'll fit right in."

"I want you so bad . . ." She throws her head back and decides to listen to me. Her warmth engulfs my shaft. I have to push up to help her accommodate my size.

"How does it feel?"

She only whimpers her answer, and I lose my train of thought. Her cream is coating my cock, and it's beyond fucking hot inside her pussy.

Her fingers clamp down on my thigh, and I feel her body tremble. "Noah . . ." she hisses out quickly and louder than necessary.

My movements are small and unnoticeable underneath the blanket, and I feel her tighten further. I bring my hand around to her neck and wrap my fingers around her throat, holding her in place as I take her.

I'm moments from busting inside of her. Holy fuck, she's gone slick around me, and I slide in deep. I feel it the moment I get her off. Her tight pussy grips me and starts to quiver uncontrollably, trying to milk me for all I have.

My fingers tighten the slightest bit around her neck, as her mouth drops open in a silent cry.

I can't hold it any longer. My cock is begging for release so I oblige it and fill her tight channel with hot spurts of come. A sheen of sweat has formed on the back of her neck, and my tongue wants a taste. I groan too loudly with my release. She moves her hand around to cover my mouth in an attempt to block out my sounds. I retaliate by biting the palm of her hand and squeezing her perfectly shaped ass.

She puts her finger to her perfect lips and tries to shush me.

We both stop moving and revel in our climax. I take the hand she is holding up to her mouth and move it down to where our connecting bodies are. I run her finger through our wet satisfaction and bring it back up to her lips. "You know what to do, ballerina."

She smiles shyly and slowly licks her finger. My cock jerks when I see her enjoy how we taste. I fucking love the way she looks when she's tasting me . . . us.

"Goddamn, Heather, you keep sucking that finger, and my cock will be hard again in minutes."

She giggles and takes my finger into her mouth, biting down hard.

I grunt and pull my hand back. "Heather . . ." I scold playfully.

"Mmm?" She tries to ask innocently.

I grab a fistful of her hair and pull her head back enough for me to kiss her as I pull out. I put my cock away and growl into her mouth, "Go clean up, dirty ballerina."

I laugh when she gasps and smacks my chest before pulling her leggings up, watching the love of my life carefully as she maneuvers out of the seat and into the aisle.

"Miss me while I'm gone?"

"Always, baby."

She winks at me for the first time, and it takes me by surprise. Fuck me . . . I'm in love.

We're back at Heather's apartment; she seems comfortable and relaxed for the first time in weeks. She's sitting on her pink couch with her leg propped up as she searches her iPad for a physical therapist who will fit her needs. I know she's dying to dance again, and I'm going to be here for her every step of the way. I have my first bar prep class in the morning, and I'm sure it will be intimidating, but I'm ready. I'm ready to leave the past behind and move forward with my life.

My phone goes off and Heather glances up at me. It's a text from Joel:

Welcome home, Ryan. We need to get together soon.

I type out a reply:

Thanks, man. We'll need to set up a time for the four of us to go out. Unless you have a plus-one?

His reply comes soon after I hit send and I move to sit next to Heather:

Nah, man, it's still just me. I heard Dillen broke things off with Coen the second he left London. What a bitch.

I almost spit out the water I just sipped:

Dude. I've got nothing to say on that topic. I've seen too many damn tears in the past week.

Tears? Because she misses Coen or because she misses that dick?

Now that is a good question.

I set my phone down before turning to Heather. "Have you had any luck?"

"Mmm, yes, I've found two. One is Dr. Miller Blythewood, and the other is Dr. Lacey Repler. It looks like Dr. Blythewood has had more experience with dancers, though, so I think I might set up an appointment with him." She looks up at me nervously, and for the life of me, I cannot figure out why the hell she just got so nervous.

She shifts so she's sitting on my lap, and I place my lips on the top of her head, breathing her in. "That sounds good, ballerina. I'll be at as many appointments as I can make it to."

"You don't have to do that, but thank you. I'll call his office tomorrow to set one up."

"Good, because you are going to be incredibly jetlagged." I stop speaking when she nuzzles my chest and bites at my right pec. "You're asking for it, Miss Lane."

"Oh? I wasn't aware," she says innocently, her voice husky with need.

I tilt her chin up and take her mouth with mine. Her soft, velvet-like tongue caresses mine, and I can't hide my fervor.

"Noah?" she asks when we break our kiss.

"What is it?"

"Have you decided when you're going to go and meet your parents? It's been weeks since they found out their son is alive, and I bet they are beyond restless to meet you."

I kiss the shell of her ear and exhale soundlessly. "I'll need to get in contact with them."

I reach for my phone and open up my email application, deciding that I might as well be the one to start this transition in my life. In fact,

I'm pleased to be taking control of my life again.

To: Henry Somer
From: Noah Ryan
Subject: Meet-Up Date

Henry,
I hope you and Ellery are doing well. I wanted to let you know that I am back in New York City. I would like to meet you soon, if your schedule allows for it. I am able and more than happy to travel to you.
Please let me know which dates would work best for you. I am enrolled in a bar prep course as of now, so weekends would work best for me.
I look forward to hearing from you.

Your son,
Noah Ryan

I hit send and look over at Heather, who was watching me type out the email. I let out a deep breath and try to tell myself that this is what needs to happen, as well as this is what I want. My family. My life.

"You're still going to come with me, correct?"

"Of course I am. I promised you, didn't I?"

"I know you did. I just needed the confirmation."

"Well, you've got it, Greek god."

"Thank you. Now tell me, would you like to go out with Joel and Coen tomorrow night? Joel was texting me earlier."

"Sure, that sounds like fun, but has Coen said anything to you about Dill?"

"I'm glad." I look at my watch and yawn. "No, he hasn't said anything since we got back . . . should I call him?"

I watch her think it over for a moment and then nod. "Yeah, call him."

I nod and hit dial and then put it on speakerphone as it rings a few times.

"What the fuck is up, man?" Coen's voice breaks through the silence.

I laugh and shake my head, leaning back against the couch. "Not shit. Just wanted to let you know we're back in the States."

"Nice, assfuck. You've been missed around these parts. Are you two going to be joining the three of us tomorrow night?"

I pause and look at Heather. She shrugs and pipes in. "Hi, Coen, I thought it was just the four of us going out?"

"Nah, not anymore, little lady. I've got someone I want you both to meet. Her name is Lana."

Her eyes go wide, and I raise my brow at her. "Uh . . . oh, okay," she stutters and closes her eyes, shaking her head slowly. I'm sure we're thinking the same thing.

"Is this a new piece of ass, or do you see this going anywhere?" All of these girls cannot be good for his pride.

"Ah fuck, man, I don't know, but I'd pay her bills. And she does this thing with her throat that . . ." He stops mid-sentence before speaking again. "Wait, is Heather still listening?"

"Damn right she is."

Heather snickers and gets off of my lap. "I'm going to bed, boys. Play nice."

"'Night, sis," he calls out and we both look at each other.

Heather breaks out a megawatt smile and mouths, "Awww" to me, before she kisses me and heads upstairs to bed. I take Coen off of speaker and pick the phone up from the coffee table.

I watch her walk upstairs before I speak. "All right, she does what with her throat?"

He laughs and starts in again. "Shit, man, does Heather deep-throat?"

I chuckle and grin. "Wouldn't you enjoy that bit of knowledge? Huh? Now tell me who the fuck this woman is."

I can hear him grin and then a beer crack open. "I met her at a club last week. Long blonde hair, perfect tits, and an ass you can bounce a quarter off of. Need more?"

"Right, the typical Coen type of woman but in all seriousness, are you good, man?"

He's quiet for a long breath, and I can tell he's contemplating. "I'm good. So where we going tomorrow?"

"Good to hear. Uhh, tomorrow . . . fuck, man, I don't know. Skydiving?"

He laughs. "You think you can talk Heather into that, man?"

"I fucking doubt it, but shit, I would be interested in doing it here in New York. Phoenix was great."

"Come on by, man, I'll hook you up. We've been slow lately so I've got the time to jump with you."

"You've got yourself a deal."

I hear Heather call out, "Noah? I can't sleep without you . . ."

I look over my shoulder toward the stairs and get up off the couch.

"All right, man, my girl is waiting in bed. I can't disappoint her," I say as I pull my shirt off as I walk up the stairs.

"Ah, enjoy the little lady, dipshit. I'll text you with details on tomorrow night soon. Bye."

"See ya." I end the call as I reach the top of the stairs and unbutton my jeans. I get them off before I walk into the bedroom where my ballerina is holding the covers up to her neck. "Are you cold?" I ask teasingly. She nods as I shut the door and walk toward the bed.

"You know that answer by now, don't you?" she asks in a sleepy voice.

I turn off the lights and get into bed, pulling her against my chest. "I do, but I seem to be your solution."

She nuzzles my chest and tangles her legs with mine before settling comfortably. "Yes, and I can't sleep unless you're in bed with me. You've pretty much ruined me for life."

For life?

"I think I can handle taking the blame for that." I pull the blankets up and kiss the top of her head, her long dark-chocolate brown hair fanning out against my chest.

"I love you, Noah."

"I love you, Heather."

How the hell did we get back here after what I did to her? I've never had anyone love me without any bounds before. I threw a ring at her in anger and was cold, even cruel to her. Yet here we are. I'm lost to this woman, and I sure as fuck hope she's lost to me.

My mind races for what seems like hours as I listen to her breathe. I have so much emotion pent up; I think I'm going to lose my shit. I can feel my heart start to race, and I'm moments from getting out of bed to pace when Heather seems to sense my unease even in her sleep. Without waking, I feel her hand drift up my bicep, and she shifts to the side. Just one touch of hers breaks me out of my marathon of thoughts, and my heartbeat returns to normal.

I slide my hand down her back to her ass, pulling her as close to me as I can without waking her. She breathes in deeply and sighs, mumbling something to herself, something that she's dreaming wildly about. I look up at the ceiling and shut my eyes in hopes of getting some decent sleep tonight.

Chapter Thirteen

JUMP OR FALL

HEATHER

We are on our way to meet up with Coen and this Lana girl. I'm rather skeptical about all of this. I'm sure Dillen would not like me hanging out with his next lay. I know she was the one who broke his heart, but I also know how much she liked him.

When Noah told me that he and Coen wanted to go skydiving today, I laughed in his face. When he didn't join in my laughter, my smile fell, and I knew that he was serious. I may have overreacted a tad with my refusal, and now I sit here, arms crossed, while Noah drives. I'm having a hard time hiding my anger and irritation. "You do realize how dangerous this is, right?"

He reaches over and puts his hand on my thigh. "I do, ballerina, but I'm licensed, and I've jumped out of a plane with Coen more times than I can count."

I don't even try to hide my scowl. I can feel my eyebrows knitted together as I stare at him. "Noah, seriously. What if something happens?

When did you become an adrenaline junkie? Why am I just now hearing that you skydive?" I hear myself huff and slam my head back against the headrest. I look over and he's got a small smirk on his face while he drives.

"Baby, you know I fucking love it when you're pissy. Relax for me, okay? It's just something that Coen and I have always done."

"Yeah? Well, it's stupid," I spit out and exhale hard.

He growls under his breath and looks over at me as he pulls up next to Coen's car. "Settle down."

I lean forward with my arms still crossed and look out the window and up at the sky, squinting as I look for bodies falling from planes. His body is buzzing with excitement and mine is telling me it's time to panic. I'm suddenly wishing I had a tiny shot bottle of liquor stashed away in my purse.

He gets out of my car and walks around to open the passenger side door for me. "Are you coming?"

Coen emerges from the building and calls out, "Hey fucker."

He's already dressed in his jumpsuit and walking toward us with a huge smile plastered on his face. I want to hate him right now. I do hate him right now. I'm sure he came up with this stupid boys'-day-out idea. Noah turns, and they do that male handshake-hug thing and then start walking back toward the building as I sit here waiting.

Ugh . . . stupid boys and their stupid toys.

I grab my bag and get out of the car when I'm suddenly face to face with a beautiful blonde woman. "Oh . . . uh, hi," I stammer out as I shut and lock the car.

She smiles brightly. "Hi, I'm Lana. I've heard so much about you."

I'm taken by surprise because I want to hate her but . . . I just can't. She's got the most pleasant smile: it's genuinely friendly.

Errr . . . sorry, Dill.

"Heather," I say and take her extended hand to shake.

She beams as we follow the men. "Are you going to be jumping too?"

My eyes go wide, and I shake my head. "No. No way. I actually think it's an insane idea." I say those last two words a little louder than necessary, so the boys hopefully hear me.

Noah turns back briefly to wink at me.

Lana giggles and nods. "I completely agree with you. I'm not into anything that puts my life at risk. I'm glad I'll have someone to hyperventilate with when they jump. I thought I was going to be the odd one out."

I watch Noah turn back and continue to walk.

Uh-huh, okay, fine, mister. That stunning wink will get you nowhere.

"No, I'll be down here too with the vomit bag up to my face."

"Well, I'll be here to squeeze the hell out of your hand," she says as we take a seat outside in the warmth of the sun.

I smile over at her and cross my legs. My foot twitches wildly back and forth, and I try to think of anything I can to keep my man safely on the ground. Thoughts of a life without Noah race through my mind as we wait. I'm in a trance while I sit there.

A few minutes pass before Noah and Coen both walk up to us. Noah leans down and presses his lips to mine. "I love you, ballerina. And fuck, you look so damn sexy."

Lana and Coen are talking softly, and I see him kiss her gently out of the corner of my eye.

I grab both of Noah's hands and pull him down. He sits on the balls of his feet, crouched in front of me.

"What, baby?" he asks as he reaches up and moves some stray hairs from my face.

"Don't go. I'll do anything you want." I lean down and whisper in his ear almost frantically, "I'll let you do me in the butt." I pull back, my eyes wide and hopeful.

His brows shoot up and his cool, stormy laugh fills my ears. "I won't be long, and we are going to do that regardless."

My hopeful face drops into a full-on pout, and I huff. *Well, that didn't work at all.*

His lips find mine again, and he stands up. "You good to go, Coen?" he asks, and I look over at Lana and Coen. He has his hand on her cheek and is looking at her like she's the most beautiful woman on Earth.

My mouth literally drops open, and I smack Noah's thigh, hissing up at him, "See, she doesn't want him going either."

He chuckles and kisses me again. "I love you. Coen, let's go, dipshit."

Both of the men smirk and walk away from Lana and I to the awaiting plane.

I'm not sure what is making my legs shake more—my nervousness for him, or him in that jumpsuit. *Holy crap, he looks hot in it.*

Lana's voice distracts me as they get everything they need onto the plane. "So, Heather, Coen told me that you are a rather popular ballerina."

I'm trying all I can not to lose it, so I grab onto her distraction. "Oh . . . umm . . . I don't know about popular." I look down at my boot and laugh. "I used to be a ballerina, but I had a fall."

She frowns. "He mentioned that too, as well as your and Noah's story. That man has really gone to the end of the world for you, huh? It's rather romantic."

I can't help but smile softly. She's right . . . everyone can see it. Everyone but me. I have been so obtuse about everything. "Yeah, he's pretty amazing," I say delicately. Before I can say another word, I hear someone whistle loudly to get our attention. We both look over, and the guys are waving to us before getting into the plane. My heart slams against my chest, and I think I'm going to be sick.

"I need a Xanax," she says before shifting uncomfortably in her seat.

The small plane comes to life, and I grimace. It doesn't even sound safe. It sounds like it's going to die. It's sputtering and revving and . . . oh God, *don't think any further.* I look over at her when the plane takes off to taxi and head to one end of the runway. "So, Lana, what do you do?"

She seems to be as agitated as I am. "I'm a professional makeup artist. I do makeup for a lot of photo shoots, and I was just hired on with Fox 5 News to do makeup for all of their anchors."

I gasp with as much excitement I can muster up. "Oh really? That's great. Maybe you can give me some tips?" I laugh.

"Oh, I'd love to, but your makeup is done beautifully. We should go have lunch some afternoon."

"I'd like that."

I look up at the sky and watch the plane take off with my boyfriend inside. My anxiety level just hit an all-time high and I start picking at my nails nervously. I'm mentally cursing Coen and Noah.

A thought occurs, and I just blurt it out. "You know . . . I don't think

I'm going to let those two hang out anymore."

"Yes, I agree, and I think that is an amazing idea. Are you joining us for drinks tonight with uh . . . Joe?"

"Joel." I smile and correct her. "Yes, I'm definitely needing drinks after this excursion. I never expected them to do this. Do you know just how . . . um . . . wild Coen is?" I try and make it sound not so bad.

"Wild? Uhm, well, sort of. I suppose not completely because it's only been two weeks. He's great, though. We met at a club when I wasn't the least bit sober. Of course he took me back to his place to . . . well, you know. He said he was just dumped and needed an escape. Unfortunately, I got incredibly ill before any of our clothes came off. So he just hung out with me for the rest of the night and made sure I was okay. So, yes, I know he's not the most romantic guy, but he cares. He truly cares in his own way."

Awww, Coen, I coo silently. "He is rather caring. You wouldn't know it to look at him because, well, he's awfully cocky. But he definitely has a big heart," I reply and look up at the sky, getting really anxious because I don't hear the plane anymore, only wind.

Shouldn't they have been down by now?

"Yeah, Coen told me about Dillen. He's actually been truly open and honest with me; I think that's why I'm really digging him," she admits, laughing. "Not to mention, he's smokin' hot!" she continues as she fans her face.

I turn and nervously ask her. "Shouldn't they have already jumped?"

She swallows hard and nods as she stands up, scanning the sky for them. "Yes, Heather, they should have been down by now."

My emotions are amped up, and I start to get teary-eyed. I once again think about my life without Noah. It would be pointless. He's everything to me. I would never be able to be with another man again. Nobody could ever compare to him—in any aspect. My heart frantically beats while I wipe my cheeks dry. My mascara is running, I'm sure, by the looks of my hand. I sniffle and look down at my feet, thinking about how I may never see him smile again. My streaming tears continue to fall, and I inhale deep breaths, trying to remain calm.

I can't. I just can't be without him. My earlier fears and apprehension of a marriage with him vanish. I want it. I want all of it with him.

Mine. My Noah, Noah as my husband. I want to have his baby. I want a family with him.

This revelation hits me so hard that it knocks the breath out of me. I hear Lana gasp, and I look over at her quickly. She's pointing to my right, and I see two parachutes headed toward us. My legs go weak and wobbly, and a huge smile breaks across my face.

"Oh," she cries out and reaches for my hand. "Let's go and get them," she squeals excitedly.

Even in my clumsy boot, I drop my purse right there and run. I don't feel any pain; I just run. To him, my boyfriend, my future. I wipe at my tears as I run with Lana, and they seem to land almost simultaneously. *Almost there, just a few more feet.* I almost sob when I crash into his chest and grip onto him. I'm clutching any part of him I can, and I can feel my body tremble.

"Oh my God, Noah, no, never again. I need you," I plead with him as I pepper his neck and jaw with my tear-drenched lips.

His arms lock around me with the parachute still strapped onto his strong, stable body. "Heather, I'm not going anywhere. I love the fuck out of you." He lifts me up, so I'm able to wrap my legs around his torso. "Hey, talk to me. What's going on?"

I can't stop sniffling and wiping at my tears, but I choke out what I need to say. "I want us. I want everything you want, maybe even more. I'm sorry it took me this long to realize it." I try to look at him through my wet lashes: his expression is blank, so I continue. "I don't want to live a life without you in it. I want everything, Noah. Everything." My breath catches on a hiccup, and I just stare.

I tolerate the discomfort in my boot as his smile lights up my world. This man has challenged almost every view or thing I believed in. He broke me down, and he has worn me on his chest proudly. I don't know how this relationship took off, but I know I'd rather have hard times with my Greek god than have to deal with them alone.

"Heather, my falling in love with you was inevitable. I'm going to be here because I love you, and when I say that, I mean it. It's not just filler, or words that are empty." He pauses to unclip something, his hand is back on me. "I need as much validation as you do, ballerina, and I will always give it to you. Now tell me why you're crying, huh?"

He runs his thumb over my cheek to dry it, but my tears are flowing steadily and a new black line forms in the wake of another.

"I thought I'd lost you."

"Lost me? Why would you have lost me?"

My tears finally start to slow, and I can see his gorgeous face. "I thought your plane crashed."

"Crashed? No baby, Coen had to piss so we went around in a circle so he could relieve himself in a fucking water bottle. I'm good, we're good."

"You swear it?"

"Yeah, I swear it. All of the bad that I've been through in life has been worth it all because in the end, you are simply the best thing that has happened to me. I get to be with the one woman who knows exactly how to send my world into chaos and fix it an instant later. Whether you see it or not, I know the depth of your love is intense and ardent. I'm not going anywhere, Heather Adalyn Lane."

I wrap my arms around him tighter than I think I ever have. "Do you . . ." I swallow and look into his eyes. "Do you still want me forever?"

"I've never stopped wanting you for forever."

He cups my face, placing his lips on mine, as he starts to kiss me painfully slowly.

Coen clears his throat, and Lana giggles innocently. I feel Noah's smile against my lips before he turns his head. "Too mushy for you, assfuck?"

Coen chuckles and makes a gagging sound, prompting Lana to smack his chest. "Coen, you jerk, let them enjoy each other." Coen straightens up as if he's been burnt by a scorching flame.

Noah pats my rear end to get my attention, and I turn to look at him. "You are in big trouble, little miss," he scolds.

"Why? What did I do?" I wipe at my mascara-stained cheeks.

He raises his eyebrow and sets me down.

"Were you not running at full speed just a minute ago?"

"Uhh . . . it doesn't hurt, I swear it."

"Don't push me, ballerina."

"I swear it."

"Don't let it happen again."

"I won't, I promise."

Lana and Coen walk over to us and her soft-spoken voice gets my attention, "Heather?"

"Yeah?"

"How would you feel about a little girl time? I can do your makeup for tonight."

Oh wow, how sweet is she?

I smile and laugh a little. "I'm sure I look like a mess, don't I? I'd really like that, Lana, thank you."

"Oh stop it, you are gorgeous. I can grab my things and meet you at your place, or you can come over to mine."

Noah kisses my cheek and sets me down on my feet.

"Whatever you'd like to do is fine with me."

I walk over to where Coen is smiling. He seems happy that Lana and I are getting along. He opens his arms to me as if he's expecting a hug, and I start smacking him on his chest hard with both hands.

"Coen, you stupid jerk! You're never doing that again!" I yell and smack him repeatedly while he tries to back away and cover himself.

"Whoa, little lady, I wasn't the one who brought up skydiving. Blame your boyfriend for that shit."

Lana laughs and goes over to stand next to Noah. I turn around and glare at him. "Ballerina . . . don't look at me like that."

"You're lucky you are my favorite pain in the ass," Coen says as he playfully takes a step back from me.

I turn back on him and point into his chest. "You guys had me scared to death! Never again."

He laughs and tries to hug me. "Awww, come on, sis. We weren't gone that long."

I shove his hands away and walk toward Noah and shove him too. "This was your stupid idea?" I glare and wait for his answer.

He surprises me by picking me up and throwing me over his shoulder, as he walks back to the building where he briefly sets me down to get his jumpsuit off. I walk over to where I was sitting with Lana and pick up my purse before heading toward our cars.

"Coen, do your guys have our chutes?"

"Yeah, don't worry about that shit. We'll meet you at Heather's place."

"Sounds good, fucker."

I'm raging mad: this entire time I thought this was Coen's doing.

As he opens the passenger side door, he sees my face and tries pre-emptive action. "It was my idea. Don't be pissed."

My nostrils flare at his admission, and I point my finger at his chest now. "Just so you know . . . you are not doing me up the butt now."

I turn and sit down in my seat and grab the door, effectively closing it on him. I'm mad, and he needs to know it. Still, a small part of me is happy it happened because it made me realize just how much I love him.

He stands outside looking in at me for a long minute before walking around and getting in the driver's seat. Silently, he starts the car and backs up before putting it in drive and heading in the direction of my apartment.

"I really like that ass of yours, though . . ."

I try my best to stay mad, so I refuse to look at him. If I look, I'll lose my nerve. He's just too stinking gorgeous. "Yeah? It's so not happening."

"I beg to differ, Heather."

I huff and look at my chipped nail polish. "Beg all you want," I mutter under my breath.

The bastard arrogantly reaches over and cups me between my legs.

I'm betrayed by my own body and my legs slightly open for him. Within an instant, I realize what he's trying to do, and I move his hands.

"Don't deny me my fun, gorgeous. You wouldn't want me denying you my cock."

"You had your fun today, remember?" I turn and look at him with an evil idea in mind. "And tonight I'll have my fun."

"Oh yeah? Will you now? I'm already looking forward to this."

He pulls into the apartment elevator, and it takes us up to my parking spot. I'm too busy formulating my plan to realize he's undoing my seatbelt and pulling me toward him. His hands glide up my neck and cup both sides of my face. Before I can try and pull back, his lips are on mine in a hurry. His tongue flicks the seam of my lips, coaxing me to open up for him.

I do.

I can't help but surrender myself to this Greek god. His lips move from mine and down my neck, nipping all the way down to my collarbone. I can barely breathe when his smoky, cool voice touches my skin, "We need to get ready. Lana and Coen will be here in a few minutes."

His voice is thick with lust, and my eyes flutter closed at the feel of his lips and teeth on my heated skin.

He takes in a deep breath and pulls back, as if it's the most painful thing he has ever had to do. Leaning back against the seat, he composes himself and attempts to rein in his monstrous erection. Then he gets out of the car and waits for me to join him before walking into the apartment with me.

Holy crap . . . what was that all about?

I walk directly into the kitchen and get out some wine glasses. I'm not sure if Lana likes wine or beer or shots, but I have it all. I'm trying to busy myself in the kitchen to keep from thinking about his lips on my body. I'm soaked between my legs, and it's highly distracting.

Noah walks into the living room and takes a seat on the couch as my cell phone rings, and it's my doorman. I quickly answer and tell him that I am indeed expecting guests. He asks me for their names, and I give him Coen and Lana's name, pausing when I realize that I don't know Lana's last name . . . *crap* . . . but he quickly thanks me and tells me that they are on their way up. I thank him before hanging up.

I walk over to the door and unlock it just in time to hear Coen's voice coming down the hall. He seems so happy, and I find myself happy for him. I open the door before he has a chance to knock, and I smile, welcoming Lana inside. "You, however, can stay out there." I direct my words at Coen, and he stares with his mouth open.

"Oh Heather . . . your apartment is gorgeous," Lana says.

I get distracted and Coen steals into the apartment and shuts the door.

"Thank you, Lana. If you can't tell, I love pink." I walk back into the kitchen and open the bottle of wine. "Would you like a drink? I have wine, beer, and hard liquor."

"I love pink, too, and if you have a sweet white wine, I'll take that, please."

She sets her large makeup bag down and walks over to the floor-to-ceiling windows. I watch as Coen joins her and snakes his arms around her from behind. She leans back against him comfortably, and they almost melt into each other. It's obvious that their feelings toward each other are intense, and I know exactly how it feels.

I feel my Greek god approach as I pour the wine. He stands beside me and runs his hand down my back to my butt, telling me he's ready to take me as soon as we are alone, but he's distracted. He's looking at his phone in his other hand.

"I just got this email." He holds his phone up so that I'm able to see and read over it quickly.

To: Noah Ryan
From: Henry Somer
IN RE: Meet-Up Date

Noah,
Ellery and I are delighted that you are back home in the States. We trust that your travels went well. We are available on the second weekend of May. We look forward to sharing our lives with you and would like to invite you to join us at our home in Southampton. Please let us know if this will work for you.

Well wishes,
Henry

I look up at him and smile softly. "So we're going then? Are you okay with that?"

"That's next weekend, correct?" He clicks on his calendar to confirm it and nods. "Yeah, I can do that." I watch him type out an email back to his father, and I smile when I feel his body relax.

I pour Lana and myself a glass of Risqué and walk over to her and Coen, handing her the glass.

"No beer for me, little lady?"

"Lana? Did you hear something?" I ask with sarcasm as I sip my wine and sit on the couch to take my boot off.

She giggles and shakes her head, deciding to play along with me. "Nope, I didn't hear a thing."

"That's what I thought."

Noah walks over and hands Coen a beer; they toast and each swallow a long drink.

I reach down and take my boot off. The throbbing I've felt for the last half-hour has intensified, and I reach for my purse. I don't normally take pain medication, but I really screwed up when I ran to Noah. "So where are we going tonight?" I ask of nobody in particular while I take the medicine.

"We can head to Marquee," Coen offers.

I nod and look over at Lana. "Is that okay with you, Lana? I'm fine with whatever. I just need to shower and get ready."

"That works for me. Would you mind if I came up and got ready too? I brought my stuff, in case Coen wanted to get ready at his place."

I am feeling an instant friendship connection with her. It would be great to have a girlfriend to do things with, since I don't have my Dill. "Of course, you can use the other bathroom if you need to shower." I look over at Noah and Coen, both seem to be checked out and playing on their phones.

"That'd be wonderful, thank you," she says politely and grabs her things before going to the bathroom down the hall.

"I'll be up to join you soon, ballerina. I need to make sure Coen doesn't fucking cheat at this game."

"Okay, boys, have fun with that." I stand up and walk past them. I decide to try and walk upstairs without my boot to test my foot. It's weak but doesn't feel too bad. If we're going out tonight, there's no way I'm wearing that stupid boot. I make it upstairs and undress before stepping into the shower, wondering if this thing between Coen and Lana is more than a fling.

I'm about to finish up in the shower when the door opens, and my naked Greek god walks in. "Damn . . ." he mutters as I bend over to finish shaving my legs.

I look up and for some reason become incredibly shy. I can wash in front of him, but shaving my legs—that's another story. I suck it up and make quick work of finishing my legs, and I turn around and face him. He's staring at where my butt was. "Don't even think about it, mister."

"Oh, I'm thinking about it, ballerina." He starts washing his tanned skin and pecs. "What do you think about Lana?"

I smile and start washing my body. "She's certainly sweet; I like her a lot." I caress my breasts with my loofah and watch his eyes darken a little more. With my plan solidified and set into action, I turn around and step back into him. "Can you get my back, please?" I ask innocently and hold out the soapy loofah.

"What are your thoughts on her?" I ask and wait for him to wash me.

I can physically feel his mood shift. *Holy crap, I've brought on a thunderstorm.* He takes the loofah and runs it across the back of my shoulders first.

"She's nice . . ." are the only words I get from him. He seems to be concentrating on me and me alone. I smile to myself, knowing I'm getting to him.

"Do you think she's right for him?"

"Huh?" He runs the loofah down to my butt and lets out a held-in breath.

I take another step back and feel his length against my soapy rear end. His breath catches, and I rub against him. Turning my head, I look over my shoulder at him. He's looking down at where our bodies are touching. "*I said* . . . is she right for him?"

"I'm going to be honest with you right now. I haven't heard a fucking word you have said." His eyes are dark, and his voice is thick with lust.

"Yeah?" I ask coyly and grind my butt into him, making sure his shaft is snug between my cheeks; I bring my arm up and around his neck to pull him from his daze

His cock flexes and hardens further. "This ass is mine. I'll fucking take it whenever I want. Is that clear?"

I angle my head and press my lips to his, sucking on his bottom lip as I moan and rub up against him. "Mmm . . ." I reply before adding, "I don't think so." I bite down on his lip and tug, before pulling my body away from his. I peek back, and he seems as if he's going to combust.

His body stands there, rigid and wanton. "Have your fun now, ballerina, but that ass will be mine when you least expect it."

I watch him rinse the soap off of his body and hear the rumble in the back of his throat, and I know, without a doubt, that he is dead serious.

I still feel like I've won this little battle between us, so I step out of the shower after rinsing off and pull on my satin robe. "I'll be downstairs with Lana getting ready."

"Keep that pussy warm for me," he calls from the shower, and I shut my bedroom door.

I laugh softly and walk downstairs, knocking on the bathroom door.

"Lana? It's Heather. I'm ready when you are."

I hear giggling behind the door, and then I realize Coen is nowhere to be found. Moments later, the door opens and Coen steps out with a grin plastered on his face.

"You always ruin my fun, Heather," he jokes and walks into the kitchen.

Lana is still giggling when I walk in.

"Hmmm," I say with a smile when I shut the door behind me. "You two look awfully cute together."

I know I should stick by Dillen's side, but if I'm being honest, they really do. I watch her blush as I run the wide-tooth comb through my hair.

"He makes me laugh quite a bit," she replies and leans forward to finish her eye shadow.

I smile and sit down on the vanity stool. "Well, that's always a plus. Laughter is good."

I'm wondering if she and I are actually talking about the same Coen. The only side of Coen I've seen is the hornball. Well, there was that one night when he helped take care of Noah with me.

"He's great, and I think this could actually lead to something, if I'm honest. I mean, we haven't had sex yet—not in the strict sense of the word—and he's been asking to see me almost every day after work."

I try to keep my composure but inside I'm freaking out.

Umm, excuse me? No sex? With Coen?

"Wow. Really? That's . . . well, that's great, Lana."

She smiles and turns to me, wiggling her fingers. "All done. Now let me get at that pretty face of yours." She instantly switches into work mode and starts matching my shade to her array of foundations.

"Okay, so your skin is, like, flawless, Heather, so I'm going to use a little foundation on you. But first, I start with the eyes. I absolutely loathe eye shadow fallout." She talks while she gets her brushes out, and I'm rather impressed. Normally when I have my makeup done, the artist just does it without really talking or explaining anything.

"What are you wearing tonight, by the way?"

"Umm, I think I'm going to opt for this black outfit that I've yet to wear. Noah hasn't seen it, so I think I'm going with that," I reply as she gently tilts my chin up with her fingers and starts to apply a primer onto my eyelids.

"Okay, cool, so we can go with any color really. How do you feel about shimmer? Or do you want more of a bold statement?"

"Oh, I love shimmer. Can we do a little of both?" I ask, and she smiles.

"Girl, I can do whatever you want."

A half-hour passes and she's completely done applying the makeup. She picks out a lighter lip gloss because she went darker on my eyes. "Do you like this color?"

I turn to look and am blown away by the emerald green color. It's bold, with a matching green shimmer over it. It's so sultry that I'm in complete awe of her work.

"Holy crap, Lana. You are freaking awesome. I love it."

She smiles at me in the mirror. "You are most welcome. Now go get this little outfit on; I can't wait to see it."

I stand and hug her briefly. The connection I feel with her is considerably sisterly, and it reminds me that I need to text or call my own sister. "Okay, you get dressed too. I'll be down shortly." I open the bathroom door and sneak past Noah and Coen who are sitting on the couch watching an action movie of sorts.

⸎

I descend down the two flights of stairs cautiously once I'm dressed, trying to not aggravate my foot. I walk lightly into the living room to where the three of them are sitting. "Is everyone ready to go?"

"Heather . . ." Lana gasps and applauds excitedly when she sees me.

She's wearing gold-glittered cropped pants and a loose fitting black button-down, which she has tucked into the waistband of her pants. The solid black heels she has on ties the look together; she looks undeniably breathtaking. I can now see why Coen is holding onto her.

Noah stands up and walks over to me. His eyes stare at mine and gradually work their way down my body.

"Holy fuck." His voice is almost a snarl as he stops right in front of me. His stormy eyes immediately fall to the V-shaped notch cut out of my top, lingering there for a moment before they move down my black jumpsuit, to my emerald green Volpi Louboutins.

His eyes narrow, and I do my best to hide my smile. "No, Heather, you can't wear those." His voice is scolding as he looks up at me.

"Oh boy," I hear Coen say in the background.

Lana giggles. "Noah, she looks divine, so don't you be a downer."

"She's going to fuck up her foot. Heather, you can't. As fucking sexy as you look, I don't want you to hurt yourself."

"I promise I won't dance, okay?" There is no way in hell I'm wearing that boot with this outfit, and I'll fight him tooth and nail on this one.

Lana gets up and walks over to us. "Noah, let her have one night where she gets to feel utterly ravishing."

I can see it in his eyes the moment he gives in, and it makes me smile. "Thank you, baby." I place a small kiss on his lips and pat his hard chest before walking over to grab my clutch.

"Who's calling for a cab?"

"It's already downstairs waiting," Coen says as he takes Lana's hand. I still can't believe that he hasn't had sex with her; I really need to tell Noah.

"You guys go on down; we'll be right behind you." I crook my finger at Noah and take the last swallow from my wine. I am so sexually aroused by the way Noah looks. I knew I would be, so I decided to go this evening without panties on, without shame. I watch him as he takes a drink from his beer and stalks toward me as I hear the front door close.

"Ballerina, you are truly killing me this evening. You look stunning, and I can't wait to show you off to every single person we come in contact with tonight." He snakes his arm around my waist and pulls me against his chest. He's wearing a dark blue button-down with a solid black tie and a textured grey vest. I run my hands from his lower torso up to his sturdy pecs.

"Why, thank you, handsome. She did a great job on my makeup, right?" I lower his hand down to my butt, inviting him to take me.

His fingers cup my cheeks, and I can feel his cock start to harden against my stomach. "She did great. Damn, I could stare at you all night."

I look down as my cheeks scorch from his sweet words. He tilts my chin up and presses his lips to my jaw. "I don't want to ruin your lipstick."

I tilt my face to his and kiss him softly. "You couldn't possibly ruin anything. Now . . . kiss me like you mean it."

The electricity crackles between us as he pushes his lips to mine, kissing me slowly, reverently, and lovingly. He hums his approval and pulls me closer to his muscled body. "You'll let me know if you need to get off of your foot, won't you?"

"Of course I will." I slip my tongue into his mouth for a brief moment. "I plan on sitting on your lap all night anyway."

His hands squeeze my cheeks, telling me he wants me too. "I like the sound of that. Are you ready to go?"

"I am." I turn and grab my clutch. "Oh, and by the way . . . Coen hasn't slept with Lana yet."

The expression on his face is one of complete shock. I think I might have just knocked the breath out of him. "Excuse me?"

I nod and walk to the door, pulling it open. "Yep. No sex."

"Are we talking about the same assfuck here?" He laces his fingers with mine as we walk to the elevator and head down to my building's lobby.

"The one and only."

We get outside to the waiting cab, and I'm about to open the door when I turn and look up at Noah. "Oh . . . and baby . . ." I lean up and whisper in his ear, "I'm not wearing a bra . . . or panties." I smile innocently and lick his earlobe before patting his chest and getting in the cab without another word.

He straightens up before sliding into the cab and sitting next to me. Lana and Coen are sitting in the row behind us, I turn around to them, and Lana is wearing the reddest of blushes; we must have caught them doing something or other.

"Heather?" she asks. "What size shoes do you wear? Because I am so stealing those heels."

"Six and a half," I say, beaming. "Let me know when you want to wear them." I sit back and look over at Noah: he's staring down at me, barely blinking. "What?"

"You fucking tease."

Mission accomplished, Heather. I place my hand on his thigh, deciding to push him further.

We arrive at Marquee and Noah pays for the ride. We get out, and Joel is the first person I see waiting by the door. "Well, look at this cab full of assholes," I hear him say above the sound of the music coming from the open club doors.

"Ah, there's the dipshit." Noah chuckles and walks over to him, shaking his hand roughly before they both pat each other's shoulders.

I wait off to the side while the guys talk shit to each other. It tugs at my heartstrings to see Noah with the guys, with all of us—his own little family.

I feel someone's hand on my elbow, and I look over to see Lana smiling. "Are you okay?" she asks.

"Oh, I'm fine. I was just thinking. When we go inside you are having a chocolate-covered pretzel shot on me."

Her eyes light up and she locks her arm with mine. "Oooh, that sounds good . . . and dangerous."

I laugh and nod. "They'll sneak up on you, for sure. I . . ." Suddenly, I'm interrupted by Coen when he walks up and leans over Lana, kissing her passionately and without warning.

Joel and Noah join us, and Joel leans in to hug me. "It's good to see you, girl. I'm glad you brought this motherfucker back."

I hug him back before looking up at him; what he doesn't know is that Noah brought me back. I look over at Noah knowingly, and he winks. *Well . . . good thing I'm not wearing panties or they'd be soaked already.*

"I'm glad we're back, Joel. What have you been up to?" I ask politely and try to ignore the hot make-out session going on beside me with Lana and Coen.

"I've been well. I'm looking forward to hearing about how the meeting with Noah's parents goes. Will you be joining him?"

"Yes, I wouldn't miss it for the world."

He smiles, and I notice that Noah's shoulders that were tense seem to relax the slightest bit. Oh Noah . . . no matter how many times I tell him I'm going, he still is so nervous that I'll change my mind.

"All right, enough of this business shit, Joel. Let's get some drinks into these ladies and try to pick one up for you . . . unless your dick is still hung up on Dill," Noah says and takes my hand, leading me through the door. Coen must be friends with the bouncer because I have no idea how we skipped that line.

Coen and Lana take a breath long enough to follow us inside, and all of us head straight toward the bar. I order us all one of my new favorite shots and stand in front of Noah. He slides his arms around my waist and kisses my neck gently.

"To answer your question, Ryan, I am not hung up on Dillen, and I don't think I need the help in finding a piece of ass," Joel comments and takes his shot, while Lana and Coen down theirs and move to the dance floor.

Noah and I take ours, and he hums deeply. "Damn, that was good."

I nod in agreement and look over at Joel as he slams his shot glass down on the bar.

"Shit, that was smooth."

"Joel?" I ask.

"Yeah?" He turns to face me, and grins.

"Thank you for helping Noah so much. Without your help, he would still be in Phoenix and living . . ." I stop myself because I don't want to turn on any emotions right now when we are supposed to be having an exciting night out.

"It's my job, Heather, and I've enjoyed helping him find himself." He looks at Noah and smirks. "This asshole would be lost without me."

"Damn right I would be," my Greek god interjects.

"If you'll both excuse me, that redhead across the bar has been making fuck-me eyes at me, and I think I just found who I'll be taking home tonight."

I can't control my laughter from his comment. Noah and I follow his eyes, and we both look at the radiant auburn-haired woman across the bar from us. She's stunning, tall, and lively.

Noah leans into Joel and says something to him. I can't hear what is being said because the music is blaring and thundering through my body.

Mmm, thundering through me. I know someone who knows how to do it better.

Joel chuckles and winks at me before walking through the throng of people to the other side of the bar. It's just my Greek god and I now, and I feel powerful knowing that I have a sort of control over him and his monstrous sex drive right now.

"Heather?" he croons and moves his hands over the material of my black jumpsuit. "I'm having a difficult time keeping my hands off of your body. You're turning heads this evening."

"Are you telling me that I'm easy on the eyes, Ryan?"

"I'm telling you that you look good enough for me to eat."

Deliberately slowly, I tease him by pushing my breasts up. By just watching me he seems mesmerized, snared in a trance, my trance. I flush at the storm I see brewing in his ocean green eyes: they suck me in and consume me. Pressing my body to his warm, firm chest, I run my hands up the back of his strong neck into his hair. His growl that I feel instead of hear is intense; it reverberates through me and sends chills down to the deepest places of my body.

He leans into me and moves my dark, straightened hair off of my shoulder and to my back, so he can place his mouth on my collarbone. His feverish lips move along my skin, bringing to life our magnetic allure to each other.

"How about we forget about this night out and head back to your apartment? I want to show you just how much you're going to enjoy my cock between these ass cheeks."

I gasp loudly as his hands squeeze and caress my behind. I'm about to cave and tell him to take me anywhere he needs me, but suddenly Lana is beside me and bumps my hips with hers. We're about the same height, so it works perfectly to bring me back to my senses.

"Are you two ready to take another shot?"

Noah gawks at me and I can see the sensual storm that was brewing behind his eyes has now turned into a lightning storm, filled with intense anguish. I bite the inside of my cheek as I slide my hands down Noah's chest. "I think that's the best idea you've had all night, Lana."

She does a little happy dance and I think orders two shots of tequila for all of us.

"Oh, Joel went to talk to that woman over there. I don't think he's going to be back in time to take his."

"That's not a problem. We'll have the extra two then."

"I like your thinking."

Noah removes one of his hands from my butt when Coen moves to stand next to him. "Coen . . ." I hear him say.

"What's up?" Coen replies.

"When the fuck were you going to tell me that you've yet to get your dick wet with this one?"

I quickly glance over at Lana, but she's preoccupied as she watches the bartender pour ten shots of tequila.

Coen laughs and places his hand on Noah's shoulder. "I don't think I'm going to push this one. I thought I had my shit in control when I was in London with Dillen, but then I met Wilde, and hell . . . my dick has never been more interested, but neither has my heart."

I almost *aww* out loud.

Lana asks the bartender to open a tab for her. I'll have to tell her later how Coen feels toward her, but I'm sure she already knows.

"Shit, man, I'm almost proud of you . . . and Wilde?"

"Thanks, fucker. Yeah, my Wilde girl. Lana Jayne Wilde." Coen looks across Noah and I to Lana, and I can tell he's dying to be close to her. He quickly moves around us and circles his arms around her petite waist as she pulls out her credit card to hand to the bartender. She giggles as Coen takes the card before the bartender can. He fishes for his wallet in his pants pocket and removes his credit card to hand to the bartender before giving Lana hers back.

Her radiant smile must send Coen into a head-spin because he almost loses his center of gravity.

Lana tucks her card into her clutch and fetches out the lip gloss she used on me earlier. She hands it to me and I apply some before handing it back to her. "Thank you."

The bartender sets the ten shots in front of Lana. "Okay, guys, here we go." She hands Noah and Coen two each, me three, and keeps three for herself.

"To new adventures and remarkable people," she declares.

"To my family," Noah says, holding up one of his shot glasses.

"Heather, do them back to back with me," Lana insists and I can't refuse.

All four of us simultaneously throw our shots back and we all chase the shot with our second and then Lana and I take our third.

Oh crap, I am going to feel this.

"Damn ballerina, the only thing I've seen you swallow like that is me."

I blush bright enough to light up the darkened club. *Holy crap.*

"Noah," I try and scold him, but I can't because that was so erotic.

Lana giggles, and I know she heard what my Greek god just said. She stops and smiles at me. "Oh my God, Heather . . . I love this song. You have to come and dance with me," she says excitedly as *Going Down For Real* by Flo Rida resounds through the club's speakers, bringing the dance floor to life.

I glance up at Noah questioningly, and he shakes his head. "No way in hell. We had a deal, remember?"

"Please . . ." I try again before reaching down to stroke the front of his jeans. He grunts and closes his eyes as his nostrils flare. I can tell he just made a snap decision.

"You have this one song. Go."

I throw my arms around his neck and kiss him heatedly before Lana pulls me by my elbow off of him and to the dance floor. Following her quickly before Noah can change his mind, I start moving my body to the music, Lana swaying right next to me. With every movement of my body I realize how much I've missed dancing. Lana and I throw ourselves into this song and drink up all we can of the vibrations that rattle our frames.

Before I know it another song is filling our ears, and I can't see Noah anywhere. We've somehow moved to the middle of the dance floor. Neither of us stop moving. I reach out for her and hug her close. "Thank you, I've missed this so much," I tell her quickly before a strong hand rests on my shoulder. *Ah crap, I'm busted.*

"I'm so excited to be out with you guys," she says before a voice interrupts us.

"Heather?" I turn around quickly and into Joel's smile.

"Oh hey," I say, beaming at him.

"Here, I got you two these." He hands Lana and I a shot, and I look at the odd-colored liquid in the glass. Lana reaches for a glass and blows Joel a kiss.

"What is this?"

"Shit, I don't know. Red ordered it. I think she said it was a Vegas Bomb? I have no fucking idea what's in it, but before I could ask, her boyfriend showed up. I acted as if I were uninterested and left with the shots. He believes he got me to leave, but what the pussy doesn't know is that he's going home alone tonight." A cocky grin that I haven't seen before emerges, and Lana and I stare at him in surprise.

"Joel!" we both say and giggle in surprised shock.

Lana moves closer to the two us. "A Vegas Bomb?" she yells above the music.

"Yeah, that's what she said."

"Yum, it's just Malibu rum, peach schnapps, Red Bull, and a shot of Crown Royal," she says without having to even think about it, but then quickly explains, "I used to be a bartender."

"That sounds dangerous." I waver before taking it, but toast her anyway before downing the shot.

She smiles and starts dancing again once she's finished it. "Do you like it?"

I lick my lips in delight and throw my arms up as I start to move my body to the beat vibrating through me. "I love it."

Joel is texting on his phone and before I know it, Noah is in my line of sight, Coen moving through the crowd right behind him. He must be having a good time, because when he reaches me, he wraps me in his arms and lifts me, colliding his lips with mine.

Coen moves around us, pulling Lana to his body, and starts moving with her to the beat of the addicting music.

I smile against Noah's lips and bite. "Well, hello, did you miss me?"

"Damn right I did. How's your foot? Be honest with me; I won't fare well with a lie from those lips of yours."

My heart melts at his concern for me, and I continue to realize I was such a fool to think otherwise. "I need to sit down," I admit and look up to meet his eyes, hoping he doesn't get mad.

His smile is almost triumphant as he sets me down and leads me back to the bar where he finds a solitary empty barstool. He helps me up onto it and spins me around, making me face him. "Does that help?"

"Yes, thank you." I feel instant relief the moment I'm off of my feet.

"What would you like to drink?" Noah raises his hand to get the bartender's attention, and I'm not surprised he gets first priority over everyone else at the bar. The female bartender leans against the bar top, showcasing her breasts for my man.

I feel a hot surge of jealousy course through my veins. "Surprise me."

He asks her for a French martini for me, and a beer for himself before turning back to me. She walks away and he takes my mouth slowly, showing her that he's mine.

A few moments later the bartender loudly places our drinks on the bar top. Noah hands his card over, but doesn't stop looking at me. Materializing out of the crowd behind us, Joel smacks Noah on the back. "Hey fucker, I'm going to steal your girl for a dance, regardless of what you say. I need to piss off Red."

I look up at Noah with interest. *How is this going to go?*

"Keep your hands to yourself, and you've got yourself a dance, dipshit."

He laughs and fist bumps Noah. "I promise nothing, dickhead." He grabs my wrist and pulls me from my stool.

Noah winks at me, and mouths, "I love you."

I beam at him as I'm dragged out to the dance floor. Taken by surprise when Joel gets behind me, I laugh. Though I can't see much in the dark of the club, I can feel his resilient form pressed up against my back. He's setting aside the FBI stereotype and taking on an entirely different demeanor, demanding control of my movements when he grinds his hips into my behind.

Oh shit, I had no idea.

He leans down and shouts so I can hear, "I'm taking her home tonight, mark my words."

I giggle and start dancing with him, trying not to put too much weight on my bad foot.

I know that his hands are on my hips but I don't feel that he's being the slightest bit sexual. I look over and see the redhead staring at us. "Joel, she's watching you. Turn it up a little, whisper in my ear or something,"

I shout over my shoulder at him.

He takes my advice and leans down. "What the hell am I supposed to be whispering? Maybe something like Noah is going to fucking eat me alive?"

That makes me laugh so hard and my head falls back against his shoulder. "Joel! Oh my God, that was hysterical." I continue to dance against him, and he laughs with me.

"No, seriously, Heather, you're going to get my ass kicked."

"Well, I hope it'll be worth it."

I turn to see where his redheaded conquest went, and when I turn back she is standing right in front of me. *Holy crap.*

"Can I cut in?" she shouts in my ear, and I look back up at Joel.

He winks down at me, and I smile before taking a step toward her. I grab her upper arms and lean into her.

"From what I can tell . . . he's hung," I say so only she can hear before I walk back to my man who's been watching me the entire time.

"Nice show, ballerina," he says as he kisses my neck.

"Yeah? Maybe I should become a famous actress instead of dancing?" I say as I reach around him and grab my martini.

"No, I like watching you dance. You're damn good at it and it's when you're the happiest."

"That's not true. It used to be when I was happiest."

"Used to?" he asks over the music before helping me up onto the barstool.

My smile widens, and I pucker my lips, wanting a kiss. "Now I'm happiest when I'm with you."

His rigid arms tighten around me and he kisses me slowly, passionately. "I love you, Heather Lane."

"And I love you. So tell me . . . were you about to kill Joel?" I ask with a smile.

He chuckles. "Were? Mmm, ballerina, I still am."

I laugh, and my head falls back. "Noah, stop. No, you're not." I smack his hard chest and bite at my lip before adding, "He's your friend."

"A friend who owes me one, big time. Are you ready to go so I can see that naked ass again, or would you like to hang out with Lana some more?"

The alcohol that's flowing through my veins has me extremely horny, and I look over and try to find Lana. "I don't see her, do you?"

He glances around the club and frowns, shaking his head. He pulls out his phone and opens up a text from Coen:

> *Hey dipshit, I'm taking my Wilde girl home. My dick may or may not be wet by the time you are reading this.*

I gasp and cover my mouth. *God, that boy is filthy.*

"It looks like I'm taking you home, Lane."

I almost drop my drink when those words come out of his mouth. Everything about that screamed Nik.

He frowns and cups my cheek. "What's wrong?"

I quickly recover and shake my head, murmuring "Nothing at all." I clear my throat and smile. "Can we go to a private booth and have one more drink?"

"Okay, one more, then we go." He leans over the bar and asks the bartender for bottle service at a private table. She smiles and tells him to follow her.

My lip curls up and I internally hiss like a cat. I hear Noah chuckle and turn back to me. "Be nice," he playfully scolds.

Whoops, that was out loud, I think.

I start to laugh at myself. "It was the alcohol."

"Good excuse. That ass better be sitting on my lap when we get our booth."

"Mmm, yes, sir," I manage to reply as I look at his tush. Suddenly I'm remembering a similar scenario just a few months back.

"What bottle of liquor do you want?"

I keep following behind him with our fingers laced.

"Heather?"

"Hmmm?" I'm staring in a dreamy haze. I can just see his naked butt right now. It's so tight and . . .

He turns and looks at me. "Ah, taking in the view, huh?"

I look up and am so incredibly turned on by his cockiness. We're finally taken to a booth that's nearly secluded, and he guides me in first. He slides in after me and asks for a bottle of Grey Goose.

I barely wait for him to settle in when I sidle up next to him.

"This seems familiar."

"It does, doesn't it?" I say.

His arms come around me and pull me onto his lap where he nuzzles my neck and breathes me in slowly. "Damn, I want to be buried inside of you."

I can feel his length underneath me already, and I'm dripping wet. "Yeah? How bad?"

"You have no fucking idea how bad. Ever since my cock slid between your tight ass cheeks, I've been visualizing my balls slapping against the curve of your pretty little ass."

My breath catches and I'm cursing myself for not wearing a dress. I boldly take his hand and place it between my legs. I can hear him groan against my neck, and it makes me feel powerful.

"You're rather enjoying teasing me tonight, Heather."

I lie against his chest and move my hand on top of his. "Touch me . . ." I breathe out. My entire body is buzzing from all of the alcohol.

He slides his hand down the inside of my thigh and over the material of my outfit to my sex.

I moan and turn my head, grinding my butt against his length. It may be the alcohol or just my good mood, but I really, really want him to take me there. "Oh God, that feels good."

Our waitress comes with our bottle and pours us each a shot. Noah stills his hand and kisses me slowly, pushing his tongue between my lips and licking my teeth.

I pull back and smile drunkenly at him, grabbing both our shots and handing one to Noah. "I have a secret to tell you."

"Tell me right now. Or I'll take my belt off right here and show you why you shouldn't tease me in public."

My entire being ignites, and I become highly aroused at the thought. My eyes are bright with excitement as I hold my shot against my lips. "Would you really?"

"That would depend. Would you let me lick that pretty ass of yours?"

I take my shot for a little more liquid courage, and I lick my lips, looking right into his eyes. "Well, that's what my secret is about." I watch as his eyes flicker from my lips to my deep cleavage and back again.

"Tell me," he says firmly.

I bring my lips close to his and let it all out. *Here we go.*

"I want you to fuck my ass, Noah. I want you to fuck it with your tongue and your cock."

His cock almost pierces my jumpsuit. "Holy fuck."

I bite down on my lip nervously, afraid I've said too much in my drunken state.

"I'll be taking you up on that invite; are you ready to go and pay into the swear jar? You're giving me blue balls."

"Wait . . . you haven't even taken your shot." I stay firmly planted on his lap and watch the room spin. He reaches for the shot, I think, and brings it to his lips before he sets it down and pours himself another and downs it.

I smile and start to laugh. "Get drunk with me." I lean down and run my tongue along his neck. "Mmm, please, baby . . . get drunk with me and then take me home and tongue fuck my ass."

I think I've caught him by surprise because his eyebrows shoot up, and instead of taking his shot he picks up the bottle and drinks straight from it. "We need to leave. Now."

Before I can even protest, he's got me off his lap and tucked into his side, walking me to the bar. I watch as he closes out his tab and anxiously signs his name. He tucks his wallet away and leads me out to the line of cabs waiting outside the doors.

I don't know if it's because I'm drunk, but I swear I can feel him shaking beside me. *Is it cold outside and I'm too drunk to notice?* I look around at the other girls in dresses and miniskirts, and they seem just fine. And then it hits me: a thunderstorm is brewing, and I'm about to be in for the ride of my life.

Chapter Fourteen

LEWD COBALT

HEATHER

The next week passes slowly in anticipation for the weekend. I didn't realize that the second weekend in May was so soon. Crap, I need to start packing since we're leaving Friday night—tomorrow night. Noah has been attending his bar prep course and studying like it's what he needs to survive. I can't tear him away from his books, but I think he might be using them as a temporary escape. It's the one place where he is so consumed by the information before him that he doesn't have to worry about the pressure of meeting his parents.

I have my first meeting with my physical therapist when we get back on Monday, and I'm excited to find out what he has to say. I cannot wait to get back into my pointe shoes and hike my leg up onto the barre.

However, I have been hiking my leg up for Noah lately. The night we went out with Lana, Coen, and Joel . . . he brought me home, and we both passed out, but he woke me up a few hours later and took me from behind as I lay against his hard body.

I've been having a difficult time sleeping so I roll over and groan, ensuring that I am loud enough for him to hear.

He glances over his shoulder at me and holy . . . whenever he wears his glasses it catches me off guard, every single time without fail.

"Are you okay? Do you need me to get your medication?"

I push myself up with my tired arms; I'm so exhausted that my body aches. I realize I must be a sleepy mess because a grin plays at his face, and I can't explain how he makes me feel.

"I need you . . ." I try to entice him to come to bed with me.

"You are so easily and naturally beautiful. I'd rather be with you than with these notes right now."

I watch as his muscles move, shifting under his skin as he takes his glasses off and sets them in their brown leather case. He gets up and comes to sit on my side of the bed, instead of his. He lies down in the space between the length of my body and the edge of the bed. In that space, he pulls me on top of his chest and cups my face. Ever so gently he presses his lips to mine, and I dissolve at his touch. Our legs automatically tangle together as our lips part company, and I lay my head down on his bare chest.

I draw in a heavy breath, taking in as much of him as I can before I let it out slowly, "I missed you."

"Mmm, I noticed. You were tossing and turning."

"See, you should have come to me earlier. I don't sleep well without you anymore."

His chest vibrates when his low chuckle fills the room. "If that's the case, which it seems to be lately, what would you say to moving in together?" His chest stops moving as if he's stopped breathing completely, or he's holding his breath.

My heart does a flip inside my chest, and I'm now fully awake. *Move in together?* The old me is momentarily frightened for a second before the new me takes over. *Yes, Heather, you love this man with everything you have. You know how you feel, and you know what the answer is.* This internal battle seems to last minutes, but really it's instantaneous. I lift my head and look up into his eyes, his wary, cautious eyes.

"I'd love that, Noah."

Relief floods his features as his chest expands, and he allows himself a breath. "Fuck, I'm not even going to ask if you're sure and risk you changing your answer," he spits out before rolling me onto my back and pressing my tired, sore body into the pillow-top mattress.

"The things you do to me, Heather. You knock me off of my feet."

The biggest smile forms on my face, and I search his eyes. "I stayed because I hoped I'd see you again," I say softly.

I see confusion flood his face. "What do you mean?"

"In Phoenix, after we saw each other at the drive-in. I wanted to see you again, so I stayed in hopes that we'd run into each other."

"I'm glad you did that," he admits as he pulls the covers over our heads to kiss me slowly.

I smile against his lips and wrap my arms around his neck.

"Mmm, you could have ravished me at the drive-in, and I wouldn't have cared."

"Is that right? Shit, I couldn't believe my luck when I saw you . . . and those shorts . . . fuck."

I laugh and lock my legs around his waist. "You liked those, huh?"

"Damn right I did. Do you still have them? I'd like to get you in the shower with those. Fuck, that white material would look great wet and plastered to your ass."

I can't help but laugh at his comment. "Yes, I still have them."

His cock springs to life on top of me and I reach my hand down and under his pajama bottoms, wrapping my fingers around his shaft to give him some relief.

"My place or yours?" he asks.

I shake my head slightly as I glide my hand down his silky yet stiff shaft. "I don't care, baby; I'll do whatever." My eyes stay focused on the massive erection in my hands as my mouth waters.

God, could he be any more perfect?

And he's all mine . . .

"Well, I prefer your bed. And moving your closet would be the biggest fucking task, so I can move my shit in here."

At this moment, he could tell me he's throwing out my nail polish collection, and I wouldn't care. Having this man on top of me and in my hands keeps me from caring about much.

"Whatever you want . . . just shut up and put this in my mouth."

I give him a long, hard stroke and look up at his face.

His tortured moan resonates with the high ceilings in my room—our room now. He lies on his back again, allowing me to move over him and take the head of his thick shaft into my mouth.

"Mmm . . . you are going to enjoy this," I say as I pull him from my mouth for a deep breath.

"Fuck, Heather."

I usually tease him before I slide down and clamp my mouth around his cock, but I can't resist him this time. I want to take what he has in store for me. I trace my finger down the muscled V leading down to his thunderous cock, all the way down to his balls. I cup them lightly until a light shiver runs up his spine. He waits patiently for my mouth again. *Holy crap, what other man waits like he does? He always thinks of me first.*

I slide my free hand down my stomach and under my pajama pants to my sex. I slide a finger into myself as I hold his cock up and place my mouth around his head. He's told me before that having both my hand and mouth on him is his unparalleled favorite. I pull his cock deeper into my mouth until he hits the back of my throat, and then slowly slide my mouth back up to the swollen head. I wrap my thumb, index, and middle finger around his shaft as my mouth works his tip. I lube up my hand with the pre-come that is dripping down his shaft as I start to move.

I can feel his eyes on me while I'm down here so I gaze up at him as I finger myself, giving him a show that he'll enjoy. I'm deliberately slow as I flick my tongue against the frenulum. I love sucking him; I love showing him the pure high I get from doing this, giving him such pleasure. I decide to make this show a little more interesting. I pull my finger out of myself and manage to get my pajama pants off with one hand as I run my tongue down the thick vein on the underside of his shaft. I have ample power over this Greek god as he lies there in crippling pleasure.

I sit up briefly and lift my butt, pulling my panties off. I hold the sheer white lace material up for him to admire before I move between his legs this time. I bite the inside of my cheek as I slide the lace material up over his cock, in one of the holes my legs go through. I leave them there, at the base of his thick erection and take him into my mouth again. His cock jerks in my mouth, and I know I've done it. I've pleased him so entirely, and he hasn't even had the pleasure of coming yet. I toss my long, straight hair to one side so he can see his shaft moving in and out from my lips.

My hand is back on him, meeting my mouth as I apply more pressure and suck that much harder. His growl rips through the room, and I moan in return, sending acute vibrations down his thick, veined gift. My breasts move as I pick up my pace. He reaches down and holds my hair back in order to have a clear and flawless view of my mouth and breasts. Instead of surrendering my mouth to him, this time I stay in control and wait excitedly for his warm spurts of pleasure to roll down my throat. My panties are hanging around his cock like it's his trophy, my triumphant Greek god. I bare my teeth the slightest bit as I move back up to his cock head. I suck him all the way to the tip before I daringly bite down.

He hisses through his teeth before warm, sea-salty liquid jets into my mouth. His long ropes of come slide down my throat, and I swallow what I can of him before he spews out of my lips and back down his shaft.

His once stiff, on-edge body relaxes, and he lays his head back against my pillow as his chest heaves for breaths of cool air.

"Fuck."

I feel victorious inside, knowing I can bring him to his knees. It's the greatest feeling in the world. I remove his heavy shaft from my mouth and leave my panties dangling around his base as I crawl up his body. "I enjoyed that."

He opens his eyes and runs his fingers into my hair. "Baby, you enjoyed that too fucking much. I'm scared for your sanity."

I move my legs to either side of his torso and straddle him. "Don't you worry your cock for one second."

He draws in a deep breath. "Fuck . . . say that again."

"Cock."

"Mmm, damn, I almost love hearing that come out of your mouth as much as I love watching my come spill from those swollen lips."

I glance over at the clock on my nightstand, and it reads 1:43 A.M.

"Get on your back, ballerina. It's your turn."

I shake my head and kiss him slowly. "We're not a tit-for-tat couple, Noah. Plus, it's late, and you have to be up in a few hours."

His hand moves from my hair and cups my cheek. I lean into his touch, closing my eyes as he whispers, "You are one hell of a woman, Heather."

"You have one hell of a cock," I mumble sleepily.

He chuckles lightly, and we adjust ourselves so I am once again in my spot. I feel his chest rumble as he laughs at my crude comment. I finally feel comfortable enough to fall asleep, and I'm moments from drifting off when I yawn.

"Oh and baby? I'm getting a new roommate tomorrow, so I'll need you to make some space in the closet, okay?"

"Damn, there's hardly any room in there for me; you're going to have to clean that shit out," he jokes—I hope—as he wraps me in his arms for the night.

I can't decide what I'm more excited about: the fact that Noah will be reunited with his birth parents or our first road trip together. I have bought so many snacks for this trip that I'm pretty sure one of us will have a stomachache before we get there but I don't let that stop me, stuffing all of it into the bag. Noah's been moody this past week, which I'm sure has something to do with his bar prep course. I'm hoping I can make him forget about everything on our way there. The smile I have plastered on my face widens when I hear my front door open and close. I know without a doubt that it's him; I can hear his slow heavy stride walking down the hall.

"Ballerina?" he calls out before walking into my bedroom.

I quickly move across the room and jump into his waiting arms. He catches me, lifting me off of my feet, so I can wrap my legs around his firm torso. His strong hands shape around my butt and I excitedly circle my arms around his neck, plastering my lips to his.

"Yay, are you finally done?" I ask as I place multiple kisses on his lips in quick succession. "Can we leave now?" I beg and squeeze my arms tighter around his neck, breathing in his fresh, clean cologne.

His smoky laugh fills the room. "I'm done for the week. I'm sorry the course ran late today. Are we about ready to go?" He pauses and kisses me before speaking again. "I fucking love coming home to you."

I pause at his words, and my eyes find his. My words are caught in my throat, and I can only nod, unable to reciprocate his sentiment. Although I love coming home to him, and I'm just as happy when he comes home to me, I just can't say it. I can't . . .

"Yes, we're packed and ready."

"Let's get going, baby," he says, setting me down gently in order to pick up our bags and carry them to the rented Range Rover.

I know that he's noticed my apprehension, but he doesn't mention it.

Dang it, why is he such a gentleman?

I follow him down the hall, grabbing my purse from the kitchen island, as well as the bag, which is overflowing with snacks. He stops suddenly, and I run into his back.

He turns to me and raises his eyebrow. "Ballerina . . . that bag wouldn't happen to be filled with candy, would it?"

I smile and look down at my bag and then back up at him, blowing a strand of hair out of my face. "Yes. It's a road trip, we have to have candy and snacks," I try to explain.

"But we're just going for the weekend. That damn bag looks like it's heavier than your suitcase."

He takes in a deep breath and it's as if he's just realized he will be meeting his parents for the first time. I hide my small frown and shrug, trying to keep the mood between us light.

"So. Do you want me to go the whole weekend without sugar? Do you even know how cranky I get when I don't have any?"

He cracks a smile and winks at me. "I like how sweet you taste, and I'd like for you to keep it that way."

I smile and am thankful that I've managed to keep his storm at bay for now. "Good. Can we go now?" I reach for my ridiculously large floppy hat and put it on.

His sinewy arms pick up the bags again as he leads the way into my apartment's indoor garage. He hauls in his bag and then my oversized pink suitcase into the back of the SUV as I get into the passenger seat.

"Do you need anything else, Heather?"

"Ah crap. Wait, I'll be right back."

I unbuckle myself and hop out of the SUV, quickly making my way back inside to grab my iPod. I may not be able to put him in a good mood, but I'm making sure he'll never forget our first road trip together.

When I come back he's sitting in the driver's seat with the engine running, entering the address of the hotel in the navigation system. It's already eight in the evening, so we won't make it to Southampton at an acceptable time for Mr. and Mrs. Somer.

As I buckle myself back in, I look over and try to make the same determined face he is. I purse my lips and lower my head into his line of sight.

"So serious."

He looks over at me and squeezes my thigh. "I'd take my belt to your ass if we weren't already running late."

My mouth drops open and goes dry.

Oh . . . oh my God, that was hot.

I smile slowly. "You wouldn't dare."

He backs out of the car elevator easily as he glances in the rearview mirror. Even the muscles in his neck make me want to jump his monstrous gift. "You just sealed the deal, gorgeous. I hope you packed my lube and some type of ointment."

I smile and reach down between my legs into my snack bag, searching. "Mmm, nope, no lube in here. And by the way . . . when did you get lube?" I ask as I pull out a bag of Twizzlers.

"I bought it a few days ago and stuck it in my shaving kit because that ass will be mine on this trip."

I gasp and smack his bicep. "Excuse me? Uhhh, no way in hell." I yank my hat off and toss it in the backseat. My fingers are clenching the armrests at the thought. "You would never fit! Are you insane?"

The smirk that forms on his strong-jawed face make my panties uncomfortably wet. "Heather, you better be up for new things because I plan on making it fit. Have you had anal before?"

I am in complete shock and watch him drive. My thoughts drift when I get distracted by his muscled forearm. He's got his sleeves rolled up over his forearms and is driving with just the one arm extended.

This man is beyond attractive.

I blink and look back up to his eyes. "Wh . . . what? No! Have you?"

His deep chuckles rings through the SUV's interior. "Ballerina, you already know the answer to that," he says as he steers into the right lane of the Queensboro Bridge.

"Is that something you really want to do? I mean . . ." I chew nervously on my Twizzler. ". . . you are huge, like, really huge. I can't even imagine . . ." I trail off.

He moves his other hand onto my thigh and cups my sex playfully. "It's a good thing I've got this pink beauty."

I choke on my candy as it goes down my throat the wrong way, coughing wildly. "Noah!" I reach over and bite his bicep once I regain my composure.

"You were all for it the other night; there's no backing out now."

I scrunch my nose as I remember our drunken outing with our friends.

He interrupts my thoughts. "What else do you have in that bag? Is there anything good for me?"

"Yes, I've got Gushers and Gummy Bears." I lean forward and search my bag again. "And . . . pretzels." I grimace, hating dry pretzels. "Oh, and suckers and Sour Patch Kids." Sitting back against the seat, I hold the snack-sized bag of pretzels in my lap, knowing he'll want them.

"The pretzels, please." He reaches over and takes some from the bag. "Thank you, baby."

I smile to myself knowingly. "You're welcome." Resting my head back, I shift my gaze sideways to look at him. He appears to be deep in thought while he eats his pretzels. I figure, what better time to have a heart-to-heart than now?

"Noah? Can we talk about something that's been bothering me?"

He glances over at me as he switches lanes to merge onto the L.I.E. "What's going on?"

"I'm . . . I want to talk about Mae." I continue to watch him, and I immediately see the invisible wall go up. The lights from the Interstate dance inside the cab of the SUV and illuminate his face.

His head tilts to the left, and I know I've more than crossed the line, but I know we need to talk about this openly.

"Well?" I prod and turn my whole body to face him.

"What do you want to talk about? She has no place in my life, Heather."

"But she raised you, Noah. You're really not going to ever talk to her again?" I trail my fingers along his forearm and can feel his muscles clench under my touch, but I continue my attempt to try to calm him. I know I'm broaching a touchy subject, but he has yet to mention her since she was charged.

"Hell, I thought you understood that I wasn't interested in having her around."

"I know but . . . ." I play with the hem of my shirt. " . . . I thought that maybe you just needed time."

"Heather, she took my life from me. The only thing I will ever be thankful for is you; I'm unsure if I'd have you without her."

I know he won't like this, but I try anyway. "Don't you think she'd like to know that we're together?"

"More than likely, but I would have liked to have known my parents."

"Maybe you could write her? Or . . . we could go see her?" I ask, sounding hopeful.

Surely he will forgive her eventually.

"Heather, don't. That's the last fucking thing I want to do. Shit, I've never even met my parents."

"Don't what? I really think it'd help you heal if you just talked to her. She's had time to think about things."

"She had thirty fucking years to think shit over. She won't change."

I sigh and resign; this obviously won't be a conversation he'll budge on. "Okay, I'm sorry. I won't talk about it again." I shift back in my seat to face forward, setting up my iPod to play through the speakers.

He reaches for my hand and laces his fingers with mine. "I'm not ready yet, I'm sorry."

"I know. I'm sorry I pushed you." I speak quietly and search for the playlist I made especially for this trip. I wanted this trip to be fun for him but I've completely screwed that up already.

He brings my hand to his lips, and he kisses each one of my fingers. "I love you."

My heart breaks just a little. I've pushed him into a corner, and he's worried about my feelings.

I'm such a jerk.

"I love you too."

He keeps my hand to his lips as he drives; the only sound in the SUV is the music I've chosen. I manage to peek over at him and he's brooding. He's crankier than ever, and it's my fault.

"You'll let me know if you need to stop, right?" I wait for his answer as his warm breath hits my hand, and I just want to curl up in his storm.

He doesn't answer me; he just drives in silence, giving me the silent treatment, and I deserve every second of it. I sigh quietly to myself, and turn to look out the window, trying to think of anything I can do to lift his mood.

After a few minutes go by, he looks over at me. "Are you hungry?"

Turning to look at him, I nod. "A little, but we can wait."

"All right," he says, before turning on my seat warmer: he knows I love it.

I lean over a little to get into my bag and look for a sucker. "Are you angry at me?" I ask softly, avoiding eye contact.

He looks over at me and winks. "Not one bit, ballerina."

My heart melts and I can't hide my smile. I squeeze his hand softly and lean over to kiss his cheek. "Mmm, you smell good," I say in his ear, before sitting back in my seat and slipping my flats off.

He glances over at me and a low, deep chuckle rumbles in his throat. "I'm glad you approve. Do you still have that perfume strip in your purse?"

I freeze momentarily and then allow myself a glance at him.

How in the heck . . . ?

"What do you mean?" I ask, feigning innocence.

His smile almost does me in—triumphant and cocky as hell. "You wrote the name of my cologne on it. I saw it in the hospital when I was looking for your insurance card."

Busted.

My face is burning from embarrassment, and I'm thankful the interior of the car is dark enough to hide my flushed cheeks. "Oh . . . umm . . ." I sigh and lower my head. "Busted, huh?"

He leans his head back against the headrest and smirks. "So busted, baby. All right by me—just as long as you don't pass it on to your next boyfriend."

I almost can't believe what I'm hearing. My heart is caught in my throat when I turn quickly to look at him. "I really hope you're joking. Next boyfriend? Are you planning on getting rid of me?"

I'm suddenly sick to my stomach. We have yet to even broach the subject of the engagement ring, and now I'm wondering if this thing between us has an expiration date.

He reaches out for my hand, and I go rigid. He frowns and looks over at me. "Of course I'm joking. Heather . . ." He sighs and breathes in deeply. " . . . I know I jumped the gun with that damn ring, and I'm sorry. I won't forgive myself for that, but I know it's not what you want . . . regardless, I'm still here." His voice isn't harsh or hard. I can hear the regret and pain in it.

I'm on the verge of tears because I have no idea how to talk about this with him. I want him, of course I do. And I definitely don't want us to be over.

"Noah? You can't say that to me. I don't even know where to begin. We never even discussed it. Do you think you really want that? Or do you think you just want that because I took your virginity?"

His eyebrows shoot up and he nods curtly. "If that's what you think . . . it's a damn good thing I returned it." He pauses to clear his throat. "I would not have bought you a ring if I didn't want it or if I wasn't sure," he adds. He looks away as if I've reached into his chest and pulled his full, all-loving heart out.

Great job, Heather. Is there anything else you want to talk about to make this trip worse?

I sigh and lay my head back against the seat. "I'm sorry. That didn't come out right, did it?" I ask but not really needing an answer.

I don't know why I continue to hurt this man sitting next to me. I reach down and grab my phone, sending Dani a text as I remove the wrapper from my sucker:

> *Sister? Are you awake? We're driving to see Henry and Ellery, and I'm making this trip suck. And no, not in a good way.*

I hit send and put the sucker in my mouth as I stare out my window.

The tension in the air is thick between us. I know I shouldn't feel hurt that he took the ring back, but it does sting a little bit, if I'm being honest. I don't know what that means . . . but I'm not even going near that to find out. *No way.*

I'm sitting here in silence, tasting the blue raspberry flavor on my tongue when my phone vibrates with Dani's reply:

> *Uh-oh, what did you do? This was supposed to be a road trip with 'epic fun,' as I recall you saying.*

I dim the brightness on my phone and type out quickly:

> *Duh, Danielle, it was supposed to be fun but I went ahead and ruined it before we even got onto the expressway.*

The song in the background changes, and it's one of my upbeat favorites, but somehow I'm not feeling too *Happy* at the moment while Pharrell sings. And neither is Noah. So instead of torturing the both of us, I reach over and shut it off.

He shifts in his seat and runs a hand through his hair. It's disheveled now, and I know he's tired. He's been spending hours studying: eight hours a day in the bar prep class and countless hours at home.

My phone buzzes in my hand with an incoming text from Dani:

> *Heather, you two need to let your hair down again and relax. I know the miscarriage and all of those fights have been hell on your relationship, but you two are so much better than that. He loves you, and you both deserve to finally be happy with each other. Stop being the stubborn ass you are and enjoy his company.*

Dang it, Dani.

I wish I could tell her she's wrong and that I'm not being stubborn but, honestly, she's right.

My phones buzzes again:

> *You love me. Now go give him road head or something. I'm sure he's anxious as hell and stressed over this situation. He needs my sister's mouth.*

Dani! You're filthy.

I look over at him and he's rubbing his strong, sculpted jaw slowly; he's obviously deep in thought over everything I've brought up.

I'm torn as to what I should do right now. Do I leave him alone? Do I let him sit there and stew and question his love for me? Or should I try and salvage this trip and make this experience for him unforgettable?

I put my sucker back into my mouth and regard him intently.

I want him happy.

My phone goes off again:

Are you sucking his cock yet?

My eyes widen and I shake my head at my sister's self-assurance. *Jeez, Dani.*

I sigh internally and shut off my phone without replying: I simply have no words for her. I toss my phone into my purse and undo my seatbelt. Without hesitating, I lean over and nuzzle his warm neck, breathing in his crisp scent. "I'm sorry, Noah. I love you, and I didn't mean to hurt you by what I said." I continue to rub my nose softly along his jawbone and bring my hand up his concrete chest, testing his mood as well as feeling for his heartbeat.

His shoulders slump as he relaxes. "You have nothing to apologize for, ballerina. You're right; I shouldn't have made that decision without you."

"Shh . . ." I shake my head slowly and bring my hand up his pec and over his muscular shoulder. My thumb grazes his neck and I can feel his heartbeat is slow and steady. "Let's not talk about this right now. Will you just try relaxing with me, please?"

He nods in agreement, placing his right hand at the small of my back as I lean over the center console. His touch calms me, and I breathe in the charming notes of his cologne that occupy my senses. "And I love you, Heather," he says as we pull up to a tollbooth.

I place one last kiss on his neck before removing the sucker from my mouth and sitting back in my seat to watch him pay the toll and drive off. His forearm rests against the steering wheel and my mouth waters. I catch a glimpse of the large vein that runs up the thick muscle and disappears underneath the rolled up sleeve. An idea pops into my head and I grab my iPod and search for a specific song. I hit play, and reach over to lower the volume as *#1 Crush* by Garbage fills the SUV. Before he can even say anything to me, I've taken his right hand and slipped his finger into my mouth. I wait and watch for his reaction.

He glances back and forth between me and the relatively empty Interstate in front of us as I twirl my tongue around his finger, tasting and savoring the flavor of his warm skin. My mouth waters around his finger for more; I'd rather have his monstrous gift pushing at the back of my throat.

I shift my body in the seat and suck his finger a little more aggressively. I'm trying my best to keep his mind off of anything stressful, and I believe it may be working. "Am I making it hard to drive?" I ask before biting down on the pad of his finger.

He grunts loudly and looks down. "You're making a few things hard, Heather."

A genuine smile touches my lips as I let go of his hand and sit back, sucking seductively on the sucker again.

"Mmm . . . this tastes so good, baby," I moan out my words as I drag the sucker across my lips, flicking my tongue out to taste it as I would the head of his cock when a bead of pre-come is offered to me. I intentionally drag the sucker slowly down to the underside of my chin. I'm getting so into this that I drop it down the column of my neck and whimper quietly.

The SUV lurches to the side as I feel his eyes on me instead of the Interstate. "Fuck."

I barely even notice the car veering off because of how turned on I am from my own carnal actions. I start shoving the sleeves of my blouse off of my arms in a hurry as I bring the sucker to my lips again and wet it with my tongue. I look down and free my heavy breasts from my bra before I place the hard blue candy on my nipple. I sensually circle it around my now peaked nipple and watch as it leaves a glistening sticky residue in its wake.

"Holy shit," is all he can manage to say.

My eyes move to the remarkably prominent bulge in his jeans, and I whimper, thinking about his girth stretching me open as he plunges into my aching core.

Arching my back off the seat, my eyes flutter closed at the feel of the sucker running over my heated skin. I can feel the sticky sugar lines that the sucker leaves along my body as I drag the cobalt blue over my skin. I cannot help but imagine Noah running his tongue along those sugary blue streaks that crisscross over my chest.

He reaches over and pushes my hair behind my shoulder as he watches me turn myself on to a point I didn't know I could take myself to. "You already taste so damn sweet."

I run my tongue over my lips to taste the sweet sugar that covers them. I open my eyes and watch my own movements, as I trail the smooth textured sucker down my stomach. I'm completely drenched just from this little foreplay show I've put on for him. "Would you like for me to go lower?" I ask seductively.

He clears his throat before he speaks. "Lower?"

I nod and put the hard head of the sucker back into my mouth before hooking my thumbs into the waistband of my leggings and shimmying them down slowly along with my red lace panties.

I can feel his storm as I sit naked beside him. The electricity between the two of us buzzes and begs for fulfillment, for some relief of any kind.

I maneuver myself to rest my back against the passenger side door and lift my leg, resting my foot on his hard muscled thigh.

His cock convulses.

With one hand on the steering wheel he quickly moves his other hand to my ankle, his need to touch me winning over. He wants to be a part of what I'm doing. He keeps glancing at me, then back to the road in quick succession as I part my thighs for him to get a glimpse of my warm, snug sex.

I think I've effectively gotten his mind off of things, and I feel high from it. I start moving my foot against his thigh and rub my toes against his bulge. A moan escapes my lips when I feel the hardness, and I teasingly lower the sucker back down my body.

"Noah? Are you watching?" My voice is hedonistic and noticeably unlike my own.

I feel the SUV slow down and he looks over at me. "I am. Show me, baby. Show me what you want."

I make eye contact with him and slip the sucker over my clit and down lower between my folds; I gasp at the odd sensation, but continue as I imagine it being the head of his shaft.

"Heather . . . I want to taste that damn sucker now. Fuck, I love that wet pussy."

Heat floods my sex and the sounds that escape me are highly erotic. His grip on my ankle tightens. "You mean taste it like this?" I ask as I bring it from my folds, back up to between my lips, and into my mouth, moaning while I suck and lick my taste from it. I've never done anything like this before, but it's a major turn-on to do this in front of him, to please him.

A long, drawn-out groan rumbles in the back of his throat, and I want to feel that same vibration running up my clit as his tongue works me to the edge of explosion, the edge of ecstasy.

I can't help but lower my hand and open myself up for him, showing him just how wet I am for him. "Look baby, I'm so wet right now." I boldly slide the sucker between my folds and push it up inside myself.

I can feel his cock flex with my foot resting on his upper thigh. "Shit."

I continue to rub his straining bulge with my foot as I play with myself, toying with the sucker. My hips move of their own accord while I twirl the sucker inside me, being sure to lock eyes with him every time I put it back in my mouth and taste my own juices coating it.

"Do you like this, Noah?" I try and make him tell me how he's feeling. I need to hear his sexy voice.

"Oh fuck it," he says brashly and pulls off onto the side of the expressway, putting the emergency flashers on and undoing his seat belt. His body moves over mine quickly as he takes my mouth, tasting my allure like I have been.

He groans at the taste and shoves his tongue deeper down my throat. My hand is still holding the sucker inside myself and I continue to play with it while he takes my mouth. I can feel my impending orgasm start to build and I decide to chase it.

His hand finds mine as I hold the sucker and I grind my hips toward our hands, which pushes the sucker deeper inside of me.

"Fuck, Heather."

I let go, and his fingers slip inside me. I grip onto his shirt tightly and reach for his zipper. "Let me see how hard you are," I demand breathlessly.

"Right here?" he snarls in urgency. "Get in the back, Heather. Now."

I smile triumphantly and crawl over the middle console, making sure to give him a show of bending over when I make my way back. At this moment I couldn't care less that we're parked on the side of the expressway. I've worked myself up so much now that there's no way I'd take no for an answer.

Noah

I'm trying to comprehend what's going on; surely this can't be a wet dream. Heather is crawling over the center console of the SUV with her pretty little ass giving me a show I've only dreamed of. The sucker in her hand is a fucking bonus. I frantically remove my jeans and kick off my shoes as I watch her sink the blue raspberry-flavored candy back into her pink pussy.

My dick is solid, rock-hard from her little show, and I know I'll be damn close to busting the moment I bury myself inside of her.

I make my way over the center console and lean down between her legs. "Mmm, these are two flavors I never thought I'd taste at the same time."

I pull the sucker out of her and kiss her unusually sticky pussy. She whimpers her appreciation and runs her fingers through my hair, locking them in place and tugging until I glance up at her. I lazily run my tongue up her sweetened clit and groan when I taste her and blue raspberry. Her other hand moves into my hair to push my mouth down on her sticky wetness as her thighs press against each side of my face.

I growl deep against her pussy and nip at her lips, pulling at her clit with my teeth. "Holy fuck, Heather, what's gotten into you?" I say muffled against her.

"I just . . . oh. I need you," she moans breathlessly. I blow warm air up her clit before I start eating her again. Her gorgeous thighs tighten around me and she digs her toes into my back and I pull away from her almost pulsing pussy. "Not a chance in hell. You are only coming when my cock is buried deep inside of you."

I smile against her smooth inner thigh when the sexiest little growl fills the SUV. I nuzzle her soft skin and kiss her before turning my head to sink my teeth into her thigh. Her skin is screaming with want and need of our connection.

She lets out a high-pitched cry. I gaze up at her and watch her tug on her sticky, peaked nipples. I move the sucker back to her pussy and push it inside of her, watching the deep blue-colored head move in and out of her achingly slowly.

"Yes," she keeps chanting and rocking her hips to meet the sucker's advances.

My cock spasms eagerly, and I push my boxer briefs down and off, freeing my straining erection. I run my hand along my dick to show her exactly how fucking turned on I am. A bead of pre-come dew's on the tip, and if it wasn't for the sucker in her fine pussy, I bet she'd pounce on me. I move closer to her again and start kissing her fervently. She bites down on my lower lip and slides her hand down my chest, "Please . . ."

"You're soaked, baby. Look at that creamy pussy."

I pull away from her lips and bite my way down to her gorgeous tits. I'm barely able to contain myself; I can feel my muscles tense and shake as my hands grip her upper arms. I'm trying not to ravage her shuddering body but damn, she's got me worked up to a point where I won't have control over my actions for much longer.

I reach down and pull the sucker out of her pussy. She moans in protest, but I proceed regardless. She's watching me, begging me silently. I smirk and place the wet sucker into my mouth and kneel up, spreading her legs wider apart.

"You've fucked with my head for long enough, ballerina; now my head is going to fuck you."

I rise up over her and feed my firm, throbbing cock into her sweet, sticky pussy with great force, moving the sucker to one side of my mouth, tasting my girl and raspberries.

She moans sweetly. "Oh? I think you're just a big tease. Unless . . ."

I leisurely slide my thick shaft out of her as she speaks.

" . . . you show me just how hard you can fuck me."

I raise my eyebrow at her words and lean down over her, wordlessly informing her that I'm in control. My tongue moves the sucker around in my mouth to the other side and I swallow the sweet, yet slightly sour juice before speaking near her lips.

"Challenge accepted, Miss Lane."

My tongue darts out and teases her parted lips. I can feel the warmth of her pussy on the head of my bobbing cock as it sits teasingly near her entrance. Her breath comes quicker, almost a pant, as I slide my hand up her flat stomach and over her perky tits. I decide to make her wait for my cock until I can feel her pussy weep for me.

"You like to torment me, don't you, Heather?" I ask as my hand slides up her throat and I squeeze with just the right amount of pressure.

My cock twitches when she lets out a gasp.

"That's right, baby. You like this part of me, don't you?"

I move my hand up her jaw before dipping my thumb forcefully into her mouth. Fuck me, her hot little mouth feels good. I tease her pussy as I rock my hips unhurriedly, grinding my swollen head against her tender clit. Her tongue twirls around my thumb and I graze the pad over her lower teeth. She bites down on my thumb as I grunt with surprise before pulling free from her mouth. I quickly tangle my fingers in her long dark-chocolate hair as I jerk and yank her head back.

Her sweet lips part, and I take her mouth hard, shoving my tongue in and fucking her mouth the way she likes. My fingers clench in her hair, and I instantly feel her pussy drip juices onto my cock. I growl and keep her head still as I press my forehead to hers.

"You like it when I'm rough? Your pussy just gushed for me. Do you feel that?"

Her mouth drops open, and she pants, and I slam my cock up, gliding balls deep into her drenched channel.

Holy fuck.

I don't even give her time to warm up to me before I fully pull out of her tightness and slam back in, savoring each solitary stroke inside of her. I pull back to look at her face, and I switch the sucker to the other side of my mouth, looking down at her as my hands are fisting her hair. Her body is riddled with tiny goosebumps as I feel her adjust to my length.

"Noah . . . oh God . . ."

I smirk and plant my feet, giving me leverage to force my cock so far into her pussy that she'll scream out as I pummel her. I can feel her stretch for me while I propel myself into her gorgeous pussy repeatedly.

"Just remember you asked for this, baby."

I growl and penetrate her tight little hole again; I've never fucked her this hard before and I'm in fucking ecstasy. She's clawing at my back and my ass, piercing my skin with her nails, and I want to be so incredibly deep in her that she feels me in her throat.

"That's right baby, swallow my cock whole," I groan and suck the juices that are pooling in my mouth from the sucker. "You wanted to tease me, didn't you? You liked seeing my cock grow when I watched you." I grit my teeth and release her hair when she gasps. She tries to say my name, but I'm fucking the breath out of her.

"You're the big tease, Heather. Not me."

I pound her pussy relentlessly, effortlessly shoving her legs wider as I glance down, watching my cock slide between her walls readily.

"Damn, baby, look at all the cream on my cock."

I pound hard again, then stop, holding myself deep.

"I want to see you suck that cream from my dick."

"Ye-yes . . . let me suck your cock, Noah," she faintly replies and her head falls back. I continue to stroke her pussy with my heavy shaft when I feel her walls grip my dick tighter.

"Yeah, baby, that's it . . . show me how you're supposed to come, Heather."

I growl and press my thumb against her swollen hood, caressing that bundle of nerves.

"Make that pussy cream, Heather."

Her legs start to tremble and I know she's going to blow. Quickly, I finger her creamy pussy while my dick pounds her. She's completely drenched my fingers and I reach down and without warning, slip my middle finger into her tight, puckered hole.

"Oh fuck yes . . ." I growl low when I feel her hot warmth around my finger, stroking her tight ring with my slick finger. Her gasp and moan steal my breath, and I have to fight blowing my load.

She's wholly losing herself to me, and I to her.

"Noah . . ." is all she can manage to say.

Seconds later an earth-shattering scream rocks the interior of the SUV when her body spasms around me. Her pussy has my cock in a vise grip as I slowly finger-fuck her ass to intensify her orgasm. I ensure that I take care of her before I surrender to my restrained climax.

I can't stop pounding her tight pussy. My jaw is clenched, holding the sucker in my cheek as I look down at her. "Do what I say, Heather . . . keep coming all over my cock. You wanted me like this— now you've got it, baby."

I ram up into her so hard, using her sweet, sticky pussy the way she wanted me to.

She throws her head back and screams, her lungs drawing in a deep breath as her body relaxes and then explodes again in another intense orgasm.

I smirk as her pussy quivers and clamps down around me. "That's it, ballerina . . ."

"Noah . . . I can't . . ." she declares, but I know otherwise.

I lean down and remove the sucker from my mouth, dragging it along her damp throat. "You like that in your ass, don't you, Heather?"

I swipe my tongue over the sticky trail I just left before sinking my teeth into her neck. Her ass clenches around my finger and I still, relishing how it feels. She's trying to speak to me, her lips are moving, but there are no words coming out of her lascivious mouth.

"That's what I thought."

She looks down at our adjoining bodies and mumbles, "I want to feel you."

I have a slight grasp on my control at this moment and her words just about knock me out. My cock jerks inside her, and I pull my finger from her ass as I thrust my dick in to the hilt.

Jesus Christ.

I grab her jaw and slide my lips over hers. "Not yet, ballerina, but soon." I start pounding away at her gushing pussy and quickly lose myself, groaning into her mouth.

She sags on the seat and in my arms. She's completely worn out. I soon slow my advances to a complete stop and smile knowingly against her lips. I take the sucker and run it along her lower lip before I pull my length out of her pussy. I watch my release bathe her pussy lips; I can't help the grin that forms on my face. I move what's left of the sucker down her overworked, fatigued, and drained body until it lies between her lips. I push the deep blue candy inside of her once more, submerging it into our orgasms, and then moving it up to her swollen roseate lips.

"Suck."

She ardently takes it into her mouth. The second our sweet and salty releases hit her taste buds, a sharp, carnal whine fills the SUV. Her eyes lock onto mine when I hear the remaining candy fragment under her bite.

"I'm glad to see you savoring this, little miss."

Her lips curl up, and her gaze is glassed over. I can't help but chuckle and kiss her forehead. "Fuck, Heather, I love you."

"Mhmm, I love you, Greek god," she musters and stretches her arms lazily until they are wrapped around my neck. "Take me to bed?"

"Bed? Baby, we're not even remotely close to home or Southampton. Get dressed and I'll find a hotel nearby."

I lift my body off of hers and grab her clothes from the front seat. She's already half asleep with her pretty little naked ass on the brown leather beneath her.

I decide not to attempt to put her bra and panties on because I'll just have to remove them once we're in the hotel room, so I grab my sweatshirt instead and help her into it. She slumps back against the seat as I try to get her leggings on. *Fuck, how the hell do women do this shit?* It takes me a good five minutes, if not more, to get them up and over her ass.

She's practically passed out from exhaustion, so I decide to leave her in the back. I lay her head down on the right-hand seat so I can check on her while I drive. Pulling her pink blanket off of the front seat, I lay it over her. I know how damn cold she gets, and I don't want her waking up because of it. I get my clothes back on with great difficulty, wondering how in the hell I got them off in the first place.

I look back over my shoulder after I get seated, and she's still passed out. I'm not the least bit sorry that I fucked her to sleep.

I look forward and am about to drive off when I realize I can't see shit. The windows are completely fogged up from our lovemaking, and it makes me laugh. I hit the defrost button and within thirty seconds, the windows are clear. I pull back onto the expressway and drive in silence, taking this time to think and drive a little farther.

How the hell did we go from arguing and disagreeing on shit to using a sucker to please her? I shake my head and chuckle to myself. This woman drives me fucking crazy, but I wouldn't trade what we have for anything in this fucked-up world. I won't let what we have end up in a tragedy.

I glance back at my sleeping beauty and smirk. She's getting bolder in this relationship, which is good I guess. She used to keep her walls up, and I tried all I could to get her to open up. Now . . . she's got no problem broaching subjects that are off-limits.

I know there is no way in hell she's going to drop the subject of Mae.

Now that she's introduced the subject, though, I realize that it's something that I'm going to have to deal with soon. I simply can't keep pushing it off to avoid the unequivocal discomfort and distress it brings me. I make a mental note to contact Joel once we get back to the city to find out more about where she is being housed and if it comes down to it, how I will be able to visit her in the correctional facility.

I think Heather's right when she said that I need to talk to Mae. It might be the only way that I will be able to fully move past this heinous part of my life.

I don't know why I thought Heather would let me just drop the subject forever. But that's what I've always done. You fuck me over, and I'm done with you forever. But not her: she's the only one I've ever forgiven. And her huge fucking heart is weighing on me and forcing me to feel things for people, even if they've done me wrong. Hell, after the way Dani talked to me in London, I normally would have written her off—fuck you and goodbye—but she's Heather's sister, and I'm learning to give people second chances.

Content with my decision, I nod and look back at Heather. Hell, she's gorgeous when she sleeps. I decide to buckle down and drive through the next hour and a half to Southampton, and to the address Henry gave me.

I don't see the house at first, but I turn down the drive as far as the gate will allow and kill my lights. What I can see is a white Georgian-style home, landscaped with uplighting, and surrounded by towering trees and a meticulously manicured lawn. From what I can see in the dark, there are four wooden rocking chairs sitting on the front porch, next to white columns that support a large second-floor balcony. There seems to be another building behind the main house, possibly a guest cottage. This home is one of a kind and radiates love and comfort, two things I would give the world to feel from my *parents*.

My nerves just kicked into overdrive as I pull away from their house. This is where I was supposed to grow up and enjoy a carefree lifestyle, but none of that happened. I search for a hotel nearby and decide on the Maidstone Boutique Hotel. It's a longer drive to Henry and Ellery's house than the hotels around here, but I'm rather enjoying the thought of spoiling Heather.

I put the SUV into park and stare out at nothing in particular. Their house is burned into my mind, and I can't help but think about what my life would have been like. What did they do for work? Do I have any cousins? Is my fath . . . is Henry some hard-ass who will be difficult to get along with? I find myself rubbing my jaw, lost in thought about my impending future.

Tomorrow, everything changes. Either I'll meet and forget them for my remaining years, or they'll be a part of my life forever. I exhale deeply and run my hand up the back of my head.

Fuck. I can't do this.

I look back at Heather, and her lips are slightly parted while she dreams. I rest my head on the steering wheel and watch her sleep. I don't know why I hadn't thought of it before, but I could have asked her what they were like. What she remembers. Hell, she didn't stay with them for much time at all. In fact, she couldn't get away fast enough. Shit . . . this was a bad idea.

I can only imagine what Ellery is like. Visions of a snooty, rich woman who's afraid to get dirty fill my thoughts.

Will I look like them?

Would I have played rugby or polo instead of football?

My little ballerina stirs and reaches out as if she's looking for me. I take a deep breath in, then let it out gradually.

I get out of the SUV and grab her purse, our bags, and my wallet. I lock the Range Rover while I go inside and walk to the front desk. The hotel is unique and gorgeous; I really think Heather is going to love this place.

A middle-aged woman with a silver pin in her pale blonde hair greets me. "Good evening, sir. Do you have a reservation with us?"

"'Evening. No, I do not. I was hoping that you'd have a room available. I know it's short notice."

She checks her computer before giving me an answer. "Yes, sir, you are in luck. We have one room available. It is called the Edvard Munch room with a king-sized bed."

"That will be great, thank you." I take my wallet out and hand her my credit card and license.

Moments later a bellhop appears and loads our bags onto the cart.

"Thank you, Mr. Ryan, you are all set. You still have an hour to place your room service order for the morning, if you are interested. Please enjoy your stay."

"Thank you. Have a good evening," I add politely and follow the bellhop up to the Edvard Munch room. I open the door, and he brings in our bags. After I tip him, he thanks me politely and walks out. I follow behind him and head back outside to the SUV.

When I unlock the door and open it, she's still sound asleep. I chuckle to myself and lean down to wake her. "Heather, baby, wake up. We're here." I brush my knuckles across her porcelain skin to try to stir her awake.

"Hmm?" she mumbles and reaches for me.

"I need you to get up and come to bed with me."

Her eyes are still closed when she nods, and I help her to sit up.

This time I actually chuckle out loud because her wild hair is stuck to her face when she sits up. "Damn, you are adorable." I reach up and move her hair away from her face as her eyes blink open slowly. I smile and help her slip her flat shoes on. "Hi, gorgeous girl. You ready for bed?"

She takes in a breath of the clean spring air and gives me the utmost glittering, sleepy smile I have ever seen. "I think so, but where are we?"

"Not far from their place," I reply before taking her hand and helping her out of the backseat.

She steps onto the ground and wraps her arms around my torso, holding me close as she takes in a deep breath.

I reach into the SUV and grab her blanket before closing the door and leading her inside. I watch as she blinks a few times, attempting to wake up and take in this gorgeous boutique hotel.

"Noah . . ."

"Yes?" I rub her back softly as I walk her inside.

"This place is gorgeous. We're staying here?"

"Yes, we are."

I lead her up to the room and open the door; she gasps in quiet awe before walking in. The room is decorated in hues of gold and black with the king-sized bed taking up most of the available space. The black head-board is lined in a golden frame, and above it hangs four different sized and shaped mirrors. An antique leather chair takes up the space in the corner, and it's all the room needs. Heather's arms tighten around me, and I lift her, carrying her to the oversized bed and setting her down.

"Is this place going to work for the weekend?"

"Noah, it's absolutely perfect." She beams up at me and pats the bed. "Come sleep with me; you look exhausted." She gives me a small frown and sits up, sudden worry flashing across her face. "What's wrong?"

I pull my clothing off and get into the bed in just my boxer briefs.

"Nothing is wrong. I'm just nervous as hell. Would you mind doing something for me? Tomorrow morning when we've both gotten some sleep, would you mind telling me about them?"

I watch her as she undresses and crawls under the covers with me. She's completely naked and looks momentarily confused about where her bra and panties are.

"Of course I will. Everything is going to be fine, okay?" she replies softly as she faces me, lying on her side.

"Thank you, ballerina." I reach out for her and pull her onto my chest where she belongs. "Why in the hell do you think you're sleeping over there?" I ask playfully as she settles on top of me and gets comfortable.

Her soft laugh makes me grin, and I reach over and turn out the light.

"I just thought . . ." she tries to explain, but I interrupt her.

"Yeah, well, you thought wrong."

That gets her to laugh again before we both start to drift off into a comfortable place. I am moments from passing out while listening to her breathe when her voice startles me.

"Noah?"

"Yeah?" I reply with my eyes closed.

She hesitates before answering me in a harsh whisper. "Are you asleep?"

I breathe out and kiss the top of her head. "Not yet, baby."

"I have to pee, and I'm sticky" she spits out quickly.

I chuckle and pat her ass. "Then go."

She lifts her body from mine, and I instantly hate the loss. "Don't listen, okay?" She asks before climbing out of bed and padding over to the bathroom naked. I smile to myself at her odd request, and then burst out laughing when I hear the exhaust vent turn on and the sink running water simultaneously. A few moments later I hear the shower start. Hell, what my girl won't do.

Chapter Fifteen

HOMESTEAD

HEATHER

We've been lying awake for a few hours now as the sun rises behind the drawn curtains of the hotel room. His thoughts must be racing because neither one of us has said a word to each other. His chest is warm, and I'm so comfortable in my spot; if we didn't have plans today, then I would refuse to move. His warm hand moves down from the back of my shoulders to the small of my back.

"Heather?"

"Mhmm?" I reply softly and nuzzle his chest.

"Do I look like them?" His voice is cool, almost dark; I know he's anxious.

His question takes me by surprise, and I have to think back to give him a proper answer. "You have your mother's eyes, I believe." I smile and look up at him. "But if I recall correctly, I think you've outgrown your dad. He's tall, but you're taller."

He listens quietly as his hands roam around my back. "Do you remember anything about them? What were they like?"

I clear my throat as I think back on that sad time in my life. I've blocked it out, but now I'll boldly jump into that darkness for him. "Well, both of your parents were extremely understanding. They knew what I was going through and were remarkably loving. Your mom . . ." I stop and smile. " . . . she would make me the best hot chocolate. It's been my favorite ever since, and I've yet to be able to perfect it."

His tense muscles relax slightly as I tell him they took care of me; of course he's more concerned about my past than his future. He's put me first since day one. "Do you think they'll remember you?"

I chew at my cheek and think on that. "I would imagine they would, but I don't know how many children they've fostered over the years. I could have been one out of a dozen."

"But you were their first?"

"Yes, as far as I know."

He presses his lips to the top of my head and inhales. "I don't know if I'm ready for this."

I can't imagine how he must be feeling, but I can hear his heart beat rapidly, as if he's just run a mile. "Hey, you're going to be just fine. You can do this—I'll be right there with you. You'll feel so much better once you've met them. Think of this as a new chapter in your life."

"Yeah, chapter thirty, in a long and seemingly empty book—with the exception of the prologue, of course. I suppose we better get up and get ready."

I move off of his chest and sit up, looking down at him as he lies on his back. "Would it help if I wore those shorts today?" I grin.

My comment brings some of the color back to his face. "Did you bring them with you?"

My smile widens, and I pinch his nipple playfully. "Yes, I did. When you mentioned them the other night, I made sure to pack them."

His body reacts by sending the slightest spasm through his chest. "Fuck, I can't wait to see them again."

Before I can tell what's happening, he scoops me off of the bed and hauls me over his shoulder, so I get the perfect view of his muscular butt as he walks into the bathroom and turns the shower on.

I can't help but smack his firm tush quickly before he sets me on my feet. "Okay, I'll shower with you, but no funny business, Noah. I know how you get." I try to keep the mood light so he stays upbeat and positive.

"Funny business? Have you named my cock now?"

I laugh and step under the warm spray. "No, but if I did, your cock's name would not be 'funny business.'"

"I'm glad you take my cock seriously, ballerina." He starts washing his chest, up and under his arms, and back up the other side until his torso is scrubbed and covered in suds.

Our shower proceeds in silence, partly because now I'm the one thinking about funny business and what I could do to accidentally slip and fall on his penis. But it's mostly because he's lost in thought as well. Last week, when we were lying in bed, he broke my heart when he whispered, "What if they don't like me?" I knew that would never be the case but how do I answer that? I know that this is what is weighing heavily on his mind at this very moment.

Once we're both showered and ready to go, I walk in front of him as we leave the hotel room. His hands come around my hips hard and fast as he pulls me back against him, "Dammit, Heather, this ass . . ."

I gasp at the sudden movement and look up and over my shoulder at him. "What? You can barely see it. I wore this maxi dress specifically for that reason. You don't need any distractions today."

And neither do I, I add quietly to myself.

His storm is brewing close enough for me to hear it. "You owe me, ballerina."

"For what?"

"For teasing me with those shorts and then deciding not to wear them in the end."

A sting from his hand warms my butt, and I step forward out of his storm clouds.

"We're going to be late if you don't control that monster."

"Monster, huh? I like that better than funny business."

I blush a deep crimson because I didn't mean to let him know how I secretly refer to his cock. He opens the passenger side door for me knowingly and watches every move of my body as I get up and into the seat.

Crap. I'm so busted.

His smirk tells me everything I need to know: he loves my nickname for him. He shuts the door quickly and moves his able body around the car to the driver's seat. He gets in effortlessly and pulls out of the parking lot, heading west down the Montauk Highway toward Southampton.

He's rubbing his jaw slowly as he drives, lost in his head—which is just as well for I don't have any words for him. The tension in the car is palpable, and I'm almost suffocating from it. I reach out and take his hand in mine, doing my best to comfort him.

The thirty-minute drive passes quickly and once we get off the highway, it takes us all of five minutes to get to the gate of Henry and Ellery's home.

I look over at him and rub his jean-clad thigh gently. "Go on, baby, I'm here."

The gate opens before he can roll down the automatic window and hit the call button. They must be as anxious to meet him as he is to meet them. Noah slowly lowers his foot onto the gas pedal, and the Range Rover moves down the driveway slowly until their home is in full view.

It's breathtaking. I inhale deeply to steady myself and speak quietly.

"I've not been here before; this is new for me too."

I hear him swallow his fear as he parks and gets out of the SUV to make his way around to me. He pulls the door open while his eyes are still locked on the front door of their house.

I climb out slowly and let the skirt of my dress fall to my feet. He takes my hand and looks down at me, cupping the underside of my chin. "If I say I'm ready to leave, we leave. Okay?"

I place my hand over his and reach up on my tiptoes to kiss him. "Okay."

He doesn't say a word; he just kisses me gently and lets go of my chin before walking side by side with me up their walkway. My heart is beating wildly, and I can feel his pulse against my fingers. We reach the front door, and he rings the doorbell, and then steps back. We're both nervous wrecks, and if I told him to run at this exact moment, I think he would.

We both hear the door handle move at the same time because our eyes shoot to each other's and then back to the door.

It opens suddenly and within seconds we're face to face with Noah's parents. There's an awkward moment of silence before they step out of the house and onto the first step. My hands are trembling, and I look up nervously at him. He's just staring at the two of them.

Ellery can't dash the tears away fast enough with her right hand while she holds onto Henry with her left.

He squeezes my hand when Henry's deep voice breaks the silence. "Son."

I think Noah's about to bolt when I feel his arm tense up—I can practically feel every muscle in his body react to that one word. Rubbing my thumb gently along the outside of his hand, I try to relax him. Before Noah even replies, Henry extends his right hand to him, and I feel Noah let go of mine.

They shake firmly as my Greek god says, "Good morning."

Suddenly and without warning, there's a squeak. Before I even know what happened, Ellery all but lunges at Noah and wraps her thin arms around his waist. She's buried her face in his chest and is crying into his slate grey t-shirt. Her sobs are racking her body, and I can't help but stare in shock—we all do.

Noah's arms are set wide apart as he hesitates to touch her, but he makes up his mind and does, wrapping his arms around his mother. A sob somehow escapes my lips, and I quickly place my hand over my mouth. *Oh Noah . . .*

He engulfs her delicate frame, and I'm melting.

My eyes tear up as I watch Noah lower his head to rest his cheek on the top of her head. He stands there, holding his mother in his arms for the first time, while she cries. He would have no recollection of being held by the Somers, so to him, this is the first time he's ever gotten the physical affection of a parent who truly loves him unconditionally. Henry and I are both captivated in the moment, watching Ellery shiver in her son's arms.

Noah surprises me when he lifts his head and ever so gently places a kiss on the top of her head. "It's okay . . ."

She sobs some more, and Noah's broad, brooding shoulders relax to a light rain shower. She loosens her arms, and Noah straightens up. Looking up at him, Ellery smiles warmly.

Her chestnut hair is shining in the warm sunlight as she speaks.

"Welcome home, Noah. Oh, look at me: I can't hold myself together. Please . . . please do come inside. I have breakfast ready."

I feel like an outsider, like I shouldn't be here.

That moment with Noah and his mother was so personal, so profoundly emotional. I don't want this moment to ever be over for him. It's better than I could have ever dreamed of. Seconds pass, and Henry steps forward. I watch in silence as he takes Noah and hugs him. The two men, who look very much alike but differ by many years, hug for a long and quiet moment. The only sound I hear is Ellery, sobbing into a tissue beside her husband and son.

Both men pull apart, and Noah swallows slowly before he's able to clear his throat. "I don't know exactly what to say; this is a lot to take in . . ." His politeness wins over his emotions as he looks over at me and reaches for my hand, ensuring I haven't run for the hills.

I give him my hand and step a little closer to him. I really wish I wasn't present right now. This needs to be just the three of them.

"Henry . . . Ellery . . . this is my girlfriend, Heather."

He introduces me and Ellery sniffles some more. They both turn to me, and I'm praying there's no recognition. Both of them smile at me, and Ellery walks over to give me a brief hug.

"Welcome, honey, we're so happy to meet you as well."

I think I relax a little because my smile isn't forced. "Thank you for allowing me to be here," I say before hugging her back. I feel relieved that they haven't made the connection; I want this to be about Noah.

Ellery lets me go after squeezing my upper arms. "My, aren't you pretty? Henry, isn't she just darling?" she asks as she turns to him.

He chuckles, much like Noah's chuckle, and steps forward, grasping my hand with both of his. "Yes, she's quite the looker."

I can't help but smile and look at Noah. He seems relaxed at the moment, his storm well at bay for the time being, as he winks at me.

"I wanted to share some of my life with you, and the easiest way I could do that was to bring Heather with me and have you meet her too."

Ellery's smile lights up when she watches Noah speak of me with such respect and love. I think I'm swooning over my Greek god.

"Noah, Heather, will you please join us inside? I'd love to show you around after breakfast. Will you be staying here tonight? But please, don't feel obligated. I have one of the guest rooms made up for the both of you. Oh . . . listen to me ramble. I apologize . . . I just simply don't know where to start."

Noah's watching his mother eagerly talk. His storm vanishes in this moment, and his grin sets my heart on fire.

"That hug was the seamless place to start, Ellery."

She covers her mouth in an attempt to stop her tears, but it only lasts for half of a second, "Come inside, please."

We follow behind them and walk just inside. Their home is warm and inviting and smells of apples and cinnamon. I feel his hand at my lower back and it eases my nervousness just a tad.

"I'm sorry; I didn't know what you'd like for breakfast so I made a few things," Ellery says nervously as we follow them into the kitchen.

I have to stifle a giggle because this sweet woman has gone over-board. Their breakfast nook is completely covered with food.

I hear Henry laugh and kiss her temple. "Honey, you've made enough for a small army."

She pulls out chairs for us to sit and hurriedly makes her way to the refrigerator, pulling out a carafe of orange juice. "You didn't need to go to all of this trouble, Mrs. Somer," I say politely and sit down in the chair adjacent to Noah. He places his hand on my thigh, and I know that he needs the connection. He's still nervous as hell, and I don't blame him.

Even though his mother and father are radiating happiness and love, it's still a tense situation. Henry's voice startles me and brings me back from my thoughts.

"So, Noah, how is the studying coming along? Your email said you were preparing for the bar exam."

He lifts up his cup of black coffee and takes a drink before answering. "It's going well. I'm excited that I get to take it this time around, but studying for it is all consuming. It's a lot to digest in a small amount of time."

Henry nods with a smile. "It's a hell of an exam, the way I hear it." He laughs and stops abruptly when Ellery smacks him on the shoulder as she joins us at the table.

"Henry, watch your language," she scolds, and then looks over at me. "I apologize, honey; I've been trying to get him under control for years."

My eyes quickly find Noah's, and he's looking right at me. I'm pretty sure we're thinking the same thing at the moment: Noah is just like his father.

My smile broadens and Henry interrupts, "What can I say? I'm hardheaded." They both laugh at their own little banter and we all seem to relax a little.

Noah nods, grinning when he says, "I think we have that in common. It's a long and tedious test, but it will be worth it. I'd like to practice family law, and I'm hoping that I'll get to stay in the city, especially after asking Heather to move in with me. That and I've got my eye on a few firms right now."

Oh yes, his storm is nowhere to be seen.

"That's wonderful," Ellery replies and hands Noah a beautiful ceramic serving bowl full of scrambled eggs. "Have as much as you'd like, honey, there's plenty here." She starts filling her plate and is about to hand Noah a basket filled with pastries when she stops. "Oh, I-I'm sorry, I didn't even ask. Do you like eggs, dear?" Her look is full of worry, and I want to just go over there and hug her. She's just like I remembered, so kind and caring, bless her.

Noah gets up and walks around the breakfast nook to her. She puts the platter of pastries down when he reaches her, and he pulls her into his arms, hugging her again. "You could serve me snails, and I'd eat it because you made it, and I love all breakfast food."

I think my ovaries have just exploded. Watching Noah interact with his birth mother is unlike anything I've ever seen. It makes me miss my mom even more, but I'm so happy at the same time. Ellery bursts into tears again, and I hear Henry chuckle.

"She's been a torrent of tears these past few days; I don't know how she has any left, to be honest."

That makes me grin, and I sip at my orange juice while Noah and his mom have a moment together.

They let go of each other, and she smiles lovingly up at him. "Okay, let's eat."

"Thank you for going through all of this trouble." He sits down beside me again and reaches for the bacon on my plate. *The bastard.* There is plenty of bacon in the dish, but for some reason, he wants it off of my plate.

I suppose that little bit of playfulness from him is good. It tells me that we aren't leaving anytime soon because he seems to be comfortable. A few moments pass, and I think I've put one of everything on my plate. I know I won't eat all of this, but she went to so much trouble preparing it all. Ellery is all smiles at the end of the table, and I can see that Noah has become even more comfortable. I listen as Ellery tells us about her nursery business. That would explain her impeccable lawn. Noah is completely focused on the two of them as they discuss how they fought over what to name it.

Henry wanted it to be something witty, while she just wanted it to be their last name.

Henry chuckles and explains, "I caved and it's now called Somer's Nursery, and I'm rather fond of it. Apart from owning a nursery, I am a physician, a podiatrist to be precise."

Noah looks knowingly at me, squeezing my thigh underneath the table before Henry continues, "I own a private practice that accepts only referrals. Heather, I noticed your boot. I'll need to take a look at that before you leave for the city. But enough about us old folks: we'd like to know some more about the two of you. So tell us, what do you do, Heather?"

My smile that was there seconds ago has now vanished.

Oh no. I'm not ready.

"Oh, thank you. I have an appointment to see a physical therapist on Monday, but I haven't seen a podiatrist here in the States yet," I reply and pick at my lemon Danish.

Ellery looks at me and asks, "Yes, Heather, what do you do?" I take in a quick breath, and my eyes find Noah's. I'm searching for any answer he can give me silently.

Noah nods almost imperceptibly, telling me that he's okay with my telling them who I am.

Am I okay with it?

Oh God, I don't know how this will go. I clear my throat and try to speak, but my throat is suddenly dry. I reach for my orange juice that Noah just nudged toward me and lift it to my lips. Ellery seems to do the same thing and sips on her juice while she waits for me to answer her. "I'm . . . um . . . I'm a professional ballerina." I speak a little softer than I intended and set my glass down. My eyes search Noah's, and he's watching his parents carefully.

I look over at Ellery, and she smiles. "Oh, that's lovely, darling. I love the ballet. We knew a little . . ." She's about to set her glass back down when she stops talking.

Yep, here we go.

I look at her directly, and she's staring at me with her mouth agape. Her hand is in midair, holding the juice when Henry speaks for the first time.

"Heather?"

I look over at him, and he's looking at me with a dazed stare. My heart rate has picked up tremendously, and I'm finding it hard to breathe. Suddenly there's a loud crash, and orange juice spills and splatters everywhere. I look over quickly at Ellery, and she's dropped her glass and is still staring at me. The moment is chaotic, and Noah pushes back from the table to grab the paper towels from the marble countertop.

Only when Noah starts cleaning up the spilled juice does Ellery blink and stand up quickly to help him. Henry places his hand on Ellery's to stop her. "Why don't we move this into the sunroom and we can clean this up later?"

I stand and watch Noah as he moves his mom's hands out of the broken glass. "I've got this, Ellery. Don't cut yourself," he says with a great reverence for his mother. I stand there nervously, waiting.

She nods and goes to wash her hands off, then turns quickly to look at me. "Heather . . . oh darling, you're so grown up." She dries her hands quickly and hurries back over to me, pulling me into her heartfelt embrace. "I don't know how I didn't see it sooner."

My lips thin into a line and I reply. "Oh please, no, that was a long time ago, Mrs. Somer." I quickly rub and pat her back.

Henry stands up and walks over to pull me into his arms next. "Heather, for those three months you showed us what it would have been like to have our son, and now you've brought him to us. What an incredible day this has turned out to be."

I can't hide the tears that well up and spill over, but I try regardless. I don't even know what to say to them. None of this was my doing. Ellery is behind me, and I can hear her blow into a tissue.

"Oh my goodness, what a morning!" she exclaims happily.

A small laugh escapes me, and I pull back from Henry's embrace. Ellery's voice is almost ecstatic when she speaks. "Come, come let's sit outside. Noah, honey, put that down, you're a guest. I won't have you cleaning up my mess."

He sets everything down and walks up to me, pulling my body into his arms. I sigh and nuzzle his chest. Ellery sighs happily and leads the way out onto their lanai.

"Who would have thought that this could be remotely possible?" I hear Henry ask, as he follows his wife and sits down in a cushioned chair. Noah laces his fingers with mine as we take the loveseat across from them.

"Heather, honey, Noah, would you like some more juice? Or a mimosa? I know I could use one right now," Ellery asks.

Noah looks at me first as if asking me the same question. I nod because I could really use one too. "I'm fine with my coffee right now, but I think Heather would be more than happy to have one with you. Thank you."

She scurries back inside, and Henry watches her retreat. He turns to us and beams. "I haven't seen my wife this happy in thirty years." He turns to look out at his yard and rubs his jaw thoughtfully. I smile because Noah has the same mannerisms as his father, and we can finally see it—together.

Chapter Sixteen

A FATHER'S INTUITION

NOAH

I've just spent an entire day with my mother and father. My earlier reservations about this encounter have been gone since breakfast. This has been one of the most amazing and memorable days in my life, and I will never forget it, no matter what the future brings for me. Heather hasn't left my side, just as she said she wouldn't, and I intend on showing her just how much I appreciate that.

I'm currently sitting in the back of my father's S Class Mercedes, listening to him tell Heather a story about my grandmother. I feel a smile play at my lips when I think back to his first mention of her at dinner.

"Your grandmother wanted to be here to meet you, Noah, but she's off on a month-long cruise to Europe right now with her . . . uh . . . boyfriend. She's quite the pistol, my mother. I'm sure you and her will get along just fine."

I feel the car come to a stop, and I'm pulled from my thoughts. We've parked out back of their home and everyone is getting out. Heather has bloomed this evening and opened up to them about her past. They've been more than polite about their questions, which I'm grateful for. I know it was a hard time for her, and it seems they've gracefully come to terms with her moving away. I get out, shut the door, and follow behind Heather and Ellery as we walk back into their home.

I'm taking everything in: this morning, day, and now evening. I think back on how worried I was and almost laugh at myself. They couldn't be more perfect, my parents.

"Noah?" I hear Henry say my name as the ladies walk into the sitting room. I turn my head in his direction.

"Yes, sir?"

He chuckles and sets his car keys in a bowl that looks as if it's made from driftwood. "Please call me Henry."

I nod in agreement.

"Have a drink with me out by the fire? It's been requested that I turn it on. Your . . . Ellery wants to make Heather her famous hot chocolate."

I laugh and watch him grab two beers from the refrigerator and hand me one. "Yeah, I'd like that," I say and follow him back outside through a different set of doors.

Shit, what am I going to talk to him about?

I step outside and close the doors behind me. When I turn back around I'm standing in the middle of a Tuscan oasis. *Damn.* Their backyard is a landscaper's masterpiece, something you'd see in a professional magazine. I watch as Henry walks over to a fire pit with multicolored glass rocks in the bottom and flips a switch.

"Fire's ready." He laughs and holds his beer up, then takes a drink before sitting down in a single chair next to it.

I smile and follow suit.

"Ellery hates firewood. She says it's nice to look at but hates the smell of smoke it leaves on your clothes, hence the gas fire." He nods at it and takes a drink. I know he's trying to make small talk to make me feel comfortable.

"It's pretty nice out here," I reply and take a drink. "Did she design it?"

He laughs and leans back, crossing his ankle over his knee. "She did. It took her almost two damn years to get it how she wanted it," he says, nodding to my right. "That koi pond has been moved twice." He laughs. "If you can't tell yet, she can go overboard with details." He then looks over his shoulder at the double doors as if he might have been caught. "Don't tell her I said that." We both laugh and it feels good . . . normal.

"How long have you been living in Southampton?"

I watch as he inhales on a deep breath and puffs his cheeks out when he exhales. "Ah, well . . ." He nods his head back toward the double doors that lead into the house. "When Heather left, Ellery decided she needed to leave the city. So I promised her we'd move and try to start fresh. There were too many difficult memories in that home."

I nod, imagining them with my ballerina. "So you've been fostering kids here?"

He shakes his head and takes a drink from his beer. I won't lie—I'm a little shocked. "No, Heather was the only one we fostered. We found it was too painful when she left and knew it wasn't for us."

"Damn, I had no idea. She thinks there were others after her. She said she was with you for three months before Dani, her sister, was legally allowed to be her guardian. Did you get to meet her?"

"Yes, we did. Dani and Heather were remarkably close from what I can remember."

"They still are. I'm sorry you had to go through losing both of us. I know it must not have been easy on either occasion."

"No, it wasn't easy, but today has made up for everything, I believe."

I raise my beer to him and nod. "Yeah, today has been really good. It's been a long time since I've felt this calm. Believe it or not, I just asked Heather to move in with me." I shake my head slightly as I recall asking her. "I didn't think she was going to agree to it, but she did."

"Ah, there is nothing in this world like coming home to the woman you love, son. You better take care of her. She's a good girl—I can tell she still is, even though years have passed since we last saw her. Now tell your old man: are you two just moving in together, or is there a possibility for more?"

I chuckle because I'm stunned. Fuck, I want so much more with my ballerina, but I don't think she's there yet. I know she told me she was when I went skydiving with Coen, but that could have easily been the adrenaline coursing through her stubborn veins.

"I'd like more. I'd like a lot more, but I acted like an ass a while back, in London. I won't get into the details, but I don't think she'd be interested in a ring from me."

"Now, now, you listen to me . . . I've been with you two for a day, and it's plain to see that you can't be apart from each other. In fact I bet—with my back to the doors—that she's looking at you right now. That is a woman who is solely in love with the man who has her heart. Heather didn't have to come out here today, and I don't think she did it for me and Ellery, or herself for that matter. She's had years to reconnect with us. Son, she did this for you."

I look up and my ballerina is looking back and forth from Ellery to myself. "I love her. I've never questioned her being the one, but I've made her question it more than once."

I chance a look at him, and he's smiling simply because he was right. Fuck, this conversation seems to be headed in a direction I'm not quite comfortable talking about with him. I suddenly feel like he's Heather's father, and I should be asking him if it's okay.

I clear my throat, searching for a change of subject, when he moves his ankle from his knee and groans as he stands up. He bends down and pats the side of my knee as I sit there looking up at him. He chuckles, a shit-eating grin on his face. "I've been in trouble with that little woman in there more times than I can count. But one thing is for certain: she knows how much I love her. And I know that Heather knows how much you love her. Call it a father's intuition."

He winks at me when he hears the double doors open, and Ellery's soft voice calls out, "Honey? Can we come join you?"

"Come on out; we don't bite."

My eyes fly to Heather's, and I see her sly grin as she walks toward us. *Yeah, I know what you're thinking, ballerina. I do bite.*

Heather joins me on the loveseat, and I reach out to take her hand. "How's the hot chocolate?"

Henry and Ellery are both watching us interact with each other. Ellery is beaming, and Henry has a grin plastered on his face.

"Just like I remembered," she says, smiling, and we lace our fingers together. I feel her thumb rub against my hand, and I know it's her way of calming me. She's gauging my mood, and I couldn't love her more for it. This woman knows me better than anyone ever has and I know now, in this moment, everything is going to be impeccable. I have her, I have my parents . . . everything is seamless.

Ellery sighs deeply, thankfully. "I'm glad you're enjoying it, darling. Now tell me, you two, will you be staying here tonight?"

Heather turns to me and I look back. I don't have an answer for her or Ellery. "I . . . oh, Ellery, I didn't bring any of my things here," she replies with genuine sadness.

"Oh, how silly of me. Of course, dear . . . will you be around for breakfast?"

Heather answers before I can even respond. "Yes, of course."

"Fabulous. Now if you'll excuse me, I know it's rather rude, but I must get some rest. It's been a very adventurous day. Please don't leave on my account. You boys have lots of catching up to do." She smiles and kisses Henry on the cheek.

I look over and see Heather hide a yawn, and I gently squeeze her thigh. "No, I think we better head back as well. I've got to get this girl her medication." I lean over and kiss her temple.

Henry smiles and stands up. "That's a good idea. Heather, I'll take a look at it in the morning, and please bring your medication with you too. Come on, we'll walk you out."

I help Heather stand, and my hand finds her lower back. We make our way back inside with a little chatter about tomorrow's breakfast menu. I can't help but laugh as I set my empty beer bottle on the countertop. "Ellery, please don't go to all that trouble again. Heather and I would like to take you both out."

Ellery beams and hugs me tightly without warning. "Let us know where to meet you in the morning and at what time. We'll be ready to go."

I look down and hesitantly wrap my arms around her. It feels foreign, her love for me. But I'm getting more and more used to it. "How does brunch sound instead of breakfast? I know Heather's medication makes her tired, and I'm afraid we may be sleeping in."

"That works for us, son—just let us know when and where. Heather dear, it's been great reconnecting with you." He hugs Heather briefly before shaking my hand.

"Thank you for having us; it has truly been an unforgettable day."

"I couldn't agree with you more."

We make our way to the SUV and say our goodbyes for the evening. I help Heather get in and buckled before I get in myself. I watch my parents, on their doorstep, wave goodbye, and it's a sight I thought I'd never see. I honk twice before pulling away and heading back down the driveway and past the gate. As soon as I turn onto the road, I have to pull off to the side and park. The tension and emotions from today finally get to me, and I just need a moment to think.

Fuck, I just spent the day with my parents.

Chapter Seventeen

UNEXPECTED FURTHERANCE

HEATHER

I'm rummaging through my purse when I feel the SUV pull off to the side. Confused, I look up and over, seeing Noah's chest heave with deep breaths.

Oh my God, what's wrong?

"Baby? Are you okay?"

I turn and am about to unbuckle my seatbelt when I'm forced back into my seat. Before I can gasp, his lips are on mine in a rush. His thunderstorm is back, and I can feel it roll over my body. His tongue seeks entry and I part my lips to taste him, to calm him. He groans into my mouth, and his hand creeps up my neck. I'm immediately wet, and he has me wanting more.

"Fuck, you were amazing today," he says between kisses as he nips and licks along my jaw.

I grasp at his shirt, pulling him closer. I can feel his rapid heartbeat beneath my fingers, and it feels as if it's going to beat out of his chest.

He's back against my lips and bites down hard. My mouth falls open in a sharp breath, and he plunges his tongue in, taking what he wants, taking what's his.

"Do you know how fucking badly I wanted my hands on you to-day?" I hear him ask over my drumming heart.

His hand hurriedly shoves my long skirt up, and he finds the apex of my thighs with great ease. Pushing my legs apart, he moves my hand to his abundant erection simultaneously.

"This . . . I've wanted this buried inside your pussy all fucking day, Heather."

He squeezes my hand, so I feel his rock-hard length trapped beneath his jeans. "It hurts, Heather; my dick is so hard it hurts."

His warm breath washes over my face, and I look up into his eyes. They're dark with lust, but there's something else there. I know instantly what's wrong. He's trying to wash away his fears with my touch. A sense of calm settles over me and I bring my hand up, caressing his cheek gen-tly before rubbing his bottom lip with my thumb.

"Shh . . ." I force his hand away from between my legs slowly. He lets me move him while he stares into my eyes. His movements are stiff, unlike himself. My poor Greek god has just been through an intensely nerve-racking experience and has come out unscathed. He's so pent up with emotion, and the only way he can express it is with his body.

Oh my baby.

I nod and wet my thumb against his tongue. "Calm down for me." I smile softly and watch as his chest that was once heaving, is now slowing with deep, steady breaths. "You're okay, baby. Everything went fine."

He finally blinks and leans forward, resting his forehead against mine. I lace our fingers together and sit there quietly, silently waiting for him to come back to me, waiting for him to process everything with-out pushing him. He's resting against me for minutes, contemplating. I watch as he nods—whether to himself or me, I'm not sure.

"I'm sorry."

My heart breaks for him, and I wish I could help him get through this. "Noah, no. Don't ever be sorry for needing me. I'm yours to keep."

I can feel his breathing slow, and I bring my hand up to caress his cheek, brushing softly against his skin, using my fingertips and then my knuckles. He moves slowly but lays his head against my chest and neck. I'm melting inside. I don't think he's ever needed me like this before. My strong, muscled Greek god is lying against my chest, needing my protection for once. I run my fingers into his hair to help him calm down. My storm might be overcast and gloomy, but he's mine.

He breathes me in and nuzzles my neck before kissing me reverently there. "Can we go back to the hotel? I need to make love to you," he asks quietly before licking a tender spot under my collarbone.

The sharp chill that runs down my body is telling enough. I cup his cheeks and make him look up at me. "I'd love that."

He moves and takes my mouth fervently. The passion and heat that we had moments ago is still there in our kiss, but this time he's controlled. He smiles against my lips, pulls back, and sits up in his seat. He doesn't let go of my hand as he puts the SUV into drive and heads down the tree-lined road.

I make sure to keep touching him as he drives. He seems lost in thought again, and I try to bring him out of his storm after almost thirty minutes of silence. "I'm truly proud of you, Noah. You made such a giant leap today."

He glances over at me and winks—that wink will kill me one of these days.

I feel my teeth sink into my lip and I stifle a moan. "I love when you do that to me."

He pulls into the hotel's parking lot and unbuckles. "When I do what?"

I unbuckle my own seatbelt and watch him. "When you wink at me."

He chuckles and gets out, walking around to my door and opening it. "Come on, baby. I want this gorgeous body naked in my arms."

He leans in to lift my skirt a little and help me out of the SUV. "Is the pain in your foot tolerable, Heather? You've been on it all day."

"I'm hanging in there. It's not nearly as bad as what it once would have been. I'll need to take my medication, though."

I feel his hand at the small of my back when he pushes me forward to shut the door. "Well, let's get you inside, and I can take care of my girl."

This man makes me swoon all of the stinking time. We get up to our hotel room and the turn-down service must have already been in because the bed sheet is pulled back, and the nightstand lamp is set on dim.

I rest my bag on the chair as I enter the room and walk over to the bed. My mind is running a million miles a minute as I sit on the bed and slowly remove my boot. I haven't even processed what happened today. I was so consumed with worry for Noah that I didn't have time to think about my own fears. I can't believe how open and loving Ellery and Henry were toward me. They could have treated me differently, much differently. But today was an outpouring of love for the both of us. Before I can think of much more, I look down and see Noah at my feet, helping my foot out of its confines. *Where did he come from?* I must have been so lost to my thoughts that I didn't even see him kneel at my feet.

He sets my boot down and reaches for my medication on the nightstand. "Do you need one or two?"

"I think one will be just fine, thank you."

He hands me one, and gets up, grabbing a bottle of water from the mini fridge. "Lie down, ballerina; you need to relax."

I take my medication and lie back to watch him move around the room. "Mmm . . . so bossy, I love it," I say, trying to joke with him. He lifts his t-shirt up and off of his torso, and my mouth goes slack.

"Do you now?"

I nod. "When you finish, can you grab me some pajamas out of my bag?"

"No. You're sleeping naked tonight." He drops his jeans and walks over to my side of the bed before dropping his boxer briefs too.

"Oh?" I play coy and roll onto my side to watch him.

He climbs over me and lies down, so we're face-to-face.

I smile and run my finger down his bare chest. "Hi."

"Mmm, hi, gorgeous."

His arms move around me and pull my maxi dress up and off, revealing my matching bra and panties.

I watch as his eyes devour every inch of my body. "Thank you for taking such good care of me, Noah. You're always so thoughtful. I always think I'm going to wake up and this will all be a dream—you won't be real."

"I'm real, baby, and I love you." He pulls my bare skin against his and locks me in his arms.

I look up at him and kiss his jaw. "I happen to love you too."

His smile is so earnest, it melts me. "You know, I never thought I'd ever hear you say that."

"Well you better not get sick of it now," I tease and press my lips to his, tasting his need.

I feel his growl rumble low in his chest, and my tongue teases him. I love teasing him; it's become my new favorite activity.

His hands move down to cup my behind, toying with the lace of my cheeksters while our tongues tease each other's.

I must have fallen asleep on him last night because when I open my eyes again, morning light spills into the room through an obscured crack in the curtains. I groan and hide my face in his chest before pulling the blanket up and over my head. He must be awake because I feel his chest move with a chuckle that I don't hear.

"Are you grumpin' already, ballerina?"

"Shh . . ."

"I'll take that as *hell yes, don't fuck with my sleep, Noah*."

"Noah . . ."

I feel him kiss the top of my head and slide out from underneath me. I am now lying on a hotel pillow instead of my spot, worsening my already grumpy morning.

"Come back?" I try and plead with him, but I hear the shower running before I can get the words out of my mouth. I reluctantly get up and toss the blanket. I'm too hot now, and it's pissing me off. I want my Noah back.

I stomp, yes stomp, into the bathroom and stand in front of the glass shower door in just my lace underwear. "We didn't have sex last night?"

He opens the door and takes in my body and mood. "Is that why you're grumpin'?"

"No . . . well . . . maybe." My sex is throbbing from the mere sight of this naked Greek god. "Why didn't we?"

He runs the washcloth over his bicep, and my mouth waters from wanting to bite him there. "You fell asleep kissing me, and I didn't want to wake you. Yesterday was the longest you've been up on your feet in weeks. You needed to rest."

"But I wanted to be fucked," I huff and cross my arms, intentionally pushing my breasts up.

His eyes go wide because I said *fucked*. "I believe another sucker is in order on our drive home, Miss Lane."

I bite my lip and almost lose my body to the memory. "Oh?"

"Mmhmm, now get in here and get ready. We have thirty minutes before we need to meet them for brunch."

I quickly remove my lacy underwear before stepping into the shower with the water cascading down one side of my body. "You really like them, don't you?"

"Yeah. They are a lot different than what I expected them to be."

"They are truly amazing," I add before completely stepping under the waterfall showerhead.

He nods and gives me that damn sexy wink again.

I need more suckers.

We're at a restaurant called 75 Main in Southampton. The French doors are open onto the sidewalk, letting in the slightest cool breeze. It took us an hour before we could actually get a table inside of this gorgeous place for brunch. Henry and Ellery have just ordered us all bottomless mimosas as we look over the menu.

When the waiter returns with our mimosas, Ellery orders the marinated portobello and vegetable salad, Henry orders the Belgium waffles, Noah gets the omelet with sweet sausage, and I follow Henry's lead with the waffles, my sweet tooth shining through.

Once the waiter walks away with the menus in hand, Henry clears his throat. "How are the accommodations over there at the Maidstone?" I smile and look over at Noah and then back at the two of them.

"I've slept really well. I actually don't remember passing out last night."

I hear Noah chuckle and feel him put his arm behind my chair. I get chills when his thumb rubs along my bare arm. "Yes, well, you are taking medication. It's either that, or I'm incredibly boring," he jokes lightly, showing his parents a new side of himself.

Henry chuckles and takes Ellery's hand. "This feisty one passes out on me every night. It's the Somer's curse, I tell you."

"I try to stay up, I really do, but I cannot seem to keep my eyes open past nine in the evening." She laughs and tries to defend herself.

"I know you do, angel, but you get up at the crack of dawn. I know your garden needs your attention too."

I almost melt at his term of endearment for her. I briefly glance at Noah and back at my surroundings, wondering if Noah ever thinks of calling me anything other than ballerina. I hear the clatter of silverware somewhere in the distance while my thoughts run wild—and not in a good way. I suddenly have questions for Noah, about the girls in his past—how he referred to them and what he did with them intimately—questions I want answers to, but I'm also unsure if I want to hear them.

"Heather, dear?" Ellery's voice interrupts my thoughts. My hearing becomes unclouded, and the room is once again loud with chatter. I realize then that I've dazed out in front of everyone. "Hmm?" I look around, and everyone is staring at me.

"Are you in pain?"

I blink and shake my head quickly. "No, no, I'm fine, Ellery." I give her my best smile, but she seems to watch me like a mother hen.

Our brunch arrives, and Noah looks at me suspiciously. He turns to whisper in my ear, "You can't hide shit from me. I'll find out what's wrong."

My reply is caught in my throat, and I'm fairly turned on by his confidence.

"Ah, before you two leave today, we need to talk in private, please?" Henry announces as Noah takes a bite of his omelet.

I sip my mimosa before drizzling syrup on my waffles. I don't reply because I'm assuming he's addressing Noah.

"Sure, that won't be a problem," Noah says and takes my hand underneath the table, playing with my mother's engagement ring.

I clear my throat and address Ellery. "You'll have to teach me how to keep a plant alive. I don't have much of a green thumb."

"Oh, I'd love to, darling. The next time you come down we'll plant something for you to take home. I have a little trick for my potted plants—I use the makings of a diaper and mix it in with the soil. It holds a lot of water and you can go days without having to worry about it drying out."

"Really?" I'm genuinely surprised but still skeptical of my ability. "I don't know. I've even killed off that lucky bamboo stuff that is supposedly hard to kill," I say in all seriousness, but Noah starts laughing.

"Well, that's something I have yet to hear. I'll help you, darling. Just let me know what plant or flower you'd like to grow before coming down, okay?"

I smack Noah's arm playfully as he continues to laugh. "Okay, I'll think of something."

"Noah, play nice," she lightheartedly scolds him.

"Yes, ma'am."

I put my fork down because I am stuffed. I watch Noah reach for his wallet and slip the waiter his card. Henry won't be happy about this, I'm sure.

I try to keep Henry occupied with a question. "Um, Henry . . . you said you'd like to take a look at my foot today. Is there a reason? Am I walking funny?" I'm suddenly nervous.

"Not that I can tell, but this is what I do. I won't trust just anyone with you, Heather. Let's head back to the house, and we'll take a look."

"Okay, thank you."

Henry moves to ask for the check when Noah helps me stand. "It's already been taken care of," Noah states before pulling out his mother's chair to help her as well.

Henry raises his eyebrow and chuckles to himself as if he's got something to hide. "Ah, we're playing this game, are we?" He winks at me and we walk out to the SUV and their Mercedes.

It doesn't take long before we're back in the confines of the Somers' Southampton home. We're all sitting in the living room with a fresh mimosa in hand.

Henry's voice grabs my attention and what he says makes me smile. "Young man, I'm not happy with that stunt you pulled at brunch, but your mother and I appreciate it."

Noah smiles and reaches for my hand. "What did you want to talk to me about?"

He clears his throat and looks over at Ellery questioningly. We both watch as she nods and smiles softly, prompting Henry to say, "Noah, come to my office with me?"

"Yeah, sure." Noah gets up and follows Henry into his office down the hall.

Ellery moves across the couch to sit closer to me. "Now tell me all about the ballet."

Chapter Eighteen

LOST IN CITY LIGHTS

NOAH

I follow Henry into his office, which looks out onto the water through oversized bay windows. It doesn't surprise me that the room has four floor-to-ceiling bookshelves, which work as a focal point, filling the room with knowledge and color—I now know from where I get my hunger for knowledge.

Henry's desk is positioned in the middle of the room with a large coffee brown leather chair behind it. He walks over to the desk and pulls out a rectangular piece of paper—a check.

"Take a seat, son, please."

I do as he asks and sit down at one of the two seats facing the desk. He surprises me by taking the seat to my right and leans back.

"Before you say anything, let me tell you a little bit of what happened after you were taken from us." He clears his throat, crosses his ankle over his knee, and starts to rub his jaw as he looks out of the window.

"We have spent thirty years looking for you, and as the years went on, it became harder and harder for us to find agents willing to help our search."

I watch quietly as he thinks back. "Your mother, as I'm sure you could imagine, was a wreck. It was a hard time for us. It always has been."

He looks back at me and swallows. "After two years of searching, your mother and I hired an attorney, and under his guidance, we filed suit against the hospital for negligence."

I'm speechless and too nervous to say anything.

"I won't go into too much detail, Noah, but there was a settlement between us and them."

"A settlement?"

"Yes, they didn't want us to tarnish their sterling reputation," he adds, "so from that settlement we received a hefty amount. Ellery suggested that we deposit the money into a bank account for you, hoping it would pay for your college tuition. As the years passed, the investment grew, and Ellery then suggested—and I agreed—that we invest some of that money into the stock market, and that is where it has been for the past twenty-odd years . . . until now." He reaches over and places the folded check on my knee.

"No, Henry, I don't need that."

"Noah, please?"

"Henry . . . I can't accept this," I say in a voice thick with emotion. I'm anxious as all hell. This is fucking uncomfortable, and I can't get out of it.

"Noah, I insist," he states and pats my knee before withdrawing, leaving that small piece of paper on my leg. "Your mother and I are so happy to be able to give you this."

I hesitate to move my hand, but I pick up the check, quickly deciding not to open it in front of him. "You did not have to do this."

I don't want to take this. I don't want a handout from anyone.

"Noah, I won't hesitate to pull the sympathy card and use your mother against you." I feel my eyebrows raise and I look over at him. He's grinning, but I know he'd do it in a heartbeat, just like I did to Heather. I pulled a card on her once, not too long ago, when I thought she was going to leave me. I can't help but laugh in shock and mock disgust.

"Damn," I respond as I shake my head and tap the check against my knee.

"Listen, son, that money is rightfully yours. Your mother and I have never struggled financially, and no, I don't know what your life was like, but you've been through more than anyone could have ever imagined. I won't take that back, and if you shred it, your mother will certainly hear about it, and trust me . . . you do not want to deal with that. I am speaking from experience here."

My jaw clenches and I stare into space, thinking. I know he isn't bluffing; I can read him well enough. My hand creeps up to the back of my neck and a thought enters my mind. With the help of this money, regardless of the amount, and what I've gotten from the diner . . . I could buy Heather a home. I could get my ballerina out of the city and into somewhere she deserves.

"Son? Are we in agreement?" he asks, breaking into my thoughts.

My hand clenches the back of my neck and I look over at him, exhaling a deep breath. "Damn, I don't know."

"Shall I get your mother in here?" he threatens.

I can't help but laugh, and he stands up, clapping me on the back. He looks triumphant as he grins. "That's what I thought you'd say." He pauses as I stand up and put the check in my back pocket. "Glad to have you home, son," he says and reaches for me. Before I can have the chance to feel uncomfortable, he grabs me for a hug. It's brief, but I feel his love for me in his embrace before he lets go. "Come on. Let's go check out Heather's foot before you two need to head out."

I follow him out and back down the hallway into the living room where Heather and Ellery are chatting up a storm.

"Ladies . . ." Henry says at our entrance, causing them to look up at the two of us. Heather beams up at me, and hell, I just figured out what else I'll be spending the money on. I wink at her, partly to see her cheeks flush and partly to let her know that everything is fine.

"Heather, why don't you let me take a look at that foot now?"

I watch as he crouches down next to her leg. I'm watching, but also my mind is racing. Things I've never really spent time considering are pushing their way to the forefront and making themselves known.

I'm startled when I feel someone touch my arm. I look down to my right and see Ellery smiling up at me. "Are you okay, honey? Henry didn't bully you, did he?"

My tense shoulders relax and I laugh lightly. I know then that Ellery knew what our brief meeting was about. I also realize that they played an excellent routine of good-cop-bad-cop to get their end result with me.

"Of course he did." I smile and put my arm around her shoulders. She's more than willing to accept my hug, and I can't thank either of them enough. "Thank you . . . it's unnecessary, but thank you." I lower my voice to help conceal our conversation while Henry and Heather talk.

Ellery doesn't let go of me as we watch Henry inspect my ballerina's injured foot, "Mmhmm, just what I thought. Heather, you're going to need to go through a month or two of regular physical therapy before you'll be able to dance, and depending on how your recovery proceeds . . . you may or may not be able to dance on pointe again."

Oh shit.

My eyes fly to Heather's face. I watch as the smile that once adorned her face quickly disappears. "Wait, what?" she asks in total surprise.

"Heather, I just want you to know what could happen if it doesn't heal correctly. I'd like to be the one you come to for physical therapy, if you don't mind driving out here three times a week. Ellery and I could drive into the city too. I want you to have the best chance of getting back on the stage and I won't trust you with anyone else."

Heather looks to me for answers, and my chest swells. Fuck, I can't help how it makes me feel that she turned to me for help. I nod slowly. "Let him, Heather. We can make it work."

"Okay," she says softly, and fuck, I just want her in my arms. She looks up at the ceiling and blinks quickly to keep her tears at bay.

I know how much she worried about being able to dance again and now she's getting her worst fears vocalized by a professional. Hell, I know she needs my touch right now just as I need hers. I move out of Ellery's arms and kneel down next to my girl. "Let me get your boot back on, baby."

Henry pats my shoulder and gets up. "Good on you, son."

She doesn't look down but nods. I run my thumb across the top of her bare foot and smile when her toes wiggle. I guess I never realized that her feet were ticklish.

"Why don't we go for a walk along the beach before you two leave?" Ellery suggests.

I smile and nudge her. "That sounds nice, don't you think, sweetheart?"

She instantly smiles and looks down at me. I don't know the reason for her smile but it lights me on fire.

"Yes, I'd love to," she answers Ellery, and I feel like we've successfully sidetracked her mini tornado of tears.

I stand and offer her my hand. She gets up and wraps her arms around my torso instead. Ellery and Henry look at each other and decide to give us a few moments. "We'll be waiting out front, dear," Ellery says as they both walk away.

I look down at the top of her head as I rub my hand down her back. "We'll get through this, Heather. I know you're upset, but it's going to be okay. Everything will work out for the best."

She nuzzles my chest. "I'm okay. I'm sorry, I don't mean to ruin this time for you."

"You couldn't ruin anything even if you tried, beautiful." I tilt her chin up and force her to look at me. "Now give me a kiss and let's take a walk."

She pushes up and presses her lips to mine. Fuck, I feel like I've needed her lips more than anything at this point in time.

I kiss her, and then move my lips to her ear. "I'm ready to get you home."

My cock grows hard when my hand trails down her throat. I feel her swallow, and she steps back, grabbing my hand. "Come on, lover-boy, enough of that," she teases and tugs at my arm. I smirk and watch her ass as I follow her.

❧

It's just over a two-hour drive back to the city from Southampton, but the traffic is ridiculous and we've been stuck on this highway-turned-parking-lot for about forty minutes now. Heather has fallen asleep in the passenger seat, and hell, she's unequivocally beautiful. After our walk on the beach, we spent a few more hours talking in their sunroom before Ellery and Heather made dinner together. It was one hell of an interesting weekend; I've learned a lot about my parents, Heather, and myself.

She loved me when I ached, when every piece of who I am was scattered across a space that I was unable to venture to alone, but she ventured there with me, and it's because of her that I haven't given up and resorted to drinking my days away. Everything about our relationship has been hard to control, but I think we've found the in-between—the place that we are both happiest with each other, and a place where we can both promise to give each other everything we have to offer. She set my damn world on an axis that didn't exist, and switched my poles around: north is now south and east is now west. As much as she's helped set my world spiraling out of control, it has not once been in the wrong direction.

I glance back over at her after moving up five inches. Fuck, this is taking forever. She takes in a deep breath before shifting slightly and stilling again, and in this moment I know she's right. Unmistakably, bravely, and honestly right: I need to talk to Mae.

I believe that everyone is brought into our lives for a reason, whether it's to help us grow or for us to help them grow. When it comes to Mae, I don't know the reason for her being in my life; I have yet to find something good that has come out of the past thirty years. Yes, I loved my life before I knew it wasn't supposed to be mine, but how can I turn back to that when it's long gone?

I need to go and see her.

I keep telling myself that I need to make up my mind about this, and now I have. It's set. I just need to make it all happen. Shit, what are my parents going to say when I tell them I'm going to go and see her?

The traffic starts to inch forward, and I follow while my thoughts are lost to the darkness of the SUV's interior. My past is my past, and it has molded me into who I am today. If I was given the opportunity to change anything, would I?

No, I don't think I would, because as much as everything has bothered me . . . I don't think I would be able to go a day poisoning myself with an altered future.

Hell, what I wouldn't give to be pounding my feet against the asphalt rather than wheeling over it right now; as much as it exhausts me, it's also the most effective way to lose myself. It keeps me from losing my mind, and spilling out for the world to see exactly how fucked up I am.

My mind switches from first to fifth gear as if I'm all of a sudden hurling down this overcrowded highway; fuck, I can't accept that much money. The check that Henry and Ellery gave me is sitting too comfortably in the pocket of my jeans.

What the hell do I do with that money? Give it away? Invest it?

I need to breathe.

I need to collect myself and being surrounded by people in metal boxes all pretending not to stare into the darkness of the metal box next to them is not helping my thought process. I'm being watched and judged in the dark while they don't know me. They don't know that I can see dawn; it may just be a speck of light, but it's what I have to go by.

I get over into the right lane of 495 to turn off the expressway at the next exit and then follow secondary roads heading west toward Manhattan. I drive another fifteen minutes before getting off at Smithtown, where I find a place to get gas and just fucking inhale without being suffocated.

The cool night breeze hits me when I get out of the SUV. I shut the door and start filling the tank up before I walk back to the driver's seat. I pause when I see my ballerina through the window, sleeping soundly. Every time I see her in all of her innocence, I have to pause and remind myself that she's mine. I have to remind myself that the path that I'm on is where I want to be, and it's where she wants to be too.

It's in this moment that I decide that I won't put us on a hiatus for anyone or any petty excuse anymore. I know what I want with her, and I trust that she knows what she wants out of this relationship too. Sure, we're on the fast track, but it's what has been working for us.

The gas pump clicks before I've even managed to open the door again. I finish up and get back into the car.

"Where are we?"

"Hey sleeping beauty. I had to stop and get gas. We're about an hour out from the city and an hour from Southampton."

"Oh? I feel like I've been asleep for much longer."

"You have been. We were stuck in standstill traffic for a while. Go back to sleep. I'll get you to bed when we get back."

"Mmm, okay." She moves and lays her head on the center console before she's lights out again, and I'm drawn back into my turbulent ocean of thoughts.

Chapter Nineteen

GENUINE VERDICTS

HEATHER

I've been in better spirits, but Noah is trying his best to keep me in a good mood. He knows I'm bummed out about what Henry told me regarding my foot. I had a feeling that something like this was going to happen. I miss dancing but I've also enjoyed my time off. I've enjoyed my time with Noah. It's been like a vacation for me, a vacation that I've needed for years. I'm lying on the couch on my stomach, searching for a movie to watch. He was rather adamant about having this time with me tonight. I can hear him whistling while he makes popcorn in the kitchen. I've tried making it myself, but it's one of the few things that I can't do. I burn it every time, so he's taken over. I sigh and drop the remote on the living room floor and lay my head on my arms.

"There's nothing worth watching," I mumble into my arms, not necessarily talking to anyone.

"Well, I'll have to disagree with you, beautiful," he says close to my ear, startling me, and I almost jump out of my skin.

I sit up and groan, "Noah . . ."

"What is it?" he asks and sits next to me, offering me the bowl of popcorn.

"I just like moaning your name."

He raises his eyebrow and laughs. "Well, that makes two of us. I quite enjoy you moaning my name as well." He winks and I have to squeeze my thighs together. I push the bowl of popcorn away and out of his lap. He watches as I crawl closer to him and lie on my back with my head resting on his thigh.

"You don't want any?" he asks and stretches for the bowl, moving it within his reach.

"No, I don't feel like it," I reply, sounding a little more bummed out than what I thought.

He grins and hands me a different bowl, setting it on my stomach. I lift my head and my spirits are lifted if only just a bit.

"Peanut butter M&M's?"

"I had a feeling you would want something sweet."

I love how well he knows me; this Greek god is someone I never thought I'd have in my life. I push his black V-neck up and sink my teeth into his side.

He grunts and his abs clench.

His hand finds the back of my head, and he pulls on my hair just a little. "Damn it; give me some warning next time." He growls that sexy growl but leaves my head in place. I can't help but smile and kiss him where I bit, before moving back out from under his shirt.

He looks down at me and runs his fingers through my hair. It's soothing, and I smile softly as I eat an M&M.

"I want to talk to you about something important," he says with a serious but soft tone.

"Uh-oh, that doesn't sound good," I joke, but I'm honestly a little frightened. He runs his thumb over my eyebrow softly, and it makes me close my eyes. I instantly force my eyes open and focus. He doesn't know that this move could render me unconscious in seconds. My father used to do that to put me to sleep when I was little.

He avoids my small joke and continues to rub my eyebrow. "What are your thoughts on moving out of the city?"

"Mmm . . ." My eyes close slowly and I try to picture living somewhere other than the city. I think about what it would be like to be Henry and Ellery, with yard work. I can feel my lips move, and I grin. "Mmm, maybe."

"Yeah?"

I can hear his surprise, and I think he's smiling, but I'm too comfortable to open my eyes. "Mhmm," I reply and continue to think about what he's asked me.

He hasn't stopped rubbing over my eyes, and I try to fight off sleep. I think he's realized that this is a surefire way to relax me. I lazily move my hand up and weakly shove his away before frowning and turning my head. He chuckles low and deep, and I hear him move the popcorn and M&M's before lying down beside me.

I turn my body into his and lay my cheek against his chest. His cologne envelops me and makes me swoon. "Mmm, you smell good." My voice is dreamy and slow.

"Oh yeah?" He starts rubbing over my eyes again. "I think that's two new things I've learned about you in the last twenty-four hours," he says quietly.

Before I can ask what he means, he offers up the information. "Your little feet are ticklish, and I can put you to sleep by touching you here," he all but whispers while he touches me.

I try and fight him off with my hand, but I'm so relaxed. "Nooo," I groan into his chest.

His hand moves lower to run over my back and down my thigh. "Mmm, but your noes usually mean yes."

I can hear that he's amused with himself but I'm too close to passing out to check and see.

"Mmm, go to sleep, my beautiful girl," I hear him say before a blanket of warmth covers me, and I fall into a relaxed and peaceful sleep.

I wake up to the sound of my phone vibrating on my nightstand. I lift my head and try to remember how in the hell I got here. Last I remember I was tucked into Noah's warmth, moments from passing out. The buzzing is persistent and annoying, and I'm about to reach over Noah's body for it when he groans and extends his arm. He grabs my phone, and I think he's going to hand it to me when he tosses it across the room. I gasp and try not to laugh.

He drags his heavy arm around my waist and pulls me down again.

"It's okay, baby, I got it," he says before falling back asleep.

I smile and lie quietly in his arms, listening to him breathe. I hear the early morning traffic down below us and cringe when a fire truck blares its horn. For the first time ever, I wonder what it's like to live away from all of this ambient noise and constant chaos.

Would I like it?

Is it something I could get used to?

I've never lived outside of the city.

Where would we live? Would we have a lawn? A lawn mower? I don't even know how to mow grass.

Would we have neighbors? Barbecues with them? Is that a real thing that happens or is it just in the movies? Would this mean more than just moving in together? A house . . . with Noah?

I start to panic but then his arms move, and he holds me tighter to him. Can he feel my heart rapidly beating while he sleeps? Is his body so attuned to mine that he knows when I'm stressed, even while he's out cold?

I start to think about that first night at his parents'. Their home was so cozy and inviting and I loved it. I loved how peaceful it was out there, away from the loud and rude city occupants. They were free to enjoy their fire pit in silence, cuddled up on the outdoor chaise if they wanted.

As soon as I saw it, I pictured myself and Noah curled up by the fire. It was such a romantic fantasy, but I dismissed it immediately. Now . . . maybe . . . could we have that?

That one single thought of me and my Greek god curled up by the fire is all it takes. All it takes to make one of the most important decisions in my life without any more hesitation.

"Noah?"

He forces his eyes open and runs his large hand down his groggy face. "What is it? Are you okay?"

I lift my head and shake his shoulder lightly.

I smile because, God, he's always thinking of me. I lay my head back down, resting my chin on his chest. "I'm okay. I just wanted to tell you . . ." I pause and watch as he nods and almost drifts off to sleep, " . . . I want to leave the city." I hold my breath while I watch him nod with his eyes closed.

"Okay, baby, we'll go out today," he speaks as he almost passes out again.

I have to hold in my laugh because he seems to have forgotten about last night. I shake his shoulder again, and his eyes fly open.

"I'm up, I'm up," he says sleepily and then closes his eyes again.

"Noah?" I try and persuade him to wake up by running my hand down his bare chest and under the hem of his sweatpants.

He groans, and I can feel him grow hard beneath me. He's never been this hard to wake up before; I briefly wonder what time he brought me to bed and how long he lay awake for. My phone buzzes on the hardwood floor again, and I move to get off of him.

"Sweetheart, come back here, please?" he says once I'm off of the bed and leaning down to pick up my phone.

I melt when I hear that word leave his lips again. Yesterday when he said it, it took me by surprise.

I grab my phone and see a handful of missed texts and phone calls from Dillen.

Dang, Dillen, it's too early.

I walk back over and set my phone on my nightstand as I climb back in bed with my man. His arms mold around my body the moment I'm back in bed. He nuzzles me and takes in a deep breath to help wake himself up. "Who the hell keeps calling, and where did you want to go today?"

"It's Dillen. And I don't think you're understanding me." I lightly drag my nails down his chest again and watch as small goose bumps break out over his skin. "I want to leave the city. Like, move away."

I think it finally registered in his sleepy brain because he tilts his head up and looks down at me with wide eyes. "Are you serious? You would do that?"

I nod slowly and watch as his eyes flicker with excitement.

I feel his chest thunder with eagerness before the smoky growl comes through his lips. He flips me onto my back onto the pillow-top bed and moves his lean, tanned body over mine, "Where are you willing to go with me?"

I look up at him, and my hands run over his chest. "I'll follow you anywhere."

"I wouldn't take you far, beautiful. I was thinking that it'd be a good place to be between my parents and here. I think I want them more involved in my life."

"I'd really like that too. They were so excited to be a part of your life; I think it's a great idea."

His lips find mine instead of answering me. "You wouldn't mind living in Long Island?"

"No . . ." I answer when he lets me up for air. Before I can say any more, he's back on my mouth again.

I can feel his girth digging into me, but my phone starts vibrating again, and I break our kiss to see that it's Dillen calling once again.

"I need to get this, baby."

He grasps my chin and holds me in place as his teeth find my lower lip at the same time that he grinds his length against me. I whimper in response.

I want him, but I've already swiped my finger across the screen along the green button, "Noah . . ."

He continues his assault against my neck and under my collarbone, as his hands travel south, spreading my legs.

"Dillen?" I try to squeak out, but his movements are so deliberate that I think he's enjoying my current torture. Noah is undressing and I'm unable to focus.

"Little shit, damn, how many times do I have to call? Oh and hi," Dill says excitedly as Noah cups my sex.

"I'm sorry, I was asleep." I look at Noah as he rises up and sits between my legs. I'm mesmerized when he grabs his thick length and strokes it, while his other hand is exploring between my thighs.

"Well, good morning, and I need you to do me a favor, okay?" She continues before I can answer her, "I need you to get dressed and come pick me up from JFK, like, now."

I gasp when his fingers penetrate me and then her words register in my brain. "Wait, what?"

She giggles and squeals, "I know right? Surprise!"

"You're here? Like, you're at JFK right now?"

"Yes," she shouts. "Come and get your best friend, you bitch!"

"Holy crap . . ." I sit up quickly and beam up at Noah.

He looks down at me with confusion marring his handsome face as I finish the conversation with Dill. "Okay, I'm getting dressed, and we'll be there as soon as we can."

"Okay, hurry, you need to hug your new roomie. Call me when you're here."

Roomie?

"Okay, love you, bye!" I hang up and toss my phone, looking up at Noah. He looks so utterly perplexed and adorable. "Dill is here," I say excitedly.

"Here? As in New York City?"

"Yes!" I sit up farther and kiss him softly, and he groans against my lips.

"What do I do with this?" he asks and looks down at his heavy shaft in his hand.

I giggle and kiss his cheek. "I'll make it up to you, I swear."

He drops his head dejectedly and growls, letting go of himself. "You're going to kill me. It's been days."

"Maybe I'll get some more suckers then."

He looks up and locks eyes with me. Before I know it, he's got me pinned to the bed. My wrists are locked in his grip above my head and his chest is pressed tightly to mine. My nipples are peaked and sensitive, and he knows it.

"Don't tease me, Heather."

Holy crap. He's serious.

"You like that sucker that much, huh?"

His fingers tighten around my wrists and he grinds his erection against my body. The sexual tension between us is thick and heavy, just like what he's got nestled between my legs. "Heather . . . say one more thing about them and I'll fuck you until you can't walk."

I want that.

I stay quiet because I simply don't know what to say. I want him more than anything, but I need to go get my best friend from the airport.

He seems to come to some sort of conclusion because his grip on my wrists is suddenly gone, and he lifts himself off my body, leaving me there breathless and weak.

"Should I let Coen know that Dillen is visiting?" He strides meaningfully into the bathroom and I hear the shower turn on.

My body is buzzing with need, but I'm going to have to put it on the back burner. I get up and follow him into the shower, doing my best not to brush up against him while I wash my body.

"Yes, I think you should tell him, so he doesn't come here with Lana, causing all hell to break loose."

He makes a painful sound as if he's envisioning it. "Yeah. I'll call him."

I try to channel my thoughts on something other than our naked bodies being mere inches from each other, but I'm having a hard time. I'm lost in thought, drifting back to the night in the SUV. I let the spray rinse my hair as my hands travel down my body and between my legs. I can still picture him above me, taking me hard. The way his biceps bulged as he braced his body over mine. The ache between my legs is unbearable. I whimper, and my eyes open in a daze. I glance down, and I'm touching myself. I'm surprised because I don't even remember doing it. I look over and Noah is standing perfectly still with his eyes locked on my body, and his jaw is tense. Before I even have a chance to be embarrassed, he speaks.

"Okay, you're done here." He opens the shower door and ushers me out, handing me my towel.

"But . . . I'm still wet."

"Oh baby, I know you are, which is why you better stay out. I don't have the willpower not to fuck you on the bathroom floor. Go get some damn clothes on before I bruise your pretty little body up."

I pout at the shower door and wrap the towel around myself. He's groaning in the shower now, and I think he's got the cold water on full blast. I hear my phone buzz in the other room, and it reminds me about the task at hand.

"Oh crap. She's still waiting." I rush into the closet and get dressed as quickly as I can, while towel-drying my hair. I dab on some lip gloss and throw my hair up into a messy, half-dried bun.

Noah comes out of the bathroom with a towel wrapped around his waist, looking like the grumpiest man in New York City. He walks past me to get dressed and mumbles something to himself about blue balls.

I make a mental note not to tease him too much today and keep my hands to myself. My lips thin as I try not to laugh. He's fumbling around in the closet and talking to himself. I almost can't take it, so I leave the room and go downstairs to wait before I start laughing hysterically.

He descends the stairs when I've just managed to collect myself. "All set, sweetheart?" he asks, and crap . . . I want to throw myself on him.

I clear my throat and shoot Dillen a quick text, letting her know that we're leaving. "I'm all ready. You okay?" I ask, and he gives me a glare. I know he's not mad at me, just sexually frustrated beyond belief.

"Yeah, and you're driving. I'll need both of my hands." He stops to think briefly and runs upstairs. He's back a minute later with a check in his hand. "I need to stop by the bank afterward."

"Okay, we'll go after we pick up Dill." I walk to the door, and he follows behind me. I'm actually excited to be driving, even in horrible New York City traffic. Today is my first day without my boot, since Henry told me it looked well enough to walk around without it.

We get into my car, and he puts the top down. "I think I'm going to invest in an SUV. Possibly like the one we rented," he says, opening the folded check once I pull out of the building and into the sunlight, "and . . . holy fuck."

I slam on my brakes when he yells.

"What? What's wrong?"

I look around, afraid that I've hit something or someone. My heart is beating rapidly as I scan my surroundings.

I stop looking around when I can't see anything wrong and look at him. He's staring at the check he went to pick up. "I . . . fuck."

I start to drive again before I get run over by a cab. "What's wrong, baby?"

"Uh . . . do you remember Henry asked to talk to me in private?"

I nod and try to maneuver my way through traffic. "Yes, is everything okay?"

He runs his hand up the back of his neck and smirks. "More than okay. Fuck, much more than okay. He told me that there was a lawsuit after I was kidnapped, and they invested the amount they received from it. This," he says and holds up the check, "is the full amount after almost thirty years of investment."

My eyes go wide and I'm sure he can see how shocked I am behind my sunglasses. "What! Holy crap, Noah."

"I believe SUV- and house-hunting are in my future."

I look over at him as he reaches for my thigh. "Where do you want to live, ballerina?"

I laugh, and he seems so happy.

Gone is my cranky Greek god and in his place is my smiling, affectionate lover. "I don't know."

I pull up to the pick-up area at JFK, and I sit up in my seat as I search for my Dill.

I keep glancing over at Noah, and he's in another place. He's staring off into the distance and rubbing his jaw. It's his habitual gesture for agitation and deep thought. I know it's not the right time to smile or swoon over him when he's got so much on his mind, but I love how much I've come to know about this man. And I can't wait to tell Dill that we've decided to move in together.

When I see Dill, she's tapping the ball of her foot on the ground impatiently and staring at the face of her watch, no doubt pleading with it. I giggle as I pull up beside her. "Why the long face?"

She looks up and screams excitedly when she sees me. "Ahhh! What took you so long?" I park and get out of the car to throw my arms around her and squeeze the crap out of her.

Not only have I decided to take a step into my future today, I also have my best friend here to talk to about it, and I'm ecstatic. "Hi, I'm sorry we took so long, but I didn't even dry my hair. Traffic was horrible as usual."

"Uh-huh! You guys were boning, weren't you?" she accuses us and smacks my butt.

I laugh and shake my head as Noah comes around to grab her bags and put them in the trunk. "Dillen, I wish I could say that it was true, but my girl shut me down as soon as she heard your voice." I watch as he grabs her for a hug.

"Noah," she squeals excitedly, "I'm sorry. Are your balls going to be okay? Shit, I'll drive, so little shit can get a fucking in the backseat."

"Oh my God, Dillen!" I shout and smack her arm. Noah chuckles and kisses her cheek before opening the door for her.

She climbs into the back and huffs disapprovingly. "Heather, how the hell am I supposed to sit back here? There isn't even room for my legs." She props her legs up on the seat and folds her arms, "you need a new ride."

"Oh, be quiet, this car is twice the size of your little box in London."

"My car was perfect for London. So I guess I should tell you why I'm here, huh?"

Noah gets in the driver's seat so Dill and I can talk. He pulls out and heads back into Manhattan.

I turn in my seat and look back at her. "Yes! What's going on? Why didn't you call me sooner?" I ask, and Noah slips his free hand onto my thigh.

"Well, things got hectic, and I just needed to leave. After your accident the company hasn't been the same. More than four girls dropped out, and they have been worshiping bitch troll ever since you left. I mean, fuck, she's not even that good. They aren't holding her at fault for your fall, and I just couldn't be around those pieces of shit, so I bought a ticket, packed my shit, broke my lease, and left. I'm glad the apartment came furnished because I didn't have to deal with any of the heavy stuff."

My mouth drops open and I look from Dillen to Noah and back again in shock. "What? Dillen! You just up and left?"

"Uh-huh. Say hi to your new roomie, little shit." She slaps a cheesy smile onto her face and points at herself.

I smile wide, and Noah looks at me. Suddenly, I remember what I just decided this morning. "Oh ummm . . ." I grin sheepishly, and Noah squeezes my thigh.

"Oh God, what? Are you guys having a baby? Heather!" She shrieks at me, and Noah and I laugh.

"No, Dill. I'm not . . . we're not pregnant. Noah and I have decided to move in together, though, but we're leaving the city."

"You are? Oh, I just got so jealous of your relationship. Dammit, Noah. Where are you moving to? And I so call dibs on your apartment, little shit."

He chuckles and pats my thigh. "Sorry, Dillen, I have to get my girl out of the city and into the suburbs."

We pull up to a bank's drive-thru for Noah to deposit his check. "I'm sorry, did I miss the wedding? Noah, not to call you out on anything, but things usually come in a specific order, but you're all over the place."

He chuckles and reaches for a pen that I keep in my center console and takes the check from his back pocket. "I have to lock her down, or I might lose her to someone more attractive than myself," he jokes with Dillen as he flips the check over, signs his name, and fills out a deposit slip.

"Oh, shut up. Have you seen yourself? Christ on a cracker, you've made me drool on multiple occasions."

He looks over at me when he puts the check and deposit slip in the canister and sends it on its way, giving me that sexy wink. "Drool, huh? That's never happened before."

"Yeah, okay . . ." Dillen says sarcastically and leans her head back. "We should all go out tonight. I'm going to text Coen and see if he's still interested in this."

Uh-oh.

I tense up and Noah looks at me knowingly. "Ummm . . . what? But you broke up. Have you two been sexting each other?"

She shakes her head and pulls her phone out of her purse. "The damn thing is dead." She tosses it back into her purse and huffs.

I'm about to speak when the bank teller comes on through the speaker. "Everything is all set, Mr. Ryan. If there is anything you ever need from me, don't hesitate to call. I've given you my personal card with your deposit receipt."

I raise my eyebrow and Dillen's mouth drops open. "Whoa . . . that's some service."

He politely thanks her and takes his receipt and the bank teller's card out of the capsule before putting the car in drive and pulling forward.

Dillen is still gawking at him, trying to find the right words in her jetlagged, overly excited brain. "I'm not even going to ask what that was about. So, Noah, where are you taking my little shit?"

Oh thank goodness that shifted her train of thought away from Coen and back to our conversation.

"Uh, I think I'd like to find a house somewhere in Long Island. I think in the middle of the island would be the best place for us to be close enough to the city as well as my parents."

"Well, that's not too far away, but I still don't like it. What are you going to do about your apartment?"

"We haven't gotten that far, but if we sell or rent, then yes, you can have first dibs."

"Thank God . . . we can't let that gorgeous place go to someone crazy."

We finally make it back to my place after driving through bumper-to-bumper traffic—at least the weather is divine and we had the top down.

Noah helps us get all of Dillen's stuff inside and into the living room where she is going to have to crash for now. I watch Dill plug in her phone and squeal excitedly when the screen comes to life. "Coen Reed, you don't know what is coming for your naked ass."

Noah shoots a *you-have-to-fucking-tell-her* look at me. "I think you'll have more luck with seeing Joel's naked ass than you would Coen's." He shrugs as she looks up at him, and I'm shooting daggers in his direction.

The bastard.

He kisses my cheek and grins. "I've got to go shower. Let me know what you two decide to do tonight . . . or who."

"But you just showered . . ."

Oh, forget it.

Dillen sits down on the couch and pats the pink cushion next to her. "Little shit? What is going on?"

My shoulders sag, and I walk over to take my seat. "Coen." I sigh heavily and place my hand on hers. "Dill, you broke up with him after he flew across an ocean to see you. I know you're not used to someone who wants you for more than your body, but Coen did. I don't know the details of what happened or when it happened, but he's seeing someone new."

"What? Heather . . . why? Is it serious?" I watch as I break her heart, even though she did it to herself weeks ago.

I can only nod because I've never seen Coen so content with life. "I would say so."

"Have you met her?"

And there it is: the question I knew I'd have to answer eventually. I don't want her to think that I'm siding against her, or rooting for Coen to move on from her, but she made a rash decision, and now it's biting her in the butt. It's what she does, though; she left the United States to dance in London with only a dream. The dance company hadn't even heard of her when she walked through their front doors. Dillen is a go-getter, whether people are ready for her or not, hence her just showing up today. Nevertheless, I'm elated that she's here, but I can't hide my friendship with Lana from her.

"Yes, her name is Lana, and honestly, Dill, I think you'd love her."

She just stares at me for a moment before she speaks. "Do you have Joel's number?"

"Excuse me?" I squeak and her lips turn up into a grin.

"I just wanted to be fucked, Heather. I'm not in love with him."

She can put up a front with me all she wants, but I know she really liked him. I've never seen her cry over a guy before.

"I'm your best friend, Dill. You don't have to put up that facade with me."

She sags on my couch and dramatically throws her arm over her eyes. "Get out of my head, would you?"

"Nope, I love being in there with you."

She leans her head onto my shoulder and sighs heavily, too heavily. "We can still go out tonight, Dill, but I'm sure Noah will want Coen there. It's up to you."

"Screw it, let's just do it. I can't hide forever in this pink paradise above the city."

"Oh come on, it's not that pink. Aside from my couch and pink blanket, I think it's rather neutral."

"I'm pretty sure you don't see pink anymore," she jokes and hugs me tightly.

Noah comes down then and into the kitchen. We both watch him in silence as he pulls out two crystal flutes, opens a bottle of champagne, and fills each glass before walking over to the two of us and holding them up. "Are we pre-gaming?"

I look at Dill and pout. "Only if she lets me try out that pretty lipstick tonight."

"Of course you can, little shit. You just have to swear not to put it on after your pretty pink lips have been ringed around Noah's cock. I'd rather not have a taste of something I can't bite into, ya know?"

"Dillen," I gasp and smack her arm. "That's mine."

She looks up at Noah and bites her lip. "Are you sure?"

"I'm fucking sure for her," Noah says in a gruff voice. "Drink up, ladies. I'll call the guys and tell them we're going out."

"Wait, do you think he'll bring that girl?" Dill asks nervously.

Noah looks at me, and nods. "Yeah, I know he will."

"Dill, just be open toward her. She's such a sweetheart and so easy to get along with. She said Coen told her about you, so please just be nice, okay?"

"Depends," she jokes—I hope.

My phone goes off and I reach for it. A text from my sister is lit up across the screen:

> I miss you, Heather. How's your foot? Are you enjoying being back? Did Noah meet his parents?

I lean back against the couch and throw myself into my reply to her while Dillen gets up and follows Noah into the kitchen to take a shot:

> Hi, sister. I miss you so much. Dillen just moved back to the city, and I'm so excited. She's crashing with us for a while. Noah asked me to move in with him, and I'm going to. We went to the Somers' house this past weekend and they were just as amazing as I remember and welcomed me with open arms. I just need my sister close by to complete my little world now.

I hit send and look down at my foot. I start stretching it and rotating my ankle like Henry told me I should. It's sensitive, but it feels good to move it around too.

My phone vibrates in my hand again:

> I'm always here, just know that. I was hoping we could all get together for Thanksgiving and Christmas. I'd like to see the Macy's Thanksgiving Day parade, so I think we should do that in New York City. And oh, I'm

so, so glad they loved having you both there. I'm sure Noah is as happy as he can be.

I reply:

I'm sure Noah would love to host Thanksgiving once he finds a house. I'm also sure the Somers would love to see you again as well. We're all going out tonight, so I need to go and get ready. I love you, and I'll talk to you later.

Her reply comes right back at me:

Have an amazing time; I can't wait to see you . . . whenever that is.

I smile at her text and reply quickly before Dillen jumps on me for not paying attention to her:

I love you. Thank you, Dani.

Two hours later, Dillen and I are ready to go when Noah yells up to us, "Baby? The doorman just called. Coen, Joel, and Lana are on their way up."

"We'll be right down. Let them in, okay?" I call down, and then turn to Dillen. "Now remember . . . be nice. All right?"

"You are going to be the death of me, little shit. You have my word," she says as she finishes using her duo brow brush. Lana would be proud to know that I know the name of my brushes now.

I hear commotion downstairs within seconds, and I take a deep breath. The guys seem to be having a great time already. I look over and Dillen makes a loud pop with her lips and puts her lipstick in her clutch.

"Mmm, let's go . . . I hear sexy men downstairs."

I follow her down, taking the stairs slowly in my heels. Dillen gets down before me, and I see Joel walk up and hug her, welcoming her back. I sigh when I get down the stairs, and Noah comes to me, snaking his arm around my waist. "Heels again, sweetheart? Is this a good idea?"

I look up and fall in love all over again. His smile is breathtaking, and he's looking at me like I'm the only woman in the world. "Probably not, but I don't want to wear flats."

"You'll let me know if it gets to be too much? Same deal as last time, ballerina, and no dancing this time. Henry would kill me," he says while he cups my face to kiss my newly glossed lips.

I pout as cutely as I can manage, giving him my practiced puppy-dog eyes. "But . . . but?"

"But nothing, gorgeous, and no matter how fucking sexy you look on the dance floor, I won't allow it. I've arranged for a VIP area with bottle service so we'll have a place to sit down."

I huff and almost stomp my foot for good measure. "Fine. But you don't dance either, okay?"

"That's fine by me. You're the only woman I want to dance with anyway."

Coen clears his throat. "Are you two going to fuck right there, or are we ready to go? Where the hell are we going anyway?"

Noah moves his hand down to my ass as he speaks to the group, "We're going to PHD Rooftop, and we'll be in the VIP area with bottle service. Are there any objections?"

I look over at Dillen, who is blatantly sizing Lana up.

"Not at all," Lana says as she walks up to hug me. "Hi, doll. How's your foot?" Her soft-spoken voice fills the room.

"Oh Lana, your dress is pretty; I want one." I look down at my foot then back up at her. "It's okay; I'm not in any pain yet." My eyes flicker over to Noah and back, and we both share a laugh.

She hugs me again and turns to face Joel and Dillen. "Hi, I'm Lana Wilde," she says politely and extends her hand out to Dill.

I watch as Dillen extends her hand and shakes hers briefly before letting go. I'm so disappointed in Dillen right now that I could swat her behind.

"Hey," is all she says before turning to Joel. "Joel, you sexy freak, are you ready to dance with me?"

Coen doesn't say a word, but he looks at Noah and shakes his head disapprovingly.

Joel is caught in the crossfire and tries to avoid the awkwardness that is radiating around these three. "Sure thing. Let's get a cab over and meet these assholes there."

"Yes, let's go," she grabs his hand and leads him to the door. "Bye, guys, we'll see you there," she shouts before slamming the door in their wake. I turn and look at Noah, and then Coen and Lana.

"Uhmm . . . so that wasn't awkward."

"My apologies, Lana. She isn't typically that rude. Loud, but not rude. I say we do some shots before we follow them," Noah says kindly as he lets go of me and walks to the cabinet where I keep the alcohol.

"Oh, it's not your fault. I figured it would be like this, but . . . if it's what needs to happen for her to get over Coen, then we'll march through. Right, babe?"

"You got it, Wilde girl. Hey Heather? I'm glad to see that boot off of your foot. How was your weekend?"

I pause before I answer. "Is this a trick?" I look around me. "Am I being punked?" I hear Noah laugh from the kitchen. "Coen is never this nice to me," I explain to a confused Lana.

"Don't push me, little lady. I'll show you my mean side. I can only deal with Dillen being a grumpy bitch tonight, so be nice. I might not be able to hold my tongue."

"I'd prefer if you didn't." Lana elbows him in the side.

"Don't you threaten me, clown! I'll have my boyfriend beat your butt," I spout off before walking into the kitchen. "You can, right?" I ask Noah playfully.

He laughs and smacks my rear. "I'd do it willingly."

"Fuck you, cocksucker."

"Coen," Lana scolds, and the three of us laugh together. She's still getting used to how these two treat each other, and I love it.

"Sorry, babe," he apologizes softly and snakes his arm around her waist.

She peers up at him. "How about you make it up to me later?"

I find myself having to look away because it's just too intimate.

"Baby?" I ask quietly as I watch him pour shots.

My Greek god reaches for me and pulls me close as he finishes pouring the clear liquid into my favorite pink shot glasses. "Yes, gorgeous?"

"Are we that cute?"

He looks over his shoulder, and then back down at me. His strong arms move around my body to lift me up onto the countertop. He moves between my legs and cups my face before taking my lips with a graceful passion.

I know what he's trying to do, and it makes me smile against his lips.

I run my fingers into the back of his hair and feel his warm skin heat mine. I instantly want to be naked in bed with this man.

"A simple yes would have been sufficient."

"I can stop," he offers, and I instantly regret my statement.

"Would you two stop? You put our relationship to shame," Lana says through a pout.

I giggle and throw my hands up. "We win!"

Noah chuckles and leans down to sink his teeth into my neck, and God, I want to be underneath him.

"Fuck, Ryan, chill your dick long enough for us to take these shots."

I squeal loudly, and my whole body trembles with his bite. I push on his hard, muscled chest to keep him at bay.

"Down, boy," I tease.

"Temptress," he says and helps me off of the counter.

We all hold up our shot glasses and do cheers before Lana and I grab our clutches, and we make our way downstairs to the awaiting cab.

It takes us fifteen minutes to go the few blocks to the nightclub before we are inside and shown to our booth, a rather large booth at that. "Noah, you didn't have to do this."

"Stop, I wanted to," he says before helping me sit down.

Dillen and Joel join the four of us, and she sits down next to me, hugging me tightly. "Thank God you're here; I missed you."

I laugh when I pull back after our hug and wipe at her smeared lipstick. "You missed me, huh? It looks like Joel was keeping you busy, though."

He shrugs and takes a seat next to Lana.

"So?" she leans in closer to me and tries to whisper over the music, "Do you think Coen will break up with her?"

I look at her, knowing exactly what she's doing. "Dill," I scold and shake my head before patting her knee. "No, I think it's more than sex for Coen."

She pouts at me knowingly and tries a different approach. "Will Joel fuck me?"

I feel Noah's hand at my lower back just then and turn my head. He's wearing a look of shock at Dillen's words, and it makes me laugh. He leans in to try and whisper in my ear, "Did I just hear that correctly?"

I lean into him and bite his shoulder before answering, "Mmhmm, we're going to have to keep an eye on her tonight."

I feel his chest rumble underneath my fingertips.

"Fine, but you owe me, ballerina, from earlier today and now. My balls are not able to handle much more torment."

I grin and drape my hand over his jean-clad thigh, leaning in to nuzzle his neck. "Awww, poor baby," I mock and lower my hand down the inside of his thigh and over his substantial bulge.

"Heather," he growls in that low, smoky voice that signals his body's in motion, so much so that I can physically feel his storm brewing.

I have to admit, I love that I can feel it. I love that I can just touch him and set his world spinning. "Yes?" I play dumb and bat my lashes.

"Don't fucking tempt me, or I'll lay you down and fuck you right here in front of your friends, and I won't give a damn." My hand is still resting on his bulge, and I grip his shaft to feel him grow and flex his monstrous cock.

"You wouldn't dare, Noah Ryan."

Ominous dark storms gather behind his eyes, and I can tell I've just pushed him too far. His eyes seem to have changed colors: they are almost leaden. A cloud of desire looms over the two of us, and I'm waiting for the bolt of lightning to strike and take me as its victim. The storm is not unpleasant: it's captivating, raw, and threatening. I know without a single doubt that this man is going to take what he wants from me now. I'm about to be under the weather—in one heck of a good way. My storm is about to ravage me in all of its sultry wrath.

All I can do is watch him. I haven't been able to look away. I couldn't even say if we were being watched. I couldn't say who was next to me, or if anyone was, for that matter. I'm locked in his intense stare.

His movements are tenacious and purposeful when he lifts me from the seat to straddle his lap. Our eyes are locked on each other's—unshakable. Despite my earlier attempt at being steadfast, I am now surrendering to the storm's surge as he violently pulls me down to meet his lips with mine. He pushes his tongue between my lips, causing my body to spiral out of control. If it weren't for his arms holding me in place, my body would go slack. This storm takes control, and there's not a thing I can do to put a stop to it now, so instead, I decide to soak it all up.

His grip on me tightens almost painfully, but I welcome it. He swallows my moans and shoves his tongue deeper, stroking every part of my mouth. I cling to him as my hips grind against him of their own accord; I can feel his full length against my panties, and I'm thrilled that I wore a dress tonight. I can feel every bit of his persistent storm.

"Ballerina," he breathes into my mouth, "don't ever make me chase after your affection. My patience is an illusion, and I don't have to prove that you're mine—you should already know."

My breath catches, and I feel my panties become drenched. He's oozing dominance, and I want more, so much more. "But I love it when you chase me."

"I won't repeat myself."

I know I caused this storm, and I know I'm going to feel the wrath of Noah Ryan, but I can't help but push him some more. I want to feel just how hard his rain hits my flesh.

"I'm ready for your storm, Noah, but you need to prove that I'm not something you're just going to play with."

His ice-cold gaze is crippling as he raises his brow. "Play with?"

I watch his storm intensify with the revelation in his voice, and I know I've got him. But he surprises me when he stands up effortlessly. I'm not only following him into the dark—he's taking me willingly. He moves quickly through the crowded room, and I can't make out where he's taking me as I trail behind him, until he pulls open a door labeled *employees only*. The room is dark and soulless. He shuts the door and turns the latch without hesitating. Before I can breathe in the cooler air, he has my back against the cold door.

"Go ahead—underestimate me."

I look up into darkness, into the space between us. I can only hear his voice and the thudding of music against my back.

He runs his hand up the outside of my thigh to the seam of my dress that is strained around my legs, which are parted around him. He doesn't let it stop him—though I doubt anything would. He digs his fingers into the thin material and rips it, as our eyes remain locked together. The heat radiating from his body can only be described as combustion generated by a lightning strike. He takes control of my mouth with his before a whimper can escape my lips that he can't swallow. He pushes his hand up between my body and the dress, the dress giving way to his heat, to his torture. He pulls back and looks down, and without a hint of indecision, he pulls the material clean across my stomach, ripping it open so he can see me.

My body is trembling and I watch his fingers flex. "I know your body, Heather. I can tell when it needs me."

I can't get my voice to work; I can't tell him that he's right. I grip the collar of his white and grey pinstriped button down and pull his lips to mine.

My Greek god's hands move feverishly over my body to get what's left of this dress off and onto the floor. My panties become his next victim as he tugs at the material with one hand, causing it to shred in his wake. I know I'm next. He doesn't speak a word but his eyes say it all: I've pushed him too far. I'm beyond excited by what he'll do to me.

He's leaning his weight against me, ensuring that I can't go anywhere. "Spread wide for me, sweetheart."

"I . . ."

Nope.

Nothing.

His hands are moving all over me—grabbing my breasts and squeezing my ass. "Fuck, I love this tight little ass," he praises me, and continues his assault. The ferocity of his hands on my body is such that I wouldn't be surprised if I'm bruised tomorrow morning.

His lips find mine as I suck in a deep breath of air, and he kisses me like he's chasing after that breath, as if it's the only and last breath he will ever take as he plunges his tongue into my mouth. His hands go from holding my chin in place to being tangled in my hair, making sure I look up at him when he breaks his lips from mine, which are already tender and raw. He bites at my top lip and moves his hand to my sex, feeling my arousal. He pushes his middle finger deep inside of me, watching as

I coat his finger with my need. My mouth drops open when he pushes against my spot, and that's all the warm-up I get before he takes that gorgeous monster out of his jeans.

I swear I can see his veins pulsing in the dark; I need this. Now.

His mouth is on mine again before moving down and nipping at every part of my skin that he can. I can't control my breathing: it's sporadic and out of control. He's doing this on purpose, making me suffer, even though I know it's killing him to have me spread in front of him, begging and ready for him to push in and stretch me out the way he likes to.

He places his head at my entrance while grabbing a handful of my hair and wrapping it around his wrist, *oh God*. He hasn't even been inside of me yet and my body is flooded with endorphins. I decide to try and fight him, to take what I want, but he's too stinking strong for me. He pushes against me to stop me, causing his cock to pound into me. I cry out in pain and pleasure. I'm slammed against the door, overcome by his cock.

Noah grunts loudly and pulls out of me the second I take his entire length. He's broken me to a point where I can't speak. He moves again before I can finish my thought or miss his thick veins sliding against me as he pulls out. Suddenly he sets me down on my feet and turns me toward the door. I have my hands braced up against the door with my ass in the air for him. He pushes my legs apart with his knee and places his warm hands on the side of my rib cage as he sinks his heavy monster into me again, and this time he doesn't stop; he's pounding my wet sex so hard that I'm being jolted against the door. I have to push back against him for this to work. He suddenly lets go of my body and moves his hands up to my neck. He splays his fingers over my jaw and neck, tilting my head back slightly and starts fucking me.

He has me up against the door with his hands around my throat fucking the life out of me . . . fucking me raw.

"Do you fucking like my cock?"

I'm still so tight that I'm mixing pain and pleasure at this point. The only thing I can concentrate on is his cock sliding feverishly in and out of me while his heavy balls slap against me repeatedly. I cry out when he moves a hand up my cheek and slips a finger into my mouth, taking full control of me. I try and suck on his finger to intensify what he's feeling, but my own screams stop me the second I try to. Just as I'm getting accustomed to this position and assault on my body, he moves a hand down to my stomach and pulls my body back against his chest.

"I told you not to tease me, Heather." He breathes heavily against my neck as he slides a hand to my breast and squeezes hard. I feel his cock twitch inside me in that moment. I'm immobile; the only movements are my heaving breasts.

He pushes up and drives in and out of me in a fast rocking motion that makes me lose my breath completely.

"Tell me why you need to come."

I gasp for breath, my fingers gripping his arms that are wrapped around me for leverage.

"Tell me why I should let you come," he slams up into me harder. "You feel how hard my fucking cock is, Heather? You did that."

"Noah . . ." is all I can muster as he holds me at the edge of my climax, holding me hostage and not letting me fall.

"No."

His teeth sink into my neck and my legs go weak. I can't hold myself up for another second as he pushes back up into me, deciding to let me fall now that he has complete control over my body. I scream out as my body is struck with waves of a storm-like orgasm.

I'm quivering, milking him, trying to grasp at his cock with my walls, but he slips free from my grasp. I hear his deep voice in my ear when his body stills. "Mmm, big mistake, sweetheart. I didn't hear my name just now."

"No, please," I beg of him.

I don't know if I can take much more, but he ignores my cries and pushes his heavy cock back into me, the head drumming my utmost sensitive spot repeatedly, and I lose myself in yet another explosive orgasm before the first one fully wears off.

"No-ahhh," I manage this time, and it will have to do because I go limp as electrifying pulses run up my nerves and into places in my body that I was unaware could feel the effects of an orgasm.

He growls and bruises my hips with his fingers. "No, baby, that doesn't satisfy me." Suddenly without warning, we collide against the door. His heavy body traps me against the hard wood and he punishes my body with his cock. He's never been so rough before but I love it. I did this.

"Fuck me, I'm taking this ass," he says as he slams into me repeatedly.

"What?" I croak out as he starts again, and I honestly don't know how he hasn't come undone yet, or has he?

I can hear him smirking as he runs his middle finger over our combined sexes and then up between my cheeks where he wets my opening, readying me for his new adventure—one that I'm not ready for, not in the slightest.

He coos against my neck and bites down. "This cock is going to love taking this tight ass. I'm going to fuck it so hard." He fingers my opening harder. "Don't fight me; your little ass wants this."

"I can't . . ." I try and force my body to move, but I'm sated and numb.

With his finger there and his cock buried inside of me he moves his other hand to my clit and starts rubbing as his cock starts to move inside of me again. I'm so slick I can hardly feel his veins rubbing against my raw walls, and I want it. I want to feel them pulse inside of me when he comes.

"Then give me what I want." He slams forward and at the same time his finger slides into my ass, causing me to cry out his name, giving him what he wants.

He groans loudly and fucks me until I'm about to break and then the door handle turns. I look up over my shoulder at him expectantly.

"Come. Now," he demands.

I let all control go and collapse, my moans swallowed by the door against my cheek and his growl that fills the small room. I don't even pretend to say his name; I can't even muster a syllable. My walls quiver and it feels like my entire body has given up because I can't even feel him inside me.

He stops moving and kisses my damp neck before nipping at me. I think he comes. We're still for a few more minutes before he slowly pulls his cock out of me, and I feel our orgasms run down my inner thigh.

"Don't let go, please . . . I won't be able to stand."

I can feel his smirk against my neck as his hand slides between my thighs. He's not only coating his finger with our mixed orgasms but three fingers are easily plunged inside of me. I can't even find a breath to comment on the amount of come before all three of his fingers are inside my mouth, stealing the breath from me . . . feeding me.

"My girl enjoys a mouthful every once in a while."

I lick and suck his fingers clean before he removes them from my mouth. He turns me around in his arms and kisses me slowly, and when he breaks our kiss he's putting his cock away and zipping up his jeans. I blankly look around for my dress and frown when I see it lying in two separate pieces on the floor. "Noah?"

He follows my gaze and I see him raise his eyebrow. The smile that forms on his face is strictly arrogant alpha male.

"I might need some help with this one. Let me get you cleaned up and I'll get Dillen or Lana in here, whoever is more sober."

I stare at him with my mouth agape. "What do you mean 'get them in here'? I'm completely naked. My panties are shredded, and my dress looks like you had a fight with it!"

"You're sure as hell not leaving this closet naked. I'm sure Lana can help somehow."

He's looking around the room, and I feel our orgasms leaking out of me, dripping down my thighs and onto the floor. I'm not even entertaining the thought of Lana or Dill seeing me like this. "No. No way, Noah."

"Don't push me, Heather. We've already had this conversation."

He pulls his phone out of his pocket and types something out before he looks up at the rack of cleaning supplies. I watch in horror as he reaches up to the top shelf with ease and pulls down a box of Swiffer refills, pulling out the fluffy apparatus, meant for dusting. He turns to me and fans the thing in front of me.

"Spread those legs, sweetheart. We don't want you a mess when you're about to have company."

My mouth just hangs open.

"There is not a chance in hell you are putting that on me. I could be allergic and then you won't be touching me for weeks."

He cocks his head to the side and stares me down. "Don't give me that shit, Heather. I've seen you use these at both your place and mine. Spread em'. Now."

I cup my hands over my eyes because I can't watch. He has never cleaned me up before, let alone with something fluffy. I'm going to die of embarrassment.

I hear him chuckle and bend down in front of me. I feel the soft cloth caress my skin and I'm suddenly relaxed. He's being sweet and gentle, and this is less embarrassing and more intimate than I thought. I peek through my fingers and watch him work gently but quickly.

Once he's done he tosses it in the available trashcan, along with my dress before checking his phone again just as there is a knock at the door. "Noah? It's Lana."

I exhale in frustration and possibly whimper as I hold my arms over my body. I look at Noah before he reaches for the door and let him know just how mad I am. "How. Fucking. Embarrassing."

"My fucking you is embarrassing? Heather, get your damn priorities straight. The lights are off," he states, and I think I've pissed him off.

He moves in front of me, unlocks the door, and pulls it open just enough for her to slip in through the crack. When he shuts it, the music that blared through is once again muted.

"Why the heck are you two in here?"

"Lana, I'm so sorry," I say from behind Noah.

I clutch at the back of his shirt and lay my forehead against him in shame. I hear her giggle before Noah speaks. He sounds just as cocky as he did moments ago. "I had to take care of business," he adds before nodding to the trashcan. "My hands got carried away, and Heather's dress paid the price."

"Is there anything in here she can wear? I didn't bring a sweater or a shawl, and I don't think Dillen did either." She stops talking for a second and claps her hands. "Noah, do you have an undershirt on?"

"Yeah, but she'll be flashing her ass to everyone if she even bends over in it," he states before reaching behind himself to touch me.

"Will you just trust me?" she insists and holds her hand out. "Take your button-down off."

I feel his broad shoulders move and I can hear the rustle of clothing being maneuvered. Lana tries to fill the awkward silence. "So . . . you guys looking for the mop n' glow or something?"

Noah chuckles and must have held up his shirt to her. "No, she was asking for it."

"Hand it to Heather," she directs him. "Heather? I'm going to need you to put his shirt on, but just simply wrap it around yourself with the collar around your chest."

Noah slips it into my hands and I shiver when I feel the warmth encompass me. I do what Lana says, and I finally feel comfortable again with just this little bit of clothing on.

"Button it up and then I'll help you with the rest."

I do as I'm told and button his shirt up my front. It's long enough to cover everything it needs to cover, but I look ridiculous with the arms hanging at my side. It's obvious I'm just wearing a man's shirt . . . at least it smells like my Greek god.

"Can we turn on the light now?" she asks, and I feel Noah move away from me.

"Yes, I'm covered up."

Lana walks up to me, and smiles sweetly. "Lift your arms up."

I do as I'm told and she wraps the arms of the button down around to my back and then brings them both forward again, tying them in a bow off to the side before inspecting her work.

"I think it's perfect."

I look down at myself and smile. It actually looks like I'm wearing a super cute grey and white pinstriped dress. "Holy crap, Lana," I squeak out.

"Well, I'll be damned," Noah says, leaning against the wall like an arrogant, sexy underwear model.

"Thank you so much; we owe you one, big time."

"Oh hush, you don't owe me a thing. Now come take some shots with me, please?"

"God, yes!" I take a step in the direction of the door and wince. *Oh holy shit. Ouch.* My eyes fly to where Noah is standing and watching.

He winks at me, and steps forward to hold the door open. "I'm still pissed," he whispers to me as we walk out and back into the crowd.

Oh yeah? I think to myself as we reach the VIP booth. Well, you're about to be furious, Ryan.

I ignore his hand at my back and scoot to the end.

He raises his eyebrow at me, taken by surprise when I move away to sit next to Lana. He takes a seat next to Dillen and Joel, and I can feel the heat from his storm envelop me when he looks up at me from across the table.

I avoid his gaze—no, his stare—and look back at Lana. "Thank you for coming to my rescue. I'm sorry you had to see that. You're a lifesaver."

"You don't have to keep thanking me. What are friends for, right?"

Coen leans over to me then. "Were the two of you fighting? Noah looks pissed the hell off. I don't think he should drink, Heather. We both know how that ends."

"He'll be fine, Coen. And no, we weren't fighting. We're okay," I say, putting my hand on his knee to pat him lightly. He tenses and refuses to look away from me.

"Holy shit, Heather, please tell me he didn't see you do that."

I scoff and roll my eyes. "Oh stop it, you're overreacting."

I decide to peek up at him, and he's staring at me like I'm torturing him. He breaks eye contact with me and reaches for the bottle of vodka. Before the waitress could even think about pouring him a drink, he's already downed two double shots. Coen clears his throat and moves my hand off of his knee. "That, Heather," he says, his eyes on Noah and the vodka, "that is him *not okay*. That is him planning my funeral, and Dillen encouraging him is not helping worth a shit."

I look back up at him, and he has a shot glass to his lips again as Dill fills another one and hands it to him.

"Dillen!" I shout over the music to try to get her attention. She looks over at me, grins, and waves happily before pouring herself a shot.

Noah takes his other shot and sits back against the booth, draping his arm over the back of it. Even in his jeans and plain white undershirt, he looks so damn sexy. He and Joel look like they're in a pretty serious discussion so I move from in between Coen and Lana and let them have their space. I move over to the end of the couch away from all of the couples and pour myself a glass of champagne that's sitting in the ice bucket in front of everyone.

While I'm staring off onto the dance floor below, I'm lost in thought, off in my own little world. What had transpired throughout the day and into the evening? What happened between us in the closet? How intense things got between us, and now . . . he's pissed at me for what I said be-fore Lana stepped in. I'm sorry, but it was embarrassing. Being naked in front of a woman you've just met recently? Being naked in front of an-other woman, period. Well, he can just stay angry.

I sit there and sip my drink when my skin begins to tingle. I don't even look—I don't have to. I know from the way my skin feels that he's locked on me. And just as soon as the feeling came, it went.

The bass through the speakers pounds through my chest as I sit there. Everyone is having a great time, flirting, drinking, and dancing. It's in this moment that I start to realize I'm the only one not having fun. What started off as a fantastic night has quickly spiraled into something entirely different. There's a storm raging all right, and I'm standing in the middle of it in a flimsy makeshift dress, all alone.

"Heather, sweetie? Are you okay?" My tumultuous thoughts are in-terrupted by Lana's sincere voice.

I plaster on a fake smile and turn in her direction. "Huh? Oh yes, I'm fine, thank you, babes. And thank you again for helping me. We got a lit-tle out of hand." I try and play my embarrassment off and take another sip.

"Oh s-stop it," she says, over-enunciating the word stop.

It makes us both laugh, and she turns back to Coen, leaving me alone with my thoughts once again. I don't notice him until it's too late; Noah pulls me up to his chest and wraps me in his arms, holding me fast. "Come dance with me."

I look up at him and almost burst into tears. I offer him my hand, and he leads me to the middle of the dance floor. We're not dancing as the crowd around us moves, but he just stands there, holding me against his chest. "I love you, sweetheart."

I stare up at this man and get lost in his dark green eyes. He's still in a state of arousal, that much I can tell.

"I love you too."

He pulls me against his chest and holds me in place; we're both unmoving. I suck in a deep breath, taking in his warm masculine scent mixed with the clean smell of his cologne, now tainted with sex. "Do you want to go home? I can stay at my place tonight. I didn't mean to hurt you, if I did. You've never not wanted to be around me . . . until tonight."

I hate how I'm being bumped into on all sides, so I move to a secluded corner where we can hear each other better. I turn and rest my back against the wall and look up at him. I'm hurt that he would even suggest that we should sleep alone, but I can't find the right words to describe it.

He cups my face and presses his lips to mine slowly. "I'm sorry."

I nod but pull away to speak. I don't want him to think I'm upset over that. "Don't be sorry—I'm fine. I'm just really sore."

"But you pulled away from me . . . and then touched Coen instead. While you could still feel me inside of you."

"I pulled away because you said you were still pissed. I intended on pushing you more to see how far I could take you," I say as he leans against the wall with his arm over my head. He loves to trap me like this. "And I just patted his knee as a friendly reassurance, Noah, not to make you upset."

"I was pissed because you said you were embarrassed that I fucked you. You were embarrassed that Lana would know what we had been doing."

I roll my eyes and shake my head. *Men.* I grip his white shirt and forcefully pull him down, his lips an inch from mine. "I was embarrassed that she would see me naked. Not that we had sex. I don't care who knows."

He looks surprised and interested with his brows raised as his hands move from my hips down to my ass in his shirt. "I don't like when you pull away from me, Heather."

"So I've noticed," I quickly reply and push my hips forward, feeling his length again. God this man is a machine.

He circles a hand around my neck and smiles. "Don't underestimate me, sweetheart."

My lips part, and my tongue darts out to lick them. Having his hand around my throat is highly erotic, and I can't help how it makes me react. "I think I enjoyed underestimating you."

"I believe you did. Now come drink with me."

I hide my pout when he takes my hand and leads me from the darkened hallway back to our group of friends. I find myself wanting him to be rougher with me; I find myself wishing he would have taken my ass.

Maybe soon?

We take our seat in the booth, and he pulls me onto his lap. Lana shoots me a drunken smile and claps her hands excitedly. "I'm so happy you two are all lovey again. Coen and I almost won for a second."

"Won?" I ask, confused, and bend forward to reach for my champagne.

"Yup, you two are the cuter couple," she huffs and reaches over Coen to hug me.

I laugh and hug her back. "You're as ridiculous as Coen is."

"Maybe I'll keep him then," she says excitedly, and my eyes dart to Dillen, who is smiling happily, sitting with Joel.

Everyone looks as if they're happy and having a good time.

Noah nuzzles my neck and bites my shoulder. "You're mine."

I look back at him. "Are we okay now? Am I still in trouble?"

"If you'd like to be, then yes, you are."

I smile at his playfulness and turn on his lap more. I lean down and rest my forehead against his, testing his boundaries with my next question.

"What would you say if I told you I can't possibly have sex with you for about a week?"

"A week? Hell, baby, that's a long time."

I kiss the tip of his nose and pull away, taking a drink of my champagne. "I guess you should have thought of that before you almost literally tore me apart, Ryan. Now you have to pay the price."

"Mmm, maybe if you're lucky I'll kiss that pussy better."

I wiggle my ass against his lap and laugh before turning my attention to what's playing out before me: Joel and Dillen. My shoulders slump minutely and I set my glass down. These two are obviously hot for each other, but I'm wondering if Dill is just playing games.

Noah seems to notice my unease and whispers in my ear, "Go and dance with Dillen."

I don't even hesitate to get off his lap and walk over to the two of them. "Dill, dance with me," I shout over the music and tug on her hand.

She breaks away from his kiss and her lips are red and swollen. "My little shit! Where did you get that dress? I want it!" she shouts back as she assesses my ensemble.

I can only giggle at my best friend as we start dancing. I make sure I'm not applying weight onto my bad foot.

"It's from Noah."

I watch my Greek god as I entice him with my body. Dill and I are dancing close like we always do and Joel joins Noah on the couch to watch.

Noah leans over and starts talking to him; I love my man and his friendships. What is more attractive than a man knowing what he wants in life? Even down to the type of people he wants involved in it.

Dillen breaks into my train of thought. "Holy fuck, Heather, he is an amazing kisser!"

Oh boy. "Dill, you can't just play with all of Noah's friends."

She stops dancing and looks at me like I've just slapped her. I stop dancing as well. "I'm not playing with them . . . we're just having fun."

I can see the hurt and anger on her face. "Dill, stop. You might be having fun, but I don't think either of those guys feels the same way."

She looks over at Coen, who is happily dancing with Lana, and then over at Joel, who is still watching us along with Noah.

"I know how much you want to be with Coen right now, and I know it hurts, but you can't hurt Joel in the process of trying to make Coen jealous. I love you, Dill, and I don't want you getting hurt either."

I reach for her hand and try to get her to start dancing again and maybe keep this from going any further, but she pulls back.

"We can't all be blessed with the man of our dreams," she spits back at me hatefully. I pray it's just the alcohol talking, but it hurts like hell.

"Dillen . . . please?" I try once more before some guy comes up behind her and starts sensually grinding his crotch into her ass . . . ugh.

She completely ignores me, opting to dance with him, and I feel deflated. I feel like the worst friend. I turn and mask my features before walking back over to sit next to Noah and Joel. They're laughing and drinking together when I sit back down. I'm hopeful Joel didn't see any of that. I wish I hadn't even been a part of it. I should have kept my mouth shut and just let her run wild like she always does. I'm barely listening to the guys' conversation when I feel a hand on my shoulder.

I turn to look and see Lana and Coen leaning over the back of the booth. "Sweetie, we're going to go back to his place. My feet are tired and he promised me a foot massage." She flashes a brilliant smile at me, and I laugh knowingly.

I watch as Coen's goofy, drunk grin slides to Noah, and he grabs Noah's shoulder. Noah looks up at him and laughs.

"Have a few too many, dickhead?" he asks, and Coen smirks before holding up his finger, and leaning in close, too drunkenly close.

Coen's words are slurred and slow as he speaks. "Lemme tell you something, Ryan. There are two things in this world that smell like fish . . . one of them is fish . . ."

He stops speaking, and Lana and I both collectively gasp in shock. Noah busts out laughing and removes Coen's grasp from his shoulder.

"Is that right, man? Had a few run-ins with that situation, have we?" Noah asks Coen, but he's too drunk to answer, and his eyes are closed as he sways back and forth.

Lana smacks him on his chest and scolds, "Dammit, Coen, you did not just say that. Agh! You and your Coen-isms."

I laugh as we watch Lana shove Coen toward the club's exit.

"Have fun you two. Text me when you make it home." I wave at her, and she blows me a kiss. I'm really, really loving Lana.

"See ya, sis," Coen manages as he stumbles out.

Noah kisses my cheek before getting up and walking over to Dillen, pulling the creep off of her and wrangling my best friend back to the booth while he talks to her.

"Heather," she squeals and hugs me tightly. "I love you too, you little shit. Can we go home? I'm fucking exhausted and drunk."

I look over at Noah, completely in shock, wondering what in the hell he said to her.

He winks at me, and I know his love for me is unconditional. Noah speaks to the waitress about paying our bill while Joel helps me get the drunkie out to a cab.

We've finally folded her into a cab when Noah walks out and climbs in the back with us, while Joel takes the front seat next to the driver. It doesn't take long to get home, but when we manage to get Dillen inside, she immediately passes out on the couch.

"Thank you for helping, Joel. You really didn't have to do that."

"Yeah, I did. I fed her the majority of those shots, so she'd stay away from Coen. I think she's got some intense feelings toward him, but I like Lana. I believe she's what Coen needs right now."

I nod in agreement and sigh as I slip my heels off. I watch, my heart melting, when Joel walks over to the end of the couch and crouches at Dillen's feet. He methodically takes her strappy heels off and covers her with a blanket. It looks like Joel has feelings for her that he's not letting on to.

Noah snakes his arm around my waist and kisses the top of my head. "Joel, you're welcome to crash here. That couch is big enough for an army."

"I don't know, man. I wouldn't want her to wake up thinking I took advantage of her."

"I don't think you have anything to worry about, man," Noah says as Dill snorts in her sleep.

I hold in a giggle and walk past Joel. "Stay here tonight. I'm going to get you two pillows."

"I'll grab them, Heather." He runs after me, and as I pull the closet door open in the hall, he snags the pillows and two blankets.

"You are too nice, Joel," I say as I snap one of his suspenders.

He winces and moves away from me. "Fuck, Heather," he says, laughing. He walks back into the living room where Noah is removing the back pillows from the couch to make more room for each of them to sleep.

I walk over and look down at her. "Should I get her into some of my jammies?" I ask Noah in particular, since he's previously seen her in her bra and panties. "That dress is going to be extremely uncomfortable to sleep in."

"I think that would be best. I'd prefer not to wake up to a naked Dillen."

"Okay. I'll be right back, guys." I smile to myself as I make my way upstairs and find some satin Victoria's Secret jammies for her to wear. With the way Joel seems to act around her, I think it could actually work. He may be just the right guy to tame her.

When I come back downstairs, Noah has Dillen sitting up next to him while Joel kneels in front of her, holding up a pink straw to her lips. "Dillen, it's just water. You need this more than you know."

I find Joel's voice soothing and rough at the same time. Any woman can see that this man is gorgeous from the inside out, and I kind of hope Dill can see it too.

Groaning, she pushes the water out of her way and tries to lie back down, but Noah doesn't budge. He keeps her sitting upright, and the men start to laugh.

"Jesus, she's a handful," Joel says through his laughter.

"Yeah, but she's got a good heart—she just doesn't know how to show it. And hell, don't get me started on her tear ducts."

I'm smiling, listening to them describe my best friend when Joel tries again. "Come on, doll, don't fall asleep just yet. You need to get some water into your system," he prods, and Noah shakes her shoulders just a bit to rattle her eyes open.

"Please, I just want to sleep," she mumbles groggily.

They both laugh again, and I walk over, unfolding the satin pajamas. "Baby, help me get her dress off?"

Joel's eyes shoot up to me, and he takes a step back. "I'll wait in the kitchen," he says, getting up faster than I've ever seen him move and goes to the kitchen, keeping his back turned to us.

I pout my lip out at Noah and mouth, "Awww, how cute."

"Who Joel?" he says softly as he holds Dillen's limp body up for me.

I nod and smile as I pull her dress up and over her head. Noah feeds her arm through one of the sleeves and pulls it around her back. "Looks like you've done this before, Ryan," I tease as I get her other arm in.

"Undressing a woman? Yes. Undressing an unconscious woman? No."

I narrow my eyes at his comment. "Is it me, or is Joel enjoying being around her a lot?" I crouch down at her feet and start maneuvering the pants around her legs. "I think he truly likes her."

Noah looks up to where Joel is in the kitchen. "Possibly. They are complete opposites, though."

I shrug at his comment and grunt when I try to get the pants up over her butt. "Are you even helping me?" I joke as I tug them up successfully, and then drop onto the floor out of breath.

Noah lays her down while his chest rumbles with a laugh. "Joel, you're a good man."

I hear him rustling in the kitchen before he comes back with another glass of ice water and a sandwich. I start to giggle uncontrollably. "Joel! How did you find the stuff to make that?"

Noah's looking at him in shock. "What the hell, man? Where's mine?"

"Dude, make your own because I'm sure as fuck not sharing with you. Heather, I just opened this thing we call a fridge. It's a great invention."

I smile and pat my belly as I lie on my back on the floor. "Nu-uh, I've got to keep my figure."

Noah bends over and picks me up, throwing me over his shoulder. "I know what I'm about to eat. Joel, have a good night. Don't fuck Dillen in her sleep, and we'll see you in the morning," he jokes.

"'Night, fuckers," he replies, and I wave to him as I'm being carried away.

Chapter Twenty

A TOUCHING SEDATIVE

NOAH

I've just woken up to my naked ballerina sprawled on top of me. I rub my hand down my face as I try to force myself to wake up. It's Saturday morning, and I'm usually studying before Heather gets up, but I don't think I should try to shift her right now.

As my eyes open and focus, I watch her sleep peacefully. I hated how hurt she looked last night when Dillen said that shit to her. There's only been a few times in my life that I've wanted to shake some sense into a woman, and last night Dillen made the cut. Heather has been nothing but sweet and steadfastly caring to her friends and family. She deserves better treatment from everyone, including myself.

She runs her hand up my chest and tilts her head up to look at me. "Good morning, beautiful, did I wake you?"

She squeaks out the cutest damn sound as she stretches and sits up. "No, my stomach woke me."

I move my hands to her hips and wink up at her. "I can make

blueberry pancakes if you'd like."

Her beautiful jade green eyes light up, and it makes me want to do more things to keep her happy.

"Mmm, yes, please," she says before giving me a full view of her ass as she crawls to the end of the bed.

I've made the pancakes while Joel and Dillen sleep, and Heather gets showered. I'm rather looking forward to Heather's reaction when she sees them curled around each other.

I wonder how in the hell he's going to talk himself out of this one.

I look up when Heather flitters down the stairs. Her eyes are focused on the living room, and she changes course from me and over to them. I watch as she creeps quietly and peeks over the edge of the couch. Her burst of excitement puts a smile on my face, and I play it cool when she hurriedly makes her way over to me. Her voice is quiet, but she's shouting her whisper, "Oh my God, did you see them?"

I wrap her in my arms, just where she should be and lift her onto the counter. "I did, but I still think we win."

"Yeah?" she sounds genuinely surprised.

"Come on, let's eat and let them wake up alone. I'm not sure I want to be in the middle of a Dillen hangover this morning."

"Good idea," she nods and shimmies off the counter before I can help the stubborn woman down. She sits so close to me during breakfast and I'm wondering what's made her so needy for my attention. We normally sit next to each other but she's damn near in my lap now. She seems okay, but something's definitely off. We've been talking in hushed voices throughout breakfast about where we're going to live. I don't know what's gotten into her, but I'm going to find out.

She's chewing quietly and I watch her with determination. She's lost in a thought, and I'm about to make her spill it when I hear someone on the couch groan. Heather's eyes flicker to the couch before she looks over at me and stands up. I grab her orange juice and stand with her, and we both quietly make our way upstairs. As soon as we make it into her room, she laughs quietly.

"Awww, I want them to be together, Noah."

"He might be what she needs, you're right."

I set her orange juice on my nightstand—mine because my things are in it. I lie down and stretch out on my back, watching her move about the room. Her mind is preoccupied, and she's cleaning like a mad woman. We haven't been together long, but I know she cleans the shit out of things when her mind is racing.

I decide to open one of my textbooks and start reading while she keeps herself busy with the duster.

HEATHER

I'm trying to keep myself busy while he studies, and the best way I know how to is to clean. Plus, it gives my mind time to race and panic and do all the things it shouldn't be doing. I've successfully cleaned every surface in my room, and I have now moved on to the bathroom when I realize all of my cleaning supplies are downstairs. I decide to tiptoe downstairs to get what I need and sneak past the living room. I hear hushed noises and whispers, and somehow I just know those two are doing things on my couch they probably shouldn't be.

I'm going to kill Dillen.

I finally sneak into the downstairs linen closet, grab what I need, and make my way back toward the stairs. I am almost in the clear when suddenly Joel's tall commanding frame rises up from the couch . . . completely shirtless.

I nearly lose my footing when I get a glimpse at what he hides from the world. I watch transfixed as he stretches his arm up into the air, before bringing his hand down to massage the back of his neck. The black ink marring his sturdy frame remains unmoving on his skin as his muscles work and stretch underneath it.

He moves his hand from his neck to his front, which I can't see, but I have no doubt that it is impeccably sculpted. Joel takes a step forward to the window and Dill growls under her breath from the couch.

I know I shouldn't be watching, but his tattoo has me in a trance. I'm trying to figure out where it starts or stops. I let my eyes roam from the tip of the tattoo that kisses his neck down to his shoulder blade. It seems to move down onto his left arm, forming a half of a sleeve, but it doesn't stop there. The tattoo spills onto his broad back, coloring his light olive-toned skin with dark lines of all different widths and sizes roaming his back. I have no idea what I'm looking at. The design is chaotic as it moves down his back to his trim waist and farther below.

I feel ashamed for admiring him, but I can't help it. What I once thought about Joel has now dissipated into nothing, and I'm left with a stranger. A ghost. A complete enigma.

Who is this man that stands in the place of my friend?

His body moves swiftly as he lowers himself back down over Dill and the last thing I see is the tip of that black ink that licks at the base of his neck. Dill's high pitch shriek and giggle break me from my trance, and I hurriedly make my way upstairs into the safety of my room.

NOAH

I must have gotten lost in my textbooks because the next time I look up the sun has set, and the room is filled with a soft glow from one of the lamps in her room. I've set my textbook aside, and I've been working on-line, prepping for my exam in a few weeks.

I look behind me, and my little ballerina is lying on her stomach on her bed. She's on her laptop, and I frown when I see a little scowl marring her face.

I shut my laptop, get up from the chair, and lie down next to her on the bed to kiss her cheek. "Hey, sweetheart."

"Hi," she doesn't look away from the screen and I grip her chin between my fingers to make her look at me.

"Hey. What's that scowl for?"

She shrugs and tries to turn away from me again.

"Heather."

I search her face, focusing my attention on those jade green eyes that belong to me. She sighs and drops onto her side dramatically. "Do you like this house?" She points next to her and I almost can't believe my ears.

I look up at it and smile. I didn't realize how excited she was about this, and honestly, I'm not concerned about what the house looks like—I just want her happy. "I'm easy, baby. I want this to be your dream."

Her growl is cute as fuck and I prop my head up on my elbow to watch her. "Hmm, I think I like this little fit-throwing thing you've got going."

"Yeah, well, I can't find anything I'm in love with."

"But you've found me, haven't you?"

"That's not what I mean," she says, pouting.

I can't help but laugh; she sounds so damn stressed. "Baby, it's a wonder you haven't had a heart attack. You don't handle stress too well, do you?"

"Noah," she whines, "I just want this to be perfect."

I have to have my hands on her. I let my fingers creep under her pajama top and caress her soft, flat stomach. "Heather, calm down, please?" I ask softly in order to calm her. "This isn't a big deal . . . what house we get. What matters is who's in it. You and I."

She lets out the breath she was holding and moves to curl into my larger frame. "Okay, but I have a question: would you like to live on Long Island Sound?"

I'm actually surprised that she's put so much thought into this. "Sweetheart, I don't care."

"So you wouldn't mind living on the water?" she tries again.

"No, Heather, I wouldn't mind." My fingers drift upward and graze the swell of her breast.

She nuzzles me and bites my chest. "Okay. Are you mine again, or are you going to study?"

I look back over my shoulder at the clock. "No, baby, I need to study some more."

She sighs and clings onto me. "No, you don't. It's all you've done all day."

I sigh and breathe in my girl's scent and hold her to me. Fuck, I wish I could lie here all night. "I'm sorry, Heather, no. I have to keep reading, or I won't pass this fucking bar."

"Okay." She pouts, but doesn't move.

I kiss the top of her head and tighten my arms around her. "Why don't you do some of those ankle stretches and look for our new home, and by then I'll be done?"

"Fine," she grumbles and fuck I'm about to laugh my ass off. I push her delicate little body away from mine, for fear I won't be able to sway her if she tries to keep me here.

She shows me her dissatisfaction by huffing and then proceeds to sit up and pull her laptop onto her lap in an attempt to block herself from me.

I can't help but laugh at her feeble attempt as I turn around and head back to the desk. I reach for the back of the chair as I pick up my glasses and put them back on.

"I want to have your baby."

I swear I almost thought I heard her say . . . but she did. I pull off my glasses and run a hand down my face to make sure I haven't fallen asleep while studying. I turn around to her when I realize that just happened. "My what?"

She looks so damn adorable sitting there with a worried look on her face. She moves the laptop off of her lap and sits there with her legs crossed over each other. Her voice is almost a whisper, and I have to close my eyes and strain to hear her next words—the ones I thought I heard the first time.

"I want to have your baby."

I set my glasses down and walk over to her, forgetting about the exam for the moment. I sit down on the edge of her pillow-top bed and take her hand. "Yeah? We have a knack for doing things backwards."

I realize then that this probably has a lot to do with the miscarriage that she's been bravely dealing with.

I'm not sure how to proceed from here. The next words that are said could either crush her or . . . fuck, I don't know anything anymore. She's still staring up at me with those green eyes and she hasn't made another peep.

"Okay . . . uh, so this is a real thing that you want? This isn't just a ploy to keep me from studying?"

She nods, and I'm unsure what she's saying yes to. "I want one . . . with you."

I drop her hand and rub my face with both of mine. I'm tired . . . yeah, that's it. This isn't really happening right now. I've been studying too fucking much. I'm under too much pressure. I chant to myself while I rub the back of my tense neck.

I think I might be going insane, but she shifts and moves onto my lap. "I've been thinking about it a lot lately. I know that it will take away my dance career, but Alexis seems to have done that already. I'm just ready to move onto the next big thing in my life, and I think that it is us. Well, I know it's us, but I want what we have to grow and what better way than with a growing belly? If Alexis hadn't intervened, we would have a little baby soon anyway. And I would be willing to share my bacon with you to make it happen."

I–holy fucking shit.

Her words are on replay in my head.

Growing belly . . . baby soon anyway . . . growing belly . . . bacon.

Finally it hits me . . . she has taken some sort of drug. "Heather, did you take your pain meds today?"

"No, it hasn't been hurting as much since I've been doing the stretches Henry has asked me to do," she says while she points her toes and turns her ankle in a clockwise rotation, followed by another in the opposite direction.

I finally exhale the breath I was apparently holding and tilt my head back to look at the ceiling. A million fucking thoughts are racing through my head. Holy God in heaven, what has gotten into her? I mean, she's right. She would be about halfway through with the pregnancy if that accident hadn't taken it.

"You've been thinking about this? This isn't just a whim? Cause, fuck, Heather, this is a really big deal."

She moves her hands up my chest and around my neck and looks me straight in the eye. "I know it's unconventional, but we do everything out of order. I want this Noah, and there is no one else I would ever want it with but you. I know it's a big deal, which is why I've only just brought it up now. I want to sit on our front porch with a pregnant belly and yell at you to bring me some more sweet tea. I want to take walks in a peaceful neighborhood while pushing a stroller. I want you, and I want this. I want something that is a little you and a little me. Neither one of us have much family, and I want for us to start our own."

I search her eyes for any flicker of indecision. She stares me down with an intensity that knocks the air out of my chest. I know now that this woman will take what she wants, when she wants it. I have to break eye contact, or I'll lose my train of thought. My arm moves around her slim waist and I drop my forehead to her shoulder. Normally the proximity of her cleavage would sidetrack me and do me in but this—this is on a whole other level. She's silent, and thank fuck, because I need quiet right now. Okay, so we haven't moved in together yet, but that's being remedied soon. We're not married . . . hell, not even engaged.

That's because you fucked that up big time, Ryan.

My lungs burn from the breath I'm holding, so I release it. We haven't discussed her foot and if she'll even dance again.

The bar.

Oh fuck, what if I don't pass it?

What if it takes me multiple tries?

What if I never pass?

I can feel my chest start to pound as I sit here in a full-on panic attack. I squeeze my eyes shut and try to block it all out. This isn't happening. Fuck me, I've never had a dad. I won't know how to be one. What do I do? Will she be crushed if I say not right now? How did we go from looking at houses to wanting a baby? How did she make that leap? My eyes open, and I'm willing myself to look up and face this beautiful woman. Face her and tell her I cannot give her what she wants right now.

I pull back and catch myself staring at her flat stomach. My hand moves of its own accord, and I lay my palm flat against her. I'm suddenly thrust back into my memories, memories of Heather lying unconscious in a hospital bed with my hand on her stomach. Touching, grasping at the missing baby that was ours, remembering how I wanted it more than anything, remembering how I wanted to believe that she wanted our child, that she'd want a piece of me inside her. A part of me growing inside her while she held onto it, took care of it, kept it alive for us. I wanted to believe that. I wanted to believe I could have that life.

I had imagined how she would look pregnant with my baby. I prayed that we could have that. And when she woke, and I had to tell her what we lost . . . it was the worst feeling in my life. Worse than finding out my entire life was a lie. Hell yes, it was worse than that, having to look my girl in the eye and tell her we lost what we made together. And now this same beautiful woman wants that with me. She wants a part of me in her. She's willingly asking for it. I'm not being tricked, coerced, or begged. She wants what's mine and wants to make it ours.

It's not an accident we're forced to think about . . . she's already thought of it and has been planning it. My thumb rubs over a small spot below her navel.

I quickly imagine her stomach growing larger every day, watching her carry our baby with joy, instead of resentment and fear. I imagine kissing her there every night, every day. I imagine how much closer it will make us, going through it together. In that instant, I know my decision. I look up at her, my anxiety and pounding heart calmed.

"Yes. I want it too."

Her eyes rim with tears, and she throws herself at me, holding onto me as if I'm her only lifeline. I move my arms around to her back and hold her fast.

"Are you sure?" She quickly moves back and runs her fingers into the back of my hair.

"Sweetheart, I want to be with you more than anything, and if this is what we both want, then I don't see why not."

My fucking heart is about to beat out of my chest when she smiles. She looks utterly happy, and I made that happen. Me. Nobody else. Her lips are on mine in an instant, and she's plunging deep with her tongue. I've never felt her so worked up before.

I lie back and pull her down on top of me. "You need to stop taking the pill."

She nods emphatically and I smirk: this little tornado of hormones has already thought of that.

"Now . . . let's start now."

Her desperate words break our heated kiss, and I feel her hands move under the waistband of my sweats. I open my eyes and look up at her. I can't help but laugh at how anxious she is.

"Heather? I'm not sure I can. I'm working with some performance anxiety right now."

She bites my lip and sits on top of my manhood. Hell, I can feel how warm her pussy is through her yoga pants.

I chuckle and hold onto her hips. "Baby, I appreciate you trying, but we've just decided on something major. He's not going to come out and play right away."

I sit up with her fully seated on my lap and move her hair off her shoulders, away from her neck.

She gives me the biggest pout she can manage.

"We should probably get you to a doctor to see when the best time for us to conceive would be."

"But I already know," she professes in a whine. I cock my eyebrow at her.

"Well, Miss Lane, it looks like you've been doing your homework. The professor is pleased."

She crushes her lips to mine, and I smack her ass harder than I mean to.

"I thought your pussy was sore."

She claws her little hands up under my shirt and up my chest. "It is . . . so sore," she says as she rocks her hips to entice me. "But I want your baby."

"And you'll get it, but we have to get the pill out of your system first."

"Gahhh," she growls and falls back onto the bed, finally giving up on her advances. And thank God, my poor balls couldn't take much more.

Who the fuck am I kidding? I can't say no to that gorgeous ass.

I move her and climb on top of her, kissing down her neck. "You win."

A week passes and Heather and I have made two trips to Long Island to see Henry about her foot. His prognosis remains the same, though. They spend an hour or two doing physical therapy while I watch or help Ellery in her garden. Heather and I have been going at it every night; I'm not complaining because I'm more than satisfied.

Heather is now sitting down at the end of the exam table in her gynecologist's office. I've told her that I don't need to be in here while she has the exam, but she's insistent; part of me thinks that she's worried something could be wrong, but why would something be wrong?

The doctor comes in and within a few minutes she's inspecting

Heather. I feel as if I shouldn't be in here.

"All right, Miss Lane, we're all done. Everything looks like it's supposed to, and I don't see why you wouldn't be able to conceive."

"That's great; could you give us an estimate as to when her birth control will be out of her system?"

Heather beams up at me as she removes her feet from the stirrups.

"Well, different studies have turned out different outcomes, but I'm going to give you an estimate of roughly three months. Now, that is just an estimate, so it could take longer, but it could also happen much sooner than that."

I'm sitting at the head of the exam table and look down at her. She's smiling up at me with her hands splayed out on her flat stomach.

"Thank you."

"It's my pleasure. Miss Lane, please feel free to call me if you have any questions or concerns. The checkout desk will have my card for you."

"Thank you, doctor," she says politely and I help her sit up as the doctor leaves the room. She's looking at me expectantly.

"Are you happy with that news, little ballerina?"

"I'm so nervous," she says as she looks down at her stomach.

I exhale deeply and rub the back of my neck. "That makes two of us."

A week passes by since we went to see Heather's doctor and I'm in full study mode, with a side of research.

Damn, I need to call Dani. And Lana and Dillen.

I decide to put down my textbooks for today while Heather is pampering herself. She says she might be too sore for my lips to graze her skin, so I'm treating her to a full-day, all-inclusive day at the spa with Dillen and Lana. I think there's still tension crackling between those two, but I believe Joel might have gotten through the tough front that Dillen puts up. Regardless, it's not my business until they decide to make it mine.

Dillen has been staying at my apartment while Heather and I look for a house on the sound. And from what I've heard from Coen, I believe

Lana might be interested in Heather's apartment too.

I open my laptop and pull up Google where my search will begin. It takes me a good three hours to secure everything before I can even call Dani. I let out a deep breath as the phone rings twice before Dani is on the line with me.

"Hello?"

"Hey Dani, it's Noah. Do you have a second to talk?"

She's breathing heavily, and I can't help but feel like I've interrupted some sort of cardio workout she was doing.

"Of course I do. How are you? Heather has been telling me about each visit you two have with the Somers. They sound like they adore you two."

"Yeah, it's been a learning curve, but I've enjoyed having them in my life. I cannot imagine what they've been through, though."

"I know, but you're all together now. I'd love to come out there and see them again."

"Well, that's kind of why I am calling. I've planned a road trip for Heather and myself, and I would like for you and Brannon to meet us there. I'm going to have Lana, Dillen, Coen, and Joel, if he can get out of work, meet us there too."

"Oh sure, we'd love to come. Where, might I ask, are we going?"

"Well, I'll set up the rooms and pay for them, since I'm asking you all to travel up. I'd like for you all to come up to Moraine Lake Lodge in Canada, on July eighteenth."

"That's rather specific, Noah. Why don't we go up for the Fourth of July instead? I'm sure there will be fireworks."

"Well, I'm taking the bar in the second week of July, and the following week we will be road-tripping up to Moraine Lake."

"Oh, that's right. You're going to kick this exam's ass—I have no doubt. So is this just a vacation?"

"Well, you could call it that."

After I got off of the phone with Dani, I go back to planning our road trip. I'd like to get my SUV before we leave. Hell, I could go to the dealership right now and surprise my little ballerina when she gets back.

But fuck, I want her to be a part of all my decision-making. I want her to be included in everything I do. She's a part of who I am: she's my future. Fuck it, I'll wait, and we'll go together.

Instead I decide to call Coen. I dial and hit call; it rings three times before he answers.

"Hey dipshit."

"What's up, man? Are you too busy with your new chick to hit me up?"

"First off, fuck you. Secondly, damn right I am. What can I do for you?"

"Lana's great. I think you might have a keeper. Listen, I need you to block off a week starting on July eighteenth."

"Can do. What's going on?"

"Heather and I are going to road-trip to Moraine Lake in Canada, and I'd like you and Lana to join us. Of course, you two would fly there."

"Oh shit. Hell yeah, we'll join you two."

"Nice, man. Her sister and her sister's boyfriend will be there too, and I'm going to ask Joel and Dillen."

I can hear him grunt over the phone. "Ah fuck. Dillen's great, but I don't want any trouble."

"You? You don't want trouble? Shit, where did this motherfucker I know named Reed go?"

He laughs. "Yeah, yeah."

I hear the front door close and Heather yells for me.

"All right, dude, I believe my girl just got back in, so I'll call you later. Shit, and tell Lana not to say anything about you guys coming up to Canada. I want it to be a surprise."

"No problem, man, you got it. My lips are sealed."

"Oh hey, before I forget . . . I think Joel and Dill have something going on. So just a heads up," I warn him. He's quiet for all of four seconds before he starts laughing.

"Damn, I feel sorry for him because I knocked the bottom out of that shit."

"Fuck, man, I don't need the damn details. I was in the other room."

"I'm not sorry, dude. But I'll let you go, and I'll let you know what Lana says."

Heather walks in and crawls onto the bed, then into my lap. She leans her head against my chest and my arm automatically moves around her, securing her in place. "Thanks, man. I'll talk to you later."

"See ya," he replies before hanging up.

I set my phone down and smile down at Heather. "Hey gorgeous girl. Did you enjoy the spa?"

"Yes, it was amazing. Thank you."

"You're welcome, baby. I hope the girls enjoyed it too, and I found a house I think you might like." I pick up my tablet and pull up the realtor website that I found it on.

"You did?" She sits up on my lap excitedly and watches me move my fingers across the screen to the website that hosts the house.

The house that I click on is on a three-and-a-half-acre property with a shingle-style, two-story house overlooking Long Island Sound in Old Field, New York.

"Noah, it's beautiful. Scroll down. What type of shingles are those? I love how they blanket the house."

"It says they are cedar. I like the floor plan. It's an L-shape with the main wing that faces the sound. And, hell, that porch is huge. Shit."

"It's gorgeous. I like that the porch is undercover and it sort of has a Japanese look to it, right?"

"I think you're right."

I click on the next picture and it shows the second wing, which hosts a three-car garage and a long driveway out to the street.

"There's only one thing I need to say about it."

"What? What's wrong with it? Did it burn down?"

"No, sweetheart." I chuckle. "I'm not into mowing the lawn. Even as much as Ellery has a green thumb, I would kill the damn grass, all three acres of it."

Her soft laugh fills the room. "Okay, we'll get someone to cut it for us."

"Thank fuck." I scroll back up and pause at the first picture again.

"Noah, are you sure you are okay with paying that amount? I can help."

"Don't worry about it, ballerina, I'll be paying it off immediately. There won't be any payments."

Her eyebrows shoot up. "Seriously?"

"Yeah. Would you like to call the realtor on this site and set up an appointment to go see it in person? It says it was listed a few days ago."

"Uhhh, yes please. Could we go on the way down to your parents' tomorrow? I don't want someone else to get his or her grubby hands on it. I love it so much."

She takes my tablet from me and starts going through the pictures again. I glance at the time and it's just past five-thirty.

"I'll call them now; hopefully they're still open. They should be, though; it's only Monday."

About a half-hour later I'm off the phone, and my ballerina is doing a dance on top of her bed. I laugh and walk over to the edge of the mattress and pull her to me by her thighs. I finally get her to stop dancing, and I lift her shirt so I can rub my nose across her flat stomach before biting at her rib cage. "You smell so damn good. You have no idea how beautiful you look."

She tangles her hands into my hair and tries to inch away when my teeth make contact with her soft skin. She moves her hands and pulls her blouse up and off of her body; now I can fully admire what's mine.

"I want to take you somewhere after I take the bar exam."

"Oh yeah?" She asks with genuine surprise and I lick around her navel.

"Mmm. How about a road trip? We'll find some romantic cabin. We could drive up to Canada and sit in front of the fire naked. You could wear your fuzzy socks—*only* your fuzzy socks."

Her giggle makes me grin, and I look up at her. "That is hardly sexy, Noah. But that sounds so romantic."

"Yeah, well, it was a good ploy. And you might as well say yes, because I've already found a cabin and reserved a room for a week."

I grunt when she grips my hair and yanks my head back. "Noah! Seriously?" She starts bouncing up and down on the bed and squeals excitedly. "Oh my God, our first vacation together."

I breathe in through my teeth because damn, she's strong. "I'm going to take that as a yes, ballerina." My fingers grip her ass and I squeeze.

"Yes, yes, yes, take me away!" She crushes her lips to mine heatedly.

I lift her off of the bed as I bite her lip. "Make me dinner, woman. Then I'll work on getting you pregnant."

"Swear?"

"You have my word."

I really want this with her now. I want a life with her. I want the family I was never allowed to have—with her. Thinking back on the first time I saw her, I knew instantly that she would make an impact on my life, but never once did I think we'd be where we are now. In less than a year, I've figured out that she's the one I'm meant to be with, and I believe we both deserve it. We've been stripped of our families and been dealt such a shitty hand of cards that I believe this is right.

Nothing in our lives has followed the plans we had set out for ourselves—they're better. I've come to realize that I can't save someone, but I can love that person unconditionally, which is what I've done with Heather. I couldn't save her from falling off of the damn stage; I couldn't save her from it ruining her dance career; I couldn't save our unborn baby, and I couldn't save our broken relationship before I left for London, but I don't think I've once stopped loving her, and I know, without having to second-guess myself, that it's what she needs.

Heather has loved life, and it has loved her right back, even though it has hindered her in ways that are simply unfair. Heather is the strongest, most loyal, and loving woman I have met. She knows her limits and sometimes tests them to see how far she can push herself, yet she knows when to pull back and put a stop to any advances.

She's made me become what I respect in a person: someone who is able to look past the disparities in life and live life for today. Heather has helped me use my struggles as steppingstones to become someone who suits me, someone who is more than a stranger in the mirror.

As I look down at her in the kitchen from the top of the stairs, I realize that any woman could throw herself at me, and I wouldn't be able to tear my eyes away from my ballerina. She stole my life. She is the sole owner of my heart. I want nothing more than to keep that smile on her lips for the rest of my life. She must feel me watching her, because she looks up and over her shoulder at me, and, hell, that smile gets sweeter each time I see her, and it breaks my soul with its beauty. My soul, my life, and this love are no longer black and white; it's all scattered with pinks and glitter. I don't think I could stand without it. She's helped me push out the poison and dilute the destructive parts of my life that felt all encompassing.

She looks down and it's as if life is in slow motion as I acknowledge the thought of her being my remedy. I've always believed that better things were coming, and she has proven to be it.

Chapter Twenty One

RUTHLESS ASSESSMENT

HEATHER

I'm anxiously pacing the living room. I've cleaned all I can in this place; I've even used my Swiffer on every surface imaginable, which got me thinking about the night at the club. I haven't talked to him since this morning, and it's now after six in the evening. I'm not anxious because I haven't seen or heard from him: I'm anxious because he took the first part of his bar exam today. I've got everything ready for dinner—I made his favorite: meatloaf, *yuck*, with mashed potatoes and candied carrots as sides. I know he knows his stuff, but an eight-hour exam is brutal for anybody, regardless of how well one knows the material. I've picked all the nail polish off my nails while I constantly check my phone for a call or a text.

This past month has flown by with my physical therapy, and we went to go see the shingled house on Long Island Sound a week ago. Other than that, Noah has been studying continuously. I'm hoping everything will pay off; he deserves this.

I finally manage to sit down and stop pacing when I hear the door open. It closes before I even hop up off the couch, and I can hear his heavy footsteps on the hardwood floor.

"Baby?" I call out before rounding the corner. "How did it go?" I ask before I take in his mood. My Greek god looks as stressed as I've ever seen him. He's wearing a look of utter exhaustion and defeat.

"Hey sweetheart," he says in a cool, smoky voice and pulls me into his arms. Oh, I've missed my man more than I thought I could. I'm melting in his arms as I press my body to his and bathe myself in his lingering cologne.

He wraps his strong arms around my waist and holds me tightly to him. He exhales a heavy breath. "Jesus, what a day. I'm pretty sure I got every question incorrect," he says in a voice I've never heard from him before. He's always so confident, never second-guessing himself, so this is new.

"Oh baby, that's not possible. You've been studying so hard. It's just nerves."

"I don't know. I think I've fucked this up already. Shit, I need to go study." He lifts his wrist up to check the time while I place a kiss on his chest.

I look up at him and frown. "No, you don't. You're going to wear yourself out. You need to eat. Come sit down. I've made dinner and it's all ready."

I pull back from him and tug at his hand. I can see that tonight I'm going to have my hands full with keeping him occupied and away from the books. He grudgingly follows me into the kitchen and lets go of my hand to make himself a drink.

Sitting down at the kitchen island with a Bourbon on the rocks, he asks, "What did you do today?"

I look up at him after plating his food and slide it over to him.

"I cleaned." I smile and try to keep him talking. "I used my Swiffer." I watch as he takes a drink, and I'm not sure if he's even listening to me.

He sets his glass down and a smile plays on his lips. "Yeah? Those things seem to come in handy. The apartment looks great. Oh shit, I think I got a phone call from the realtor." He pulls his phone out and taps the screen a few times before her voice comes across on speakerphone.

"This message is for Noah Ryan and Heather Lane. Please give me a call back at your earliest convenience. I look forward to hearing from you. Bye now."

I smile after I hear the voicemail. "Do you think we got it?" I watch as he sets his phone aside and picks up his drink again.

"Doubt it," he answers me in a dejected voice.

I can't help but frown. I know he wants the house just as much as I do. My Greek god is so disheartened tonight, so I decide I want to console him in some way. I hop up onto the kitchen island and move his plate out of the way, moving my legs to either side of him in front of me. "Noah?"

"Mmhmm?"

He's staring into his glass as he twirls the liquid around and around, listening to the ice clink against the glass. He doesn't even notice that I've moved in front of him. "Aren't you going to eat?"

He sighs heavily and places his hand on my thigh. "I'm really not hungry, baby."

"Hey . . . come on, you can't go hard at this tomorrow if you don't eat." I rub his hand that rests on my thigh and try to tilt my head to get into his line of sight.

He finally looks up at me with weary eyes. "If I eat, can we just go to bed?"

I nod and rub softly under his tired eyes with my thumb. "Yes, baby."

He kisses my thumb and I lean down to press my lips to his. "Don't ever doubt yourself, Noah. Okay?"

He nods in agreement before helping me off of the island and onto the seat beside him. Quietly he picks up his fork to start eating; relief floods me.

He remains silent as I force myself to eat what I made for him. It's not that I didn't do a good job—I just hate meatloaf. But it's his favorite, so he says. He's too absorbed in thinking about his exam to even notice that I haven't really eaten. I decide that I can't eat any more than my carrots and potatoes and get up to scrape my plate. I'm cleaning the kitchen up to give him time to eat and when I turn back around, he's gone.

His drink is still there and his food is barely touched. I look down the hall and see the light on upstairs. "How in the heck . . . ?" I trail off to myself. I make my way quietly upstairs and find him sitting at the desk. My professor has his glasses on and is back into study mode. He's thumbing through his books—looking up what, I have no idea. I lean against the doorframe and watch him in the dim light. My heart breaks for this man as I watch him push himself harder and harder. I cannot watch him do this to himself any longer.

I push off from the doorframe and walk over, gently rubbing my hands up his back and over his shoulders. He stops what he's doing and drops his head in defeat. He doesn't say the words, but I know his mind has finally given up on him tonight.

"Come to bed, baby," I say softly in his ear.

His hand comes up and rests on top of mine while he takes his glasses off with the other. I watch with a heavy heart as he drops his glasses onto his open books and pinches the bridge of his nose. He reaches over and turns the lamp off and just like that, my professor has retired for the evening.

I tug at his shirt and lift it off of his rigid chest. He pulls it up over his head the rest of the way before undoing his jeans and stepping out of them. "I want you naked in my arms, ballerina."

I nod and watch him crawl into our bed. "Okay, baby, I'll be right back."

The last thing I see of him before I walk out of the room are his boxer briefs sliding down to his ankles and his muscular tush getting under the comforter.

I know this isn't the time to think dirty thoughts, but *dang it.*

I tiptoe downstairs to finish cleaning up the kitchen before turning the lights off. I find myself hoping that he can hang in there for one more day. I don't know what to do for him in this situation.

When I make my way back upstairs and into our room, he's sound asleep. He's on his stomach with one of his muscular arms outstretched onto my side of the bed. I can't stand the thought of waking him so I can lie in my spot, so instead I get undressed and crawl in beside him. I snuggle into his side and drape my arm over his lower back, doing my absolute best to hold my tired Greek god, my exhausted professor.

When I woke up this morning, I was in bed alone. I never felt him get up nor did I hear him get ready. After my eyes adjusted to the light, I looked over at his desk and saw almost every book opened and piled high on top of each other. He must have been furiously trying to cram the every bit of extra information into his head before he left. It's been seven hours now—seven long, excruciating hours. There isn't a thing out of place in this apartment. I know that pacing doesn't help my nerves, so I decide to sit down and text Dani:

Hey big sister, I miss you.

I type out and hit send. It takes her just a few minutes to reply back as I sit down on the couch and wait for my Greek god to walk in through the front door.

Hi sissy. I miss you too! Brannon is reading over my shoulder and told me to tell you that he's jealous that you don't miss him.

I giggle and reply:

Awww! I do miss him too! He's just a butthead and trying to start trouble, though.

She replies shortly after I hit send:

He said you better watch out because the next time he sees you, he's going to show you just how much trouble he can be. Okay, I don't even want to know what he has planned. So tell me, how you have been? Also, I think I want to move back to New York City. I miss you too much.

I gasp and sit up straighter, my fingers having trouble typing fast enough.

What! Are you serious? I would pee my pants if you did.

My phone buzzes in my hand before I have the chance to set it down:

I just pouted so hard at Brannon that I think he's going to try and make it work. I won't have a problem transferring to my PR agency's NYC division, but it's just his company here. I'm so giving him until the end of the week. I want to be able to hug my sister whenever the fuck I feel like it.

My fingers dance across the screen as I type out my reply to her:

And I so want to rinse your mouth out with soap whenever I feel like it. Tell Brannon I will love him forever and ever if he makes it work.

I'm glancing back and forth between my phone and the front door.

Oh he'll make it work all right because he's not getting my mouth around his big ole' dick until he tells me we're moving. And yes, he's still reading over my shoulder.

I gasp.

DANI OMG STOP! I don't want to think about his penis. Gahhh!

I'm about to toss my phone across the couch when the front door opens, and my Greek god fills the frame. My phone goes off again, but I drop it and leap off of the couch hurriedly to jump into his open arms.

"Baby! You're all done." I pepper his face with kisses as he holds onto me. His chuckle makes me smile, and I feel like my boyfriend is back.

"Thank fuck that is done. I sure as hell better pass that shit too. Mmm, I missed you, my ballerina," he says with a smile on his face before he holds onto my butt and lifts me off of my feet to kiss me as if he hasn't been able to kiss me in months.

I squeeze him as tight as I can while we kiss, pouring all my love into it. "I've missed you. Even though you've been here, you've been distant."

"I'm sorry, baby, I know it's been hard on you, but I'm all yours, and I'm damn ready to get our first vacation started."

I'm smiling so big that my cheeks hurt. "I can't wait! Can we go pack now?"

He steps further into the room and kisses me slowly before moving his lips down my neck, "Definitely, but first we need to call our realtor."

My head falls to the side, and I get chills. His lips are so soft and the way he breathes against my skin is such a turn-on that I have a hard time concentrating on much else. "Uh-huh . . ." I say, but I'm not quite sure what I'm responding to.

He continues biting at my neck playfully while he pulls out his phone and dials. It rings on speaker, and I'm lost to him.

I have no idea what's being said. All I feel are lips and hands and teeth. My fingers grip his t-shirt and pull.

Noah talks to her between nips, and I'm too lost to even realize that he's already hung up the phone until his lips find mine again. "What do you think?"

"So good . . ." I breathe out with my eyes closed.

His arms are around me again as he pulls his lips away from mine. "I don't think we're talking about the same thing, sweetheart."

My eyes open, and I'm saddened at the loss of his lips on mine.

He runs his hand into the side of my hair and smiles. "What's wrong, baby?"

I smile and shake my head. "Nothing, why?"

"You're not excited that we got it?"

I stare at him for a moment before his words register. "Wait, what?"

"Mmm, you were too preoccupied with my lips to realize what she said, weren't you?"

I nod and stare at him, impatiently waiting. "Well? What did she say?"

"She said they accepted our final offer on the house and then proceeded to congratulate us while my lips were on your porcelain skin."

"WE GOT IT?" I shriek.

"We got it, baby. It's ours."

I don't know what to do. I want to scream, and jump up and down, and kiss him all over, "Ahhh! Oh my God, don't mess with me, Noah Bradley Ryan."

"I wouldn't dream of it; I'm serious."

I smack his hard chest and squeal with excitement. "Noahhh! Oh my God, we bought a house!"

"Damn right we did. I need to drop off a check in the morning before we head out on our road trip."

I plaster my lips to his and jump up, wrapping my legs around his torso. "I love you, my professor."

He chuckles and smacks my butt playfully. "The professor is gone for a while, sweetheart. I'm not picking up another book until I have to."

"I think I like the sound of that. I'm ready to be selfish and hog you to myself for however long we're going for."

"Well," he says, "it's going to take a minimum of three days to drive up there, depending on the route you want to take. We can either drive through the US and stop in Chicago and then enter into Canada from North Dakota, or we can enter through Buffalo, New York, and drive through Canada for the majority of the way."

I pretend to think on it, but I already know my answer. "Let's go through Buffalo and on up. I've already seen most of the US."

"You've got yourself a deal, ballerina. Let me get you pregnant, we'll pack, and then we'll be ready to go in the morning."

I laugh hysterically at his flippancy over getting me pregnant and bite at his neck before squirming out of his grip. "Deal. Come on, lover boy . . ." I make sure to sway my hips as I walk in front of him. As I walk up the stairs, for the first time ever, I'm battling between sleeping with this man and doing something else. I want him to get me pregnant, but I am so stinking excited for this trip.

It's the morning of our road trip and I'm elated. Noah woke up an hour before I did to go pick up a rental SUV from the airport. I kind of hope it's similar to the one in which he had his sweet way with me.

I've had the most fun packing for this trip. I can't be sure, but I think my lingerie pile far exceeds my clothing. I am currently sitting on my bag, trying to zip it closed when I hear his deep voice call out for me after the front door shuts. "Sweetheart? You better be up and ready. We've gotta hit the road."

"I'm up and I'm ready, but I can't get this thing to shut," I yell out, and I hear his footsteps come up the stairs. I can't wait to see him; no matter how many times I watch him enter a room, he still makes me forget to breathe.

He walks in with that confidant strut, and his sexy grin knocks the air out of me. "Well, hello, gorgeous." His cool voice reverberates through my chest and he leans over to zip my bag up effortlessly.

I wallow in my appreciation of this gift to women that belongs to me. "Thank you."

"You're welcome. Now get that gorgeous ass downstairs, so we can drop off the check for our house."

"Eeek!" I squeal and hop up, smacking him hard on his tush. "Meet you downstairs."

"Move that ass, sweetheart," he says as he picks up our bags and follows me down the flight of stairs. I grab my purse and iPad before holding the front door open for him.

"Did you get your snack bag?" he asks as he stops to let me through the door first.

I scoff and hold my hand up to show him the large Victoria's Secret duffel that is filled to the brim. "You seriously think I would leave home without it?"

He laughs and we walk to my garage spot. I stop dead in my tracks when I see an identical SUV to the one we had a while back.

"Fond memories, Miss Lane?" he whispers sexily into my ear.

"Yes, indeed, Mr. Ryan."

Once the SUV is loaded and we're both in our seats, I dig inside my duffel and pull out a blue raspberry sucker, unwrap it, and pop it in my mouth.

I look over and he's watching me with a cocked eyebrow. "Really? Are you going to tease me with it before we even leave the building?"

I push the sucker to one side of my mouth so he can see it pressing hard against my cheek, "Yup."

His nostrils flare as he inhales deeply, and I grin. "This trip is going to be so much fun!" I tease and pull the sucker from my mouth to place a loud kiss on his lips. "Get moving, honey!"

I watch him lick his lips as he pulls out of the garage and into Manhattan traffic to meet with our realtor.

It took us just over an hour to sign paperwork for the house and hand over the deposit check to our realtor. We still have the closing next month, when the final contracts are signed. To my surprise, my name was on all of the paperwork too. He's made sure that this house is ours and not his alone, and I love him all the more for it.

We're finally on our road trip, and I'm elated. I hold my hand over my chest and feel my rapid heartbeat. "Oh my God, Noah, I'm freaking out. We're going to live together, like, officially," I squeal excitedly and clap my hands in quick succession. I'm so happy I'm having a hard time containing it.

He reaches for my hand and laces our fingers together before bringing my hand up to his lips. "You're all mine, ballerina. I'm incredibly excited to officially move in with you."

My heart melts, and I'm smiling from ear to ear, but then a thought suddenly crashes into my mind. *Oh crap.* My smile falls and I try to think about how to broach this with him. He must notice the change in my body language because he glances over at me questioningly.

"Can we make a deal?" I ask as I chew on my lip nervously.

"That depends . . ."

I scowl and sit back. "Okay fine, I'm not moving in."

"Hey," he prods gently, "of course we can make a deal, sweetheart. What's on your mind?"

I snap my head back around and look at him with a hopeful expression. "I can't pee in front of you. What the heck am I going to do if we live together?" I throw my hands up and am quite animated when I speak.

"We pretty much live together now. Do you have a problem peeing while I'm around?" I can tell he's holding in a laugh as he waits for my response.

"Yes. Yes I do." I throw my arm over my eyes and lay my head back against the headrest. "Oh my God, what if . . . ugh . . . kill me now."

I can feel his hand on my inner thigh before he speaks. "I love you. There are no what-ifs. I don't like those two words side by side: they challenge everything they are put in front of. It's time to let go of what you can't change, ballerina. We both want this to happen, correct? And it's happening."

I stop and hold my breath. *Okay, this is happening.*

"But what if I have to poop? And you're there? Then what?" My voice raises in panic as I throw my arm off my eyes to look at him.

"Would you like your own bathroom?" he asks sweetly because I think he realizes that I'm serious about this, but then his smile cracks and he tries to swallow his laugh.

My nostrils flare, and my eyes widen as I watch him laugh. I start smacking his bicep and shoulder repeatedly while he drives. "I'm serious, Ryan!"

"Whoa, I think you might need a fucking. Heather, I love you, and with everything we've been through, there is no way in hell you are going to scare me off."

"What if I puke in front of you? That's so unattractive," I prod, testing him.

"I'll still love you, Heather. Are you trying to test my love for you? Is that what is going on?"

"No. I'm just checking." I stubbornly look away and out the window. "What if I need you to get me *ladies' days* stuff?"

"Then I'll get it with a six-count box of cupcakes."

I can't help it when a smile breaks out on my face, and I look at him, rolling my eyes. "You're ridiculous, you know that?"

"Possibly, but I couldn't care less if you see me taking a piss."

"Yeah, I know," I mumble and dig through my purse.

He chuckles and watches me as he drives, looking back and forth between me and the highway in front of him. "Do you want to stay in Buffalo tonight?"

"No." I shake my head and slip my shoes off, curling my feet up in my seat. "I want to road-trip and drive until we're too tired to continue. Then we'll stop to sleep. That's the fun of these adventures. And I plan on making this unforgettable."

"You've got yourself a deal, gorgeous. I'm glad I put you down as a driver too."

I pout. "Heyyy. I'm not driving, I'm a copilot."

He winks and gives me that sexy smile before kissing my fingertips. "Oh and Heather?" he prods as I look dreamily out the window.

"Hmm?"

"You better get over this aversion to going to the bathroom in front of me. If I'm going to get you pregnant, you bet your ass I'm watching my baby being born," he says matter of factly, and my mouth drops open.

"Uhm no. That's not happening, Noah."

The look that he gives me is deadly and I instantly feel like cowering into my seat.

"Excuse me?" His voice is dark and cold.

"Why would you want to see that?"

I feel like he has a slight grasp on his sanity by the look in his eyes as he looks from me to the road and back again. "You're serious? I've seen you in every intimate way possible already."

I scrunch my nose up at the thought of him seeing things at the end of the bed whenever I do give birth. "I don't know."

I watch his fingers grip the steering wheel as he looks forward. "Heather Lane, you will not deny me that opportunity."

Oh.

His dominance radiates off of him, and I can physically feel it wash over me. I reach my hand out and splay my fingers on his bicep. "I think you're right. I don't like the thought of you seeing all of that, but if you want to . . ." I sigh heavily. "Can we just have fun, please?"

I know that what I've said bothered him, but if I'm being honest, his dominance is such a turn-on.

"Yeah, we can. Now come over here and make it up to me."

I smile because his storm is gone for the moment. "Mmm, I'd love to." I lean over and start kissing his neck, nuzzling him, and breathing in his cologne.

I can feel the rumble in his throat, and I swear it makes me clench my legs shut.

"You smell so good." I nip at his earlobe and sit back before I do some horrible things to him.

"I'm glad you think so. Let me know when you need to stop."

"I'm good," I reply happily and put my bare feet up on the dash.

I can feel his eyes on my freshly pedicured feet, and it makes me giggle. "I think this foot fetish might have actually turned into a real thing, Ryan," I taunt him

"It's a possibility." He clears his throat: it sounds thick with what . . . tension . . . lust? "How's your foot feeling, sweetheart?"

"It feels great—the best it's felt in a long time."

"Good."

As I'm about to turn on the radio, my Greek god surprises me with a revelation. "You know I'm fucking your ass on this trip, right?"

"Excuse me?"

I'm staring at him in disbelief. "You know you'd like it," he coos and brings my hand to his lips. "You enjoyed my finger in your ass not too long ago."

I bite down on the inside of my cheek as I think about his finger inside of me, making my orgasm so much more intense. "Maybe."

He laughs deeply and licks my finger. "I fucking knew you would love it."

I squirm in my seat as I watch him drive and change lanes. I know this is probably absurd, but he looks so sexy driving and in charge. Changing the subject, I ask, "Are you glad to finally be done studying?"

"You bet your pretty little ass I am." I can tell he's smirking to himself.

The bastard.

Chapter Twenty Two

MONUMENTAL MOVEMENTS

HEATHER

For the last three days, Noah and I have had the most amazing time. I've never laughed so much in my life. My cheeks hurt from smiling, and I feel closer to him than I ever have. We've bonded over this road trip and I can tell that he is completely carefree. He smiles all the time and has been more affectionate than I ever thought possible. He's clearly thought this trip out—when he had the time to do so, I'll never know. We've stopped along scenic routes and have taken pictures of the beautiful scenery. He's even humored me and taken selfies with me with the mountains in the background. I've been sending pictures of us to Lana, Dillen, and Dani, and they all have been swooning over how cute we are together. I must admit, I really caught an amazing specimen of a man and I don't ever plan on throwing him back. I've tried to be more comfortable around him regarding my bathroom breaks. So instead of asking him to make a pit stop, I just tell him I need to pee. I know he's enjoying it because he smiles like nothing else when I tell him.

I've even gotten him to talk about Mae, and it never resulted in an argument.

I think we're on the final stretch of the road trip before reaching our destination, because he turned off a main road awhile back, and we're headed through a two-lane road lined with gorgeous trees and snow-capped mountains. Everything looks like it belongs on a postcard. I'm in awe every time we round another corner.

I'm stunned into silence when we turn again, and I see the most beautiful cerulean lake. It takes me a moment, but I see a lodge ahead and Noah slows the SUV. "Oh my God, Noah, are we staying here?"

He reaches for my hand and squeezes. "Damn right we are. The lodge looks over the lake. Welcome to Moraine Lake, sweetheart."

I can't even describe how enchanting this place is. He parks under the entrance to the lodge, and I get out. I'm in a trance, it seems, as I walk away from him and the lodge. I go as far as my feet will take me, to the edge of the grass, and I can peek through the trees at the beautiful aquamarine water. The sun makes the water glitter in the distance, and I think I've actually died and gone to heaven. The colors that surround me are unlike anything I've seen in my travels throughout North America. I can't believe I'm standing in the midst of such beauty. Suddenly I feel him behind me as he snakes his arms around my waist, holding me to him. His lips caress my neck before he asks, "Do you like it?"

"Noah, it's incredible. I cannot believe you found this place."

He chuckles against my skin and gives me a squeeze around my waist. "You constantly seem surprised by what I'm capable of."

"It's just that I've traveled so much . . . ." I stop because it seems ridiculous to say that I've never seen anything so captivating before. "Noah, I love you."

He turns me in his arms at that moment and lifts my chin with his finger. "I love you more than you know, Heather." He lowers his lips to mine, and in that instant the wind picks up, tossing my hair around wildly. I can only imagine what we look like in this embrace with this scenery surrounding us—picture perfect. He releases me a moment later. "Let's get checked in."

I nod excitedly and hug him once more before we walk hand-in-hand up the path to the lodge.

I've traveled all over the United States and have never been so enamored by any one place as much as I am here. While he checks us in, I'm drinking in my surroundings. Like a little kid full of excitement, I want to run around this paradise to see every square inch of it. I must be fidgeting without realizing it because he squeezes my hand, and I look over at him. He's smirking as he looks down at my feet, and I follow his eyes. Without realizing it, I've been tapping my foot impatiently.

"Am I taking too long, Miss Lane?"

I grin and stop tapping my foot. "Yes, hurry up," I joke.

He holds up the room key in front of me. "All done, baby. Should I grab our bags first?"

I shake my head and tug on his hand. "Can't they take it up for us?" I plead.

"I'm sure they can." He turns to the front desk agent to ask her, but she's already nodding her head.

"We'll have the bags brought up. Enjoy your stay, Mr. Ryan," she says, clearly drooling over my Greek god.

"Thank you." He smiles his panty-dropping smile and leads me to the elevator bank. "You seem to be enjoying yourself already, little miss."

"Well, my man is spoiling me—of course I'm enjoying myself."

We make it up to our floor and then down the sunlit hallways to our room. Noah opens the door to our room, and I gasp when I step inside: it's a split-level suite with floor-to-ceiling windows.

The curtains are drawn, so the room is bathed in an abundant amount of warm sunshine. My eyes are drawn to the king-sized bed, as it's the first thing I walk past. The headboard and footboard are done in a shiny oak to fit the ambiance of the lodge. I run my hand along the smooth, rounded surface of the footboard and am briefly caught daydreaming about gripping it tightly with Noah's body behind me. I shake my head to clear my thoughts as I step down the two steps into the sunken living area, which has a river-rock-faced fireplace. Just outside of the large window is our own private balcony overlooking the lake and mountains. I've noticed that there are no telephones or televisions in the room: it's a complete getaway. This lodge is a dream: everything is nature-inspired and oozes comfort.

My hands reach for the double doors, and I open them in unison. The breeze that blows in is crisp and inviting. "Oh Noah, look . . ." is all

I can say. I step out onto the balcony and lean against the railing, taking in the beautiful sight before me. "It's just perfect," I say to myself in a whisper.

I feel Noah move beside me as he appreciates the view. "Damn, I saw pictures of this place online, but none of it does it justice."

The balcony has just enough room for two cushioned chairs and a small table spacing the two, with a private hot tub on the other side. I look over and up at him. "This is so perfect, Noah, thank you."

"I'm glad you like it, ballerina."

The bellman comes in and drops off our bags. Noah walks back and tips him, taking the rental car keys from him before he leaves. "I sure as hell hope you brought your bikini, ballerina. Get your little ass into the hot tub."

"I like it when you're bossy, and of course I brought it."

Fifteen minutes later we're in the hot tub looking out at the lake as the sun starts to set. The sky is illuminated with warm color, radiant red and auburn hues that kiss the snowcapped mountains.

We're both quiet as I look over at him. He's got his head lying back against the tub headrest, and he's gazing straight up, looking at nothing in particular. I'm wondering what he's thinking about. "Does this feel good after driving for so long?" I ask, trying to pull him from wherever he is.

"You're damn right it does. But then again, so will that ass on my cock."

My head shoots up off the headrest and I look straight at him. I can feel the wet tendrils of escaped strands clinging to my neck as the rest of my hair sits on top of my head. He's unmoving, just staring up at the darkening sky.

"What?"

"Which lube would you prefer? Flavored or unflavored? I bought one of each."

My mouth is agape. I can't even answer his question. He's totally serious, isn't he?

"Well?" he pushes.

"Uhh . . . I."

The water ripples as he moves toward me. "We'll go slow,

sweetheart." His lips are on my neck before I realize I have yet to breathe.

I now realize that he's been trying to get me relaxed this whole time. And holy hell, it's working. My arms and legs are so relaxed, and now he's working his lips against my neck; my only reaction is to moan.

"I'll take that as a yes . . ."

The electricity between us is palpable and I'm caught in its flare. I trust this man with my life, even when the skies grow dark, and his storm becomes immeasurable. I'm ready for him.

His arms move around me, caging me in as his lips assault my body with a welcome shock of targeted current. He knows what he wants and where he wants to go.

I cannot see underneath the bubbled surface, but I can feel one of his hands slide underneath my black lace bikini bottoms to the side of my left cheek. I jolt in front of him as his teeth almost break my skin as his lightning splits the night sky. His storm is radiant and full of powerful wonders, as his descent on me looms closer, darker.

This man is his own electrical storm, and the charged region of his gorgeous anatomy is ready to strike an uncharted place on my body. His large hand moves to cup my cheek instead of my sex. He takes his time to work me up, and I fantasize what it would feel like to host him there. With the water pressing against us, he moves his finger between my cheeks and up, touching me, causing the vibrating electricity between us to sing.

"Don't stop."

"Where do you want me to touch you?"

His question reminds me of the first time he ever touched me, and I know I made the right decision that night.

"Everywhere," I counter.

His other hand is on me in an instant, grasping my chin, forcing it to the side as he bites down on my overheated skin. I can feel his heavy gratitude for me pressing against my belly as he touches me.

"Make those sounds for me, Heather." His voice is highly erotic as he begs me, his lips making their way down between my breasts and his tongue playing at the edging of my bikini top. I oblige his request and wail tenderly, begging him for more and whispering his name.

He reaches his hand around to my strapless top and easily unhooks it. The second he gets it off, I slide my hand up his wet, warm chest and up around his neck before pushing my breasts up against him. My nipples are hard, tender, and peaked, while bolts of electricity zap through my veins.

He cups my breast with one strong hand and kneads me, while his lips surround my nipple. My back arches, and my fingers run through his wet hair.

"Oh yes, Noah."

I moan when he sucks, and then nips with his teeth. I glance down and lose my breath when he looks up at me in the same moment that his tongue and lips surround my other nipple. He loves to watch my pleasure, and I, his. The hand that is beneath the water never caresses me where I'm silently begging him to be. He's teasing me, forcing me to show him just how much I want him.

"I need to hear you say it, Heather," he prods and releases my nipple. He rises and looms over me, his lips red and full from his assault on my upper body.

I look up, and I know my eyes are dark with lust.

My breathing matches his.

My sex is aching for his touch, and I'm about to combust.

I maneuver my legs and wrap them around his waist, trying to pull him closer to me. "Noah, please . . . I need you. You've got me so worked up."

I'm begging and he's smirking down at me, shaking his head. I whimper—I'll keep begging if I have to.

"Not good enough, sweetheart." He lowers his head and his lips are a mere breath away but not touching mine. "Beg for me to touch you, Heather."

Every piece of me aches for this man. I would exchange years of my life for him to touch me—touch me like only he does—every day. Each time our bodies connect, the feeling that overtakes me is almost more than I can handle.

He must notice that I'm utterly lost to him in this moment, because he lifts me out of the water before cautiously stepping out of the hot tub. As soon as his feet hit solid ground, his lips are back on me as if they never left.

He takes me back inside the room and up the two steps that lead to the end of the king-sized bed. Removing his lips from my neck long enough for him to throw the comforter off of the bed, he lays me down on my back. My chest is heaving as he moves over me. His hand moves down my rib cage as I stretch out on the bed. I don't care that we're wet or smell of chlorine; I just care that he wants me as much as I do him.

His hand is back underneath my lace bottoms, pulling them down so he can see me, all of me, lying before him. I can't help but run my hands down to my breasts and pull on my nipples to relieve some of the tension that is percolating through my pent-up body.

"Fuck, I'm going to enjoy this," he states and leans down to kiss down my rib cage, down to my hipbone, and close to his destination at the inside of my thigh.

His teeth sink into delicate flesh on my inner thigh, and my legs automatically try to close. His hands grip my knees to keep them open and in place. I can feel him inhale my arousal, and it makes my cheeks blush.

"I won't be rough with you right now, but fuck do I want to be . . ." he says as he bites again but licks soothingly afterwards.

He lifts himself off of my wet body to remove his swim trunks, before going over to his duffel and pulling out two types of lube. "Which do you want, baby? Strawberry or unflavored?"

"Unflavored."

He walks back over to me with his phone and the lube, one in each hand. Before he puts his phone down, soft, erotic music fills the room. It's now dark outside, and there is only one warming light on in our suite.

"Are you ready?"

"I think so."

Tossing the lube next to me on the bed before climbing on, he starts kissing up my neck all the way to my ears, where he pauses to nibble on my earlobes before locking his lips with mine. One of his hands tracks down my body, while he uses the other to prop himself up—I'm ultra-aware of every move he makes.

"Grab the lube, baby."

I'm so freaking nervous that I'm practically trembling on this bed. I've never thought I'd be doing anything like this, but then again, I trust this man completely. He sees the indecision in my eyes, I'm sure, because he leans down and starts kissing my neck again slowly, passionately. My tense body relaxes once again, and I know he can feel it. He wraps his arm around my waist and turns me, putting my back to his front while we lie on our sides. I can feel his warm breath on the back of my neck and shiver when his lips follow my collarbone and down the curve of my shoulder. I can feel his hard length against my butt as he pays special attention to my aching sex with his fingers. He's going so slow with me, and I appreciate everything he's doing to make me feel comfortable.

"Mmm, there you go baby, just relax for me."

He reaches for the bottle and I hear him open the cap of the lubricant before he runs a finger down between my cheeks to my puckered opening. He lazily circles me there, applying the slightest amount of pressure. I barely gasp because it feels so good, but it's hard not to be tense when I know what's coming.

"Just lie there and enjoy this, baby; it's going to take some time. I'm not going to hurt you," he tenderly whispers in my ear between licks and kisses.

"I know. I trust you."

He nips at my shoulder as he slowly sinks the tip of his finger into me. He removes his finger briefly to apply more lube before he rims his finger around me again. The lube is frigid against my heated skin as he applies some more with his free hand.

I exhale an audible sigh, and I can feel him grin against my neck. "Mmm . . . you do like it, don't you?"

"Yes. Give me more, please?"

I can feel his cock twitch against my behind when I say that, and he slides his finger in deeper. "Fuck, you're so tight. I'm going to enjoy every minute of this."

I close my eyes and relish the feel of this unexpected and delightfully full feeling. It's a different sensation than having him finger me—alien and one I'm not accustomed to—yet it's so intriguing. I wonder if he can bring me to an orgasm like this?

I reach back and stroke his length because I need to feel him. He takes in a deep breath and sinks his teeth into me, and I feel naughty. It's like he's offering me something forbidden. He's tempted me, and I want more. I love that this will be ours: both of our firsts, our dirty little secret.

I start to rock back against him, making sure to rub his length between my cheeks. "Do you like that?"

"Damn, baby, more than you know."

A heated moan escapes from my lips when he teases me with a second finger. He slides his available hand over my skin to my sex where he starts stimulating my clit, applying the perfect amount of pressure.

I can feel his body vibrate behind me as a growl escapes him. My grip on him has become tighter, and I'm shamefully writhing in his arms.

"You have to let me know when you want more, ballerina."

I nod. "I want more," I boldly state and squeeze him hard.

He starts pushing his fingers in and out of me slowly, yet I can tell he's eager to do this.

"More, Noah . . . I'm ready."

I turn my head and meet his eyes. The love for me in his eyes is more visible than ever before. He presses his lips to mine as he takes his cock from my hand. "Are you ready for my head?"

I whimper against his lips and nod slowly. He slides his cock between my cheeks easily and then he's there. I try and relax, but this is just too much. The slightest amount of pressure he's applying is more than I can handle. I bite down on my lower lip to keep from gasping, but he's just too big. Oddly enough, I do feel a little give before a burning sting of pain and pressure. Holy hell, this will never work. My breathing picks up, and I can feel all of my abdominal muscles tense.

"Shh . . ." he whispers in my ear before kissing down the back of my neck in a much gentler fashion. I hear the bottle of lube open and he applies some to our wanton bodies.

I try exhaling, but when he tries pushing in again, my body rejects him, and I quickly press my hand against his bare thigh, halting him.

"Stop. Oh God."

He doesn't move an inch; he waits for me patiently as the minutes go by. His lips are on my skin and his fingers push into my wet sex slowly. With each thrust of his fingers he hits my spot, which makes me ache for him in a place I've never wanted anyone to fill before. I position him again at my opening and breathe deeply. "Just let me go slow, okay?" I beg in a whisper.

"Take your time, baby. Just relax and take me."

I lie there for another silent moment before I push back against him. I'm beyond surprised that when I push back, my body gives way to him just a little. He doesn't move a muscle; he just continues to kiss me and finger me attentively. Before I know it, I'm back to being completely relaxed because I'm in charge.

The pressure is intense, but the initial sting is gone, and I am beyond horny for this man. He's being so patient with me that I want to give him this. I gradually push back again, and I feel him tense behind me. I hear a muffled growl, and then his fingers start working faster against my clit.

"Noah . . ." is all I can manage to say before my body breaks out in a rush of warmth. We've been lying here for what seems like an hour, but I've finally done it. I've taken him, even if it's just his head.

"Fuck yeah . . ." I hear him say in my ear.

A triumphant smile plays at my lips. "You feel incredible, Noah. I can't describe it."

His forehead drops to the back of my head, and he's breathing in deeply. His fingers stop playing with me, and his hand moves to grip my thigh.

"Baby, I can't fucking move, or I'll come, right here and now," he admits, groaning to himself.

I bite my lip and reach back to wrap my fingers around the rest of his shaft. I want to know if I can take more of him. I push back slightly, and his head slides in some more. And now I'm taking some of his length. I have to pause and let myself adjust because the pressure is still overwhelming. His hand is now the one gripping my thigh, begging me to go slow.

"Heather . . . fuck, do not move," he almost begs, but I decide not to listen. It's finally feeling good enough to move, and I want to try and take all of him.

His fingers are still circling my wet clit as I push back again. The moan that comes from my Greek god is one I've never heard before. It sounds like he's in torturous agony, but I know that he's overwhelmed by how tight I am.

"Mmm . . ." I go slick between my legs when I hear him. I feel so powerful like this. "Don't stop me . . ." I slide back and forth and feel myself stretch for him. "Oh Noah . . . it feels so good."

I cannot believe I'm doing this and can't believe how incredibly amazing it feels. I know without a doubt that he can make me come like this. He grabs my hips to slow me down. His fingers dig into my skin, and I can feel him shaking behind me.

I know that he's on the verge of breaking, and I'm loving the fact that I can be the one to do it. I'm torn between making him come and making myself come. It all feels too good. "Noah . . . I love your cock—fuck me," I beg and try to force my hips back. He wanted my ass, and now he's barely taking it.

He grits his teeth and breathes out heavily before he bends and pushes my legs up. "Let me take control . . ." he hisses in my ear.

I reach back, refusing to give up control at this moment, and halt his movements. I can feel his large frame tremble behind me, and his breathing has changed to a pant. "Noah . . . you're going to make me come," I moan out, knowing he won't be able to handle it. My body is finally getting accustomed to the feeling of him inside of me, and I'm so close to my climax. I want to take this from him.

He hisses through clenched teeth, and I take that as my cue to make my move. I'm trembling inside with nothing for my walls to grasp on to. His cock isn't fully seated inside me, but I can't describe how it has me so close to my climax. "Noah . . ." I manage to cry out as I slide back and forth, taking this from him. I can feel everything, every single movement we make, every time his cock twitches inside of me.

Everything.

My head falls back against him and a guttural moan leaves my lips. "Fill me up, Noah . . . give me your come," I demand as I slide back over and over again while he tries to stop me unsuccessfully.

"Heather," he groans, and I whimper in response, which does him in. He pushes his hips up, and his body goes rigid as I feel his length twitch and then start to pulse inside of me.

I gasp, and my body goes tight when his hips lunge forward, sinking his cock deeper. My Greek god is growling into my ear, and I lose myself when I realize I've taken what *he* wanted to take from *me*. I made him come. I dominated this experience, and it is so hedonistic that I come so hard, the feeling unlike anything I've ever experienced.

His arms move around my waist, holding my back against his

strong, damp chest. I throw my head back against his shoulder so he can watch me lose myself to him. My lower lip is caught between my teeth, and I can't hold in the noises escaping me. "Oh fuck . . . baby, yes."

His hips spasm again as he jerks inside of me. "Fuck," he growls.

I can feel his fingers running up and into the back of my damp hair. His fingers fist with strands of my hair locked between them. And, oh crap, I know what he's about to do. My orgasm hits its crescendo when he tugs, pulling my head back. My mouth falls open at the sensation. My eyes close as he takes my mouth and takes control again, because I'm still lost in my orgasm as he recovers. He takes it all from me because he wants it all, just as I did. My body is buzzing, and I feel like we're out of this world, or we're spinning uncontrollably in a fit of orgasms. We stay like this for a long moment as I attempt to regain what's left of my libido.

NOAH

I've completely lost track of how much time we've spent in this bed tonight. I haven't even pulled out of her, and I can't fucking wait to get back into her. Her body shines with the sheen of sweat coating her flawless skin. There's a bead of perspiration on her left nipple that I want to wrap my mouth around and make her scream like she did earlier. To please her, I thrust my hips up and into her once more before I slide my cock out of her tight opening. Damn, I don't know how she got me to fit, but she did, and she completely did me in.

Once I'm out of her, she turns around in my arms and runs her hands into my hair, and down the back of my neck.

"Can we do that again?"

"You bet your little ass we can. Did you enjoy that?"

"Noah, I don't think there are enough words in the English dictionary to describe how unbelievable that was."

"Go get your glorious ass into the shower while I call housekeeping and have them change the sheets out."

I watch her sit up, and I can tell she's still trying to find her center of balance. She stands up, giving me an impeccable view of her ass, the ass that I finally took . . . the ass that held me captive until I couldn't breathe any longer.

I get up and grab my Galaxy, calling the front desk to ask them to come and change the bedding. The woman tells me that there will be someone up to the room in a few minutes. Heather has the shower started by the time I hang up; I don't hesitate to join her. The bathroom is already filled with steam when I walk in. I shut and lock the door before stepping into the shower with Heather, who has her hand stretched out to the wall, holding herself up as she stands under the waterfall showerhead.

The water beads down her body, and I'm enthralled by my girl. I stand in front of her, and she moves into my arms, unable to hold herself up anymore. "Wore yourself out I see, sweetheart."

"Mmm," is the only response I manage to get out of her.

I start washing her down, touching her in every spot I can, as she leans against me for support. "Noah?" she asks softly.

"What is it?"

"I just love you."

Fuck, this woman has me by the balls. "I love you too."

I hear a male voice announce housekeeping, and I know I need to keep Heather awake and in the shower for a little while longer, so the dude can change our bedding. There's no question as to what we were doing on the bed: the lube is still out and our damp clothes are strewn all over the floor.

"Take me to bed?" she asks as I rinse the shampoo out of her hair.

"Let me get you finished up, and then we'll go to bed."

"Okay, but can I wear your sweatshirt to bed? It smells like you."

"You don't have to ask, Heather. Of course you can."

I finally get all of the suds out of her hair before putting her conditioner in. I need her to smell like my girl, and not chlorine.

"The bed is all made up. Have a good night," the male voice says through the door, and I hear the suite door shut.

It takes me a few more minutes to get her rinsed off and for me to get washed up, but once we're done, I help her out of the shower and wrap her in the warm white towel.

I can't help but smirk when she walks over to my luggage and rummages through it, grabbing my sweatshirt that she loves to wear and pulling it on, sans bra and panties.

As I'm drying off and about to pull on my boxer briefs, I notice her hand move to her stomach and a little frown forms on her face. "Heather? Is everything all right?" I mask my concern as best I can and watch her. She crawls under the comforter, which is weird because she normally waits for me to lie down first.

"My stomach doesn't feel good," she replies quietly.

I'm not going to lie: I'm instantly hoping she's pregnant. But then I walk over and look down at her, and her beautiful face is scrunched up in pain. "Baby? Can I get you anything?" I pull back the comforter and lie next to her on my side. I hate that she feels ill. There's only been a couple of times in our relationship that she hasn't felt good, and I've hated every one of them.

"No, I'll be okay," she replies, and I can tell she's uncomfortable. Her arms are wrapped around her midsection, and I move her arms out of my way. Slowly, I lift the sweatshirt to reveal her flat stomach. I watch to make sure I'm not hurting her, but I brush the backs of my knuckles against her stomach softly. Her eyes flutter closed and I repeat the motion over and over again, in no particular order. Using my fingertips on occasion, tracing her lower rib cage, and around her navel, I'm doing all I can to make my girl feel better.

Within minutes I find myself daydreaming in the quiet room. The only sound I hear is her quiet breathing. She's fast asleep and free from pain, which was my end goal.

I decide to take this time to think and make sure she's okay before I even think about sleeping myself. What if she is pregnant? I chuckle at the thought.

Well, damn, that didn't take long, Ryan.

I know she really wants my baby, but does she really even know what that shit entails?

Do I?

My fingers trail lazily against her stomach, and she shifts in her sleep. I stop moving and wait for her to get comfortable again before I continue caressing her. It's one of those things you find out about your significant other as you go. I found out early on that she calms down with my touch, so naturally, when she wasn't feeling well one night, I tried rubbing her stomach gently. To my astonishment, it worked, and so I've been doing it ever since. Thankfully she doesn't move again, and I'm too afraid to move her, so tonight she'll just have to lie beside me, instead of in her spot. My mind has never been clearer than at this moment, and I really don't know what to do with myself.

I don't know what to do with my spare time now. All of my waking moments have been spent thinking about studying. Now that's gone, and I'm at a loss for what to do. Part of the reason for this trip was to help me relax after what seemed like a fucking lifetime of studying. The other reason was for Heather. She deserves this trip more than I do. My girl has been through so fucking much that I just needed to do something nice for her. I needed to do something to show her how much she's loved—by myself and everyone else in her life—hence, this vacation. It took some planning, but she's worth it, and it's the one thing I knew she would love.

The next morning Heather is up and brushing out the knots in her hair by the time I wake up. "Mmm, good morning, gorgeous."

She turns to look at me. Her eyes light up, and she tosses her hairbrush before jumping on top of me. "You're awake," she says before scrunching her nose up.

"I am, are you okay?" I ask as I wrap her in my arms.

"Yes, my butt is a little sore from last night, though," she nuzzles my bare chest before biting into my shoulder.

"Mmm, then why are you so chipper this morning?"

"I want to go canoeing. I woke up and saw the canoes on the dock, and I want to go. Please? Can we?"

"Of course we can. We're here for just over a week. Come on, go get dressed."

She jumps off of me and runs to the other side of the suite where our bags are. She starts digging through her pink suitcase and pulls out a pair of jeans, long black socks, a plaid shirt, her Hunter rain boots and her sunglasses. She gets dressed and heats up her curling iron to do her hair. I get up and lazily stroll into the bathroom to brush my teeth.

"Noah? Can we get breakfast first? I'm starving, and I want bacon."

"Bacon it is, baby. We'll head downstairs. I believe they have breakfast every morning."

Twenty minutes later we're seated at a table for two, looking out at the lake. We eat breakfast quickly, and I down a cup of coffee while she steals a strip of bacon off of my plate.

"Okay, I'm done," she says excitedly while wiping her hands on the linen napkin.

"All right, let's get going."

I take her hand as we walk outside and down to the dock, where we meet a gentleman who instructs us on the canoe and where on the lake would be a great place to paddle out to. He holds onto the end of the canoe, as I take Heather's hand and help her down into it, before following her in. We're handed our oars and told to have a good time.

"Are you ready, ballerina?"

"Are you kidding me? I was born ready, Greek god."

We're gently pushed away from the dock, and we both start paddling, each of us with an oar on either side of the canoe. I'm surprised we didn't have to establish who gets what side.

"I can't believe you found this place. I'm still trying to take it all in."

I pull out my phone and take a picture of her, her back turned to me with the lake, trees, and mountains in the background. No matter how dramatic the beauty is around her, she's still all I see. I quickly set the picture as my phone's wallpaper before putting it back into my pocket and sinking the blade of the oar into the water. Tranquility and silence surrounds us; the only sound is the slicing of the oars through the water repeatedly as we slide along the glassy surface.

We spend an hour paddling around and exploring the lake, before we head back to the docks to get out of the cold. Hell, it's colder up here than I thought it was going to be.

We take a seat in the common area in the lodge, in front of a vast fireplace that heats up the room. I watch as she takes her rain boots off and props her feet up on the ottoman in front of us. I follow her lead and remove my shoes before pulling her into my side.

"Damn, baby, you're cold."

"But it was so worth it. Plus, now I have an excuse to be in your arms for the rest of the night."

"I like your thinking. Oh shit, I almost forgot to tell you that I made plans for us tonight, so don't double-book us."

I'm stoked for Coen, Dillen, Dani, Brannon, and Lana to fly in this afternoon. They have flights into Calgary International Airport. I have a rental SUV set up and ready for them once they all get in. I just hope that Dillen doesn't do anything stupid because Lana is coming. Lana and Heather have gotten rather close, and I didn't want to be the one to jeopardize their friendship if I didn't invite her on this vacation.

"Tonight? What are we doing?"

"You'll have to wait and see." I'm thankful that a waitress comes around with a tray full of mugs of steaming hot chocolate, because it distracts Heather for the moment.

"Oh, I love everything about this place, Noah," she says as she reaches for a mug. She wraps her hands around the white mug before she blows on the steam.

I kiss the top of her head as we watch the flames in the wood-framed fireplace dance over the logs and behind the bars that hold the logs in their grate. The whispers of others around us are barely audible as the flames crackle lively and bathe us in their warmth and light.

Chapter Twenty Three

INFINITY

NOAH

The day goes by leisurely as we lounge around the lodge and make small talk. After dinner, we get our coats on and head outside for an evening stroll. The sunlight is fading hastily, leaving pink hues of color running across the sky. My ballerina seems to be transfixed by and incredibly enamored of her surroundings at the moment, and in a way I'm thankful. I need this ten-minute walk to gather my thoughts.

"Oh!" she pauses mid-step along the path and tugs at my hand. I look down beside me at her, and she's peering across the way about twenty yards out.

"Noah, look!" she gasps quietly, and I follow her gaze. I chuckle when I see two deer grazing and walking lazily beside each other.

"Yeah? Is this your first time seeing wildlife?" I ask her, a little surprised.

She only smiles and nods. "Oh my God, they're so pretty. I want one."

"In your dreams, sweetheart. Watch your step," I add as we walk over the roots of an ancient subalpine fir tree. I step up onto a rock and help her clamber up, and then do the same for another and another and before too long, we're higher than the lodge.

"It's getting dark, Noah. Shouldn't we head back?"

"Nah, we've got a few more minutes. Come on." I squeeze her hand to encourage her. I'm glad she doesn't put up a fight as she walks next to me.

"Oh my God, what if there are bears out here?" she asks and I keep her hand in mine because I feel she's about to bolt and run in the other direction.

I laugh but keep my voice low. "There undoubtedly are bears out here, and with as much candy as you ingest, your blood probably tastes like honey, so stay close."

"Noah, that's not funny," she scolds, walking closer to me. "I think we should turn back now. I'd rather not fall down these rocks."

"Settle down, girl, I won't let anything happen to you."

We're walking in almost complete darkness—well, I'm walking and dragging her along.

I step up onto a larger rock formation, which acts as a platform over-looking the lake; I look back at Heather to offer her my hand when I realize that the rock is half as tall as she is. I chuckle and hold out both of my hands to her, wrapping my fingers around her wrists with her doing the same to me, so I can lift her up and onto this larger rock.

"My, my, my, Greek God, are you trying to show off?"

I laugh because she weighs practically nothing; it's like lifting a cracker.

"Hardly," I reply.

As soon as I know she's steady on her feet, I take her hand and lace our fingers together. I know this is the perfect spot because I can see it from here. I feel her shiver beside me, and I pull her in front of me to wrap my arms around her tiny frame. It's pitch black now—just what I was wanting.

"Noah, what are we doing up here? I can't see a thing. Are you try-ing to kill me and dump my body off the edge?" she kids, but it's a hor-rible joke.

"Shh . . . I have a flashlight. We'll be able to get back just fine." My eyes are adjusted, and I'm surprised that she can't see it yet. Is she that unobservant?

"What? You've had a flashlight this whole time?" she whispers loudly and half turns to look up at me.

"Yes, ballerina, I'm not going to go traipsing through the mountains without a flashlight at least." I laugh and kiss her forehead. "Now turn around and look. Do you see it?"

"See what? It's pitch black out here."

I wrap my arms around her and turn her around to face the dark area below us where the lake is nestled between the mountains. She gasps and covers her mouth when she sees it: a vast constellation of stars and galaxies light up the night sky as it gets darker. The iridescent beauty of the Milky Way slightly reflects in the glassy cerulean lake. It's a vertically stretched panorama of the most awe-inspiring view.

"Is that what I think it is?"

I grin to myself because I've been able to give her the twinkling stars she always dreamt of. And not just any stars, but the Milky Way. This feels good, being able to do this for her. It's taken so much time and planning, but her reaction is well worth the wait. I peer up ahead of us and stare into the millions of stars. The pitch-black night sets the glistening stars off effortlessly, and the snowcapped mountains provide the unspoiled setting. There's not a more unblemished place on this earth. I move my arms from around her and slowly crouch down beside her. She's too completely awestruck and engulfed in what she sees above us to even notice.

"Heather?"

"Mmm?" she says before she turns and glances down at me. "Noah?"

"Heather, from the moment I laid eyes on you, I knew it was a pivotal moment in my life. I set out to leave you in my past, but you danced your way back in, and I couldn't be happier. You are the most beautiful creature I've ever seen and I am so lucky you wanted me—I adore you. I want to wake up to you every morning, fall asleep with you in my arms every night. I want to grow old with you, and I want nothing more than to live a long and fulfilling life with you by my side. I want to make you happy in every way possible. Being with someone has never been so simple or pleasurable before. I'd walk to the ends of the earth to have you for the rest of my life."

I reach into my jacket to retrieve a little blue box from the inside pocket. She's watching me intently when I shift from a crouch onto one knee. Her eyes glow under the starlight when she realizes exactly what I'm doing—damn I could get lost in those jade green eyes.

"You're the most precious gift I've been given, and I want to take care of you. If what you need is for this to be a long engagement, I'm more than okay with it. I want—no, I need—to be promised to you in any way I can be."

I open the unmistakable blue box and reveal a three and a quarter-carat pear-shaped diamond, hand set in a diamond halo platinum ring, while I watch and gauge her reaction. I can feel my heart palpitating savagely against my chest.

"Heather Adalyn Lane, will you do me the extreme honor of becoming my wife?"

HEATHER

My heart feels like it's going to explode in my chest. I have such a burst of energy but I can't move. I'm rooted to the spot.

He reaches for my hand and runs his finger down my left ring finger. "Heather?"

"Noah, are you serious right now?"

He looks up into my eyes as he waits for my answer. I glance down at the blue box in his hand and at the most gorgeous ring I have ever seen. I can't seem to find my words, not a single one as a tear runs down my cheek.

He brings my hand to his lips and places a kiss to my ring finger. "Baby?" he prods.

"Of course I will! I love you so much. My answer is yes, yes, yes, Noah. Yes, I'll marry you."

He smiles a smile I've never seen before, and he drops his head before shaking it in . . . what? Disbelief?

"Yes? Damn, baby, I love you so much." He gets up and takes the ring out of the box, before slipping it onto my left ring finger. My heart does a somersault and aches all at once. I love this man so much that it physically hurts.

"Yes . . ." I repeat softly.

Without warning, he picks me up and takes my mouth in a passionate kiss. I throw my arms around his neck and kick my legs up behind me as I start to kiss my man.

My fiancé.

His arms tighten around me, and I know that this is real. I followed my heart, and it led me to this man. He makes every moment I'm with him feel like magic. I've decided that, yes, I want to spend the rest of my life with him, and I want the rest of my life to start right now.

He pulls back from me and takes my left hand, pressing his lips to the oversized diamond. I look down at it shining on my finger and squeal excitedly, "Noah, we're engaged!"

He chuckles and kisses up and down my neck. "You're damn right, sweetheart. You're mine forever."

"I know. Oh Noah, I'd choose you over and over again without any doubt. I love you."

He sighs heavily and pulls back to look at me. "You had me worried for a minute there, baby. I was about to beg." He gently moves my hair away from my face.

I look down at my ring and giggle. "You took my breath away. You've given me every dream I've ever had in the span of one evening. You're my happily ever after."

He drops his forehead to mine. "Jesus, Heather, you've made me the happiest man alive. Thank you." Lifting his head, he presses his lips to my forehead while he holds me snugly in his arms.

I turn my head to the side and look out at the beautiful scene before us. I will never forget this day as long as I live. I'm committing everything to memory: the rocks, the mountains, the lake below us, and the Milky Way . . . all witnesses to our engagement.

His hands move down to the small of my back. "Would you like to call your sister? Or my parents?"

I shiver and nod, taking one last look at the view. "Yes! Can we go back? I'm freezing, and I want to look at my engagement ring."

He takes his jacket off and places it around my shoulders and I gratefully slip my hands into the comically long sleeves. I take in a deep breath because I'm surrounded by all things Noah.

"Let's get you warm, ballerina."

NOAH

This night couldn't have gone any better, and right now I'm on cloud nine. She looks like a vision sitting there on the floor in front of the fire in her pink satin robe. That smile hasn't left her face since we've been back, and fuck does it feel good because I put it there. She was distracted during our bath, looking down at her hand continuously. I guess it was a good distraction, though.

She's currently on the phone with her sister. Her words are running together as she tries to tell Dani what our evening entailed. Heather looks back at me on the couch quickly and cups her mouth. "What? You knew?" She listens for another second before responding. "He asked you? Seriously?"

She turns her head and narrows her eyes at me cutely before pointing at me. *Well, it seems as if I'm in trouble.* I wink at her, and she beams up at me.

They talk for a few more minutes before hanging up. I get up to grab the bottle of champagne that has been chilling in the ice bucket and pop it open. "Would you like to call my parents next?"

"Yes!" she exclaims and looks up at me from the floor. I adjust my pajama bottoms before sitting down next to her, filling her champagne flute.

Once I set the bottle down, she shifts and moves onto my lap as she dials Ellery's number. "I hope we're not waking them up," she adds as she sips on her champagne before leaning back against my bare chest.

I kiss the top of her head and wait for Ellery to answer. There's one more ring before her voice is on the line.

"Hello?" she answers with a little hesitation. I smile because I know that she's nervous as hell right now. I clear my throat and answer before Heather can.

"Mom? She said yes."

Heather quickly turns around and looks at me with the biggest smile on her face. It's the first time she's heard me call Ellery *Mom*.

"She did? Oh honey, I'm so happy for you both. Hold on, Henry wants to hear the news too." She takes a few moments to figure out how to put us on speakerphone and when she does, my future Mrs. Noah Ryan starts telling our story to my parents—our parents.

After I relive our engagement again through Heather's memory, I hear my mom blow her nose loudly on the other end. I chuckle, and I hear my dad chuckle as well. "We couldn't be happier for you two, son," Henry speaks up.

"Thanks, Dad. We'll need to go out to dinner when we get back next week. Oh damn, I don't think we told you, but we got the house too."

We both flinch a little when Ellery's high-pitch squeal comes over the line followed by more nose blowing. "Oh goodness, this is the happiest day ever. You two are getting married, and you'll be closer to us too."

"We will be," I say. "You're both part of our lives."

"Oh honey, you both mean so much to Henry and I. Listen, we've already spoken about this, and we would love to pay for the wedding. I understand that money is no longer an issue, but please let us do this. Heather? Darling? You wouldn't mind, would you?"

She freezes on my lap and I move the hair away from her shoulder, pulling her robe down and kissing her skin softly. "Mom, we haven't discussed anything yet, but that's not necessary."

"We know it's not, but we would like to do this for you two. I don't know how life brought the two of you together, but I'm not going to stand in love's way. We're going to encourage it. And I do not want to hear any ifs, ands, or buts about it."

I drop my head back against the couch cushion with an exaggerated sigh. "Dad? Mind talking some sense into her please?" I feel Heather move and straddle my thighs and start kissing my chest. My fingers find her long, soft hair as Henry speaks.

"I'm on this side of the battlefield, son. I highly suggest conceding, because Ellery sure has her ways."

I drop it for the moment because I don't want an argument. Not on this night. "We'll talk about it when we see you guys. Okay?"

"All right, darling, just answer me this: have you decided on a date?"

My eyes are closed with Heather's lips on my chest when she stops kissing me. I open my eyes and raise my head to look down at my girl. She's looking at me, her eyes are twinkling, and a smile is forming on her face. "Well," she says, "I've always loved the snow . . . so I was thinking of a winter's date."

Chapter Twenty Four

A BEAUTIFUL MARVEL

NOAH

It's the morning after the best evening of my life.

Heather has agreed to marry me, and damn, I could not be more contented.

She stirs on top of me—her favorite spot—clad in her lace underwear. I've made the decision of a lifelong commitment to my ballerina, and I've never seen that spark shine so bright inside of her. That ember that won't go out in my life—the one I won't let go out—has grown into a glowing fire by night, one that can be seen by anyone. I place my lips against the top of her head and breathe her into my awakening senses. She lets out a deep breath and stills again, once she can feel the warmth from my bare chest.

I shut my eyes and replay the evening in my mind: from the Milky Way to the phone call to my parents. I grin when I remember the shock on Heather's face when she heard me call Ellery *Mom* for the second time. As for the first time, I will never forget that day as long as I live.

After I had made the decision to ask Heather to marry me, it just seemed right . . . seemed like the right time. Heather and Henry were in his office, working on her physical therapy, so it was just the two of us in the room. I was watching Ellery busy herself in the kitchen—she'd insisted on making me a pie. I couldn't get her to sit her ass down, so I just sat there and watched. I was sitting there at the island, my arms crossed over my chest, when something just told me . . . *now is the time* . . . so I didn't fight it.

"Ellery?" I used caution when forming my next words. "Could I ask you to help me with something?"

She smiled and looked up at me as she wiped her hands on her apron, dusting it with flour from her fingertips. "Of course, darling, what is it?" she asked, not hesitating to walk around the island to stand next to me. Even with me sitting, I was still a foot taller than her, it seemed. My heart was pumping wildly in my chest, and my foot started to tap quickly. I looked down at her genuine smile and instantly felt a calm wash over me. It caught me by surprise, because Heather had been the only other woman to be able to calm me just as quickly.

"I'm going to ask Heather to marry me, and I'd love it if you would help me choose the perfect ring."

I couldn't help but laugh when she gasped and threw her arms around my neck. "Noah! Oh honey, yes. Oh, I'm so happy for you! Of course I'll help you!" She was beaming when she pulled back to look at me and placed her palm on my cheek.

"Thank you . . . Mom."

She stood there taking in the word, as if it hit her in the heart, before she just ripped her apron off and grabbed me by the hand. "To hell with the pie. It can wait."

That was the first time I've ever heard anything resembling a swear word from my mother's mouth. We told Heather and Henry that we were going out to lunch and then just outside of the city to one of Ellery's favorite places to get supplies for her nursery business, which bought us some time to head to Tiffany's in the heart of Manhattan.

She was more than a help. When I first picked out a ring back in London, I chose it in haste. The only thought in my mind was keep her, keep her, keep her. That turned out to be a disaster. This time, with my mother by my side, the selection process was much different. She perused the glass cases with a keen eye. She forced me to really think about Heather and what I could see my ballerina wearing. I laughed when she actually smacked my arm and scolded me when I told her that Heather would like anything that glittered.

"Noah Ryan, behave," she scolded.

"Yes, ma'am," I replied with a smirk.

Finally we came to the section of diamonds that were pear-shaped. I knew immediately that this was what my girl should have on her finger.

I'm snapped back from the memory when Heather bares her teeth, sinking them into my pec.

I grunt and look down at her. "It's not nice to bite your fiancé, Heather."

"It is if he likes it." She giggles and sits up animatedly. "Can we go canoeing again? I loved it so much."

"We can do whatever you want, but first I'm in dire need of a full breakfast."

"You've got yourself a deal, handsome. I'll go get ready, and we can head down. I think that I'll order that hot chocolate again." About to run her hand through her hair, she pauses to admire her ring. "I'm never taking this off."

I laugh briskly and sit back to admire her face. "I'm glad you like it. Ellery made sure I put a lot of thought into it."

"She did? She's amazing, Noah. I can't believe this is happening. I can't wait to show the girls when we get back to the city."

Heather swings her legs off of the bed and twirls once, before almost skipping to the bathroom to get ready for the day. I glance down at my watch on the nightstand and bolt out of bed. *Shit.*

"Heather? Don't take too long. I don't want them to close breakfast before we're able to get down there."

Her giggle makes my cock throb, and I have to keep my mind on breakfast. I walk into the bathroom to get ready too, while my hands grope her ass aggressively. "Mmm . . . you would think after last night that you ate enough," she jokes as she raises onto her toes to get closer to me.

"I could never get enough."

It doesn't take us long to get ready and leave the room for breakfast. I make sure to smack her ass cheek before leading her out of our suite and down to the main dining room, where the smell of homemade breakfast wafts over us. I look down and she's entirely oblivious to her surroundings. She's back to looking at her hand. I chuckle and lean down to whisper in her ear, "Should I leave you two alone, or would you like to join us for breakfast?"

"Mmm? Us?" she asks quietly.

"Yes, us, you little shit," Dillen announces loudly and jumps up from her seat.

Heather looks up quickly and gasps before Dillen collides with her in a hug. "Little shit, let me see it right now." I grin and walk over to shake Brannon's hand when he stands up and then let go of him to hug Dani, welcoming them.

"Holy crap!" Heather squeals before jumping up and down collectively with Dillen. Within seconds, all the girls are hugging and giggling while Coen, Brannon, and I watch in amusement.

"All right, let's see it," Lana says softly, and Heather holds up her hand for all three of them to see, which gets a collective sigh.

"Fuck, Ryan, you just upped the game to a standard that neither Coen nor I would be able to meet," Brannon says before making his way over to hug Heather. "Congratulations, sassy toes."

Coen smacks me on the back. "Way to go, fuckhead. When do the babies come out?"

"Hell, man, whenever she wants them—which is now. Keep that shit to yourself, though."

"Now? You're fucking with me, right?"

"No, dude, we're running full steam ahead. We've both lived through our own personal hells and it's time that we get to be happy. I'm happy, man." I stop looking at Heather for a second to see what he's thinking.

"I know you are, and I'm here with you all the way. The only time you get to forget about me is when you have spit and baby shit all over yourself."

I laugh and shake my head. "Not a chance in hell, bro."

"Fuck that, man, fuck that."

Heather looks over at us, prompting Coen to step forward and hug her. "Congratulations, little lady. Welcome to our family."

"Awww, Coen, I love you too." She hugs his neck and turns to Dani and hugs her again with tears in her eyes.

"When did you guys get here?"

"We all got in last night."

"You jerk. You were here last night already and didn't tell me?" She wipes at her eyes and lets go of her sister.

"Of course I didn't tell you! Your fiancé would have skinned me alive."

I watch as Heather spins on her toes to face me and steps into my arms, burying her face in my chest. "I love you so much, Noah. Thank you for this."

I kiss the top of her head as everyone takes their seats, giving us a minute to ourselves before we join them for breakfast.

"You're welcome, sweetheart." I kiss her lips gently before looking at those eyes that swallow me whole. "I hope you enjoy your surprise. You could call it an engagement gift." I wink and pat her ass.

She nods enthusiastically and kisses me once more before we let go of each other, and I pull out a seat at the table for her.

"Has everyone ordered?" I ask the table and reach for a menu, handing it to Heather before grabbing one for myself while my available hand rests on Heather's thigh.

"We have, but we asked them to wait to bring anything out until you two arrived," Lana says sweetly. She's sitting on the other side of Heather, sipping her water. I can't begin to imagine how awkward this trip started out for her. I make a mental note to remember to thank her individually for coming out and supporting us.

Heather puts down her menu and starts talking to her sister about the lodge. I know she couldn't care less about what to order right now, but I also know what she'll eat. I find it funny that not too long ago, I had no idea what this girl wanted regarding us or even her life, and now I'm able to order breakfast for her because I know her that well.

Damn, life has changed. I fucking love it.

"She'll have the blueberry pancakes with bacon and orange juice, and I'll have the Santa Fe omelet with bacon and coffee, just black, please," I tell the waitress before she leaves.

Heather starts to tell our story again while my coffee is placed in front of me; I know she won't get fed up with telling it. She loved last night as much as I did. Lana has Heather's left hand in her two hands turning her engagement ring from side to side in order to get a better look at it.

This right here is family.

My parents and Joel might not be here, but we're blessed to have each and every one of them in our lives.

Chapter Twenty Five

TENEBRIFIC TRAGEDY

HEATHER

"I can't believe you pulled something like that off, Noah Ryan," I try and scold him as I straddle his lap fully clothed in my tight jeans and white camisole.

Naturally, his hands move around to my rear and squeeze. "I've told you before not to underestimate me, sweetheart. You shouldn't take me lightly."

My fingers run up into his hair and I tug hard, pulling his head back as I rise up onto my knees. I try and tower over him but I still seem to fail. "You're really going to get it later for keeping such a secret from me."

"Get it? If you keep swaying your hips against my cock like this, I will fuck you."

"Uh-uh . . ." I tease and sway my hips again. "You don't have time for that. We're meeting everyone downstairs in ten minutes." I tease his lips with my tongue and smile; I'm just feeling too playful.

"I only need three minutes."

He grabs hold of my hips and flips me onto the bed as he moves his body over mine, biting down my neck and pushing his hands between my breast and my bra. He pushes my bra down and my under-wire pushes my breasts up for him perfectly. "Don't tease me with something I can't have, especially if it belongs to me."

I'm incredibly turned on by his dominance, and I'm happy to know that I can provoke him in just the right way. "I can do whatever I'd like . . . know why?"

"Because you'll have my name by winter's end," he says as his lips sweep down my throat to my breasts, taking one nipple into his mouth and biting it sensually.

I nod because I've lost all speech. The only sounds coming from my lips are whimpers of delight.

He moves to my other nipple and bites softly and then stops everything to look up at me. "You should get dressed, ballerina; we wouldn't want to keep everyone waiting."

A loud, frustrated growl works its way out of my throat, and I huff. "No! I was supposed to be teasing you. You always turn it around on me."

His warm, smoky laugh fills the room, and he helps me up, kissing me slowly. "I love you."

I manage the cutest pout I can and furrow my brow. "Tease," I simply reply and put my girls back in place. I decide not to return the sentiment as I walk over to grab my riding boots and slip them on.

"Stubborn," he retorts as he puts on the thin jacket that he wore when he proposed to me.

"Ah! Noah!" My mouth drops open in surprise as he gives me a wink.

That cocky, suggestive wink.

One smack on the rear and an elevator ride later, we're standing in front of our friends, deciding who should ride with whom.

"Okay, so, let all us girls ride in one car and the guys in another," Dillen announces.

I look up at Noah and pout, which gets me a kiss on my lips and another smack on my butt. "I'll see you there, baby."

I smile because he's so stinking affectionate. "Bye, handsome."

The men go ahead while Dani runs upstairs to grab her camera. "Have either of you been horseback riding before?" Lana asks Dill and I.

"I have! Ahhh, I love horses. They're so beautiful. Have you, Dill?" I bump my hip against Dill so she'll reply to Lana politely. When that doesn't work, I look over at her, and she's studying her nails, picking at them and trying not to pay attention to Lana.

So help me God.

After an awkward pause, Dillen finally looks up at me, and smiles politely. "I haven't, and I'm not going to lie . . . I'm scared shitless. What happens if I fall off?" she asks Lana anxiously.

Lana smiles and seems excited that Dillen is talking to her. "Just hang on with those long legs of yours, and you'll be just fine."

"If I fall off, one of you three needs to save my broken ass," she says with a giggle and leans over to hug me. "I'm so happy for you. I'm sorry I've been a stuck-up bitch."

I frown and hug her back. "Dill, stop, you haven't. I know things are awkward," I whisper in her ear. "But Lana is super sweet; give her a chance." I swat her butt and she jumps back laughing.

"Look at you, little shit, getting all handsy."

Dani is making her way downstairs as Lana smiles at the two of us. "How long have you two known each other?"

I look at Dill and scrunch my nose. "Too long. She's a pain in my tutu."

We all burst out laughing as we walk out of the lobby and get into the rental vehicle. Dani gets into the driver's seat, and Dillen gets in front while Lana and I pile into the back.

I grab Dani's camera and start snapping selfies of Lana and I. "Hurry, Dani, I want to see Brannon get on a horse for the first time," I whine from the back.

"Oh hell yes, I need to see that too."

We drive for the next thirty minutes while taking pictures the entire way. Once we arrive at the stables, I see my fiancé and the two men hanging around the horses waiting for us.

We all get out of the car, and they start whistling at us. I can't help but smile: this is by far the best time I've had with my new little family.

The guys start laughing when they see us put on our newly purchased cowboy hats that we bought at the local gas station.

"Howdy, boys," I say in my finest Southern accent as we walk up.

"Howdy?" Noah asks as he takes in my little outfit, and I just know he's wondering what I'd look like in just the boots and hat.

I squint up at him through the sunlight, and he pulls me to him by a knot at the front of my tied-up flannel shirt. I thought it was a cute ensemble for today's little outing.

"Yes, howdy." I lean up and give him a chaste kiss before turning around to face our group. "Okay, I want that black horse. Nobody touch him—he's mine. Brannon, you should take that short, stumpy pony since it's your first time." I laugh at my smart-mouth comment.

Dani giggles with me and takes my hand. "I knew there was a reason you were my sister, sassy toes."

Brannon growls under his breath, "Watch yourself."

A fit of giggles takes over me, and I'm holding my stomach, bent over with laughter. I can hardly talk I'm laughing so hard.

Dani hugs me tightly. "I love you. Now let's ride. I'm excited to see these men's reactions."

We all walk over to the guide and go over the safety measures. I keep looking over at Brannon, and he's paying attention like his life depends on it. I keep my hand over my mouth because I'm afraid the laughter will just spew out of me.

Dillen must notice too because she nudges me in my side when the guide asks if anyone has any questions. Coen pipes in, "Will Noah still be able to get Heather pregnant after this little adventure?"

Dani's eyes shoot toward me and light up excitedly. "What? Are you serious? A baby? Oh my God, I'm going to be an auntie soon? I better bust out your baby blanket, sister."

"Ah shit, man, I don't want to think about the saddle before I'm in it," Noah says jokingly and the guys all chuckle.

I look over at Noah questioningly and purse my lips.

He told Coen? Oh my God, he really wants to be a daddy. Holy hell, I want to jump his bones right now.

He winks at me again, and I swear if he does it once more today, I'm going to attack him in public and beg for him to make love to me.

Dani is bouncing up and down excitedly on her toes. "You should name her Danielle . . . just a thought."

I grab Dani's wrists and make her stop. "Stop it; I'm not having a baby." I laugh and squeeze her cheeks. "Besides . . . I'm a virgin," I say as I flip my hair over my shoulder and walk away, swaying my hips. I smile when everyone busts out laughing at me.

"With that ass? I doubt it," Coen calls out as we all get up onto our horses.

Noah walks past Coen and smacks the back of his head, before coming up behind me to help push me high enough to swing my leg over. Once I'm astraddle, he gets on the horse beside me. I watch as Lana leans over and kisses Coen, while he helps her get her feet into the stirrups; Dillen notices, but her mood doesn't shift.

One of the instructors helps Dillen up, but she doesn't even try to flirt with him. I'm in shock, actually. She just gets her feet into the stirrups and looks back down at her phone, red-faced, timid, and texting. I look beside me and Noah is just watching me. "See something you like, cowboy?" I tease and shimmy my breasts at him.

"I like everything I see, future Mrs. Ryan."

Dang it, he's too freaking sweet, and I love him to pieces. I blow him a kiss and adjust my rear end in the saddle before making my horse turn.

"Why aren't we going yet?" I say to nobody in particular when I notice Brannon has two men helping him up on a stubborn-looking palomino. I bust out laughing. "Awww, poor Brannon."

"Draw attention to it, why don't you, sassy toes?" Brannon spits back playfully as he finally gets up and takes hold of the reins. Our guide takes off, and Dani is the first to follow him.

"I love you, Brannon," I shout and watch his horse fall in behind Dani. Then goes Dillen and Lana, who are followed by Coen. I'm fine being the last in line when Noah speaks.

"Get going, cowgirl. I won't have you last."

He nods in the direction of the line. I'm not sure if he's just being protective, or if he wants to stare at my rear all day, but I move my horse regardless.

We're about five minutes into the trail, and Coen has been groaning the entire way. "I doubt this is doing my balls any good. My dick is about to fucking fall off."

I laugh hysterically, and my head falls back. I almost lose my hat in the process as it falls off and almost blows away before I grab it. "Oh shoot!"

"Dammit, Heather, quit horsing around." I hear Noah behind me, and I turn around.

"Hey grumpy butt, what's your deal?" I ask with a pout.

"My deal? Baby, I don't need you getting hurt. Please be careful."

I stop and think for a moment about how protective he is over me, and I love it. The riding is out of his control, and he's exercising any amount he has. "Okay, I'll be careful." I turn and wiggle my butt at him before looking back over my shoulder.

His shoulders stiffen as he sits up taller. "Heather . . . so help me God."

"You'll what? Spank me?" I taunt.

"I'll do more than that. Pay attention, Heather. I'm not joking around."

I sigh and drop my head back again, making a disgusted sound like a scolded schoolgirl. "Yes, sir." I mumble. I look ahead and hear the others chattering to each other happily. I take this moment to actually appreciate my surroundings: it's exceptionally beautiful up here. The crisp mountain air is a tad chilly, but the bright morning sun makes it bearable. I can hear water trickling off in the distance and the birds chirping from nearby branches. This truly is an amazing vacation with my family. I can't imagine a more perfect place—no wonder my parents loved it here.

"Heather!" Noah shouts my name, and I'm snapped from my daydream.

"Huh?" I blink, confused and look up. I gasp and quickly pull the reins to the left, nearly escaping my death as I've basically drifted to the edge of the trail.

"Baby, what is going on? Please pay attention," he demands again, and the rest of the group grows quiet.

"All right, we're done here," I hear him say as I pull back on the reins and stop my horse. I'm actually shaken up, and I clutch my chest.

Okay, I really need to pay attention.

Moments later he is at my side. "Heather? Are you trying to give me fucking heart failure? Shit, woman."

"It happened so fast. I'm sorry."

He reaches for me and takes my hand. "Calm down; we'll head back soon."

I shake my head and take a deep breath as our horses snort and shift their footing. "No, I'm okay. I just got sidetracked by the view. I'll pay attention. No more horsing around, I promise." I flash him a reassuring smile while I give him his pun back.

He squeezes my hand gently. "I want you to enjoy this, sweetheart, but please be careful. You're my world."

"I will, I swear."

He gives me his charming smile and nudges my chin gently. "Better catch up then, cowgirl; they're waiting." I look up and the group has stopped up ahead as they wait for us.

"Ride next to me?" I ask, and he nods.

We talk amongst ourselves about the scenery and our little group while we continue on our trip. We discuss how Dillen is actually being polite to Lana and how they seem to be getting to know one another. We jointly laugh at Coen and how he keeps complaining about his family jewels and how they'll never properly work or feel normal again.

And we can't help but laugh at Brannon, because his horse doesn't seem to want to walk in a straight line and it won't stop crapping every six minutes. Dani keeps complaining about the smell and the two of them are arguing back and forth, and it's cracking us up.

"Well, I can't really help it, Danielle," he calls back over his shoulder. "How am I supposed to keep this damned donkey from shitting in your path?"

The whole group can't help but lose themselves to laughter, and I almost pee myself because of it.

With Dani's camera still in hand, I snap a few shots of the group. As we come to a rest area for the horses to take a break and drink, I take a wonderful picture of Lana and Coen smiling at each other and holding hands while sitting on their horses. "Awww," I sigh out loud at the two of them. I look over and find Dill on her phone . . . again. I smile and take a picture, reminding myself to caption this one as *Talking to Joel—again.*

"Heather!" Dani calls out to me. I turn my head to look at her, and she's making the signature 'duck face' you see most girls making in photos. I laugh at my sister and quickly take the photo.

"Perfect, Dani, just perfect."

She points over at Brannon. "Quick, take his picture." I look over and see him shouting at his stubborn horse while it decides to bend down and take a dip in the freezing cold water.

"Motherfucker!" he shouts and tries to pull on the reins. We all laugh, including our guide.

"Awww, poor Brannon. He's having such a hard time." I laugh and take a few more pictures as the guide gets off his horse and manually leads Brannon's palomino out of the water and onto dry land.

We all decide to get off our horses and stretch our legs as this is a two-hour ride through the beautiful scenery.

"Ahhh shit, my balls," Coen groans and walks bow-legged over to sit in the grass.

Moments go by while I admire our family. The only people who are missing are Joel, Henry, and, of course, Ellery. I'm sure she would want to sit side-saddle, though.

I wouldn't have any of this if I hadn't met Noah, or if he chose not to follow me—twice. I can't believe how much he loves me. It takes me by surprise time and time again, when he truly shows it without holding back.

I look over and watch him from afar while he sits with Coen in the grass. They're both laughing, giving each other hell, and it makes me smile. It makes me happy to see him finally have a full family—we both do. There's no doubt in my mind that Coen will be his best man at our wedding. He's been there for Noah through thick and thin. I snap a quick picture of the two of them and look around.

Dani jumps on my back and squeals excitedly, "I'm so happy for you, Heather. You've found your prince charming . . . I mean Greek god . . . in a golden-sash toga."

I pull back and smile sweetly at her. "He's everything I need. Thank you for giving him your blessing. I can't begin to tell you how much it means to me that you did. Dani, I know I'm not getting married for a while, but would you like to be my maid of honor?"

She stills and her eyes glass over. "Heather, of course I will. Oh sister, I love you."

"I love you too." I sniffle and hug her again. I lower my voice, so only she will hear me. "Do you think Brannon would like to be involved too?"

"I think he would love to be. He's like your older brother, Heather. I think it'd be great if you let him walk you down the aisle. He's always been so protective over you, for years now. That's just my suggestion; you don't have to do it unless you love the idea."

I nod and squeeze her to me as she does the same. "Thank you. I love it."

The guide gets back up onto his horse. "Saddle up, gang, let's get going."

The remainder of the tour is scenic and beautiful. I'm in love with this place. I know the resort that my parents honeymooned at once a year isn't too far from here, and I'm suddenly overwhelmed with love and the knowledge that they died together. They died in the one place that they could never get enough of, and I know that they would have loved Noah. They would appreciate how much he holds me up, how much respect and loyalty he has for me. He's offered me the world again when I thought it was gone, and it's only now that I realize that that baby of ours must be safe in my mother's arms. She'll take care of it until I'm able to finally meet it. A tear slides down my cheek as we come to the end of the trail, the trees opening up onto a wide-open area where the stables are nestled.

Noah is at my side helping me down from my horse moments after we stop, ensuring that I'm still in one piece. I try to hide my clouded eyes, but he notices. He wipes his finger across my cheek before kissing where my tears ran. "I'm here, baby," he says to me softly, and it's about all I need for the tears to well up again.

I feel a hand on my back and look over my shoulder to find everyone standing behind us. Dani frowns at me when I turn around and lean against Noah. "Heather? What's wrong?"

"It's just . . . I think Mom and Dad would have loved Noah, and I know that they are showering that unborn baby of ours with unconditional love up in Heaven."

All of them go soft at once. Lana moves closer to Coen as he wraps his arms around her, pulling her into his side. I've never seen him so happy and content before. Dani reaches for my hand while Brannon steps closer behind her, and Dillen starts to sob on her own.

"I love you all. Thank you for being here and making this trip unforgettable."

I feel Noah kiss the back of my head and snake his arm around the front of my waist. "Don't cry, sweetheart."

I smile and half laugh at myself. "I'm sorry." I quickly dash my tears away. "Should we head back and have drinks in front of the fireplace?"

"Yeah, and ice my nuts," Coen pipes up.

The girls giggle while Noah and Brannon agree with him.

Dani grabs the camera and hands it to Noah. "Noah? Take a picture of all us girls?"

"Sure, no problem." He holds the camera up as we pose in front of him while Coen whistles. "Fuck, we're some lucky bastards."

"Damn right we are," I hear Noah say behind the camera. "Okay, now just the sisters," he says, and we stand there giggling and hugging each other for the camera.

"I want these photographs, Dani," Noah says proudly as he takes the picture. "So much so that I'm going to hold onto this damn thing because the last time I asked for pictures of Heather, well, I'm still waiting on them."

I laugh, and she huffs. "Oh, give me a break, Noah. I've been busy!"

Brannon laughs and chimes in, "Busy riding my dick."

"Oh shit, I think that fucking alcohol is needed," Coen pipes in as Lana giggles.

"Heather, I need a Bellini, or something stronger, if this is where the conversation is headed," Lana says shyly.

We all laugh and everyone is starting to walk to the cars. "Wait!" I shout and rush over to our guide. I ask if he'd take a picture of the whole group and the guys start groaning. "This is the last one, Heather. You're getting camera-happy," Brannon replies as we all crowd together.

The guide graciously takes our picture a few times before Noah thanks him, tips him, and takes the camera back. "Let's get going. How would you ladies like to drive back?"

"Duh, Noah, girls in one car, hot guys in the other," Dani says, patting his chest as she walks over to give Brannon a kiss.

"All right. Separate me from my fiancée all you want, trouble. She's always going to be mine," he jokes with my sister, and I love the relationship that is forming between the two of them.

"Fat chance, bud," she replies back, and I give my Greek god a kiss.

"See you in a little bit, baby. I love you."

"I love you too." He smacks my rear as he opens the back door for me to get in and closes it behind me.

I roll down the window and yell at my sister, "Dani, quit making out with him already. I'm starving."

She flips me off as she walks away from Brannon backwards, telling him that she loves him.

I blow Noah a kiss and turn to Dillen and Lana as Dani gets in. "Crap, you guys, my legs are actually sore. You'd think I'd be used to riding by now."

Dani starts driving and the guys follow us out onto the two-lane highway. "Heather, you little whore," Dillen says excitedly, "you ride that man too much."

"Shut up, I do not. I'm a virgin, remember?" I grin, and Lana laughs her head off.

"Uh-huh . . . then what happened to your dress at the club that one night? It just fell to pieces because of poor workmanship?"

"Possibly?"

"Excuse me? What happened to your dress?" Dani asks curiously as she eyes me from the rearview mirror.

I can't hide the blush that creeps up my cheeks. "Uhhh, well, see what happened was, there was an earthquake, and my clothes just kind of fell apart."

Lana cackles, and Dill turns around in her seat to face me. "There was an earthquake that night?" she asks with sincere curiosity, and Dani's mouth drops open.

"Holy shit, Dillen, you really are an idiot."

"Danielle Torin Lane, you watch your mouth, young lady. And you know I was too busy with Joel's mouth to notice a damn thing, little shit."

I laugh hysterically at the two of them. "Was that it or the massive amount of alcohol you consumed that night?"

"There's a slight possibility that it was both. Now shut your mouth, little shit. Don't make me come back there."

Lana yelps as a sudden downpour opens up over us. She pushes the button for the window to close repeatedly, but it refuses to close the entire way. "You have got to be kidding me," she squeals and tries to close it again, but it doesn't work.

I pull my flannel shirt off and move across the backseat to tie it up. We eventually get the open part of the window covered and I sit back. "Whew."

"Thank you, Heather," she says sweetly. "I'm wet, and Coen isn't even in the same car, dammit."

I freeze and look up front to gauge Dillen's reaction to Lana's comment. She seems to pause for a moment but then smiles, suddenly shouting, "Holy shit, Lana, we're Eskimo sisters."

Whew, I was not expecting that reaction.

Dani makes a face when the rain gets harder on the windshield. "I must say, Coen is gorgeous, but is he any good in bed?"

"Yes!" they both say in unison, and Dani and I laugh.

Dani and I both look at each other in the rearview mirror. Our eyes meet knowingly before we smile brightly at each other.

NOAH

The rain is coming down hard and I'm glad I'm the one driving. Giving up control in a situation like this makes me tense. Coen is groaning in the backseat, holding his nuts. "Fuck, dude, are you hitting every pothole on purpose?" he complains and I laugh.

"I'm sure you've had your nuts ridden harder than today. Chill the fuck out; we're fifteen minutes away."

"Yeah, yeah."

I turn the wipers on as fast as they can go to try and see better when we reach the two-lane bridge. The girls turn onto it first, and I follow behind. Shit, it's really coming down.

I sit straighter and try to squint, seeing only their taillights in front of me. "Damn, I wish I had my glasses," I comment to nobody in particular.

Coen laughs from the backseat. "You still wear those fucking things?"

"Damn right I do. They seem to get me ass every time I wear them too, so you can go fuck yourself, dipshit."

"Shit, Lana just needs to see me, and she fucking strips."

"Dude, I've heard you fucking before. I don't need any further details."

There have been a few cars passing by as we head back to the lodge, but the roads are mostly empty. I can see a large white SUV coming down the other side of the bridge. I look back at Coen in the rearview and chuckle when he gives me the finger.

I look back at the road and am instantly confused. I hear a distant pop and then someone's horn up ahead. I slam on my brakes when I see the girls' grey SUV swerve to the right. Their brake lights light up bright red. In that instant my heart stops. The white SUV that is headed their way almost collides with their SUV, and I hear two horns honk before both vehicles swerve in opposite directions. The rain is coming down too hard to see anything, but suddenly the white SUV stops, and I watch in horror as everything happens in slow motion.

"Oh fuck!" is all I hear from Coen before my ears start ringing. My heart slams against my rib cage and my adrenaline skyrockets. It all happens so fast, yet insanely slow as I watch it happen, frame by frame. The SUV that Dani is driving suddenly collides with the guardrail and the rail shatters like it's made of matchsticks. My heart drops to my stomach, and I can't make a sound as I watch their car plummet off the bridge and out of my sight into the water below.

I slam on the brakes and put the Range Rover into park. I can't feel my body moving as I get the seatbelt off, and I swing the door wide open. I sprint ahead to where a few feet of the railing is missing from the side of the bridge. I don't hesitate for a second as I see that corner of the bumper sink into the dark water. I dive into the water, journeying into the dark nothingness. The water gives way to my body as I swim down in search of the grey SUV. The water does not resist my movements as I finally see the car in a foggy haze. I have to go back up for air before I can swim any further, before I can get to my girl. I propel myself up with as much energy and force as I possibly can until I feel the harsh and heavy raindrops hit my face.

Brannon and Coen are standing at the edge of the bridge when I surface to draw in a lungful of air. Coen dives in, and I go back down to where I last saw the SUV before I know if Brannon jumped in or not. The frigid water is not solid but it feels like stone against my body. I finally reach the vehicle as Lana is pulling her body out through the window. I grab her and make sure she's conscious, and able to make it up to the top on her own. She's panicked, though: she looks petrified. I push her up toward the water's surface and follow her through the bubbles to the surface to get another breath, as well as to make sure Brannon can get her to the banks of the river. When we emerge from the depths, she starts to panic as I hand her off to Brannon who starts swimming her to the water's edge.

I take a long, deep breath and dive back into the dark waters. When I eventually make it down to the car, Coen is pulling Dillen out through the window and swims her up. She seems to be conscious, but I don't let it distract me to get Heather and Dani out. That's when I see her: the only thing holding Heather down is her seatbelt. I maneuver my body through the almost too-tight gap of the open window to Heather's side. Her lips are sealed shut, and I want to give her my breath. I want to watch her inhale fresh oxygen that will stop her from suffocating in this heavy liquid stone. I press my lips to hers and push the breath of air I'm holding into her mouth. When she doesn't respond I start working on her seatbelt, trying to get it unclipped, but it won't fucking budge. She's unconscious, and I'm fucking glad I can't see her thrashing and gasping for air.

I look toward the front for Dani just as Brannon manages to get in through the window of the SUV and thank fuck because there's no way in hell I could choose. Brannon gets into the front and gets Dani's seatbelt off with ease, before getting her out of the window while I struggle to free Heather. It feels like hours go by when I finally get it open. I move the belt from around her limp body as Brannon pulls Dani out of the vehicle. I make sure that Heather's not caught on anything before I attempt to move her. Once Brannon has Dani through the window I move backwards and get out of the window before I pull her out with me. The car creaks and protests as the weight of the water pushes it farther into the depth of the river. I push myself off of the roof of the car while holding onto Heather as I struggle to get to the surface, and bubbles escape from her nose.

As soon as I breach the surface, I inhale a burning breath. My chest feels like it's on fire, and I cough as I swim to shallow water with Heather in my arms.

"Fucking call someone!" I cry out as loud as I can to the bystanders on the bank. There seems to be more people than just us, and they're standing around one body with Brannon leaning over it. I can't worry about that: the girl in my arms is unconscious.

"Help! Somebody fucking help," I scream over the rain as I lay Heather's cold, lifeless body onto the muddy, slanted riverbank. I start breathing against her lips—her blue-rimmed lips.

I can hear girls crying . . . *Dillen and Lana?*

I start performing CPR on Heather, trying to remove the water from her lungs. As much as mine burn right now, I know hers are ablaze.

"Come on, baby. Breathe. Breathe!"

My arms burn as I put all my weight against her chest. I can feel her sternum crack under the pressure and I hear it break. I'm yelling for help as Coen joins me. He's breathing life into her as I continue building pressure in her chest. My life is flashing before my eyes. My girl is dying right before me and all I can feel is numbness.

All I hear are screams.

Mine.

The girls'.

Coen's.

Brannon's.

The paramedics'.

It may have been minutes but it felt like hours. But they finally arrive and push me away.

I fall backwards onto my ass as I now struggle to breathe. They block my view of her. I've already lived through this before. This cannot be real. Coen pulls me to my feet, and I look back over to Brannon on his hands and knees while they work on Dani. Dillen and Lana have been pulled aside to be examined, but all I can think of is Heather. The lump in my throat is about to suffocate me. Coen steps over to Brannon to help him up and, fuck, the look of agony in his eyes must be the same as what he sees in mine. I turn my attention back to Heather and wait for a reaction out of her.

My vision blurs, and my body finally starts to shake. I think I'm going to lose my shit. I can't believe what I'm seeing, what we're going through. This isn't happening to us. The wailing I hear from Dillen is unbearable, and I cover my ears in protest. I turn my back on the whole scene. I can't watch them cover her. I can't. I just fucking can't. I can't have that vision stuck in my head for the rest of my life. It can't be the last thing I see of her. I feel my knees buckle, and a painful cry fills my ears as I clutch my chest.

My own cry.

How am I going to tell her when she wakes up? How am I going to look at her and tell her she'll never see her sister again? How do I tell her that we all did all that we could to save her, to get her to breathe again? What words do I choose to tell her that the weight of the water was too much for her, and that her heart stopped, while hers will continue to beat wildly?

The only thing I can seem to hold onto is the thought that I could have done more; if I had done more to save her life, then we wouldn't be in this brightly lit hospital room where I can smell the death wafting through the hallways. We should not have to say goodbye like this.

She has her hand over mine, trying to calm my numb and un-inflatable heart. It isn't working, and it won't. I've dealt with loss before, but this . . . this anguish is all consuming. My feet feel like cinderblocks, and I haven't been able to move my arms because they weigh as much, if not more, than the inconceivable weight of the water which held her down. The indescribable agony she felt, that I felt. I lost count of how many breaths I took that she couldn't. I don't remember pulling her out or breathing the frigid air of what I could into her lips. My eyes close, and all I can see is her frigid blue lips on her soft face. Those lips that I'd kill for sealed shut with her last breath.

I'm brought back into the current moment when Lana releases my hand to take the cup of ice water from Coen. I don't bother lifting my head when he hands me mine. I can still hear the faint beeping of the machine, telling me just how much I failed.

I'm certain I won't be able to take her suffering. I won't be able to help. This is beyond our control, and I feel like death. The room is quiet, and I look up at her lifeless body and over at Brannon. He's just as inconsolable as I am. Dillen had to be sedated to numb her pain and devastation, and I wish nothing more than to join her.

I'd do anything to bring her back.

I had to be the one to identify her body.

The others couldn't do it for me. I needed to be the one. I wasn't strong enough to help her . . . to help them all, so I punished myself.

Our lives are broken.

Our family is no longer whole.

Our entire lives were ahead of us, and now I can't see past the dark, all-consuming water that stole her away. How can I get past this tragedy?

One by one, they leave: first Lana and then Coen. It's just Brannon and I. We look at each other, both knowing that our lives will never be the same, forever changed. A dark, malevolent cloud will hang over us until it is our time to go.

"I'm sorry. I'm sorry I couldn't save her." My voice cracks, and I lose it.

We both do.

Both of us lose it for the women in our lives. The two sisters that meant so much to us, that meant so much to each other.

Nothing will ever be the same again. It will take all I have to call my parents, to tell them of this deplorable news. They will want to pay their respects to her; I know she was important to them, and they will want to be there for me as well . . . to be there for all of us . . . to be there when they bury her.

I look down toward my feet, hoping that when I look up again, none of this will be in front of me. That the machine that is breathing for her, keeping her alive, isn't really there, but the sound is excruciatingly loud. I swallow the crippling guilt before I open my fist to reveal Heather's engagement ring to my red, swollen eyes. The pear shape is pressed into my palm, a painful reminder of a fraction of the pain she must have felt hours ago. When I turn the ring over, it catches the fluorescent lighting, making it sparkle like it never has before.

I'm revolted that it can still shine while her light is out.

Epilogue

I do not know what the time is, let alone where I am. I have yet to grasp hold of this unfathomable dark nightmare that I'm engulfed in. Scenes from the accident and every excruciating hour since have been on replay in my head. I will continue to punish myself with these scenes, these memories as I sit in this over-sanitized, fluorescently lit hospital room. I did not get to see her last free breath through those ice-blue lips, because I was unable to push myself further to save her. It's because of me that she lost her last breath, that she expired.

I've been in this position before, but this is exponentially worse. Maybe that moment in time prepared me for what I need to do now. I have to look her in the eye and give her the worst news possible. I have to tell Heather that her sister has passed on, and she's now with her parents once again. That I'm all she has left.

This is the second time in my life that I've dealt with death. I've gone thirty years without being close to someone who has passed. The first . . . was my child. My unborn baby perished before I even knew about its existence. And now, Danielle.

My future sister-in-law.

How do I find the right words this time around? Brannon left Heather's bedside about ten minutes ago, leaving me on my own with my fiancée. I can still smell the water from the river on my clothing; the damp musty smell hasn't allowed me to fully breathe since my body hit the dark waters.

I can't describe the pain I felt when I thought I had lost her, when her body lay cold against the muddy, rocky riverbank. I struggled to stand, and all I could hear were screams as the bile rose in my throat. Now, moments from now . . . I'll hear it again, when I tell the woman I love that her last and only relative is gone.

"Noah."

I glance up to the head of the bed where Heather's eyes are open and peering at me questioningly. She's lifted the oxygen mask up and off of herself. I get up and move the two feet closer to her. I'm emotionally fatigued, and I know it's just going to get worse.

"Leave that on, sweetheart," I manage as I take her hand in mine, running my thumb over her cold fingers to soothe her anxiety. She tries to sit up as she looks at me with confusion and panic.

"Noah? Dani . . . Dillen . . . Lana? Are they okay?"

I let out a deep, unsteady breath and look away from her as I speak. "Lana and Dillen got out unscathed, but Dill is sedated in the room next to this one right now."

I watch as her eyes flicker through my words. They dart from side to side, going over what I said. She sits up and a hopeful plea escapes her lips. "Dani? What about Dani? Is she hurt? Did she have her seatbelt on?"

My heart shatters when the tears stream down her cheeks. I run my tongue over my teeth to fight the emotions that are in turmoil as her eyes beg for me to answer her. I bring her fingers to my lips and shake my head. The tears I've been fighting off for hours now emerge and line my eyes. "I'm sorry."

Her eyebrows knit together in confusion before she sits up straight with great effort. "Where is she, Noah?" Her voice is shaky yet demanding. I can hear the hope and pain in her voice all at once.

"Heather. Sh-she's no longer with us." I force myself to kiss her fingers, to try and soothe this in any way I can, but I won't be able to stop the reaction, depression, and hurt that will ensue now. She rips her hand away from mine, and it stings like a slap to the face.

"No! Don't say that, Noah. Tell me the truth."

The tears steadily fall down her cheeks as her chest heaves, and she starts to hyperventilate. I don't have any more words for her, only sadness in my eyes as I stand and lean over to her. I wrap my arms around her shoulders and hold her to me as she struggles to break free from my grip. The screams that I knew I'd hear are ringing loudly in my ears. She's fighting me, kicking her legs furiously and smacking me repeatedly.

"No, no! Please, no. Not my Dani! Please?" She screams a bloodcurdling wail, and I struggle to hold her in my arms as she fights me.

I don't try to fight her movements. I hold her against my chest as she struggles wildly. "I'm so sorry, baby. I tried all I could to get all of you out before . . ."

I can't finish that sentence.

Although I have her safe in my arms, I can still see her in the dark water as her hair floated around her. I would not be able to live without this woman; I don't know how Brannon is.

She's heaving in my arms, and my grip tightens to hold her. She screams her sister's name over and over again, and I know I won't be able to calm her with just my touch. She's beyond that now.

"Shh, sweetheart, I'm here." I hold her head tight against my chest and feel the tremors rack her tiny frame.

"Noah! No!" She smacks my chest once before she simply cannot scream anymore as her emotions and tears nearly choke her.

"I know, baby, I know." I kiss the top of her head and listen to the powerful sobs that fill the room.

"Are you sure?" she glances up at me, begging me for this not to be true in a voice that is drowning in emotion.

I briefly close my eyes to escape that painful look staring back at me. I nod once and open my eyes to see her face crumple in pain before she loses it once more.

I move to sit on the bed and shift her into my lap to ensconce her in my warmth. "I know that nothing I say right now will take this pain away, but I love you, Heather."

She doesn't respond to my words, and I'm not sure if she even heard me over her own screams, but it's all I can do right now.

We haven't moved in over an hour. I can't tell if my ballerina has fallen asleep, or if she's decided to stay mute.

Heather's nurse has come in to check on her more than three times now, but she won't budge. I watch as the nurse locks eyes with me, and I see sadness in hers as well. She knows the situation. She knows my ballerina lost her only sister.

I press my lips to the top of her head as the nurse walks up to us. "Miss Lane? I just need to check your vitals, and I'll be on my way."

She's unmoving, and the nurse pleads at me with her eyes. I gently move her away from my chest and lay her back against the bed as it sits upright. The look that is on her face terrifies me and will haunt me until the day I die. She's staring off into the distance and looks catatonic. There's no life behind those eyes anymore. It looks almost as if I'm once again staring into Dani's empty eyes as she lay dead on the cold rocks.

I move to the other side of the bed so the nurse can get to Heather, but I don't stop touching her as the nurse wraps the blood pressure cuff around her bicep. "I'm not going anywhere, Heather."

I have to look away because her eyes are black and soulless, unlike Heather's.

The nurse takes her time checking Heather over. I don't think she wants to disturb her in any way.

"Mr. Ryan, I'm going to send the doctor in soon, but her vitals seem to be back to normal. In my opinion, you should be able to take her home within the hour. Miss Ascher is being woken up as we speak, with the other two in the room with her."

I nod and look back at my girl, reaching over to move a stray hair from her face. She doesn't budge an inch or even blink. "You'd like that, wouldn't you, baby? To go home?" I ask her and try to get anything out of her. I can't even imagine what she's thinking right now.

She stays mute. Unmoving.

"Thank you," I say to the nurse as she gathers her things and walks out of the room.

I look at my left hand, which is still fisted around her engagement ring. I open my fist; my knuckles feel raw and strained.

"Sweetheart? Would you like to put your ring back on?"

I rub her ring finger with my thumb and slip her ring on for a second time. It shines like never before, but her light is still out.

She moves toward me, and I think it's my cue to take her back into my arms. Before I can sit down on the hospital bed, she's trying to move onto my lap and curl up in my chest. I get up and onto the bed and make sure she's physically comfortable, because I know the thoughts running through her head are anything but comforting.

"Why?" Is all that comes out of her mouth.

And fuck me, I could never give her a proper answer.

"I don't know, sweetheart, it was just her time."

I know that comforting her won't take the pain away and that it will just cushion it, but I don't have another choice. Holding her is all I can do for her right now. This grief that she's feeling will only intensify, and I'll be ready to provide the comfort that she needs to get her through it.

She starts to cry again, but this time it's soft and full of mourning. The full depth of what's happened has sunk in, and she's embracing it all. I look up when I hear the door open, and I lock eyes with Coen. He looks tired and weakened by the events of today. He sees Heather crying in my arms and doesn't say a word; he just walks over to where we sit on the bed and wraps his arms around her as well. I've loved him like a brother, but right now he just solidified that status. He's comforting his sister. My girl.

Her hand fists my shirt, and I know she needs to feel loved and wanted, and we're giving as much of it to her as we can. I watch as she moves her hand from my shirt to Coen's hand.

"I'm here, sis. I always will be."

I close my eyes and choke back my feelings. Fuck, these two are going to kill me.

There's a knock on the door and the doctor walks in, his voice resonating throughout the room. "My apologies. Do you mind if I come in and take a look?"

"Come on in, doc, and tell me I can take my sister home."

Coen and I move out of the way and watch as he looks Heather over. He seems to be pleased with her recovery because he nods to himself and then checks her monitors.

"According to her vital checks, I believe she will be just fine to travel back to the lodge tonight. I do suggest that you take a day or two off before traveling home. Mr. Ryan, you told me that she doesn't fly, and I believe driving down to New York City right now wouldn't be a good idea. I'd like to ensure she does not have any effects from the accident."

"Okay, great," I nod and reply, but everything about this is anything but great. "Is there anything that she can take for pain? Anything I need to watch out for?" I ask and he pulls me over to the side.

He starts going over a few things to be on the lookout for regarding depression and suicidal thoughts. I listen carefully and watch as Coen moves to Heather's side, crouching close to her. She leans against him, and I'm grateful that he's here, supporting her and myself. I know that he's trying to avert her attention while we talk. My hand moves to my jaw, and I rub it as I listen to what he's telling me.

Suicide?

She might try to kill herself? Not on my fucking watch.

He stops talking, and we both look at Heather when she asks in a tortured cry, "Did she suffer?"

I look over at him for his answer and watch as his lips thin. He shakes his head and talks to Heather gently. "No, she didn't. The coroner is not yet finished with his report, but from what I've been told, she did not have any water in her lungs. It looks as if she passed immediately as a result of the collision."

Heather doesn't respond to him; instead she turns back to Coen and buries her face in his shirt, muffling her sobs.

"I want to go home, and I want my sister back."

My stomach knots at her heartache, and Coen looks up at me with just as much anguish. He's at a loss for words. We all are. I have to stop the fresh sting of tears that threaten to give many of my emotions away.

Her doctor tells me that she's all set to go as soon as she's ready. I thank him before he exits, and I walk over to Heather and Coen.

"Baby? Let's get you dressed into something warmer than this gown. We can go back to the lodge now."

I watch as her petite frame trembles against Coen. We both stare at each other, both of us unsure of what to do for her. She doesn't respond to me; she just cries. Coen shakes his head minutely before trying. "Sis? Brannon is just down the hall waiting for you."

Her head snaps up, and she gasps before covering her mouth. "Oh Brannon. How is he? I need to see him."

I nod in agreement and help her move off the bed as she tries to get up. "He's having a hard time too, sweetheart."

Coen moves back toward the door. "I'll go gather the crew while you help her get changed, bro."

"We'll see you in the lobby."

"I'll see you in a few, sis."

He gets a faint smile from her that isn't truly hers as he walks out of the room.

I walk over to the pile of clothes that Lana bought for the both of us.

"I'm sorry that I'm a mess, Noah."

I turn to her with a pink 'I heart Canada' t-shirt in my hand. "You have nothing in this world to be sorry for. Don't ever apologize for mourning."

She sniffles and pulls the blue gown over her head, leaving her naked and shuddering.

"If this was easy, then that love you had for each other wouldn't have been true. The reason why this is going to be difficult is because of the bond you shared with her. I cannot replace that, and I doubt anyone will ever be able to in your lifetime. Everyone grieves in their own way, and I'm going to be by your side through it all. Please don't push me away when you need me."

The salty tears are back, and they steadily move down her cheeks to her jawline and then drop onto her exposed breasts as she nods in agreement.

Heather refused to be rolled out in a wheelchair to the rental SUV; instead, we're walking down the hallway of the Banff—Mineral Springs Hospital's emergency room. My arm is locked tightly around her as we round the corner, where we see Brannon staring in our direction while the other three stand next to him, trying to console him in any way possible. When he moves toward Heather, the others take a step back, and Coen signals toward me, informing me that they are going to be waiting in the SUV.

"Heather."

"Oh Brannon."

She walks out of my arms and straight into Brannon's brotherly grasp. He hugs her tightly. "I'm so sorry, Heather."

"I'm sorry too."

I don't know how life will go on after this devastating loss for the two of them, but I'm sure they will lean on each other for guidance through their grieving.

"I wasn't ready to say goodbye to her," Brannon says, and he angrily wipes at his cheeks.

Heather doesn't say another word. Instead, she buries her face into his chest as emotional sobs rack her frame.

Brannon leads her out into the cold air, as they speak quietly to themselves, before he helps her into the SUV. My phone buzzes in my front left pocket and I reach in and pull it out, not recognizing the number calling as my eyes follow the two of them out of the double glass doors.

"Hello?"

"This call may be recorded and monitored. You are receiving a collect call from an inmate, Mae Ryan, at the Arizona State Prison Complex—ASPC Perryville—Women's Treatment. Do you choose to accept this call?" a robotic voice asks me on the other line.

Oh fuck.

My heart stops for what seems like the millionth time in one day. My feet stop of their own accord, keeping me from moving another inch as I make up my mind in an instant. My reply is cold and clipped. "Yes."

THE END

Be on the lookout for book three:

An Expiration Date
The Date Series

About the Authors

The co-authors come as a package deal with extravagant ribbons laced on top. Their combined enthusiasm is seen as a pink sunrise, uniquely captivating. They share a love for writing, fictional romance, passion-fruit tea lemonade, sweetened and shaken on ice, as well as the color pink. Their combined efforts to share their internal monologues, since they share a brain, can be found in The Date Series.

Jess

Jess is a registered dental hygienist by day and a contemporary romance author by night. She currently resides in the Greater St. Louis area with her husband. When Jess isn't writing (meaning her characters aren't demanding her undivided attention), she enjoys reading books, scouring Pinterest, collecting fountain pens, and traveling with her husband.

Sasha

A self-published author by night and all around busybody by day, Sasha is an international baby, born in gorgeous South Africa. Her cultured lifestyle is one that many don't get to experience. Four countries, and a co-author later, she has published her first book of The Date Series. When she's not preoccupied with her imposing owl fixation, she's hashing out new ways to translate a titillating and libidinous scene onto a page.

Stay in contact with Jess & Sasha (JSAuthors)

www.JSAuthors.com
Facebook: /JSAuthors
Twitter: @JSAuthors
Instagram: @JSAuthors

Please find and follow our Pinterest board, *JSAuthors*, to see small snippets of our inspirational photos for *A Winter's Date*.

Acknowledgments

We would each like to thank every single person who has encouraged us to pursue this series and our dreams.

I would like to thank my parents, Andrew and Vanessa, for everything you do. You both encourage me to continue to chase after this new adventure in my life with guns blazing; it would be impossible without you. In addition, I would like to thank my brother, Tynan, for the faith that you show in my work. I love you all to the ends of the earth and back again.

~Sasha

I'd like to thank my husband for his continued support, patience, and understanding on this amazing journey. To my sister, thank you for your love and constant excitement about this series. You've given me many things to write about! I'm sure you know by now who inspired Dani and Heather. And to my parents, family, and friends: thank you for your support and encouragement. Your excitement for this book/series is heartwarming, and I'm so happy you enjoy it. Mom, thank you for getting me hooked on reading! Without it, I wouldn't have ever attempted this endeavor. I love you all.

~Jess

Collectively, we thank the following people for the time they contributed to making this series what it is today:

To Lisa Aurello: finding the right words to thank you for all that you do and have done for us is nearly impossible. We're incredibly honored to be working with you on our novels.

To our betas: Dani Naas, Ashley Scales, Jillian Crouson-Toth, Ninfa Zito-Maisano, Linda Russell, Kelly Williams, and Erica McKinley. Thank you for all of your advice, love, and effort you constantly give us.

You ladies are truly amazing in every sense of the word.

To Mark Thomas, Greg Sandifer, and Jason Epps: thank you for contributing to help build some of Coen, Joel, and Noah's banter. Keep the good lines coming!

To Judi Perkins: your talent is exceptional. Thank you for providing us with yet another gorgeous, and one-of-a-kind book cover.

Last, but certainly not least:

Thank you for reading *A Winter's Date*.

-JS